THE HANDYMAN

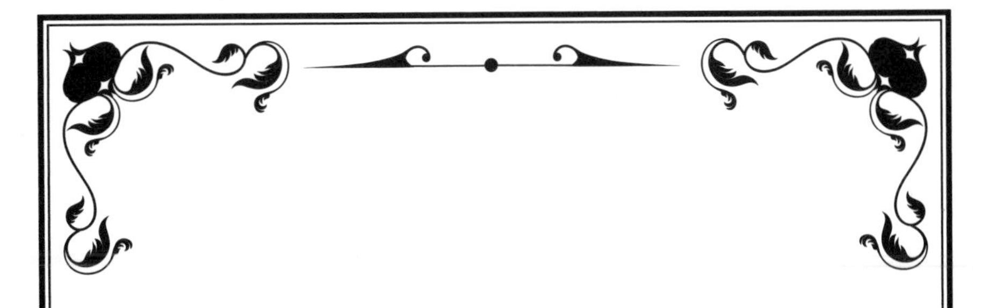

THE HANDYMAN

BENTLEY LITTLE

Cemetery Dance Publications
Baltimore
2017

This book was previously published as a signed Limited Edition hardcover
in the Cemetery Dance Publications Graveyard Edition series.

Cemetery Dance Publications
132-B Industry Lane, Unit #7
Forest Hill, MD 21050
http://www.cemeterydance.com

First Trade Hardcover Edition Printing

ISBN: 978-1-58767-616-1

PART ONE
DANIEL

ONE

BUSINESS HAD BEEN slow for most of the summer. So as much as I resented it, I was working on a Sunday morning, nearly two hours from home, showing a one-bedroom cabin in Big Bear to a young couple looking for a weekend getaway. It was the only property in the area within their price range, which meant that it was, in realtor parlance, a "fixer upper." No view, no lot to speak of, and not only had the previous owners been allergic to maintenance, but the structure itself had issues obvious to even the most unobservant layman: stains on the ceiling from leaks in the roof; a sagging wall where a window had been installed with no consideration given to the location of load-bearing beams; a series of crooked shelves in the half-kitchen; a ridge in the incorrectly laid tile where two sections of flooring did not meet properly.

None of these drawbacks seemed to deter the young couple, however, who were positively giddy over the prospect of owning a vacation home in the mountains—no matter what shape it was in.

Still, as I led them through the rooms, the problems with the place were so distinctly noticeable that, at a certain point, it became comical. Looking at the shoddy construction in the bathroom—an unpainted plywood counter inexpertly built around the small sink—the husband shook his head, chuckling. "It's like a Frank house," he told his wife.

My breath caught in my throat, the rationalizing excuse I'd been about to offer suddenly forgotten.

Frank house.

I couldn't believe what I'd heard, and I looked more carefully at the man and woman, whom I'd seen until then only as buyers. They were a good decade or two younger than I was—in their mid-twenties, I suspected—and appeared to be Southern California natives. The man, Brad, a computer programmer, had one of those weird little squarish goatee things and wore a Bing Crosby-looking hipster hat. Connie, his wife, was blond and tan, with the standard issue big boobs and jeans so tight that everything was outlined.

I spoke carefully, making a special effort to keep my voice calm and noncommittal. "What did you say?"

"Oh, nothing."

"Did you call this a 'Frank house?'"

"It's kind of a private joke."

"What's a 'Frank house?'" I pressed.

"It's nothing."

"What is it?"

"You really want to know?"

"Yes," I assured him.

Brad laughed. "Okay. I grew up in this house in Tarzana. My mom still lives there. The neighborhood sort of grew up around us, but when we moved in about twenty years ago, the house was by itself on the edge of the city. The guy we bought it from was the guy who built it, a guy named Frank. I was really little, so I don't remember much about him, but my dad always said he was one of those guys who tries to pass himself off as an expert on everything. According to Frank, he'd invented this energy-saving heater and air-conditioner for our house, and he'd installed some kind of plumbing system that recycled sink water to fill up the toilets. The place was supposed to be state of the art when it came to the environment. Only nothing worked. The toilets didn't flush. The roof leaked. And things kept falling apart. Not right away, but over the years. And each time something happened, my dad would curse out Frank and say, 'This damn Frank house.'"

"Tell Mr. Martin about your mom's laundry room," Connie said.

"Daniel," I said reflexively. "Call me Daniel."

"Okay, so last year, my mom was watching TV. At night. And she hears this huge crash from the kitchen area. She goes back to check it out, and the entire floor of the laundry room's collapsed! The washer and dryer have both fallen into this hole in the middle of the room, and the sink's been pulled on top of them and water's spurting everywhere from the burst pipes. It turns out that Frank hadn't put in enough support beams for the floor. After they looked at it, everyone was amazed that it lasted as long as it did. Pure luck, according to the contractor who fixed it."

Connie shook her head. "And the weird thing was that, under the floor, they found all these rolls of wallpaper. Dozens of them!"

"Twenty six," Brad confirmed.

"Frank had been storing them down there in the crawlspace."

"That's why I called this a Frank house," Brad said. "It kind of reminds me of the home where I grew up."

I returned to realtor mode. "So this should be nothing to an old hand like you. Now, we haven't finished going over everything, but it seems like you're favorably inclined. So if it turns out that you two do want to make an offer, I'd bid two to three thousand lower than asking price since the place has all these problems. We might even try to get the seller to have some of them corrected before sale, though I doubt we'll get anywhere on that."

Brad and Connie looked at each other. "We are interested," Brad said.

"Good! Then why don't we go back to my office, I'll put in a bid, and we'll see where things go."

I was on automatic pilot. I sounded helpful, engaged, competent, professional, but inside, I was none of those things.

Frank house

I looked around the poorly built cabin, feeling cold.

At that moment there was only one thing on my mind.

There were more of them.

TWO

I WAS TEN YEARS old when my parents bought the lot in Arizona.

We were on a two-week vacation, visiting relatives in Colorado, obnoxious redneck cousins who pretended to like me and my brother when the adults were around, but tortured us once the parents were looking the other way. On the return trip to California, my dad had scheduled a three day stop-off in Arizona, deciding that if we were going to go to the Four Corners area, we should take the opportunity to see the Grand Canyon. It was nice to be with just our immediate family again, and as we travelled down from northern New Mexico on the unlikely named Highway 666, I was, for the first time on the trip, genuinely happy.

The book *Blue Highways* had been a bestseller a few years prior, and my dad had read it and been inspired. He wanted to travel the country using back roads, so rather than drive Interstate 40, we took smaller roads through the overlapping reservations of western New Mexico and eastern Arizona.

In the backseat, between me and my brother Billy, was a pile of books. On top was a Sunset publication titled *Indian Country*, and when we weren't playing one of the travel games we'd gotten at McDonald's, I used the book to check out where we'd been and where we were going. There were maps inside, and photographs, and descriptions of scenic sites. I looked up the Hubble Trading Post, which a sign on the side of the road had said was 75 miles ahead. "Can we stop by the trading post?" I asked.

"Sure," my dad said.

Scattered here and there across the flattened landscape were Hogans and houses and trailers. Up ahead was a gas station and a surprisingly large Basha's supermarket. Billy had to go to the bathroom, so my dad pulled into the parking lot and we went inside, looking for a restroom.

Ours were the only white faces in the grocery store, and we were the only ones speaking English. Everyone else was talking in a Native American language—Navajo? Hopi?—and I understood for the first time what it must be like for immigrants coming to this country. Actually, we *were* immigrants, I realized. These were the original residents of this land, and to them we were foreign interlopers.

It was uncomfortable for all of us, and my dad went into the bathroom with Billy while my mom and I remained close together outside the door. As soon as Billy was done, we were back in the car and on the road again.

We spent the night at a hotel made out of red rocks adjacent to the Cameron Trading Post. Perched on the edge of a gorge carved by the Little Colorado River, the hotel's claim to fame was the fact that Waylon Jennings had spent his honeymoon there. Other tourists besides ourselves were staying at the lodge, and even without a swimming pool, Billy and I had fun.

The Grand Canyon, when we reached it the next morning, was so massive as to be overwhelming. We drove from lookout point to lookout point, and the canyon was so enormous that, over the space of twenty miles, the views were nearly identical. It was only the differences at the top, where we were, that brought some variety to the landscape, and we spent most of the day exploring Grand Canyon Village, the touristy collection of hotels and shops and historic buildings that lined a populated stretch of the south rim.

Still wanting to stay on the side roads, the AAA map's blue highways, my dad did not take the interstate to Phoenix the following day but instead followed a patchwork of smaller rural routes out of

Flagstaff and over the Mogollon Rim, a massive plateau which my Sunset book said was home to the largest stand of Ponderosa pines in the world. Driving down the south side of the escarpment, we saw a small town nestled in a broad valley between heavily wooded hills. The two-lane highway wound in a switchback to the bottom, where tall pine trees cast dappled shadows on the blacktop. Ahead, a green sign at the side of the highway marked the town limit.

"'Welcome to Randall,'" Billy read aloud. "'Founded 1881, Elevation 4,260 feet, Population 4,260.'

"Hey!" he said. "The population's the same as the elevation!"

"That's weird," I told him.

"Believe it or not!"

"Not *that* weird."

It was another mile or two before we saw the first building in town, a church. One of those little white-steepled ones you see in movies. The small parking lot before it was dirt, and behind was a stand of dark green Ponderosas. It looked like something out of a Norman Rockwell painting.

So did the quaint downtown that followed. There was a brick hardware store with adjacent nursery, a video store, a bank, a fire station, a pharmacy next to a doctor's office, a bakery, a jeweler's, a barber shop, a feed and grain store, a couple of gas stations, a post office, a grocery, a laundromat, a library and several other businesses that lined both sides of the highway for three or four blocks.

My mom thought it was the cutest town she'd ever seen, and instead of just passing through, she had my dad drive down side streets, through neighborhoods of cottages and cabins and single-story homes. Behind the houses was a trailer park, and past the trailer park a dirt road that led to a series of large cattle ranches. The sky, far bluer than it ever appeared in California, was filled with white puffy clouds, and though this was Arizona in the summer, the temperature was pleasant, the area cooled by a gentle mountain breeze.

"I could see myself living here," Mom said.

We ate a lunch of hamburgers and fries at a restaurant called The North Fork, a dark bar-like place with wood paneling and pictures of fishermen and their catches framed on the walls. Afterward, my dad filled up the car at a one-pump gas station that had a stuffed moose in front of the office.

We already had reservations at a motel in Phoenix, and we'd lose our deposit if we didn't show. Otherwise, we would have spent the night in Randall at a cute rustic inn next to a running stream, where my mom had my dad take a picture of me and my brother before we headed out.

It was well over a hundred degrees when we reached Phoenix, too hot even to swim, but it was getting late anyway, so we got a pizza, brought it back to our room, watched TV, went to bed, and the next morning headed for home.

Back in Anaheim, sitting in our sweltering, un-air-conditioned house, we thought about that little town in the pines, and one night when we were sitting on the back porch, looking over our neighbors' roofs at the Disneyland fireworks exploding in the sky to the east, my mom said, "It would be nice to have a little vacation home someplace like that, where we could go hiking and enjoy the fresh air and spend our summer vacations away from it all."

"It would, wouldn't it?" my dad agreed.

"It would."

"All right, then. Let's do it!"

Dad was an impulsive guy, and while that sometimes drove my mom crazy, it made life a lot more fun for us kids. On the way back from the dentist, for example, immediately after we'd had cavities filled, he might decide to stop off and get ice cream. Or, instead of going to the hardware store as he'd originally planned, he would take me and my brother to the miniature golf course. Like I said, it often irritated my mom, but this time she had no problem with it. She was giggly and excited as my dad talked about the logistics of buying a second home, and that night Billy and I went to sleep knowing that, even though we weren't rich, we might soon have our very own vacation house.

One of my dad's friends had told him about a new development in the home trade, pre-fabricated houses, and the next weekend our entire family went out to investigate. There was a company that made and sold pre-fab houses in Corona, and we drove down the Riverside Freeway to where a grouping of model homes were on display in a field adjacent to a gigantic lumberyard. There was a traditional cabin, a small A-frame, a medium-sized A-frame and a large A-frame, as well as a hexagonal house topped by a bubble-like skylight that looked like a landed UFO. The houses were surprisingly affordable and came with everything except carpets and furnishings. Shingled roof, tiled floors, wall paneling, overhead lights and switches, kitchen counters and sink, stove, bathroom sink, toilet and bathtub; all were included, along with the basic construction materials, interior plumbing and wiring. All a person had to do was put it all together. Or, in our case, hire someone to put it all together.

It was the mid-sized A-frame that appealed most to my parents, and we walked through the model twice. The first floor consisted of a living room, an open kitchen with dining counter, and, down a short hallway, a bathroom and bedroom. But it was the upstairs that captivated Billy and me. If we bought the house, the high-ceilinged loft would be shared by both of us, and we were already planning how we would divide it and where we would put our beds.

Downstairs, the salesman was trying to pressure my dad into buying a house today. The kit was only $15,000—the price of a car!—and it could be delivered within a week.

"Well, actually, if we were to buy one, it would be for a place in Arizona. I'm pretty sure it would be too expensive to ship it—"

"Oh, we have a branch in Phoenix," the salesman said. "In fact, you could even purchase a kit today, and we could have our Phoenix branch ship it to your property."

"That would be great," my dad told him. "*If* we had property. We're still in the looking stage right now."

"Take my card, then. And when you're ready, give me a call. I'm sure we can arrange something satisfactory."

We were all excited as we drove back to Orange County, and to the cheers of me and my brother, my dad announced that next week we would be returning to Randall, Arizona.

Our family didn't have a lot of money. My dad was a junior high science teacher and my mom was a substitute English teacher. But my parents did have summers off, which we usually spent going to the beach or doing fun free things around Southern California. We were exactly the kind of family who could really make use of a vacation home because we would be able to spend a lot of time there.

I heard my parents talking low in their bedroom that night when they thought I was asleep. "Do you really think we can afford it?" my mom asked.

"It's not that much," my dad assured her. "We can refinance the house and use the extra money to buy a lot and that A-frame."

"But we'll need to pay someone to build it."

"I think we can swing it. Don't worry. Things will work out. They always do."

Their voices got lower after that, so I couldn't make out what they were saying, but the tone sounded positive, and I fell asleep dreaming of all the cool posters I would put up on the roof/wall of my new loft bedroom.

We did indeed return to Arizona the following week, after my dad had had the car checked out by a mechanic buddy of his to make sure it was still in good enough shape to travel. We'd driven it far already this summer and didn't want to tempt fate, but everything seemed to be in working order, and I helped my dad change the oil, we washed the car together, and early Monday morning, well before sunrise, we were on the road.

This time, my parents had made reservations at the Knotty Pine Lodge in Randall, and we arrived in town mid-afternoon, checking in and dropping off our suitcases before heading downtown to a setback log cabin that housed one of the local real estate offices. The agent was a pretty blond woman with a thick Southern accent who my mom later said reminded her of a beauty pageant contestant. My dad told the woman what we were looking for, but seeing that we were from California and assuming that we were wealthier than we were, she tried to steer us to large houses on large lots, a crude and tactless maneuver I'm proud to say I've never used in my own career as a realtor. We were interested in none of the properties she showed us, but while being driven around in her oversized silver Buick, we passed several empty lots with signs that read "For Sale By Owner."

After we thanked the agent and left, my dad drove us back to one of the owner-offered lots. There was no one around, but we got out and walked around the property—a rather small piece of land with a lot of trees—before my dad wrote down the telephone number listed on the For Sale sign.

He seemed to remember where all the lots were, because he drove down a narrow road, around a house-sized boulder and through a neighborhood of ill-kept shacks until we reached the next for-sale-by-owner property.

It was at the third lot that we came across two couples clearing brush. They hadn't been there when we'd driven past with the realtor, but now they were apparently trying to get the land in shape for selling. The man who seemed to be in charge was a bald older guy wearing thick black-framed glasses and striped overalls that made him look like a train engineer. He was directing the two women to rake up leaves, while he and the other man concentrated on clipping branches.

"Hello!" my dad called from his open car window. We'd pulled up parallel to the workers and Dad waved at them from across a small culvert. "Are you the owners here?"

"We are," the man with the glasses said, walking up. He gestured toward the other man. "You interested?"

My dad turned off the ignition and got out of the car. The rest of us got out as well.

"I might be," Dad said.

"I'm Frank," the man said. "That's my wife Irene, and my brother-in-law George, and his wife Betsy."

My dad jumped the culvert and held out his hand. "I'm Andy. Andy Martin." He gestured toward the For Sale sign. "How big's the lot and what're you asking for it?"

Frank didn't answer right away. "I live right across the street there, in that house. Built it myself."

We all looked over at the home opposite the lot. Two stories, red with white trim, it resembled a barn as much as a house. A rock chimney ran up the left side of the structure, and two upstairs windows to either side of the doorway gave the impression of a face. A gravel horseshoe-shaped driveway took up most of the land between the house and the street, with scrub brush and a single pine tree in the center of the U.

"George and I, we bought this property together for investment. George and Betsy live down in the Valley." At the time, I had no idea what this meant. I thought they lived in some nearby valley, but I learned later that when anyone in Randall referred to "the Valley," they meant the Phoenix area, which Arizonans had dubbed the "Valley of the Sun." "We thought it was probably a good time to sell. And since George is retired now, he and Betsy can use the extra money."

"What're you asking?" my dad repeated. "And what's the size of the property?"

"It's a quarter of an acre, nearly half an acre with the greenbelt." Frank pointed. "The land in back is owned by someone, but we've never seen him, don't know who he is, and the lot's never been built on. Probably an investment. The greenbelt runs along the side there, fifty feet wide, and that gives you some privacy with the Davidsons' cabin, although that's a vacation home and they're hardly ever there."

"The price?" my dad prodded.

Frank stroked his chin. "Truth is, we haven't really figured that out yet. We kind of put the sign up before we were ready. We were planning to clear off this dead brush, trim a few trees and bushes and see if we couldn't get a little more for it. We bought the land about seven years ago, off the guy who sold the Davidsons their place, and paid twelve hundred for it. We were thinking we could probably get three for it now."

Dad had picked up a little information about the area from our tour with the realtor. He squinted skeptically at the lot. "Are there sewer hookups, or is this a septic tank situation?"

"Septic. Sewer line's still three streets away. They keep promising it's coming, but I've heard that for five years now, so don't hold your breath."

While my dad continued to discuss details of the property with Frank, and my mom started talking to the two women, my brother and I walked through the lot. To us, it was a revelation. Unlike our home in California, with its ranch-style house placed between a front lawn and a back lawn, this land was wild. There was a kind of path that led through the brush, and it appeared to be a trail used by animals; I could see hoof prints in the dry dirt. The predominant vegetation consisted of large bushes with thick red branches and small green leaves that I later learned were Manzanita. There were pine trees as well, most of them small, with pale weeds that grew within the thin branches of sticker bushes. Birds flew up from their hiding places as we approached, and a squirrel froze when he saw us, thinking we wouldn't notice him, before speeding off through the underbrush. Near the back of the lot was a big tree that was definitely not a pine but looked more like one of those huge sprawling oaks, usually home to a clubhouse, shown on the covers of children's story books. I looked up at the thick branches forking off from the wide sturdy trunk and saw where we could hammer beams and planks and make a tree house of our own.

"How about twenty-five hundred?" my dad was saying as we walked back. "That's more than double your investment, and a pretty good price for a lot with no sewer hookups."

"We were thinking three."

George nodded. I don't think he'd said a word since we arrived. Off to the left, my mom and the two old ladies were laughing about something.

"Maybe we'll keep looking," my dad said, turning away. He motioned us back toward the car.

"Who you gonna get to build your home?" Frank asked. They must have been talking about the pre-fab house while we were exploring.

"I don't know yet. Why? Do you have a suggestion?"

Frank gestured across the street. "Like I said. I built my house from scratch. You pay me two thousand to put your kit together—and you won't get a better deal than that; not in this town—and we'll let you have the lot for twenty-five hundred."

George nodded.

"I don't know..." my dad said.

"You talk to anyone in town. Frank Watkins does quality work."

"Are you in construction?"

"I was. But I'm retired now. More of a jack of all trades these days. Why don't you all come in and look at my house? Check out my work before you make any decisions."

So we all walked across the street, where Frank and Irene gave us a tour of their home, Irene pointing out knickknacks they'd gotten from various trips, Frank showing off the fireplace he'd built, the wet bar he'd made. He did seem to know what he was doing, although he told us the upper floor was still unfinished and consisted of plywood floors and open walls.

"I work on it when I get a chance," he explained.

Billy and I were allowed to go back outside and explore, and when my mom called us back, my dad was shaking Frank's hand and everything had apparently been decided.

My dad was smiling. "You got yourself a deal," he said.

THREE

"...AND THAT ONE idea of mine saved the U.S. Air Force over *three* million dollars."

Frank was sitting on a stack of lumber, talking to Del Stewart, who was leaning against the side of his pickup truck drinking out of a thermos. So far, both times we'd come by to check on the progress of our house, Frank had been lounging around and talking. Meanwhile, the house wasn't getting built. After telling us that he could put the whole prefab home together in less than a month, he'd only managed to construct the skeleton of a cinder block foundation in the first nine days.

Del was the man Frank had hired to help him. A lean, taciturn man with long greasy hair and a wardrobe that seemed to consist of a single pair of dirty jeans and a faded Lynyrd Skynyrd t-shirt, he looked like the kind of guy who would rob a house rather than build one.

We walked up, and I could tell from the way my dad said "Hey, Frank, how's it going?" that he was getting frustrated. The first time we'd driven over from California, four days after they'd delivered the building materials, we'd expected to see the frame of the house constructed. After all, as Frank said, building a pre-fab house was like putting together a model: all the parts were there, they just had to be joined. But when we arrived, Frank and Del had only managed to clear a section of the lot where the house was to stand, and string some twine between stakes to mark the area.

This time, only my dad and I had made the drive, Billy and my mom choosing to stay home rather than make the nine-hour trip to Randall.

"I thought you'd be a little farther along," my dad said diplomatically.

"We've been working on the plumbing," Frank assured us. "Right now, we're just waiting for the building inspector to sign off on it. Then we can go on to the next step and start on the frame." He showed us where he and Del had installed a septic system and put in a main water pipe that went out to the street. In addition, they'd cleared a section of dirt for a driveway, and built a culvert over the ditch.

Seen in that light, Frank had accomplished quite a bit, but there was still no way that the house would be done in another two-and-a-half weeks. Not at this speed.

As it happened, the building inspector arrived as Frank and my dad were talking. He did indeed approve the plumbing, which allayed my dad's fears and let him know that Frank *did* know what he was doing, and allowed Frank and Del to start work on the frame. My dad and I stood around and watched for awhile, my dad even helping a bit, before the two of us went off to have lunch. We returned to California the next day, feeling good, knowing the house was finally going to be built.

It took nearly two months to finish construction, and the summer was practically over by the time Frank called to tell us that the work was done and we could move in. My mom had been searching for cheap or secondhand items with which we could furnish our vacation home: getting an old dresser out of Grandma and Grandpa's garage, some bed frames from the Salvation Army, mattresses from a discount warehouse, our old coffee table that we'd stored in *our* garage, my aunt Alice's discarded couch. Though there were still plenty of things we needed, we rented a U-Haul trailer, piled in what we had, and took off for Arizona.

Our first impression was that the house still wasn't finished. The model home had been a dark redwood color, but the A-frame on our lot was the pale yellow peach of unpainted pine. Frank had obviously been waiting for our arrival, because he was crossing the street from his own house, keys in hand, as we got out of the car. He handed the keys to my dad. "She's all yours."

He began explaining which key was for which door, but Billy and I were already rushing forward. Peeking in the front windows, we saw an empty living room, the kitchen beyond and the stairway that led up to our loft. Mom, Dad and Frank were soon behind us, and with a loud "*Ta Da*!" my dad unlocked and opened the door. We walked inside.

The walls were made out of cardboard.

At least that's what it looked like to us.

Frank told us it was drywall.

"Where's the paneling?" my dad asked. "The model home had paneling."

Frank shrugged. "I don't know what to tell you. This is what got delivered. If I'd known there was supposed to be paneling, I would have asked about it, but I assumed that this is the way it came and you were going to finish it yourselves."

"We don't know how to do that," my dad said.

"I'll show you," Frank promised. "It's easy."

We stood in the middle of our small empty living room, looking around. Not only did our vacation house look like its walls had not been put up, but the floor was plywood. None of us could remember what the floor of the model home had looked like, whether it had had carpeting or tile or linoleum, but it had not been bare wood.

"I don't know what to tell you," Frank said when we pointed this out to him. "Maybe there was some sort of deluxe package offered, but the kit you bought had no finishing materials provided at all."

There were sinks, however, and a toilet, and a shower-bath combo. There was even an electric stove installed (although no refrigerator).

Upstairs, in our loft, the deficiencies weren't quite as noticeable. The floor was still bare plywood, but our side walls consisted of the slanting A-frame ceiling and actually looked pretty good. The front of the loft overlooked the living room below and had a bare wooden railing, so it was only the back wall, with its single small window, that had the cardboard-covered drywall.

Frank invited us over for dinner that night, and my mom gratefully accepted. We had no groceries, no refrigerator, and with all the unpacking we had to do, dinner would have been, of necessity, a pretty makeshift affair. But Frank said his wife Irene was making hamburgers and told us we could come over whenever we wanted. "Whenever you get hungry," is how he put it, and that gave us time to unpack the U-Haul, get our beds set up and arrange what little furniture we'd brought.

Even my parents had not realized how many things were needed to stock a vacation home, and after a long night sleeping on bare mattresses (we'd forgotten sheets), we went out to the Randall Café for breakfast and spent the rest of the day buying the day-to-day necessities we'd need if we were going to keep living in the twentieth century. One shocking omission was a television, and here both Billy and I put our feet down. While it was cool having our own vacation house, there was no way we were going to spend the remainder of the summer without a TV. My parents must have felt the same way, because one of the first places we went that morning was the local thrift store, where we bought a used black and white set. It was only temporary, my dad promised. As soon as we had a chance, we'd go down to the Valley and charge a new color one. Billy and I would inherit the black and white set for our room upstairs. We could only get two stations—channel 12, the NBC affiliate out of Phoenix, and channel 4, the NBC affiliate out of Flagstaff—but NBC had some good shows on in the mid-1980s, so we were pretty happy.

Frank did indeed teach my dad how to tape up and plaster over the sheets of drywall, and the entire family ended up painting both the inside and outside of the house. We also bought peel-and-stick tile that we laid down on the floors.

By the time we finished all this work, the summer was pretty much over. "Not much of a vacation," I grumbled.

"Consider it a working vacation," my mom said.

"It builds character," my dad joked, but then he wrapped an arm around my shoulder, squeezing it. "We'll make it up next summer."

There were three days left before we were going back to California, and Billy and I spent them exploring. We hiked up the hill behind our little neighborhood and found what appeared to be an Indian ruin at the top. There were several square foundations made from rocks and adobe, and though we didn't find the arrowheads we were hoping for, we did pick up some black and brown pottery shards that we put in our pockets. We also walked into town—with our dad's blessing but against our mom's wishes—and, with the allowance we'd been given for all our work the past weeks, bought ourselves cherry slushes from the Dairy Queen. Billy also bought a map of Arizona ghost towns in a tourist shop. I thought it was a complete waste of money, but he tacked it to the sloping ceiling above his bed so he could look at it as he fell asleep.

What we didn't see, either in town or on our street, were other kids. There had to be some, but from our perspective, Randall seemed like a retirement community. There were old people everywhere, and the two boys we did see, down by the Circle K, were tough looking and older than us, wearing CAT hats and cowboy boots, and we walked a long way around just to avoid them.

On our way home, someone honked at us, and, startled, we turned to see Frank's pickup truck. He offered us a ride, and Billy and I just looked at each other. The dangers of hitchhiking had been drilled into us ever since we could cross a street, and we'd been warned never to take rides from strangers. Frank wasn't exactly a stranger, but neither of us had ever gotten into the car of anyone besides our parents or the parents of our friends, and that made this a monumental decision. Would we get in trouble if we rode with Frank? Would our parents get mad at us because we didn't get their approval first?

In the end, we decided to keep walking, and Frank laughed, said, "Suit yourselves," and drove off.

I looked over at Billy and saw that he was glad we hadn't let Frank give us a ride. I wasn't sure why, but I was, too. We were both tired of walking, but somehow even exercise seemed preferable to being stuck in a pickup cab with our neighbor from across the street. We didn't discuss it, though, and walked the rest of the way back in silence. Frank's pickup was parked in his driveway when we arrived, and Frank himself was standing on the gravel in front of our house, talking to our dad, who called us over. "I just want you to know," he said, putting one arm around each of our shoulders, "that if Frank offers you a ride, it's okay. We know him; he's not a stranger."

Dad, as usual, had known exactly why we'd done what we'd done, and we nodded to show that we understood, although when Billy and I glanced at each other, it was clear that neither of us regretted not accepting the ride.

Frank's last name was Watkins, but for some reason he wouldn't let either me or Billy call him "Mr. Watkins." He wanted us to address him as "Frank," the way the adults did, and after a short disagreement the first time it came up, my dad gave in. It was the first time we'd ever called a grownup by his first name, and it definitely felt weird.

But then...Frank was weird.

We were lying in our beds in the loft that night, each of us staring up at the slanted ceiling. My parents had invited Frank and his wife over for dinner, and they'd stayed so long that Billy and I had had to go to bed before they left. Downstairs, we could hear Frank telling my parents in detail how the town council had asked him to help design and build an addition to the town hall. Eventually, goodbyes were said, the front door opened, and there were footsteps and voices on the wooden deck as my parents walked outside with Frank and his wife.

"Finally, he's gone," Billy whispered. I hadn't been completely sure until then that he was still awake.

"Frank?" I whispered back.

"Yeah."

We were silent for a moment.

"I don't like him," Billy said. "He *stares*."

I knew exactly what he meant, but I was a little surprised that my brother had picked up on that. The truth was that Frank had an unnerving tendency to look at you for too long both before and after he answered a question you'd asked him. It was a disturbing habit, and for some reason, it made me think of an alien trying to be human. There seemed to be an incomprehension in that gaze, a sense that he was attempting to access information that would indicate the proper way to behave, as though he didn't know how to respond in a human manner. It was a ridiculous idea that I knew made no sense, but the feeling was there, and the thought occurred to me that since he obviously wasn't an alien, maybe he was crazy.

The idea scared me, because I honestly believed it could be true.

As strange as Frank was, however, it was actually his wife Irene who haunted my nightmares.

I wasn't sure why. She was a nice woman. Around adults, she seemed to round off Frank's rough edges, and with kids she had kind of a grandmotherly air. In my dreams, though, Irene Watkins was just...creepy. In real life, she was thin and old and wrinkled, but all of those features were exaggerated by my imagination, and in my nightmares she was a hideous crone whose decrepit visage chilled my spine.

In one dream, I had awakened in the middle of the night and Billy was gone. My parents weren't in the house, so Billy was my responsibility, and I ran down from the loft and through the small house searching for him. He was nowhere to be found, but I heard a noise outside, and when I pulled aside the curtains and looked through the window, I saw him running across the street to Frank's. The house was dark, but I could sort of see it in the moonlight, and the front door was wide open. Billy ran inside, and in that instant the two upstairs windows lit up, the front of the house turning into a cubist version of Irene's face. The light in the right window flicked on and off like a winking eye, and the dark doorway widened and grew until it had turned into her toothless mouth smiling malevolently at me. From somewhere inside, I heard my brother screaming in terror.

Then I woke up.

Another time, I was dreaming but I thought I was awake, and I looked at the window between my bed and Billy's and saw Irene's wrinkled face floating in the air outside, staring in at me.

By the light of day, however, Irene was as nice as could be, and whenever I thought about my nighttime fears, I felt embarrassed. I even felt sorry for Irene because Frank was such a domineering, overbearing personality and I thought she deserved someone nicer.

Still...

Even though I liked having a vacation house and I liked Arizona, it was definitely something of a relief when we returned to California and the real world.

FOUR

WE SPENT CHRISTMAS vacation in Randall, and while Billy and I got to see snow for the first time, the holiday still wasn't as much fun as it usually was. Ordinarily, we would open our presents Christmas morning and then spend the afternoon with our friends in the neighborhood playing with those presents. But we had no friends here, only our parents and each other, so while Christmas morning was great, the afternoon felt kind of lonely. Frank and Irene came over later in the day with some homemade peanut brittle. It was clear that Irene would have dropped off the present, said "Merry Christmas" and left, but, once again, Frank overstayed his welcome. He still had a staring problem, and if my parents didn't notice it, Billy and I did, and we went outside as quickly as was polite to play with a remote-controlled Jeep that Santa had given Billy.

We were happy to go back to California the day after New Year's.

Summer was slightly better because we were allowed to invite friends. My friend Kenny was scheduled to come first, and he stayed for a week. He drove over with our family, and his parents picked him up the following weekend on their way to the Grand Canyon. In between, we hiked and hung out, and actually met a kid named Wyatt who lived down the street. Billy's friend Luke was supposed to come over a few weeks later, but I guess the trip was too far for his parents, and they called to cancel a few days prior.

It was near the end of August that Frank and Irene announced they would be moving. Frank said he'd been offered a job by IBM, because the company wanted him to help reorganize one of their facilities in San Francisco. Even Billy didn't believe that, but both he and I were glad Frank was leaving. Although we'd seen him less this summer, our interactions with him had been ever more uncomfortable. It even seemed sometimes that he purposely waited to drive into town until Billy and I were walking, just so he could offer us a ride. My new friend Wyatt, from down the street, thought Frank was weird as well, and he said that his dad told him Frank was leaving town because he "had to." What that meant, we weren't sure, but it didn't matter. The important thing was that Frank would be gone.

Irene would be gone, too, and I was glad of that as well. She was a nice woman, and I felt sorry for her, being married to Frank and all, but I still had occasional nightmares about her, and the last one had been a doozy. In it, I was lost in a maze, wandering endlessly through pitch black corridors with only a faltering flashlight to provide illumination. Hearing an odd susurration behind me, I turned, shone the flashlight—and saw Irene crawling on the floor toward me, her eyes wide and white, her mouth an open black hole. I awoke sweating and ready to scream.

The For Sale sign went up in front of Frank's house a few days later. It said "For Sale By Owner"—"Why should I pay someone else to do what I can do better?" he told my dad—and it sat there ignored for the next two weeks, with not a single person stopping by to look.

"Maybe you'll still be here when we come back," my dad said before we returned to California.

"No," Frank said. "I need to be in San Francisco by October first."

"What if the house doesn't sell by then?"

"Oh, it'll sell," Frank promised.

"Well," my dad said, holding out his hand. "Keep in touch. And thanks for everything."

"I have your address and phone number," Frank said.

That made me feel weird. It was a gut reaction, but, glancing over at Billy, I could tell he felt the same, and the two of us hurried back into the house before our dad made us say goodbye and shake Frank's hand.

Frank not only had our California phone number, he used it. A month after we'd returned, he called my dad to tell him that he and Irene had sold the house. The problem was, he said, that movers were taking all of their furniture to San Francisco on Monday, but the deed transfer papers were to be signed the following Wednesday, and he wouldn't have the money in hand until that Friday.

"So either we sleep on the bare floor of our empty house," he told my dad, "or we waste money on a motel, or...well, I hate to even bring it up, but I was wondering if we could rent your house for the week. It'd be handy for us because it's right across the street, and Irene could clean our place up and get it ready for the new owners, and it'd give you a little extra cash, say, a hundred dollars?"

"Of course," my dad said. "After all you've done for us..."

"I'll winterize your house before we leave so your pipes won't burst, and I promise we'll be as careful with your place as we would with our own."

"I trust you," my dad said.

THE call came shortly after breakfast the next day.

Someone had broken into our house.

Mom, Billy and I heard my dad's side of the conversation, so we pretty much knew what had happened, but he filled in the details as soon as he hung up. Apparently, Frank and Irene had gone over to our house with their clothes and toiletries, intending to use the key we'd left them to let themselves in, when they discovered that the door was unlocked. Walking inside, they saw that a floor lamp had been knocked over, and books and knickknacks had been swept off their shelves and onto the floor. The cupboard doors in the kitchen were all open. Nothing had been stolen as far as Frank could tell—the TV and stereo were both still there—but he called the sheriff and filed a report. The sheriff's office was going to leave the file open until we got there and could verify ourselves whether anything was missing. Unfortunately, he and Irene were leaving in two days, and since there was no way my dad could get over to Randall until the weekend, they were going to miss each other. But Frank said he would leave the sheriff's report on our kitchen counter, along with his new phone number in San Francisco, in case we needed to get ahold of him.

"They didn't steal anything?" my mom repeated.

My dad shrugged. "Teenagers, probably. Most likely, they broke in and had a party. Besides, we don't really have much worth stealing. Most of our stuff there is secondhand. Not the kind of thing thieves are looking for."

My dad wanted to drive over to Arizona alone on Saturday and speed back on Sunday, but my mom wanted to see the damage for herself, so we all ended up going, leaving about three o'clock Saturday morning and arriving in Randall just before noon.

Wyatt must have seen our car coming up the street, because he and his brother rode up on their bikes and were putting down their kickstands just as we had gotten out and were walking toward the deck. "I thought you guys were selling the place," Wyatt told me.

I shook my head.

"Then why were you selling all your furniture?"

I frowned, not understanding. "What?"

Then I heard my mom's startled gasp as my dad opened the door to the house.

"What the hell?" my dad said.

Billy and I hurried up the steps of the deck, Wyatt and his brother following. Inside, the house had been cleaned out. Our couch was gone. So was the coffee table. A chair and a freestanding lamp were still there, but an end-table and the lamp that had been on top of it were not. The TV and stereo were missing.

Mom wandered inside, stunned. "Where is everything?"

I turned toward Wyatt.

"That's what I was talking about. Frank had a garage sale and was selling your stuff. That's why I thought you weren't coming back."

"*He what?*" Dad's face was so red I thought he was going to have a heart attack. Wyatt backed away from the fury in his voice.

"It's okay," I told him. "My dad's not mad at you."

"No. I'm not." Dad took a deep breath.

"Yeah, Frank had a garage sale in your drive there. For two days. I thought you guys knew. I thought you told him to do it."

"Did you buy anything?" I asked.

Wyatt shook his head. "We didn't. I don't know who did, but some people around here might have."

My mom was shaking her head. "I can't believe Irene would go along with something like that. Unless Frank..."

"*I'm* filing a report with the sheriff," my dad declared. "Don't touch anything. It's all evidence."

Billy had already run upstairs to see if any of our stuff was gone, and I followed him.

"Don't touch anything!" Dad called out.

Luckily for us, the loft seemed to be untouched. Our posters were where they should be, our beds were there, our dresser, Billy's toys, my books and videotapes. I hurried back down. "Nothing's missing," I told my parents. "I don't think he went upstairs."

"Thank God," Mom breathed.

"Fat old bastard probably couldn't *get* up there," Dad muttered. He used the phone to call the sheriff's department, and two cars were in our driveway ten minutes later. Wyatt and his brother had gone home, but we were waiting for the sheriff on the deck, my dad adamant that we not touch anything in case there were clues or fingerprints. Of course, Frank had lied—he'd never filed a report about the "robbery"—but it turned out that he was not unknown to law enforcement.

"Ask anyone in town," Frank had said proudly when my dad had originally questioned him about whether he had the construction skills to build a house, implying that he was well known for the quality of his work. My parents had never done so, but they definitely should have, because we learned now that, in Randall, Frank was famous—or infamous—for being a braggart and a liar who had performed shoddy construction work on a number of houses in the area. He owed money to several people for jobs he hadn't finished after being paid ahead of time, and there were accusations that he had stolen building materials from several homes that he'd worked on. I remembered Wyatt saying that his dad had told him Frank was moving because he "had to," and that made sense to me now.

Dad told the sheriff and his deputies everything he knew: that Frank and Irene were supposedly moving to San Francisco, that Frank said he'd been hired by IBM, that Frank's in-laws, George and Betsy Robertson, lived somewhere in the Valley.

"Betsy Robertson?" the sheriff said. "She used to be the secretary down at the town hall. I know old Betsy. Didn't know she was related to Frank, though." He shook his head, chuckling. "Bad break."

We all exchanged glances. We'd been told the Robertsons lived in the Phoenix area. Why would Frank lie about that? Why would George and Betsy let him?

We went to see the Robertsons immediately after the sheriff's men left, getting their address from the local phone book. It turned out they lived in the poorer section of Randall, in a battered trailer behind the downtown. Our whole family drove over, parking in the weeds on the side of the dirt road that ran past their trailer. I'd expected the sheriff's deputies to beat us there, but questioning Frank's in-laws didn't seem to be high on their list of priorities, because there was no sign of the law.

We walked through the yardful of dried thistles to the front door, Dad knocking firmly on the metal until it was opened by Betsy. "Yes?" she said, then, recognizing us, "Oh, you're the people who bought the lot! Come in, come in."

The interior of the trailer looked like my grandparents' house: flower-print couches, generic landscape pictures on the walls, shag carpet.

"We have some questions about Frank," Dad said.

We heard a disgusted groan from the other side of the room, where George was reclining in an easy chair. "What's he done now?"

"He robbed our house and skipped town."

George and Betsy looked at each other.

My dad explained it all, from Frank's announcement that he'd gotten a job with IBM in San Francisco, to his offer to pay rent to stay in our house for a week, to the "robbery" Frank claimed to have discovered.

George looked tired. "At least they told you they were going. Neither of them said word one to us. We found out they moved on Tuesday when Betsy called up Irene to get a pound cake recipe from her."

"I got that weird noise and the message that said the line was no longer in service."

"So I drove over there to tell Frank and Irene their phone was having problems and...they were gone. I saw a 'For Sale' sign in front of the house. Frank had come over a week before to borrow a socket set, and he hadn't even said anything about it."

"Irene's your sister, right?" Mom asked Betsy. "And she didn't tell you they were moving?"

"Told us nothing. Never heard about that job or San Francisco or...anything." She seemed upset, almost as though she was about to cry.

George looked at her sympathetically. "Don't worry, dear. She'll call."

"Has Frank ever done anything like this before?" Dad asked. "Has he ever stolen things from people?"

The two of them shared a glance. We all caught it.

"Is that a yes?"

"I don't know," George confessed. "I've wondered sometimes." He gestured about him. "Frank's helped us remodel the place several times, even built a storage shed in the back and added a laundry room off the kitchen. He told us the materials were left over from other jobs that he'd done, but...I always wondered if maybe he didn't steal them."

"Frank was never the same after the war," Betsy admitted. "Oh, he was always Frank, but...something happened to him in Vietnam, something changed him. He never would talk about it—to hear him tell it, he had a great time over there, was a big hero and was responsible for many successful missions—but when he got back, he was different. More secretive, I guess. He was always up for socializing and always one with a good story, but he kept himself, his real self, more private than he had before. At least, that's the way it seemed to me."

"That's it exactly," George agreed. "I've known Frank since we were in grade school. He was always a bit of a rascal, a smart-ass even, pardon my French, but after the war..." He shook his head. "There was a darkness in him after the war."

"And the way he treated Irene sometimes..." Betsy sighed sadly.

Billy nudged me with his elbow. This was getting at it. This was the Frank we'd known, the one who'd made us so uncomfortable that we'd rather walk a mile up a hilly road on a hot day than spend three minutes in a truck with him.

George thought for a moment. "I had the feeling Frank had *learned* something over there in Vietnam. Not just *seen* something—every soldier sees things he wishes he could forget; I can attest to that—"

Betsy nodded somberly.

"But Frank...it was like he'd somehow learned some sort of secret, and it...changed him. He never said anything like this, mind you, this is just my opinion, but after the war, I always got the feeling that Frank knew something he wasn't saying, something he couldn't tell anyone, and it made him a little bit...off."

We were there for awhile longer, Dad and Mom trying to find out more about Frank and where he might have gone, and though we didn't learn much, the overall impression I had was that George and Betsy were *relieved* Frank had disappeared, and, more than anything else, that odd observation stuck with me.

We didn't ask them why they had lied about living in the Valley.

Before heading back to California in the morning, we stayed overnight in our bare-bones house. Dad made one last stop at the sheriff's office on our way out, got a copy of the incident report for insurance purposes, and the detective assigned to the case promised he'd call and let us know if there were any developments.

There were none.

Over the next few months, Dad called the Randall sheriff's department at least once a week, trying to "light a fire under them," as he said, but the news he received was always the same: nothing. No one had seen Frank, our stolen furniture had not turned up anywhere, and it was highly unlikely that the case would ever be closed.

We returned to Randall for Easter vacation. We'd spent several weekends scouring thrift stores for replacement furnishings, and a U-Haul trailer once again accompanied us to Arizona, filled with what we'd found.

"This house smells weird," Billy said, sniffing the air as soon as we walked in.

He was right, it did, but Mom just told us to open the doors and windows and let in some air. The minute she walked into her bedroom, though, she rushed back out, gagging. "It's in there!" she managed to croak, and then hurried into the bathroom where we could hear her throwing up into the toilet.

Something like this, Billy and I had to experience for ourselves. Holding our noses, we walked through the kitchen and down the short hall to my parents' room. The stench was powerful enough to break through the barrier of our plugged noses, and we didn't get any farther than the doorway before we dashed back out through the front of the house and stood breathing the fresh air on the deck.

"There's something dead in there," Dad announced after investigating for himself. His stomach wasn't as delicate as ours, and he hadn't run away like the rest of us.

"What do you think it is?" Mom asked from the kitchen, still holding a hand over her nose.

"Hard to tell. Rat, maybe. Mouse. Raccoon. Whatever it is, I'll find it."

But twenty minutes later, having moved almost everything except the bed and dresser into the hall, with clothes from the closet piled atop the bed, there was still no sign of what could be causing the stench. "It must be under the house," Dad reasoned. He got a flashlight from the junk drawer in the kitchen, and we followed him outside, where he opened up the small trapdoor that led to the crawlspace under the A-frame. The terrible smell wafted out through the opening but was not as strong as in the bedroom. Poking his head in, Dad shined the light around, then immediately jumped back. "Jesus!"

Billy and I pressed forward, trying to see in. "What is it? What is it?"

He pushed us back. "Call the sheriff," he told Mom, his face white. "Now."

"What is it?" Billy demanded.

"Dead dogs," he said.

Mom hurried back inside to call the sheriff, and we could hear her running footsteps on the floor of the house. Dad shone the light into the crawlspace again, and this time we saw what he was talking about. Dead dogs, four or five of them at least, with a big German Shepherd lying on top, were piled in the dirt directly below my parents' bedroom near the rear of the house. It was a shocking and inexplicable sight. The eyes of two beagles whose heads lolled in our direction glowed silver with the reflected illumination of the flashlight. One of the animals was partially white, and on its fur we could see dark clumps of dried blood. The only sounds were our heavy breathing and the buzzing of seemingly hundreds of flies.

I couldn't help myself. I threw up. I managed to jerk my head to the right before it happened, but it was still too close for comfort, and both Dad and Billy jumped back with expressions of disgust. I went over to the hose and turned on the faucet, washing off my face and hands.

Mom came back. "They're on their way." She glanced at the square black opening under the house. "Who do you think could've—"

Dad looked at her. "Frank."

I could see that.

I imagined him in the middle of the night, skulking through the forest, between trees and bushes, going from house to house, looking for dogs that were tied up in their owners' yards, then killing the animals and carrying them over his shoulder back to our place. I shivered. Just the thought of it freaked me out.

How had he killed them? I wondered. Poison, probably. He couldn't have shot them because someone would have heard.

Why our house, though? We were letting him stay there. We were nice to him.

None of it made any sense.

The deputies who accompanied the sheriff were the same ones who'd shown up last time, and it made me wonder how big the Randall sheriff's department was. It was probably closer to Mayberry than Anaheim, I thought, and despite the bizarre, horrific nature of this crime, I doubted they'd be any more successful in finding Frank than they had been up to now.

Mom took me and Billy away from the crawlspace opening and out to the front of the house while Dad explained what we'd found. From Frank's old place across the street, three kids and a woman carrying a baby came walking toward us. The new owners. Their last name was Goodwin, and, as it turned out, the dad, who was at work, was a mining engineer. He'd been transferred here from Clifton by his company, which was reopening a copper mine in the nearby foothills that had been played out in the 1950s, but which today's extraction technology had made once again viable. The eldest boy was a teenager and quite a bit older than me, but the younger one, Mark, was twelve, about my age. The oldest girl, Janine, was a year younger than Billy, and the littlest was a baby.

Mrs. Goodwin and the kids had walked across the street because they were curious about the two sheriff's cars in front of our house. Mrs. Goodwin seemed a little concerned, maybe thinking we were the type of people who were always getting in trouble with the law. But Mom explained what had happened, that we had smelled something horrible and had discovered a rotting pile of dead dogs that Frank had left under our house.

"Frank?" Mrs. Goodwin said incredulously. "The Frank who sold us this house?"

Mom nodded.

"I can't believe it!"

"Oh, believe it," Mom said, and proceeded to tell her about our stolen furniture and the garage sale, and our discovery that Frank was infamous around town for not completing construction jobs and not paying back money he owed.

Dad and the deputies walked out from around the side of the house. One of the officers used the radio in his car to call the office, while the other one wrote something down on a clipboard as he spoke to the sheriff. Dad approached us. "They said they'd gotten reports of five missing dogs in this area of town over the past three months. I think that's them."

"So Frank killed them?" Mrs. Goodwin said. "And hid the bodies under your house?"

"Looks that way," Dad said.

"Jesus," Mrs. Goodwin breathed. "What a sicko."

"Oh, this is Melanie Goodwin," Mom said, making introductions. "And this is my husband, Andy."

The three of them talked while we kids tried to casually make our way over to the side of the house. We were just starting to get to know the Goodwins, so even though Billy and I had no desire to see those dogs again, we were willing to let our new neighbors check them out. The crawlspace door was still open, but when we actually got there, Janine and Mark held back with me and Billy, while Dean, the teenager, poked his head into the opening. He came back looking queasy and a lot less brave than he had a moment before.

"Hey, you want to come over to our house?" Mark offered.

"Sure," I said, and the five of us headed back out to the street.

"Where are you going?" Mom asked, always alert.

"Over to their house," I told her.

"It's all right," Mrs. Goodwin said.

We walked across the street and tramped over the gravel driveway. "How long have you guys been here?" I asked Mark.

"About two months. Two *long* months."

I smiled.

"You know," Mark told me as we approached the front door, "I think our house is haunted."

"Dill weed," Dean said scornfully, pushing past us into the house and "accidentally" hitting Mark's head as he passed by.

I shivered, thinking of Irene. Looking up at the second floor windows, I recalled my nightmare where the front of the house had turned into her face and she had swallowed my brother.

Janine walked inside, followed by Billy and Mark. I entered last. Dean had already plopped himself down on a couch in the living room and turned on the TV. Janine was introducing Billy to their new kitten, who was running crazily around the dining area, chasing imaginary playmates between the legs of the table and chairs.

"Let's check out my room," Mark said. "It's upstairs."

None of us had ever been on the second floor of Frank's house. While the downstairs looked different with the addition of the Goodwins' furnishings, there hung about it the same off-putting, off-kilter atmosphere that I remembered. It was not a comfortable home, and I felt even more uneasy walking up the steps to the second floor. Frank had hidden the stairway in what looked like a closet next to the kitchen, and the narrow passageway was darker and steeper than it should have been.

At the top, the open landing offered access to two bedrooms and a bathroom. Mark headed straight into the closest bedroom, but I paused for a moment, struck by something that seemed familiar, something I could not quite put my finger on—

The walls.

"That's our paneling!" I said.

Mark turned around. "What?"

I pointed to the walls. "I recognize it from the model home. That was supposed to be our paneling. Frank stole it."

I ran downstairs to get my parents. Dad was again talking to the sheriff, but Mom and Mrs. Goodwin came along with me, and I showed them the paneling on the second floor.

"That bastard," Mom said under her breath. I could not remember ever hearing her swear before.

Mrs. Goodwin looked nervous. "We didn't know anything about this..."

Mom waved her hand dismissively. "Don't worry. It's not your fault. And we don't need it anymore anyway. But just the thought that Frank would steal from the house that we hired him to build..." She shook her head. "Every day, it's something else. I just wonder what we're going to find out next."

What we found out next happened the day before our vacation ended.

The Goodwins were good people. Back in California, we barely knew our neighbors. My friends and Billy's friends were kids from school, scattered all over the neighborhood, and my parents' friends were mostly people from work. The Harshbargers, the old couple to the right of us, we barely saw, and the Jorgensons, to the left, we didn't really like and mostly ignored. But from day one, it was like we'd known the Goodwins forever. They weren't just our neighbors; they were our friends. The dads got along, the moms got along, and we kids played together nearly every day, except Dean, who was too old for us, and the baby, who was too young.

Mark and Dean shared one of the upstairs bedrooms, while Janine, being a girl, got her own. But Dean had apparently been complaining since before they'd moved to Randall that he needed his own room and was too old to be bunking with his little brother. Frank's house had a basement—which I hadn't known about—and Dean was pushing to make the basement into his own room. Kind of like Greg's cool attic pad on *The Brady Bunch*, I imagined. The basement needed work if it was ever going to be anything other than storage space, and Mr. and Mrs. Goodwin told Dean that if he cleared it out, cleaned it up and painted it, he could have it. So he spent almost that entire week trying to get his new bedroom in shape. One day, he even gave me and Mark a dollar each to help him move a half cord of firewood from the basement to a spot outside under the rear deck.

It was Saturday, the day before we were supposed to head home.

We were awakened by screams from across the street.

Morning in Randall was always quiet, the forest silent save for birdsong, wind and the occasional far off muffled whooshing of cars from the highway. So the screams of Mrs. Goodwin sounded even louder and more shocking than they would have ordinarily. It wasn't a case of us wondering what was causing the noise; we knew exactly what it was. In fact, I thought for a second that Mr. Goodwin had gone crazy and was slaughtering his family.

Dad was up and out the door before the rest of us had even thrown off our covers, and by the time Mom, Billy and I had dashed across the street in our slippers and pajamas, he was already inside the Goodwins' house. The front door was open but the screen door was closed and, unsure if we should walk in uninvited, Mom knocked loudly. "Melanie?" she called. I could hear the fear in her voice.

Mark opened the screen, his mom right behind him. Both of them looked sick.

"What is it?" Mom asked. "What happened?"

"There's a skeleton in the basement!" Mark blurted out.

Mrs. Goodwin was nodding. "Dean got up early to work on his room before breakfast and replace some rotted boards, only behind the boards was a body."

"A skeleton!"

"A skeleton," she agreed, her voice just this side of panic.

"A kid!"

"It looks like a child," she confirmed.

I wanted to go down there and see, but Mom was holding tight to both my hand and Billy's. "Did you call the sheriff?"

"They're supposed to be on their way."

I looked at my mom, and I knew exactly what she was thinking, because I was thinking it, too.

Frank.

Mrs. Goodwin went to get the baby out of her crib. Dean, Dad and Mr. Goodwin came up from the basement, and we all stood outside on the porch, most of us in our pajamas, waiting for the sheriff to come. I didn't get to see the skeleton, but the descriptions being bandied about painted a vivid picture for me. Mr. Goodwin estimated the boy's age at about three. Mark said the body was crouched or sitting down, so it could fit into the tiny space dug into the dirt behind the wall. Dean said the skull still had some skin on it. Rotted blackened skin. He was trying to come off as tough, but he wasn't pulling it off, and his cracking voice was a mixture of sorrow, sadness, fear, curiosity and confusion.

"I wonder how long he's been there," a subdued Billy wondered.

"We don't know," Dad told him. "The medical examiner will have to figure that out."

Mom invited the rest of the Goodwins over for breakfast, while Dean and the dads stayed to wait for the sheriff. The moms went into the kitchen, and I turned on the TV so everyone else could watch cartoons while I went upstairs and changed into my clothes. Even with the light on and the morning sun streaming through the window, the loft seemed darker than it should have, and I thought about Frank's staring problem and the dead dogs under the house and the skeleton in the basement across the street, and I quickly took off my PJs, pulled on pants and a t-shirt, and ran back downstairs.

The sheriff and a deputy arrived in the same car moments later, and a few minutes after that an ambulance and fire engine pulled up. They were all still there a half hour later when we finished breakfast. A reporter from the newspaper was taking pictures. This was obviously a big event in Randall—it would have been a big event back in Anaheim, too—and as soon as Mark and I finished eating, we headed across the street. I didn't bother to ask Mom if I could go, because I knew she'd say no. The two of us just took off, sneaking between the ambulance and fire truck in the middle of the street and hanging around the periphery of the crowd gathered in front of the Goodwins' door, where Dad, Dean and Mr. Goodwin were talking with a fireman, the sheriff and his deputy.

No one seemed to know who the boy was. Did Frank and Irene have a secret son? A retarded or deformed kid they kept locked in the basement? If so, had he died accidentally or had they killed him? Maybe Frank had kidnapped a kid from another town or state, tortured him in the basement, then hid his body in the wall after he died. None of the options were good, and the onlookers grew silent as a paramedic walked past them into the house carrying an empty white zippered bag. I assumed they were getting ready to bring out the boy's skeleton.

"Can't you find Frank and arrest him?" Dad asked the sheriff. "Jesus Christ, what does he have to do, kill someone in front of you before you go after him?"

"We *are* after him," the deputy said defensively. "We're not just sitting around twiddling our thumbs. And we've alerted a lot of other police and sheriff's departments, too."

"Don't worry," the sheriff said calmly. "We'll get him."

"What about his in-laws? George and Betsy? Maybe they know something about this."

The sheriff rubbed the back of his neck. "Funny thing about that..."

But it wasn't funny. It turned out that the trailer had burned down, and nothing was left but blackened earth. One of the firemen said it had happened about a month ago. Propane explosion, he explained, started by a leak near the water heater.

"Were they—?" Dad asked.

The sheriff shook his head. "Never found hide nor hair of 'em. Which is why they're still persons of interest. No sign in the ashes of any bones or...anything. I don't know if the explosion was deliberate or they left before it happened or left *because* it happened, but they're gone."

"We put an APB out for them, too," the deputy said.

It took the rest of the morning for the kid's skeleton to be brought up. Pictures had been taken, they'd gone over the basement for fingerprints or other clues that might point to the identity of the boy or whoever had walled him up, and I'd long since gotten bored and gone back to our house, when Mark came running over and told us they were bringing up the body. Luckily for Billy and me, Mom was in the bathroom at that moment, so we took off without telling her, running across the street and standing next to Dad for protection, in case she caught us.

After all that, we couldn't really see anything. The skeleton was brought out on a stretcher, already sealed up inside the white bag, although I could kind of make out the outline of a body.

Soon after, the officials left, and Billy and I went home with Dad. I didn't know what the Goodwins were doing or how they'd be able to sleep tonight in a house where a dead body had been found. The entire family came over later in the afternoon, when we were packing for our trip back to California, and thanked us for all our help. I assumed they were saying goodbye, and I felt sad. I'd just gotten to know Mark, but already I considered him one of my best friends, and I'd been looking forward to hanging out during the summer. Now the idea of spending those three months alone with my brother depressed me—although at least I still had Wyatt down the street.

A lot of stuff had happened since we'd bought the house in Randall, but I wished for the first time that we *hadn't* bought the house. While the dead kid would make a great story to tell my friends once I got back to school, deep down, I would rather not have known about it. I was pretending to be cool, but the thought of spending vacations across from that house kind of freaked me out, and when Dad woke me early the next morning to get ready for the trip home, he pulled me out of a dream in which Irene was pushing Billy's dead body into a crevice in the basement, her ancient wrinkled face all smiles, while Frank stood on the stairs watching her and nodding approvingly.

FIVE

THE ECONOMICS OF vacation home ownership turned out to be not as simple as my parents had originally thought, especially when things started to fall apart. At first, it was a leaking toilet. The plumber who came to fix it shook his head and said he was surprised it hadn't leaked immediately because the bonehead who'd installed it hadn't put in a required gasket. After that, we had a blackout, because, the electrician said, Frank hadn't wired the house properly and one of the circuits was being overloaded. Then the roof leaked during a summer monsoon, and the roofer told us after he'd patched the spot that there should have been a layer of tarpaper under the shingles. He warned us to expect additional leaks in the future unless we had the entire roof redone.

"This damn Frank house," Dad said after each new disaster.

That year, my father had to get a summer job to make ends meet. There weren't that many part-time job openings in Randall for a middle-aged man who was only in town between the last week of June and the last week of August, but he managed to get hired at the lumber yard. Wyatt from down the street had moved, though we never found out why or where, but the Goodwins still lived in Frank's house—surprisingly, after all that had happened—and for that I was grateful.

"I wouldn't live there," Billy confided to me. "It's probably *really* haunted now."

I felt the same way, but I didn't want Billy to know that, so I pretended to be braver than I was. Mark even invited me to stay overnight there a couple of times, and I did. Although...

I didn't like the house.

Part of it was the skeleton in the basement, of course. But part of it was the fact that Mark was right—it did feel haunted. As I lay on the floor in my sleeping bag while my friend snored in his bed, I heard creaking on the stairs, as though someone was walking slowly up. No one was—and I knew that even at the time—but the sound was definitely real, not a figment of my imagination, and there was no explanation for what caused it. The house had cold spots as well: one outside the upstairs bathroom, and one near the kitchen downstairs that I knew everyone must have felt but that no one commented upon. The cold spots might have been a result of air seeping in from outside due to Frank's shoddy workmanship—except this was summer, and the air outside the house was even warmer than the air inside. What could definitely *not* be put down to poor workmanship were the glimpses of movement I occasionally spotted in my peripheral vision. It happened while we were eating dinner with the entire family—a dark shadow that seemed to slip quickly from the entryway into the short hall that led to the master bedroom—and it happened while I was alone: movement behind me in the bathroom mirror while I brushed my teeth; a figure far taller than Janine passing from the landing into her bedroom; a shifting of the darkness behind the partially open door of Mark's closet.

More than ghostly encounters, however, it was the house itself that made me feel unsettled. The doors did not seem to be in the right places; they were always too far to the left within a wall or too far to the right. And the views outside the windows were not what I thought they should be. In Mark's room, for example, the window opposite his bed should have looked across the street at our house—but it was the *other* window that faced that direction, while the one opposite the bed faced the forest. Strangest of all, each time I closed my eyes and opened them, the walls seemed to have just stopped moving, as though they'd been in motion until that second and had only clicked into place when I opened my eyes.

I said nothing to anyone, however, and, in truth, the subject of the house hardly ever came up. I suppose the Goodwins wanted to forget what they'd found in the basement, so no one mentioned it, and life continued on as though it had never occurred—although I noticed that Dean's new bedroom was what had formerly been his dad's den, next to the master bedroom, and the basement was once again used only for storage.

The weird thing was that no one had discovered who the skeleton boy was. There were no missing kids in town, and though the sheriff's department had sent out photographs and dental x-rays to every law enforcement agency in the state, perhaps the country, no one had ever responded. No grieving parents came to claim what was left of the body, and I think everyone kind of assumed that it *had* been Frank's boy.

I know I did.

June and July passed by quickly. It was nice having friends living right across the street, and Mark and I, and Billy and Janine, spent most days together, hiking, riding bikes, listening to music, hanging out. We didn't even have to invite friends from California over that summer, and one night, upstairs in the loft when we were about to go to sleep, Billy said, "I think summer's more fun in Randall than it was in Anaheim."

"I think so, too," I told him.

YOU never know which conversation with someone is going to be your last. If you did, you'd probably make it more meaningful, probably talk about important subjects, personal things: hopes, dreams, regrets. Feelings.

My last conversation with Billy was a disagreement about cartoons. Specifically, whether the new batch of *Ren and Stimpy* episodes, the first in a long while, were up to the show's usual standards.

Billy said the new cartoons were just as good as they'd always been. I said they weren't funny and the voices sounded off.

I've thought about that morning many times since then, played it out in my head with a hundred different outcomes. Sometimes, in my imagination, we talk about our plans for the future: what we want to be when we grow up. Sometimes, we talk about our parents, the good, the bad and the ugly, because we're the only two people in the world to have the shared experience of living with them.

But the truth is the truth, there's no escaping it, and the truth is that my last words to my brother were banal criticisms of a long-forgotten kid's program. And his to me were childishly mundane rebuttals. There was nothing special or significant about what either of us said, and the only reason I remember that conversation to this day is because of what came after.

And what came after was death.

It happened during a commercial. Billy had to go to the bathroom, and he hopped up from his seat on the floor and ran past the kitchen, down the short hall, and—

The floor gave way beneath him.

I saw him fall, heard the crash, heard the scream. The sound of collapsing wood lasted longer than my brother's cry, and I knew instantly what that meant. Filled with horror, I ran over to where he'd fallen through the floor. Mom, washing dishes in the sink, had immediately turned around and was already there, and Dad rushed out from the bedroom, where he'd been changing his clothes.

Billy lay beneath the house, impaled by what looked almost like a spear: a sharpened triangular board embedded in the ground and now protruding from my brother's midsection, blood gushing all around it and spilling onto the earth. His eyes were wide open, and he seemed to be staring right at me.

Dad pulled me back from the opening just as Mom fainted and started to fall. He let me go, causing me to drop back onto my buttocks, while grabbing her around the waist and keeping her from collapsing. His own face was sick with shock, a terrible expression I knew I would never forget. Back in the living room, I could hear the voices of Ren and Stimpy arguing, and I laid on my back and stared up at the ceiling and started to scream.

I was a kid and left out of the deliberations and details, so I don't know how everything happened or what transpired, but the funeral was held in California. We drove back in a completely silent car, and Billy was transported somehow to a mortuary in Orange County. He was buried at an old cemetery in Anaheim across the street from a restaurant called The Original Pancake House. The day was hot and sunny, and the new suit my mom bought me itched. There were no kids there—family friends and relatives had not wanted their children to be exposed to death so intimately—and I was alone with a bunch of adults and a small coffin that didn't even look real. We weren't churchgoers, but there was a minister who stood at the head of the open grave and talked about loss and grief and pretended to know my brother.

I stood there numbly, feeling more alone than I ever had in my life. Billy and I hadn't always gotten along, but we were brothers. We slept in the same room, we ate our meals together, we brushed our teeth together, we played together when our friends weren't around. I was closer to him than to anyone else in the world, and now he was gone, his body about to be buried amidst all these strangers.

I had never seen my dad cry before, but he cried that day. Everyone cried. Then they lowered the small coffin into the hole, we each threw a handful of dirt on top of it, and then the funeral was over.

"He's not even buried!" I shouted when my parents started to move away. My voice was too loud and broken up by sobs.

But Mom told me that's how it was done: the people at the cemetery would finish filling in the grave once we were gone.

I folded my arms and refused to move. "I'm not leaving!" I announced.

"Daniel," Dad said gently.

I appealed to him as someone who should know better. "That's Billy!" I yelled, pointing into the open hole. "We can't just leave him like this!"

He looked at me, put a sympathetic hand on my shoulder. "You're right," he said, and the people who had started to leave came back, and we all stood there as employees were found who filled in the hole. Dad said a few more words when it was done, thanked everyone, and people drifted off until only the three of us remained, looking down at the rectangular mound of dirt. We stood there quietly, thinking our own thoughts, and it was Dad again who put a soft hand on my shoulder and said it was time to go.

The house when we got back seemed quiet and empty and unbearably sad.

In the days that followed, someone from either law enforcement or the insurance company, I don't know who, examined the accident site at our Randall house to determine what had happened. According to my dad, it was concluded that the structural design was flawed, with too much stress being placed on an area of flooring with no underlying support. How that part of the hallway had lasted as long as it had was a mystery, since it should have failed long before this. And why it had collapsed under Billy, the lightest of us all, rather than under someone heavier, was something that no one had an answer for. My parents planned to sue the makers of the pre-fab kit—"For everything they have," Mom said bitterly—over the faulty house design, but found out that the company had been made aware of that problem almost immediately and had instituted a fix. For our year and the year before ours, before the problem was permanently rectified with a remodeled kit, an extra beam was added to support the wood over the hallway, along with steel brackets to install the beam between two existing supports. Moreover, to protect themselves from lawsuits, the company had required recipients of the fix to sign for it.

And Frank had.

He had simply not installed it.

The only question in my mind was whether Billy's death had been an accident, the result of poor workmanship, or whether the collapsing floor had been intentional, some sort of trap. It was the sharpened board directly beneath the spot that made me wonder. I thought of Frank's alien stare, and the way he waited to drive his truck until Billy and I were walking so that he could offer us a ride, and as crazy as it sounded, I could see him setting us up that way on purpose.

He'd ripped off our furniture.

And our paneling.

And piled dead dogs in our crawlspace.

And now he'd killed Billy.

Our family did not survive the loss of my brother. My parents accused each other of setting the stage for Billy's death. My dad blamed my mom for wanting a vacation home in Randall in the first place, and my mom blamed my dad for hiring Frank to build it and for not seeing the sharpened board when he helped the sheriff and his men take the dead dogs out from under our house.

We never went back to Randall. The house and all of its furnishings were sold without any of us returning to Arizona, and after a year of terrible screaming fights alternating with deep cold silences, the two of them separated, me and my mom staying in the house, my dad moving to a nearby apartment. They both worked for the same school district but they did not see each other on a daily basis. In fact, I'm pretty sure the only contact they had was when I was passed off from one to the other.

My dad died in a car crash when I was sixteen, and my mom cried through the entire funeral. Until that moment, I thought they'd hated each other, but obviously something was left of her feelings for him—more than something—and seeing how much his loss affected her made it more acute for me as well. I thought I'd been getting along fine with the weekend visits and occasional summer sleepovers, but suddenly I was aware of all I'd missed, the little intimate everyday things that amounted to a real relationship. I remembered Dad tucking me in at night when I was little, sitting next to me on the couch watching TV, taking me to the hardware store with him to buy some small item he needed and, afterward, stopping off to get an ice cream cone. Despite everything everyone said about spending "quality time" with kids, I realized that it was "quantity time" that was more important. I never cared *what* I did with my dad, I just wanted to be with him for as much time as possible. It sunk in that we would never have time together again, and I understood, as I hadn't up to that point, how far apart we'd drifted after he'd moved out of the house. Staring at his closed coffin, I felt unmoored in the world, adrift. I still had my mom, but my dad was gone, and I would never be able to ask his advice on buying a car or making repairs or applying for college or any of the thousands of other things that would come up in my life. I sobbed through the rest of the funeral myself, crying for my dad, for my mom, for me, for Billy, for the lives we should have had but didn't.

I was in college when my mom passed away. In those pre-cell phone days, I was called out of my Principles of Economic Theory class by a delivered pink call slip and told to go to the Administration building, where I was informed by an elderly secretary that Mom had collapsed at work and was in St. Jude's Hospital. The school had no more information than that—I don't think the hospital's privacy policy allowed them to reveal anything else to a non-family member—so I hurried out of the building and across the massive parking lot to my car. St. Jude's was less than ten minutes away. I got there in record time, speeding but not getting caught, and swung into a green 15-minute visitor's spot, dashing through the building's entrance to the Admissions counter, where I was told that she was on the fifth floor, in Intensive Care.

"Can I see her?" I asked.

"You can go right up. Just wear this." She'd written my name on an adhesive sticker, and I affixed it to my shirt pocket, hurrying over to the elevator.

The ICU was structured like a wheel, with a nurse's station at the hub and a series of rooms arranged around it. My mom was in Room

D, lying on a raised bed that took up much of the small space. She was surrounded by monitoring equipment. There were wires everywhere and a tube shoved down her throat, so she could not speak, but she was alert enough to squeeze my hand when I grasped hers. I realized that I had not held her hand since I was a child. In fact, the last time I could remember doing so was in Randall, when she came with us to buy a root beer float at the Dairy Queen one time and held onto both me and Billy as we crossed the highway.

I was informed by a doctor that she had had both a heart attack *and* a stroke, and that the stroke had affected not only her cognitive abilities but some of her organ functions. The doctor gave it to me straight: she was not expected to live, and even if she did, the brain damage she'd suffered was irreversible and no amount of rehab could bring back what had been lost.

Mom had the eyes of a miserable dog, sad helpless eyes that stared up at me and seemed to be pleading for an end to this agony, although at that point I'm not sure she even knew who I was. I thought of the people I'd seen on the news who advocated for euthanasia, who fought entrenched medical bureaucracies and lengthy court cases in order to relieve their loved ones' suffering through assisted suicide, and I realized that I wasn't one of those people. As selfish as it might be, I didn't want my mom to die; I wanted her to stay alive as long as possible. At the same time, I wanted to let the hospital handle everything. I was content to just be there and hold her hand and not have to do any of the thinking.

She hung on for three endless days, days in which I slept in the chair next to her and left only to go to the bathroom, grab a quick bite to eat from the hospital cafeteria, or rush home to take a quick shower and change my clothes. She couldn't have been in much pain because they kept her heavily sedated at all times. For all intents and purposes, Room D of the ICU had been turned into a hospice, and I was with her when she passed away. The doctors and nurses told me it was coming—their instruments recorded the failing of her body—and I remained in place, holding her hand, speaking soothingly to her, though I had no idea if she could understand me.

They had turned off the sound on the monitors so I would not have to hear that maddening beeping, but I could see the line graphs diminish from mountain peaks to small foothills, and at the moment all of the lines went flat, I felt a sudden heavy limpness in her hand and saw that her chest had stopped moving.

She was dead.

Both of my parents were dead.

Would they still have died if Billy had survived? There was no way to know, but so many variables would have changed over so many years that I found it hard to believe that my mom would have been in the exact same physical condition she was today, or that my dad would have been driving in his car at the exact time that the unlicensed driver who hit him would have sped through that intersection.

In other words, they'd probably still be alive.

It was a notion I'd had before, but that was a dangerous line of thinking, and each time the idea intruded upon my thoughts, I pushed it away, not wanting to get bogged down in an endless spiraling chain of what-if scenarios.

Even if Billy had lived and they *had* each died at the same time in the same way, I would have had someone to share it with. Billy would have been experiencing the same loss, and we could have gone through it together. But I was all alone, untethered in the world after watching the last of my family pass away before my eyes.

"She's in a better place," an overweight nurse told me as she and the doctor began unhooking the equipment.

I wanted to cry. I wanted to smack the pious look of pity off the nurse's face. I wanted to scream out my frustration and demand that someone else's mother be taken instead because I had already given enough in this life. I wanted to run out of the room and out of the hospital and drive away, never looking back. But I shut it all down. Before I allowed any emotion to take hold, while the numbness still remained, I shut it all down.

I shut it down.

SIX

IT HAD BEEN years since I'd thought about Frank, but after showing Brad and Connie that cabin in Big Bear, it all came back, and I knew I had to talk to Brad's mother.

Frank House.

On Monday morning, I met with the couple at my office back in Orange County. I'd been trying to think of a way to get Brad's mother's phone number or address, but luckily for me, she was co-signing the loan with them, so I had all the information I needed in the paperwork. Pretending it was related to the sale, I called her the minute the two of them left my office, making an appointment to meet her at her house in Tarzana. It was the house I really wanted to see, and she agreeably allowed me to meet her at her home.

There was construction on the Santa Ana Freeway and a traffic jam on the 101, but I'd given myself plenty of time and still arrived a few minutes early. The house, I saw, as I pulled up to the curb in front, was a single-story structure set back from the street. In what may or may not have been a freaky coincidence, it was painted the same red barn color and had the same white trim as Frank's old house in Randall.

I got out of the car, pressed the button on my key to lock it, and walked up to the front porch. Before I could even ring the bell, the door was opened by an elderly woman with a heavily made-up face, dressed in tight brightly colored clothes far too young for her age. "Are you Mr. Martin?"

I nodded my acknowledgment. "And you must be Mrs. Simmons."

"Call me Sandy." She opened the door wider. "Come in. Would you like something to drink?"

"No, thank you," I said politely. Stepping over the threshold, I glanced casually around the living room in which I found myself.

And stared at the walls with a shock of recognition.

They were covered in our wallpaper.

I identified the pattern immediately, though I hadn't seen it in decades.

Re-experiencing a smell associated with childhood could bring back a flood of forgotten memories, I knew, but the sight of that wallpaper did exactly the same thing for me. Seeing it again, looking at those beige southwestern designs on that off-white background, made me feel like I was a kid again, on vacation in Arizona with my family, and I was instantly overcome by a profound sense of loss.

The emotion must have shown in my face because Sandy Simmons was suddenly looking at me with an expression of concern. "Are you all right?"

I forced myself to smile. "Fine," I said. "I'm fine." Glancing away from the wallpaper, I looked through a doorway into the kitchen. There was something about the doorway...

The frame.

Yes. I'd seen it before, too, though it took me a moment to realize where.

In George and Betsy's trailer home.

I was surprised I'd even noticed such a detail, but I had, and for some reason its appearance had stayed with me. I hadn't been able to identify it at the time, but as a realtor, I now recognized it as distressed wood trim, of a type that had been very popular thirty years before.

Were these just coincidences? I didn't think so. As with the Goodwins' house, Frank had apparently taken bits and pieces from projects on which he'd worked—our A-frame, George and Betsy's trailer—and used them in the construction of this building. I looked around. How many other things, I wondered, had been stolen from jobs that he'd been hired to do?

Not sure of how to broach the subject, I held out the folder I'd been carrying, my ostensible reason for coming over. I'd Xeroxed all documents pertaining to Sandy's co-signing of her son's loan, and though it was a lie and totally unnecessary, I told her I needed her initials on several pages. We sat down on the couch, I took out a pen and handed it to her, then flipped through the documents and had her initial the bottom of sheets where Brad and Connie had signed.

Casually, as though making small talk, I said, "Brad mentioned that this was a Frank house."

She laughed. "You'd have to know some family history to get that one..."

"We had a Frank house," I said. "In Arizona. When I was little." I gestured toward the walls. "In fact, that's our wallpaper. Frank must have stolen it so he could use it for his own house here."

Sandy was no longer laughing, and when she spoke I detected an uneasiness that hadn't been there a moment before. "That was Frank," she said.

I told her the tale of our vacation home and the Goodwins' house, leaving out the parts about the dead dogs, the boy's skeleton and Billy's death, but leaving in Frank's stolen furniture garage sale, and the fact that he'd taken our paneling and used it in his own house. I let her know what we'd learned about Frank from others in town after he'd left.

Sandy didn't seem surprised by any of it. She leaned forward. "I never told Brad this because it would've freaked him out, but underneath all that wallpaper, when the laundry room collapsed, there were *bones*. Animal bones—cats, guinea pigs, what have you—but a *lot* of them. Like someone had been killing pets for years and storing their bodies under the house."

"Frank," I said.

She nodded. "I think so. Don't ask me *why* I think so, but I do." She shivered. "There was something...not quite right about that man. I never trusted him. My husband didn't either. Oh, we joked about him and made fun of him, especially about what a terrible builder he was, but I think we were also a little...I don't know. *Nervous* isn't the right word, but it's close. Even if he *had* stayed nearby, I don't think we would have asked him to fix any of his problems. He was an uncomfortable man to be around, if you know what I mean."

I did.

"The stare," I said.

"You noticed it, too!" She laughed again. "Yeah, he would always stare at you in that weirdo way when you were talking to him."

"And there were those big pauses."

"Right," she said, "as though he was translating whatever you said into a foreign language that only he understood." There was no laughing now, only remembrance of Frank's odd behavior.

I took a deep breath, decided to plunge in. "There were dead dogs under our house," I said quietly. "And the house across the street, Frank's house, the one he lived in, had the body of a dead boy walled up in the basement. Well, not a body exactly, more of a skeleton. He'd been dead a long time."

Sandy looked stunned.

I explained how the Goodwins had found the dead boy, how both Frank, his wife and his in-laws had disappeared, how his in-laws' trailer home had exploded, and how the police had never found hide nor hair of any of them. I gestured around. "And then, all these years later, I find that Frank Watkins moved here, built another house and did exactly the same thing."

"Watkins?" Sandy said, frowning. "His name was Warwick. Frank Warwick."

A fake name. This was a new wrinkle. But not entirely surprising.

I shrugged. "Maybe that's why they couldn't track him down."

She waved away that suggestion. "Criminals use aliases all the time, and *they're* caught. My bet is that your small town police force was just incompetent. I mean, here he was, only one state away and starting all over again."

She got no argument from me. "Did you meet his wife when you bought the place?"

Sandy put a hand to her cheek. "Oh, the poor thing! I felt so sorry for her. She seemed browbeaten, living with that man."

"Irene was her name, wasn't it?"

"You know, I think you're right. Irene. That sounds familiar. But Frank was the one we remembered. What a blowhard! Even without all—" She waved her hand around. "—*this*, he was so obnoxious that I couldn't have forgotten him. Which reminds me, do you want to see the house? I could take you around."

It was why I'd come, and I followed her, noting with my realtor's eye a hodgepodge of styles, due no doubt to the variety of stolen materials used in the building's construction. In the hallway, I recognized wainscoting from the Goodwins' house.

Frank's house.

We walked to the master bedroom. "Do you happen to know where he moved?" I asked. "Did he tell you or your husband anything about his plans?"

"Funny you should say that. He was bragging to Stephen that he was going to Detroit, that one of the big automakers had been impressed by an idea he had to make their workplace more efficient and he'd been hired as a consultant at some outrageous salary. I probably wouldn't have remembered that, except Irene let slip that she wasn't looking forward to moving to Las Vegas because she hated the heat and wasn't a big fan of gambling. The men were talking in the living room, and us women were over in the kitchen, but sound carries, and as soon as she said that, Frank shot her the hardest look I'd ever seen in my life. She immediately shut up. Honestly, it was like he wanted to kill her. She was such a frail, frightened little thing to begin with, and she seemed happy to have someone to talk to, but as soon as she let that cat out of the bag, she shut her mouth and never said another word." Sandy shook her head. "It wouldn't surprise me to learn that he beat her after that, because that's what it looked like he wanted to do, and that's what it looked like she was afraid of. Anyway, I never forgot that, and if you ask me, I think they moved to Las Vegas. Although, for some reason, he wanted us all to *think* he was moving to Detroit. Like I said, I never trusted that man."

We stepped into the master bedroom. It was larger than I'd expected, and nicely furnished. The adjoining bathroom contained both a sunken tub and a shower. But I didn't like it. I didn't like any of it, and after a quick inspection, I moved back into the hall. Sandy led me into what had been Brad's old bedroom, but was now her "workspace." There was a long table covered with assorted crafts in various stages of assembly, a treadle sewing machine, and a desk piled high with scrapbooks. It was the type of room Irene would like, I thought with a shiver. In my mind, I saw her ancient wrinkled face, and as though I were a child, goosebumps popped up on my arms.

Was Frank still alive? I wondered.

That was the question. If he was, he would have to be in his nineties—he'd been old even when I was a kid—but that made no difference to me. I didn't care if he was on his deathbed. The lying, cheating bastard had killed my brother, and I wanted to confront him. Maybe the law couldn't prosecute him (*or maybe it could*, I thought hopefully), but there might be something I could do to make his last years miserable.

It wasn't just a question of whether Frank was alive, however. That wasn't the reason I'd needed to see the house. There was something *else*. Something that had always been in the back of my mind, but that I'd refused to acknowledge. Mark Goodwin had told me the first day I'd met him that his house was haunted. I'd believed him, without question—I'd sensed it myself—but to me it hadn't been the presence of ghosts that had made the house feel that way, it was the fact that it had been built by Frank. There'd been the same sort of off-kilter feeling to our own house, though it had taken me awhile to notice it. I believed it was the cause of the nightmares I'd had, and I believed it had led to the bad luck that had followed us since we'd first set foot in that A-frame.

There was nothing logical or rational about the notion, and to be honest, it was more of a vague feeling than an actual belief, but it was one of the reasons I was here.

I was getting the same vibe from this place.

"This is going to sound crazy," I said. "But did you ever suspect that your house was, well...haunted?"

It was a long time before she responded, which told me the answer even before she vocalized it. "I think it is," she said. "I've always thought it was. When we first moved in, I had a hard time sleeping. I'd hear noises at night, like people moving around in rooms that I knew were empty. I'd get up to go to the bathroom, and I'd hear silverware clinking in the kitchen, as though someone was eating. Or I'd be lying in bed, and I'd hear the laundry room door open. Things like that. Wind, too. I'd feel cold breezes sometimes. Once, I even thought I saw something, a kind of shadow in my dresser mirror."

"Why didn't you move out? Why *don't* you move out?" I realized that that sounded like a self-serving suggestion coming from a realtor, but it wasn't meant that way, and that was not how she took it.

Sandy shrugged. "I guess I just got used to the place. I pretended nothing was happening for Brad's sake—have to be strong in front of kids, you know—and after awhile it became like background noise. Nothing ever happened. Not really. I never felt threatened or in danger, so I just ignored what I heard or what I saw. Or what I *thought* I heard or *thought* I saw. Nothing ever actually hurt me."

"Your floor collapsed," I pointed out. "That could have killed you."

I was thinking of Billy.

"I suppose," she acknowledged, "but it was so long after the fact, that I never even put it together with...that other stuff."

"Until now," I prodded.

She sighed heavily. "Until you brought it up." She looked at me soberly. "Was your house haunted?" she asked. "Was Frank's old house?"

I nodded. "Yeah, I think they were."

In the silence following my admission, I heard what sounded like a light knocking coming from within the room's closet. In my mind, I saw Irene, older than old, standing inside the closet and tapping on the door with a long witch-like finger. Sandy met my eyes, and I knew she heard it, too. The rapping continued. It probably had some perfectly logical, utterly ordinary explanation—air in the water pipes, a barometric differential causing a wooden beam to expand and contract, a mouse in the walls—but I was afraid to open the door, afraid to check, and we left the room, walking back down the hall toward the front of the house.

"So it still goes on," I said.

Sandy nodded. "Yes, it does."

SEVEN

SEEING THE SIMMONS house and hearing Sandy's stories about Frank got me thinking. Before this moment, I had never had any desire to return to Randall, but now I was curious. I wanted to see the town. I wanted to see our old vacation home.

I wanted to find out more about Frank.

There it was. I didn't know why, or what I could possibly hope to learn, but maybe if I saw those locations through adult eyes, from a more worldly perspective, I'd find something out about the man that I hadn't known before. There was a nagging feeling at the back of my brain, a sense that if I could understand who Frank was or why he did what he did, I might be able to find him. And make sure he was punished for his crimes.

For Billy.

There was a definite pattern, I realized after talking to Sandy Simmons. All of Frank's houses incorporated stolen materials, and all of them had bodies or bones buried somewhere within their construction. It was a *thing* with him. There seemed something ritualistic about it, and that led me to the part of all this that I didn't want to think about.

The supernatural part.

I was not a skeptic. No realtor is. We've all had encounters with properties that seemed off somehow, that didn't feel right, houses where we didn't want to spend time alone, where we quickly put up our signs, set out our flyers and left as fast as possible. But this was less vague, more specific, and the fact that these *hauntings*, for lack of a better word, were connected to a single person—Frank—made me feel distinctly uneasy.

But no less determined to get to the bottom of it.

So I thought I'd take a few days off and drive back to Randall. That was the good thing about being a realtor: the hours were flexible. It had been a tough summer, and I was still treading water financially, but the commission from the Big Bear cabin sale, as small as it was, allowed me at least a little leeway, and once my end of the paperwork was completed and filed, I intended to take a short research trip.

Two days later, my work done, I decided to speed over to Randall on Friday, returning on Sunday, thinking that would give me enough time to snoop around and see what I could find without significantly impacting my job.

I left the Lincoln at the office and took my van to meet Teri for lunch at Don Jose's, intending to tell her of my plans and explain why I had to break our date for Saturday. The Lincoln was a show car, meant to fool clients into thinking I was hugely successful and doing better than I was (luxury cars, even crappy ones with rolled-back odometers like mine, made prospective homebuyers feel comfortable). My actual ride was an eight-year-old Honda Odyssey. I'd bought the van because it was supposed to have a stellar safety record, but mine must have been made on a Monday since it had given me nothing but problems from the get go. My previous vehicle, a Ford Explorer, had lasted over 200,000 miles before I decided to trade it in. But this pile of junk had barely half as many miles on it, and had already had to have the motor mounts replaced twice. Last year, on a trip to San Diego, it had died right in front of the nuclear power plant at San Notre, and I'd had to wait two hours for a tow back to Orange, where I found out that it needed a new transmission. Oh, and a new front axle. When I told my tale of woe to Jim Gibbons at the office, who also happened to have a Honda van, he said, "Yeah, they do seem to have problems with their transmissions."

As it turned out, his transmission had been recalled. But when I went online, to see if there was a recall for my year, I found out that it was only for the three years prior. I was out of luck, and I had to shell out nearly two thousand dollars to have my axle replaced and my transmission rebuilt. The damn thing still made mysterious noises when I braked or when I accelerated, so I only drove the van locally.

Since there was no way it would be able to get me all the way to Arizona, that meant I was going to have to rent a car for the weekend.

Unless...

I suddenly had an idea.

I could convince Teri to come with me and we could go in her car.

That was a big step, though. Maybe too big. Teri and I had met last year at the birthday party of a friend from college, had hit it off and were now kind of, sort of, almost semi-dating. It was not really anything serious, but a weekend trip in her car would definitely kick the relationship up a few notches. Did I really want that?

Did *she* really want that?

Maybe it would be better to shell out the money for a rental car after all.

Teri was already at the restaurant when I arrived, waiting for me on a bench outside the front door. She looked damn good, as she always did, and I gave her a quick kiss, put my arm around her waist, and we stepped inside. I ended up telling her about my visit to the Simmons house, and a little about Frank, and about my planned weekend trip to Randall.

Apparently, she thought I was inviting her. "Oh, I wish I could go," she said, "but there's no way I can take off Friday. In fact, I may even have to come in on Saturday." Teri worked in the IT department of an Orange County-based bank. She put her hand on mine. "Maybe next time?"

"That's okay," I told her, and then the waitress arrived, and we ordered.

Rental car it was.

I remembered large parts of the trip to Arizona. Landmarks. Specific gas stations, even. A McDonald's in Quartzite where we'd once stopped for lunch. A rest area where Billy had thrown up after seeing an overflowing urinal. The inspection station at the border with its display case of desert bats and bugs.

A lot had changed since I was a kid. The Phoenix area had grown tremendously and had spread much further into the desert than I would have expected, Subways and Wal-Marts crowding out saguaros and ocotillo on new roads that led to new subdivisions. But the route to Randall was still a two-lane highway, and the town itself had changed hardly at all. On the way in, I saw signs for a new development, The Pines, that apparently offered luxury vacation homes to rich people from the Valley, but that was an anomaly. The lack of jobs in this area had kept the town small, and it was still just as cute as I remembered it. A few of the businesses had changed—the video store was now a Starbucks, and the bakery was now a pizza restaurant—but the essential character of the downtown had remained the same.

I drove slowly, looking for the turnoff to our old neighborhood, not positive I remembered where it was. Although the clouds in the sky were more white than gray, the streets were wet and the air was filled with a unique scent I hadn't smelled since childhood: forest rain. I rolled down the car window to better take it in, breathing deeply, feeling happy, feeling sad, recognizing the deep earthy odor of dirt, the lighter smell of fresh pine needles, the clean scent of water, all of it mingled together and suspended in a humidity that was comforting rather than heavy. It brought me back to those monsoon summers we'd spent at our vacation home, and though I'd come here in pursuit of information about Frank, I was suddenly overcome by memories of my dad, my mom and my brother, filled with a feeling of loss so strong that I almost pulled the car over.

At that moment I saw our street, recognizing it by the ponderosa pine on the corner. Miraculously, it had not been chopped down, although the formerly vacant lot where it stood was now occupied by a two-story house with a two-car garage.

I turned, heading up the winding road, past trees much taller than I recalled and many more houses than I remembered. I rounded the curve where I'd fallen off my bike, glanced over at the ditch where Mark Goodwin had found the rotting body of a dead raccoon. A powerful sadness settled over me. I had not expected this reaction and wondered if I should turn around and leave. Maybe coming here had been a mistake.

Then I found our old house—

—and saw a camera crew out front. With trucks and lights and a crowd of technicians. And a group of neighborhood residents behind a barrier of sawhorses, watching it all.

What was going on here?

I pulled to a stop at the side of the road and got out of the car. A couple of heads turned my way, but I was not nearly as interesting as whatever was being filmed, and the few neighbors who'd noticed my arrival decided to ignore me. I walked up to a young man wearing a Weird Al Yankovic t-shirt. "What's going on?" I asked.

He said that the crew in front of us was preparing to film an episode of *Ghost Pursuers*, a basic cable show that purported to investigate "real" haunted houses. I wasn't familiar with the program, but most of the gathered onlookers seemed to be diehard fans. One of the stars of the show, a man everyone was calling "Petey," stood just behind the sawhorses answering questions, signing autographs and posing for selfies.

"Who owns that house?" I asked Weird Al, pointing to our old A-frame.

"No one now. The old guy who lived there killed himself. That's why they're here."

The news made me feel strange. We'd bought that pre-fab kit. The house had been built for us. We'd spent summers and vacations there, and no matter what cosmetic changes had been added since, I knew every inch of that A-frame intimately. The thought that a man had committed suicide in one of our rooms left me feeling queasy inside. I wanted to hear more specifics, but a man with a megaphone announced "Quiet on the set!" and everyone stopped talking.

Petey had moved away from his adoring fans and was standing in the center of the street between Frank's house and ours. "We're here in Randall, Arizona," he intoned. "The most haunted town in America."

The most haunted town in America? When had that happened?

"Cut!" the man with the megaphone yelled, and they shot it again, from a different angle, then from another angle, before the megaphone man finally yelled, "Got it!" and workmen started moving equipment onto our old driveway, now covered with blacktop rather than gravel.

I pushed my way to the front of the crowd. An attractive young woman on the other side of the barricade was texting on her cell phone, and I tapped her on the shoulder. "Excuse me," I said. "Are you one of the ghost hunters?"

"Ghost *pursuers*," she corrected me. "And yes, I'm Deb," she said in a tone that indicated I was supposed to know who that was.

"Well, I know a little bit about that house," I said. "My family built it. I used to spend my summers here."

Deb seemed far less interested in my story than in her texting. She moved forward so I could push a sawhorse aside and pass through the barrier. "The producer and director are over there," she told me, pointing.

I walked past a group of men mounting a camera on a track to where a tall man with a gray Sam Elliott mustache was talking to a short, clean-cut younger man wearing earphones around his neck. I assumed they'd be talking about the show, but they weren't.

"Korean chicks love anal sex," the man with the mustache was saying.

"Why?"

"Because it's painful and it's difficult to get through, and they think that makes it worthwhile. It's a cultural thing."

"So your girlfriend..."

"Every day." The man's proud grin faded, and he scowled at my approach. "Who are you and what do you want?" He motioned to someone over my shoulder, indicating that I should be removed.

"I'm a guy who used to live in that house when I was a kid. My dad had it built for our vacation home. And I know why that house across the street is haunted, also. But if you don't want to hear about it..." I started to turn away.

"No! No! We'd love to hear your story!" He waved away the man he'd just called over to kick me out. "What did you say your name was?"

"I didn't, and I'm not going to."

"That's fine, that's fine." He was gesturing to someone else. Two bearded men in their early to mid-twenties strolled over from where they'd been sitting on nearby chairs. "I'm Scott Spencer, producer of *Ghost Pursuers.* These are our writers slash researchers, Evan and Owen. Tell them whatever you know—or let them interview you about what you know—and then maybe we can get you on camera as an expert or a local or a local expert or...we'll figure it out."

I wasn't about to appear on camera. It would erode my professional credibility—no one wanted to buy a home from someone who'd appeared on *Ghost Pursuers* talking about haunted houses. But I was definitely willing to provide them with background information. I'd never seen the show, and on air the pursuers might pretend to be the height of journalistic integrity, but off the air, the team responsible for the show was desperate for anything that would help them fill time. I could have lied through my teeth and told them a tale about the spawn of Bigfoot and they would have used it. But, as it happened, I was legitimately able to fill in some gaps on stories the researchers had already unearthed. They told me that they were calling Randall "the most haunted town in America" because of these two supposedly haunted houses situated directly across the street from each other, and I relayed the story of Frank and the dead dogs and the dead kid, although I left out any mention of Billy.

"We can stretch this to two episodes!" the producer said excitedly. "That one house is small, so I didn't think we could get twenty-two out of it, but with this guy—" He hooked a thumb in my direction. "—we might just be able to put in enough background that it'll cover up when our specter-cams don't find anything. Which they never do," he confided to me.

Evan and Owen looked at each other. "Two episodes?" Evan said. "I don't see why not. We've done more with less."

"Yes!" Spencer shouted. He rubbed his hands gleefully. "This puts us at least half a week ahead! I want two new scripts from you ASAP," he told Evan and Owen. "Leave the first ten as is. We'll keep what we have for the initial foray, but prep the pursuers that the rest is being revised." Barking orders, he headed toward Deb, still texting in front of the crowd, while he motioned for Petey and another man standing on the sidelines to join them.

According to Evan, Will Grouse, the old man who'd been living in our house, had told friends and family for at least two months before he hanged himself that he'd seen and heard things he could not explain and that he feared he was losing his mind. The place across the street, Frank's house, already had a reputation for being haunted and had been vacant since the height of the recession, when the last owners had walked away from their mortgage and the bank had foreclosed. It was a neighbor from down the street, where Wyatt used to live, who had emailed *Ghost Pursuers* about the homes.

Evan turned to me. "We'll take you in with us," he said. "You show us around, let us know where the pursuers should train their cameras, where you found the dead dogs, where... Well, just tell us whatever you can about each room. I understand that you don't want to be on the show, but if you could feed us some info that *another* talking head could say, that would be great. Do you know the other house, too?"

I nodded.

"Excellent. Then we'll cover them both."

Either sound carried or the producer's ears were tuned to everything going on around him, because Spencer suddenly left Deb, Petey and the other pursuer and hurried over. "We need you to sign a release before you go in," he said.

"Why?" I asked.

"Because we film everything, every interaction with the location. Hand-held. Just in case we catch something. And if you happen to be in the shot, well, we need your permission if we incorporate it into the broadcast."

"No," I said.

"No?"

"No."

"Then you can't go in."

I shrugged. "Then I won't tell you where the haunted parts are, and you won't know where to look. I suppose you could probably figure it out by trial and error, but time is money, right?" I met the producer's eyes. "Your call."

"Damn it!" He took a deep calming breath. "Fine. Go in and show them what to look for. But film it," he ordered his crew. He turned his attention back to me. "If we do see something, maybe you'll change your mind about participating."

"Doubt it."

"Make sure you keep him out of it, then. Over the shoulder shots only."

With Evan and Owen leading the way, and a pony-tailed cameraman following right behind me, we made our way past a table covered with boxes of donuts, past groups of men setting up equipment, and up the steps to the deck of the A-frame.

It had been a long time since I'd been here, but the boards felt the same under my feet, and my body's sense memory moved me forward as though I'd never left and had been living here all my life. The house's paint was peeling, and a wrought-iron security door had been added since my day, but the place was far more familiar to me than I would have expected it to be, and I felt a tightening in my gut as Owen held the door open and I walked across the threshold.

We'd sold the house furnished all those years ago, and, amazingly enough, our bookcase was still there, painted white now instead of stained walnut. The stove was the same, too, although the refrigerator and all of the other furnishings were new to me. The couch was in the same spot as our couch, however, as was the coffee table, and while I knew that the small space offered only a limited decorating range, the continuity still made me feel more at home than I would have expected.

My eyes kept glancing toward the spot in the hallway where the floor had collapsed.

Where Billy had been killed.

"Feel anything?" Evan asked. "Sense anything?"

I shook my head, not trusting myself to speak. In my mind, I could see my mom in the kitchen, cooking dinner, my dad on the couch reading a book. I felt tears welling in my eyes and forced myself to remain focused on the present. "So where'd the old guy hang himself?" I asked.

Owen pointed to the stairs leading up to the loft. "There," he said, "from the top railing." I wasn't sure I'd heard the second "writer slash researcher" speak until this point.

Looking up, I felt something. A slight sense of vertigo as my eyes found the A-frame's peak. Gooseflesh rippled my arms as I started up the stairs.

The loft that had been my brother's and my bedroom was now storage space. A cockroach scuttled under a pile of boxes as I turned on the light.

There was definitely something here. It might have been from the suicide, it might have existed before, but the feeling in the loft was one of uneasiness. In my mind, unbidden, flashed the image of Irene, wrinkled, skeletal and grinning, hiding behind one of the piles of boxes, waiting for me.

"Any stories about this floor?" Evan asked.

I looked toward the back wall. There was only a narrow pathway through the center of the loft. The areas where our beds and dressers had been were entirely blocked by boxes. I wondered what had happened to all of my posters that had been left behind when we sold the place. "The hanging man should be enough," I said.

"Nothing happened up here?"

A wave of *something* passed through me. It was a physical sensation, like thick gummy air hitting me and moving on. I suddenly felt nauseated. I shook my head. Turning, I walked back down the stairs, pushing past the cameraman. "But if you're looking for ghosts, that's a good place to start."

I paused in the living room to catch my breath. The nausea had passed, but my heart was pounding. I was frightened, not in the abstract intellectual manner of an adult but in the direct instinctual way of a child.

Owen was frowning. "Did you sense something up there? It looked like...like you got scared or something."

"I think I might have a touch of food poisoning," I lied. "I just felt like throwing up for a second."

"Nausea," Evan said. "That's a good reaction. Make a note of that," he told his partner. "Give it to Deb. Have her get nauseous. We won't mention you at all," he assured me. "Don't worry."

I looked toward the spot in the hallway where the floor had collapsed, but quickly glanced away, knowing I needed to steer everyone away from that area. Not that I thought my brother's ghost was hanging around, waiting to be contacted. But if by some miracle such a thing were possible, I didn't want it to be with this crowd, and I didn't want it shown on TV.

"How about the kitchen?" Evan asked. "The hallway? The bathroom? The back bedroom?"

"The bedroom," I said, though I'd never had any weird feelings about my parents' room. "The dogs were under the bedroom." I led the way past the kitchen and down the short hall. As though on cue, a dog barked somewhere in the neighborhood, which wouldn't have seemed so creepy had not the temperature dropped a good ten degrees the second we passed through the doorway. I glanced around to see if the others had noticed it as well, and was relieved to see that they had.

Evan was grinning. "Thank you, Jesus!" he said. "Finally, a real one!"

"That window might not be closed all the way," Owen said in a half-hearted attempt to play devil's advocate.

"It's *warmer* outside," Evan snorted, "not colder." He looked at me. "Any stories here?"

"Just the dead dogs."

"Good enough. We can milk this one. Why don't we go out and you can show us where you found the dog bodies, how it happened and all that."

Ten minutes later, we were through. In a way, I thought, trudging back down the short driveway toward the street, it was better that all of these people were here. It allowed me to look at the house objectively and kept me one step removed from emotions that probably would have overwhelmed me had I been all alone. As it was, I was filled with a profound sense of loss as I recalled walking up this driveway with Billy and my parents for the first time.

Scott Spencer broke away from a discussion with the director. "Well?"

"I still don't know if we can get twenty-two minutes out of it," Owen said. "It is a small house."

"If we incorporate background..."

"Maybe," Owen said doubtfully.

"You need more background information?" I asked.

Spencer grinned. "Lay it on us."

I told them about Frank's in-laws, George and Betsy, describing how their trailer had blown up in a propane explosion about the same time Frank and Irene had skipped town, and how their bodies had never been found. I was glad to be sharing this information and hoped they'd use all of it. I wasn't sure when this episode would air, but maybe Frank would see it. It was why I was cooperating with the program. While they might be using me, I was using them, too. We were each getting something out of this.

What would be Frank's reaction, though, if he did see the show? Nostalgia for the good old days? Would he be proud of his accomplishments or worried that someone was on his trail? Hopefully the latter. My goal was to scare him into making a move, doing something that would help me find him. I still wasn't sure what I would do if I did, but I reassured myself with the knowledge that there was no statute of limitations on murder, and I was pretty sure a modern forensics team could easily tie him to that dead boy in his basement.

And maybe between now and then I'd be able to dig up a few other things as well.

"Now check out the Lee house," Spencer told us. "See what you can come up with."

"Frank's place?" I said.

"What was this Frank's last name?" the producer asked.

"Watkins," I told him.

"The Watkins House," Evan said, trying it out. "That sounds better. 'The Watkins House.' Has a nice ring to it."

Spencer shook his head. "Too close to the *Whaley* House, which we just did last season. Stick to the script."

"The Goodwins lived there after Frank," I said helpfully.

The producer snorted. "Goodwins? That's not scary at all. Keep it the way it is."

The writers and I walked across the street, still shadowed by the cameraman. I hadn't been inside Frank's house for over three decades, but it looked almost exactly the same as I remembered.

It *felt* the same.

"Jesus!" Owen exclaimed the second he walked through the door.

His partner looked over at him. "You feel that, too?"

"We all feel it," I said. "But that's only the beginning." I moved forward, glancing behind me, remembering the glimpses of movement I used to see in my peripheral vision, the dark shadow that slipped almost unseen from the entryway into the short hall leading to the master bedroom. "I thought you guys checked this place out already."

"*We* didn't," Evan said. "Mark, yes. And the location scouts. And the director. But we're just the writers. We do as we're told."

"This is a gold mine," Owen was saying.

I'd forgotten just how *odd* Frank's house was, with the doors in the wrong places and not where you'd expect them to be, the angles of the rooms slightly off in a way that wasn't actually noticeable but that made you feel a little dizzy. The windows didn't let in as much light as they should, and, as I remembered, directions seemed off in here, as though the inside of the building had a different orientation than the outside.

"Where's your stolen paneling?" Evan asked. "That's a good hook."

"Upstairs."

But I didn't want to go upstairs. Being here was much more intense than I'd thought it would be, and compared to the relatively benign environment of our old vacation home across the street, much more malevolent.

Malevolent.

That was it exactly. There was a maliciousness here. This was not the vague, diffused air of the paranormal that hung about our A-frame, but a far more focused, concentrated and *intentional* haunting. At the same time, my connection to Frank's place was much less personal, so I didn't feel the need to gloss over things or hurry through the rooms. In fact, I *wanted* to take my time. I wanted to study Frank's house, learn from it. After all, this was not only a house he had built, this was where he'd *lived.*

"So can we start upstairs and work our way down?" Evan asked.

I nodded reluctantly, not trusting myself to speak.

"Good blueprint for the show, too," Owen said. "Starting at the top, ending up in the basement where the body was found."

"We like to end shows with the cause of the haunting," Evan explained. "That way, it's structured like a mystery, with a payoff at the end. Keeps viewers from switching."

There was a cold spot by the kitchen in the same place I remembered. Back then, we'd all ignored it, pretended we didn't notice it, but Evan and Owen moved around in it, commenting, trying to find its diameter, while the cameraman filmed it from every possible angle, hoping something would show up on playback.

"Excellent," Evan said.

"There's another one upstairs," I said.

"All right. Lead on."

I didn't want to be in the lead. Even as an adult, even in the daytime, with three other men and dozens of crew members and onlookers on the street outside, I was as frightened as a child alone at night. Frank's house could do that, and, not for the first time, I wondered how Mark and his family had been able to stay here.

Whatever happened to Mark?

I didn't know, and I'd never thought to find out. Obviously, the Goodwins had sold the house, but when? How long after we'd left? And where were they all now? Did they ever think about their days in Randall? Were they still in Randall?

When I got back, I was going to see what I could discover, try to track Mark down.

The narrow stairwell was dark. I started walking up, but after five steps or so was filled with the overwhelming certainty that I was by myself and no one was behind me. I knew that wasn't possible, but I paused and looked back nevertheless, grateful to see Evan, Owen and the cameraman. The sensation returned the second I turned around, though, and I had to force myself to continue up the stairs.

At the top of the landing, I saw movement off to my right, in what had been Janine's room. "There's something in there," I said, moving aside so the cameraman could get a look. He went in first, and Evan followed, flipping on the light as he entered. Owen stayed outside with me. "Do you see anything?" I asked.

"Not yet," Evan replied. "What did you think was in here?"

"I don't know. A figure. I thought I saw movement." I stepped forward, through the doorway—

And a shadow detached itself from the darkness within the open empty closet.

Lurching into the center of the room, it jerked about like a spastic marionette, moving toward the cameraman as though drawn by the opportunity to reveal itself. Stumbling backward, then turning around in a panicked attempt to get away, I saw what looked like a woman reflected in the medicine cabinet mirror in the bathroom across the landing.

An old woman.

Irene.

No! I looked quickly away, my eyes glancing toward the room that had been Mark's. I saw something sitting on the empty floor, a stunted dwarfish figure with an oversized head rocking back and forth in time to some unheard music.

I ran down the stairs. My heart was pumping so hard that I could feel it in my throat. I had no idea if the others were following me, and at that point I didn't care. Speeding past the kitchen, through a cold spot, I ran out the front door and into the driveway, not stopping until I hit the street.

Scott Spencer and several crew members, as well as the crowd of neighbors outside the barricade, watched me, surprised and curious. A few of the rougher looking technicians wore mocking expressions, but the producer was ecstatic. He knew he had something good here, and he hurried over just as Evan and Owen emerged from the house, their faces blanched.

"Well?" he said.

"Get the pursuers in there now," Evan advised. "It's Amityville."

Spencer hurried off. "Petey! Deb! Ralph!" He was shouting orders to the makeup people even as he rounded up the stars. Abandoning their cranes and dolly tracks, cameraman, sound men and other crew members started scrambling.

I frowned, noticing that our cameraman was missing. "Where's—" I began.

"Filming the basement," Owen said. "That's one brave motherfucker."

He was right. There was no way in hell I'd have gone into that basement, especially not alone.

"I'm going to get my laptop," Evan told me. "Then you can fill me in on everything you know about the place."

"They're going in right now," I said. "You're not going to have time."

"It's a real one. They can just respond to what they see. And if they fuck up, we'll have better lines they can re-record later. What we need from you right now is stuff for the background narration, to fill in the blanks between shots of the house."

The cameraman came out, well before anyone else was ready to go in, and he headed straight for Spencer. I followed Evan and Owen over, and we looked through the camera's small playback screen at the trip into Frank's. It unfolded just as we'd seen it, although...

It looked fake on the screen, somehow. The shadow in Janine's room wasn't exactly cartoony, but it was well within what even a moderate television special effects budget could do, and I was surprised to find the scene so unbelievable. Spencer, however, was euphoric. "Even if we get nothing with the pursuers, we still have this! Home run!" he announced loudly.

The cameraman didn't catch anything in the bathroom, but there was a slinking movement of shadow into Mark's closet, even though the dwarfish thing on the floor was gone. None of it looked particularly realistic, and I was not only disappointed but confused as to why that should be. It was the reason, I supposed, that every footage or photo of a ghost or UFO always proved so inconclusive, and I thought that maybe I'd been too quick over the years to dismiss claims of the supernatural.

Oddly enough, it was the basement, where nothing had happened, that the *feeling* of Frank's house really came through. There were no moving shadows, no eerie figures, and even the section of wall where the mummified boy was found had long since been repaired. But when the camera zoomed in on a yellow vinyl chair that had been left behind by the house's most recent occupants, a wave of cold washed over me. The chair looked utterly ordinary, but something about it was fundamentally wrong in the way all of Frank's house was wrong, and that sense leaped out of the frame at the viewer.

"Wow," Evan said.

I was not the only one who'd noticed it.

The cameraman nodded, shut off the playback. "That's why I left," he said. "I got scared." He met Spencer's eyes. "Make sure they go down in the basement. We'll get ten minutes just out of that."

The producer was already leaving. He nodded in acknowledgment as he excitedly instructed the three ghost pursuers about what they needed to do once they were in the house.

Evan glanced to the left at Frank's place, then to the right at our old A-frame across the street. "What's his name? The man who killed the dogs and the kid and built these buildings?"

"Frank," I said.
"Jesus," he breathed. "Who the hell *was* this guy?"
That's what I wanted to know.

EIGHT

I CHECKED IN WITH the sheriff's office while I was in town, stopped by the local newspaper office, even quizzed some of the neighbors gathered around to watch the filming. I was impressive to the neighbors because I seemed to be somehow involved with *Ghost Pursuers*, and I took advantage of that, getting them to open up and talk more intimately and honestly than they would have otherwise.

But it had been a long time, and the truth was that I knew more about Frank than anyone else I met. The reputation of the haunted houses might have spread all the way to Hollywood, but Frank was practically unknown even in his own town. I returned to California disappointed by how little I had learned, yet at the same time filled with an even firmer resolve to connect the dots, to find out how, why and where he was building these houses with stolen materials and buried bones.

I remembered George and Betsy saying that Frank had changed after he went to Vietnam, that he was somehow "darker." What did that mean? And what was *that* part of Frank's journey?

As soon as I got back, Teri wanted to know about my trip, and I thought about telling her the truth, but in the end I didn't. *To protect her*, I told myself, but I was not sure that was it. Or at least not entirely. It was a small club, the people whose lives had been affected by Frank, and an exclusive one, and I didn't think anyone outside that circle could really understand the truth of what it meant to have lived in a Frank house. Sure, I could describe it and try to explain it, but Teri would still be on the outside, and I wanted her to stay that way.

I thought back to what I'd seen in Randall. Experiencing the sort of supernatural encounter that had only been hinted at before had invigorated me, and I vowed to track Frank down. For my brother, for my parents, for me.

The best place to start was obviously with the houses. Frank never used a real estate agent, apparently, so I couldn't track him down that way, but property tax records were easy enough to obtain, and though the going would be slow, I figured I'd be able to find him eventually if I stuck with it. The problem was that he probably used a different surname each time. And it was nearly impossible to track down just a "Frank." He could also move anywhere in the country. The only leads I had were the fact that he seemed to keep using a last name that began with "W," and Sandy Simmons' hunch that Frank and Irene had moved to Las Vegas after selling their house in Tarzana.

So I spent my spare time doing research—although, as luck would have it, I didn't *have* much spare time. The real estate business ebbs and flows, and for one of those unknown reasons entirely unrelated to other economic conditions, our office caught a wave. All of our agents were suddenly listing and showing and selling, and as quickly as it had come, my dry spell evaporated. I knew it wouldn't last, knew I had to strike while the iron was hot, so as much as I wanted to pursue Frank, I pushed that aside and got busy selling. It had been over three decades, and a few weeks more wouldn't make much difference.

Still, whenever I had an extra moment, I made phone calls, sent emails, looked up records. I sometimes thought it was stupid and pointless—and I didn't completely understand the sudden need, after all these years, to chase Frank down—but something had been awakened within me. I was not by any stretch of the imagination a religious person, and I didn't believe in fate or mystical signs, yet I couldn't help ascribing some import to the fact that I had sold that

Big Bear Cabin to a man who had grown up in a Frank house. I wouldn't go so far as to say that I thought there was a *reason* it had happened, but I'd been made aware that Frank had continued on after Randall, doing the same thing elsewhere, and I had to follow up on that. I had to know.

I found myself wondering if Sandy Simmons had any paperwork from when she and her husband had bought the house from Frank, thinking the title transfer alone might give me some information to work from, and I called to ask. She wasn't answering, but I left a voice mail and told her to call me back at her earliest convenience. Fudging the truth a little, I hinted that the reason for the call had something to do with her son's purchase of the cabin, thinking that it might make the call seem more urgent.

It was Brad who called me back, nearly two days later. I could tell from the tone of his simple greeting, "This is Brad Simmons," that he was distracted and upset by something far more important than a glitch in his sales paperwork.

"Thanks for returning my call," I told him, "but, actually I needed to speak with your mother."

"She's not here," he said, and the hesitation that followed let me know that he wasn't sure whether he wanted to tell me any details. "She's in the hospital," he said finally.

"Oh my God," I said. "What happened?"

Another pause. "The house collapsed. While she was sleeping. It just...the roof just fell in on her."

"Is she all right?"

"She's in a coma."

It was the Frank influence. I knew it in my bones—

bones

—though there was no way in hell I could prove it to anyone.

I shivered. "I'm sorry," I said. "I hope she gets better." I had no idea if that was stupid and insensitive to say under the circumstances, but it was the only thing that came to me. I found myself wondering *how* the roof had collapsed. In my mind, I saw it spontaneously crumpling at a focal point directly above Sandy's bed.

It was, I realized, the second time the house had tried to kill her.

"What were you calling about?" Brad asked. "What did you need? It sounded like—"

"It's nothing," I assured him. "Just a question I had, and it's already been taken care of. I'm sorry to bother you at a time like this. Really. Everything's fine."

"Okay." He didn't sound entirely convinced, but I swore again that there were no last minute problems with the sale and promised to call him if anything came up.

"Don't worry about a thing on this end," I told him. "Just take care of your mom."

I hung up, feeling shaky.

The talk of houses left me wondering once again what had happened to the Goodwins. Had Mark and his family endured accidents and problems and tragedies like everyone else who'd lived in a Frank house? I had a feeling they had, and part of me wanted to know the details, but part of me didn't.

I decided to put off looking for Mark until I could gain some emotional distance. Hearing about Sandy Simmons had shaken me, and while it could have been a completely random accident, unconnected to anything else, I didn't think that was the case. At the very least, it was Frank's poor construction skills that had led to the roof's collapse, and whether or not there was a supernatural element involved, it was still Frank's doing that had led to this.

I redoubled my search efforts, and they finally began to pay off. A Frank Watson in a town called Biscuitville, Texas, had transferred ownership of his house to someone else in 1976. A Frank Wilson in Bernalillo, New Mexico, had sold his small ranch house in 1982. Someone named Frank Wilton had bought, remodeled and sold a fixer upper in Las Vegas in 1993. I found eight homes all together, eight possibilities. There were pictures of most of these properties from subsequent sales with legitimate realtors, and from all of them I got the same vibe I got from Frank's Randall house, from our vacation home, from Sandy Simmons' place: the sense that there was something off, something wrong, something weird.

Were all of these Franks *him*? And which, if any, was his real last name? George and Betsy would know, if—

George and Betsy.

I stared at my computer screen. Of course. George and Betsy. I thought for a moment. There'd been no bodies in that propane explosion, and, knowing the Randall Sheriff's department, even if they had tried to track down the couple, they probably hadn't put too much effort into it. It was quite possible they were still alive somewhere. They'd both be old, *really* old, but if they were alive I still might be able to track them down. I knew their last name, Robertson, and while it wasn't that unique, there probably weren't too many George *and* Betsy Robertsons who were married to each other.

Unless they'd changed their names, too.

I slumped in my chair, disappointed.

Of course they had.

Still, it couldn't hurt to check, and I spent a couple of hours using every program, app and website at my disposal to try and find them.

Nothing.

Feeling defeated, I scrolled back through the real estate photos I'd saved. They definitely seemed like Frank houses. They had that *feeling*, though no two looked alike. The one in Texas was two stories and sort of Victorian looking. It seemed far too professionally built to be all Frank, and I wondered if he'd been working for a construction company at the time or if he'd simply remodeled an already existing structure. The one in Las Vegas was little more than a shack, a small ramshackle one-story building that reminded me of a third-world slum dwelling. He could have definitely built that. One, in Pocatello, Idaho, was a double-wide trailer with an added-on carport.

Like George and Betsy's.

I stared at the picture. The more I thought about George and Betsy, the more suspect they seemed to be. First there was that story about them living in Phoenix and buying our original lot as an investment. They hadn't lived in Phoenix, we'd found out from the sheriff; they'd been longtime residents of Randall, and Betsy had been a secretary at the town hall. So why had they lied? And why had they bought the lot and why had they sold it? Then there was that thing about Frank and Vietnam, how he'd come back changed. Maybe he had, but if he actually was "Frank Watson," he hadn't come back to Randall but to Biscuitville, Texas—and had apparently moved to several states in between. There was also the mysterious explosion that had destroyed the Robertsons' trailer. Had they set it? Had Frank set it? Why? And why had they disappeared after that?

I wondered if either of them were even related to Frank or Irene.

The confusing part was that there seemed to be threads of truth woven through the lies, so it was impossible for me to tell where the lies ended and the truth began.

Between showing houses, I kept up my search.

I'm not sure when exactly I decided to take a leave of absence, but I started calculating expenses *vis-a-vis* my bank account, and at some point made the decision that I could afford to take some time off and check out some of these Frank houses in person. I needed to see them for myself, and I honestly thought I might be able to ascertain his whereabouts (or his fate, if he were dead) from what I might learn by visiting those locations and talking to people who'd been entangled with him. It had become an obsession, this search. I realized that, understood it on an intellectual level, but on an emotional level it was still something I felt compelled to do. All of my feelings involving Frank had been bottled up since Billy's "accident," since the deaths of my dad and my mom, and everything had started leaking out when I learned that Brad had grown up in a Frank house, that I was not the only one, that the man had kept on doing what he did long after Randall. I told myself that I might be in a position to not only see that he was punished for his past crimes but make sure that he was stopped so he could never do it again.

I made an itinerary. The houses were literally all over the map, and if I were going to do this, I had to decide how I wanted to proceed, where I wanted to go first: I could visit the houses in chronological order, or in reverse chronological order, or closest-to-farthest, or farthest-to-closest. Eventually, I decided to begin with Las Vegas. It was the one real lead I had, the one house, thanks to Sandy Simmons, that I was almost positive was his, and it happened to be the one nearest Southern California.

I hadn't seen Teri for almost a week, and I felt guilty about that. We'd kept in contact primarily by text, talking only once or twice over the phone. Our last actual meeting had not even been a date or a dinner or a long conversation but a quickie in the bathroom of the real estate office at lunch on Monday. She needed it, I needed it, we had a very limited amount of time, so she dropped by when everyone else was out, we locked the bathroom door, I pulled her pants down, slipped on a condom, bent her over the sink and took her quickly from behind. She was gone before anyone else in the office returned.

If I was going to be gone for awhile, I needed to tell her, and I needed to do so in person rather than over the phone, or through a text or email. I owed her that much.

We met at a Chili's located in the parking lot of a mall. Inside, the place was crowded. On the opposite side of the restaurant, as we walked in, waitresses were singing "Happy Birthday" to an old man surrounded by his family. The waitresses presented the old man with a brownie topped by a single burning candle. "Make a wish!" his family exhorted him. "Make a wish!"

We sat down in a booth suggested by the overenthusiastic server. I'd always hated restaurants like this, but they were part and parcel of the world I lived in, the glad-handing realm of real estate, and not for the first time I wondered how I had ended up in this life.

It was probably because of Billy.

Probably because of Frank.

But there was time enough later to feel sorry for myself and bemoan my off-track existence. Right now, I needed to let Teri know that I would be gone for awhile.

"I need to go on a business trip," I lied.

"Where?" she asked, curious.

"Nevada, maybe Texas, New Mexico..."

"Road trip?" she said. "Sounds like fun."

The expression on her face was one of eager anticipation, and I realized with a sinking feeling that she thought I was inviting her.

Not knowing how to tell her that I didn't want her to come with me, I said, "It won't be fun. And I'm not sure how long I'll be gone."

"That's okay."

"I thought you couldn't get time off."

"Things have calmed down. It's a slack time for us. And I have plenty of vacation days saved up."

The waitress stopped by to take our order, animatedly introducing herself and rattling off an impossibly long list of specials. Teri ordered a chicken fajita platter and a margarita, while I just asked for a side order of French fries and an iced tea.

"Are you sure?" the waitress prodded. "We have—"

"I'm sure," I said.

"You don't—"

"I'm not hungry."

Teri waited until the waitress left. "Not hungry?" She grinned mischievously. "I bet I know something you'd like to eat." Her eyes glanced almost imperceptibly down at her lap, and I laughed. I was going to miss her sense of humor when I was gone. A sharp small pang of melancholy told me that I was going to miss more than that, and I realized that despite my determination to keep this relationship light and casual, within the past few months it had somehow developed into something deeper.

Maybe she *should* come with me.

No.

I liked Teri. A lot. Which was why I didn't tell her about my real mission. I needed to protect her, keep her out of it. And, in a weird way, I needed her to be a kind of anchor, to keep me grounded, to maintain my connection with the real world of jobs and relationships and practical matters so I didn't go floating off permanently into the nebulous world of quests and ghosts and the mysteries of Frank.

Besides, I might not come back.

I don't know what made me think that, but as soon as I did, I realized that the possibility had always been at the back of my mind. It was behind the feeling of sadness that had been dogging me all day, and it was the real reason I was reluctant to get Teri involved.

I was not sure if I thought there was the possibility of physical danger or if I thought something might happen that would cause me to abandon my life and career and never return, but I was filled with the sense that a big change was coming, that after this my life would never be the same.

It took awhile, but I eventually dissuaded her from coming with me, convincing her to save her vacation days so that we could take a real trip, a fun trip.

The next day, I called around to find the best deal on the smallest rental car possible, knowing that I might need it for awhile. There were some loose ends that needed to be tied up both at work and at home, and it was another week before I was actually ready to take off. Officially, I would be on leave for one month, but there was the understanding that it could be extended. I shifted my listings and in-process sales to May Lam and Mike Rivera, dividing the workload based on who I thought would do a better job with each individual property, and made sure that everyone in the office had my cell number in case they needed to get in touch with me for anything. After deleting information so there was nothing private on my computer, I gave Mike my password should anyone need to access my files.

I spent that night at Teri's, and we tried things we'd never tried before. She couldn't possibly guess what was really going on, but I think she understood that I was not actually going on a business trip, and she made me promise that I would call and text her every morning and every evening. It was almost as though she, too, had a premonition of danger. But neither of us spoke of that, and we parted the next morning with a kiss, the way we always did.

For a brief moment, looking out at her through the driver's side window of the car, I considered inviting her to accompany me—and I could tell that she would say yes—but I knew this was something I needed to do alone.

Waving, I drove off, headed home, packed my bags, and started for Las Vegas.

NINE

THE HIGHWAY WAS crowded, and what was supposed to be a three hour trip took five. I should have either left earlier or picked a day other than Friday to drive to Las Vegas since a lot of Southern Californians were obviously playing hooky and making this into a three-day weekend.

I'd been to Vegas only once before, two years ago, to attend a real estate convention, and I hadn't been impressed. The resorts that looked so spacious and inviting on television commercials had turned out to be right next to rival hotels and directly abut the street, while the strip had seemed to be jammed with perpetual traffic.

I was looking now for the real Las Vegas, the part of the city where people lived, not the part where visitors came to vacation. I'd programmed the address of Frank Wilton's house into my GPS, and when I reached the center of town, it told me to take an off-ramp, exit the freeway and head north, away from the strip. In an area bordered by seedy bars and abandoned buildings but marked by new housing developments, I passed two subdivisions under construction and there, between a recently completed gas station and an as-yet-unopened post office, the GPS announced that I'd arrived at my destination.

Where Frank's shack had been torn down.

I guess that was something I should have expected, although the possibility had not even occurred to me. Just as surprising was the fact that nothing had been built in its place. There was only an empty lot, flat and weedy and surrounded by new buildings. I felt a huge disappointment. This was the most recent listing for a "Frank W" house I could find, and I'd been hoping the current owners could tell me where Frank had gone from here, or at least point me in the right direction.

I'd been in the car for a long time, so even though there was nothing to see, I got out and walked around. I don't know what I expected—to pick up some sort of creepy vibe from the flat ground? To feel an unseen presence in the open space?—but there was nothing. As far as I could tell, this was an ordinary vacant lot, and though I walked its length and width, looking down at the ground for some left behind object that might indicate it had once been part of Frank's house, I did not find anything.

Still, in this revitalized area, flush with new construction, the spot on which Frank's house had sat was conspicuously empty.

That had to mean something.

Unsure at first what to do, I finally took out my phone, went online and accessed property records for the lot. I found that it was owned by an investment firm, Southwest Land Trust. Calling the number provided and leveraging my real estate credentials, I worked my way up the phone ladder and reached a "property consultant," who looked up the site for me and said that, yes it had once been owned by a Frank Wilton, but the company had bought it off a subsequent owner and had no information on Mr. Wilton. Southwest Land Trust had had the onsite structure razed in anticipation of building a liquor store at the location but had run into some setbacks. There was nothing weird, nothing mysterious. It was a zoning issue, pure and simple, and since the issues seemed to have been resolved, construction would probably begin soon.

This was a bust, and I was temporarily thrown, not sure of what to do. In spite of my initial plans, I was tempted to head back to Orange and give it all up. Confronted with the fruitlessness of my efforts, this entire trip suddenly seemed a waste to me. What had I been thinking? I'd gotten so wrapped up in the Frank narrative after learning about the Simmons house in Tarzana, that I'd allowed it to consume my time and energies in what was proving to be a really unhealthy way.

But I was not wrong.

Brad's mother was in a coma because her house had collapsed.

And both Frank's house and our vacation home in Randall were going to be on a ghost-hunting TV show.

And Billy was dead.

Billy.

I couldn't give up now. This was just a temporary setback. I had to press on, even if I was by no means convinced that it would lead anywhere. I stared at the vacant lot, thinking. What I really wanted to do right now was go straight to that first house in Texas. My hunch was that it could teach me the most about Frank. Since New Mexico was on the way, however, it seemed stupid to pass by the house in Bernalillo without stopping, so I decided to go there first before moving on.

I did some quick calculations. Bernalillo was a good ten to twelve hours from Las Vegas. Even if I left right now, there was no way I'd get there until after midnight—and I certainly couldn't wake up the owners of the house at that time—so I figured I'd just drive as far as I could, and then stop someplace when I got tired.

I sped through Arizona and ended up spending the night in a fleabag motel in the New Mexico border town of Gallup, having Taco Bell for dinner and McDonald's for breakfast before setting off for Bernalillo.

From the photo I'd seen and the description "ranch house," I expected the dwelling Frank built to be out in the countryside. But, to my surprise, it was located on a cul de sac pretty close to the center of town. Bernalillo itself seemed as though it was a community from *old* Mexico. Many of the houses were adobe, and mine was the only Caucasian face I saw. While the town's rural roots were front and center, however, there were newer shops and subdivisions spreading out from the original core, and I passed an Arby's and The Store before my GPS told me to turn right off the main street.

I pulled to a stop. The house looked just as it had in the photo I'd downloaded. It was cute, and seemingly well-constructed, which made me wonder if Frank had actually been involved with this one. Maybe "Frank Wilson" was *another* Frank, having nothing to do with my guy, and I was wasting my time here.

I got out of the car and went up the front walk.

An elderly Hispanic woman answered my knock. She didn't seem to speak English, and I didn't know enough Spanish to string together a sentence she could understand. Talking slowly didn't help either of us communicate, so she called over her husband. He emerged from somewhere within the house, and though his English was slightly better, it was not great. We struggled through introductory pleasantries, and I tried to explain why I was here, but they both looked confused. When I asked them, "Did you buy this house from Frank?" however, their demeanors changed. The name "Frank" had a galvanizing effect, and I saw the man's expression harden as the woman crossed herself.

Jackpot.

"Frank *es* bad man," the husband said. "*Muy malo.*"

I nodded to let him know I agreed. "Yes," I said. "*Si.*"

"Why you want to know about Frank?"

I wasn't sure how to answer that. "The police are looking for him," I decided to say. "I'm trying to help."

The man translated for his wife, and the idea that the police were after Frank brought a smile to both of their faces. Introducing themselves as Arturo and Maria Garcez, they let me in, and I noticed with a shiver that, while smaller, the house seemed to have the same floor plan as the first story of Frank's Randall home.

I nearly tripped over a bump in the rug and could tell as my foot explored the spot that it was a floorboard that had not been properly aligned. Typical Frank job. As though reading my mind, Arturo gestured at the ceiling above our heads. I could see a dark stain on the white painted plasterboard. "The roof leak," he said. He pointed ahead toward a back door that led from the living room into the yard, outlining the door in the air with his finger. "And wind blow through cracks."

Glancing into the adjacent kitchen as we walked into the living room, I recognized Sandy Simmons' sink faucet. I was only able to identify it because the design was so unique, and the sight of it confused me. Frank always stole things from one project to use on another, but how had that worked here? Had Frank stolen it from himself? Or had he stolen both faucets from another job? I didn't know, but the one thing of which I was certain was that the faucet *was* stolen.

That was Frank's MO.

So were the bodies and bones.

In the living room, I looked around. On top of a narrow table against the wall were framed photographs, most of a small boy. In the center was one photo larger than the rest, the child in his Sunday best. The frame was wrapped in black ribbon.

My heart sunk in my chest.

There was no way I was going to ask about that—but then again, I didn't need to ask. I knew he was their son, and I knew he had died, probably in this house.

Maria was speaking quickly in Spanish, and Arturo translated as best he could, letting me know that his wife thought the house was cursed. Wherever they lived, she'd always had a garden, but in this yard, all of her plants died. Their dog had run away shortly after they'd moved here. Whether they used a fan or the fireplace, the living room was always hot in the summer and cold in the winter, although that was not true for the rest of the house. Her face twisted with hate, and in the midst of the Spanish, I heard the word "Frank."

"Why don't you move?" I asked, still speaking slowly, as though that would help me be understood.

Arturo's eyes flicked involuntarily toward the pictures on the table. He shook his head. "No."

I didn't press.

"What about Frank?" I asked. "Do you know where Frank is? Do you know where he went?"

Arturo looked straight into my eyes. "No. But if I find him, I kill him. I *kill* him."

I might not have learned anything new, but what I'd already known I had confirmed, and at this point that seemed like progress.

It was still mid-morning, and if I left Bernalillo right now and drove eight hours straight, I'd be able to reach that first Frank house, in Texas, by late afternoon. There was nothing more to be learned here, so I thanked the Garcezes for allowing me into their home, promised to let them know if Frank was found and caught, filled up my tank at a gas station and started off.

It was the longest and most boring drive of my life, and Biscuitville, Texas, when I reached it, was the saddest little town I'd ever seen. It was not a cute little hamlet that had fallen on hard times, but a place that had *never* been cute. Literally three blocks long, the town consisted of buildings made from tan bricks and unpainted boards the same color as the surrounding flatlands, everything covered with a dusting of brown dirt and black diesel exhaust.

Parking my rental car on the street, I walked into a dingy café, hoping to get some information about how to get to Frank's house since my GPS did not seem to recognize this area of the state and the three streets I'd passed were not marked. A little bell tinkled as the door opened, tinkling again as it swung slowly shut behind me. Even the people here were ugly, I thought, looking around, and a depressing gloom settled over me as I crossed the scuffed floor to where an overweight waitress stood behind the colorless counter, frowning.

"Excuse me," I began.

"Yeah?" Her voice was too loud and tinged with a defensive belligerence. She seemed to sense somehow that I was not here to buy anything and apparently considered me an annoyance. I could feel the hostile eyes of the other customers boring into my back.

As a realtor, I was used to dealing with all types of people, but the atmosphere in the café was making me very uncomfortable. I forced myself to push those feelings aside. "I'm looking for Tulane Road."

The waitress snorted. "The B and B?"

Had Frank's house been made into a bed-and-breakfast? "I don't know," I admitted. "One-eleven Tulane Road's the address."

"B and B's the only thing out there." She stared at me with unveiled disdain. "You know the address but don't even know what it is?"

A couple of men laughed harshly.

I ignored them. "How do I get there?"

She looked out the grimy window. "That your car?"

"Yeah."

"Turn it around. Tulane's the first street on your left."

I thanked her for the information, but she'd already turned away, and I passed between two tables of sullen diners on my way out the door. The café wasn't exactly crowded, but it was nearly dinnertime, so it was probably as full as the place ever got.

Now that I knew which sun-faded strip of asphalt was Tulane, I found it easily, and while I had to drive a mile or two out of town to reach it, the waitress had been right: the bed-and-breakfast was the only building on the road save for a collapsed barn and the crumbling foundation of a house that had never been built.

It was obviously not a very successful business (after all, how many visitors could they expect in Biscuitville?). The homemade sign was faded almost into illegibility, and the parking lot was a square of hard packed dirt where a yard should have been, its only vehicle an ancient El Camino up on blocks.

The building itself bore the signs of amateurish construction common to seemingly all of Frank's projects. I saw crooked steps leading up to a slanted porch, an off-center front doorway, a poorly mortared chimney and numerous areas of patched roof that didn't match the original shingles. The rooms, I was sure, would have windows that didn't open or that let air seep in from outside. The wiring would be substandard; the plumbing wouldn't work the way it was supposed to.

It was late, and since I had nowhere else lined up—and there were no other towns for miles—I decided to stay the night. I also figured I'd be able to get more information out of the owner if I were a customer. There certainly wouldn't be any problem finding a vacancy. Walking up the creaky steps, I knocked on the closed front door.

The woman who ran the B&B was old and tired and didn't look as though she'd ever been happy. As she informed me when I told her I needed a room for the night, she was the owner, operator and only employee of the establishment, so I wasn't to expect what she called "hotel service."

"I don't serve meals here," she said as I signed in. "But there's food over to the café, if you want. Breakfast, lunch and dinner."

I thought of telling her that the word *breakfast* in "Bed-and-Breakfast" ordinarily meant that that meal was served to guests in the morning, but I didn't want to antagonize the woman. I needed to quiz her about Frank, and I knew she wouldn't want to answer any questions if she felt insulted. It didn't look as though she wanted to answer questions anyway, but I started off with a general query. "How long have you had this place?"

She stared flatly at me. "Since it opened."

This wasn't going to be easy. I kept my voice light and casual. "And when was that?"

"What's it to you?"

I wondered if she was any relation to the waitress at the café. "This place kind of reminds me of a B and B I stayed at back in Colorado. Guy named Frank owned it."

She reacted to the name, and my heart started pounding. "He built the place himself—" I continued.

"Frank Watson?"

Watkins, Warwick, Wilson, Wilton, Watson...

"Yeah, that's him."

"He's the lying son of a bitch who sold me this place." There was real anger in her eyes.

I decided to take a chance. Pretending to look around the living room/lobby, I said, "The place looks nice."

"You don't know shit, mister."

The hostility in her gaze and the solid finality of her tone made it clear that she considered the conversation over. Rather than press the issue, I decided it was better to wait for another opportunity.

I was lucky to have brought along my checkbook, because the bed-and-breakfast was unable to take credit cards. I wrote out a check for an exorbitant hundred dollars, thirty more than I'd spent the night before in Gallup, and the old woman—she hadn't even told me her name—gave me a room key and led me silently down the hall.

I had to admit, the room was nicer than I'd been expecting, certainly nicer than the peeling paint on the exterior of the house had led me to believe. A brass bed with a quilted cover occupied the center of the room, and some sort of dried wildflower arrangement decorated the wall behind it. To the left of the bed was an antique dresser, and to the right a small round table with two facing chairs, a tray on top of the table holding an empty water pitcher and four glasses. Against the wall next to the door, facing the bed, was a doorless armoire housing a pre-flat screen television set.

I was told curtly that there was no ice available, but that I could fill up the pitcher with water from the sink in the bathroom at the end of the hall.

"Do other guests—" I began.

She cut me off. "You're the only guest."

"Is that bathroom for both of—"

"My quarters are in the basement."

The basement.

I nodded. "Okay."

"There's no hotel service here," she reminded me again. "And I don't like to be disturbed. If there's an emergency, press this to call me." She pointed to what looked like a doorbell button on the wall. "Otherwise, I'll see you in the morning. Checkout time is anytime after eight."

She walked away before I could ask any questions or even thank her.

I hadn't eaten anything since a Subway sandwich lunch in New Mexico, but I didn't want to go back to that café, so when I took my suitcase out of the car, I also grabbed the can of Pringles that I kept by the front seat to snack on while I drove. Though warm, my ice chest in the back still had a couple of Coke cans left, and I brought one of those in with me as well.

It was late afternoon, easing into early evening, but still too early to shut myself up in my room, so I decided to do a little exploring and see what I could find. The old woman hadn't told me where I could and couldn't go, and I decided to take advantage of that. If she caught me nosing around somewhere I wasn't supposed to be, I'd just plead ignorance.

Once in the hall, I heard the woman's footsteps going up the stairs to the second floor. Knowing where she was gave me some freedom, so I quickly walked through the open rooms of the first floor, checking out the bathroom, a supply closet, the living room and adjacent family room. I didn't go down to the basement, not wanting to invade her privacy, but I did peek into the kitchen, which looked shabby and seldom used. I saw an old gas stove and an ancient Frigidaire. Hearing footsteps start down the stairs, I decided to check out the grounds. I'm not sure what I was looking for—

signs of buried bodies?

—but I went outside through the front door, and walked carefully around the building. The sun was going down, bathing the west wall of the house in hazy orange. To the east, across the flat prairie, the sky had already darkened into night.

There was no cellar door, no small windows at ground level, no indication that the bed-and-breakfast even had a basement. What was it like down there with no windows? I wondered. It had to be dark and claustrophobic.

And the old woman *lived* down there?

I thought of the Goodwins' basement and the skeletal remains of the boy they'd found.

If there were any bones here, they were probably in the basement.

With a loud *smack!* a rock hit the side wall, barely missing my head. There was a rustling in the brush off to my right, and another rock came sailing out, landing near my feet.

What the—

"Hey!" I called out. I dashed over to see who was throwing things at me.

A naked child ran away through the tall brown grass, giggling.

I blinked, caught a glimpse of bare skin before it disappeared.

That wasn't possible. I stared at the still swaying grass. Had I really seen what I thought I'd seen? What *had* I seen? A naked kid? A chill ran down my spine. But where had he come from and where did he live? The bed-and-breakfast was the only extant building on this road, and in the direction the youth was heading, there was only desert. Could a child really cross miles of rough ground on bare feet?

Was it even a child?

I was afraid to find out, which is why I did not chase the figure but slunk back inside the B&B. In my room, I peered out the window at the darkening landscape. I saw nothing, but a rock hit the side of the house next to my room, making me jump, and I immediately pulled the drape shut. Turning on the light, I sat down on the bed.

What the hell was happening out there?

In my mind's eye, I saw a band of naked feral children crawling through the brush, waiting for me to come outside again.

To kill me.

It was a crazy thought, but at that moment it did not seem at all farfetched.

Taking out my cell phone with trembling hands, I called Teri, grateful to hear her voice. I couldn't really fill her in on what was happening, but I filled her in on where I was, told her about my long drive today, about what a pit Biscuitville was, about everything that wasn't important. Talking to her calmed me down. She told me about in-fighting in her department at work, and let me know that she'd driven by the real estate office on her way home because she was thinking about me. Too lazy to cook, she'd picked up a veggie burrito from Mother's Market and was heating it up in the microwave even as we spoke.

Hearing all this made her feel far away. And she was, I realized. Southern California was almost halfway across the country. I glanced toward the closed drape. Biscuitville was like some alien land, a place I had not known existed, that I wanted quickly to escape and that I never wanted to see again.

"I miss you," she said before we hung up.

"I miss you, too," I told her.

I almost added, "I love you," but didn't. That was the distance talking, and the last thing I wanted to do when I returned was walk back some embarrassing statement I'd made out of loneliness. Although, staring now at the black screen of my silent phone, I thought it might actually be true. Maybe I did love her. And if she'd made a special effort to drive by my office when she knew I wasn't there, just because of its connection to me, maybe she felt the same.

That probably should have made me feel better, but it made me feel worse, and I ended up turning on the television for company. I sat through two commercials, one for medicine that apparently helped old men get erections while they were folding laundry with their younger wives, and one where an elderly actor tried to convince people to gut their children's inheritance by signing up for a reverse mortgage. I felt weighed down by everything. When the nightly news came on, even though the top story was about a school shooting, I felt strangely comforted because at least the anchor and the set and the reporter were familiar.

The news ended and an entertainment program came on. Feeling braver and more settled, I pulled open the drape. Outside, the sideways smile of a new moon hung low in the sky. I could hear crickets and cicadas, but the only sound of human habitation in this land was the far off noise of a pickup's engine. Looking in vain for any sign of the naked child, I saw only clumps of grasses and brush that in the darkness resembled Horta-like monsters encroaching on the bed-and-breakfast.

Had I seen what I thought I'd seen or had I imagined it? And, if I had, was it connected to the Frank house?

It almost had to be.

With nothing to do, I ate my dinner of Pringles and Coke while watching a drug smuggling documentary on CNN. I tried to check my emails, but something was making my phone slow, so I sat on the bed, channel surfing. The first *Men in Black* was on TNT—wasn't it always?—and though I'd seen it a hundred times, I stopped flipping to watch it. I'd had a long day, and before the first commercial, I was starting to doze. Feeling sleepy, I took off my clothes, turned off the TV and crawled under the covers.

I was awakened much later by a banging sound. Sitting up groggily, I wasn't sure for a moment where I was and thought the noise might be someone knocking on the front door of my house in California. Then I recognized the room, realized where I was, and thought maybe the old woman was trying to wake me up for some reason.

A burglar? A fire?

No. The noise wasn't coming from the door, I quickly discerned, but from somewhere on the floor above. It was a steady beating, the sound coming every few seconds in regular intervals. I closed my eyes, lay back down and waited for it to go away, but it didn't. The banging continued, got louder if anything, and finally, I swung out of bed, slipped on my pants and padded over to the door, opening it.

In the hallway, the noise was even louder, as though someone upstairs was hitting a baseball bat against a wall. I'd come out because the noise was annoying, had awakened me, and I wanted it to stop. But it was too loud, too insistent, and the whole situation seemed more than a little threatening. The fact that there was no sign of the old woman was unsettling, too. Looking toward the stairs, I tried to tell myself it was water in the pipes or a heavy wind outside that was making a branch hit the roof, but I couldn't make myself believe it because I knew it wasn't true.

Someone was upstairs.

Hitting something.

The banging continued.

I walked slowly up the steps to the floor above, thinking how like the stairway in our A-frame this was and wondering if Frank had based these stairs on those in our vacation house, stealing the design just as he had stolen so many other things.

No, he couldn't have. He'd built this way before he'd moved to Randall.

The banging grew louder.

At the top, a weak yellow light illuminated a small landing. I stepped onto the floor, seeing two doors in front of me. One open. One closed.

The open doorway revealed a room that was pitch black.

That was where the pounding came from.

I wanted to run back downstairs, run outside, get in my rental car and never come back. But I remained rooted in place.

The noise suddenly stopped.

"Hello?" I said tentatively.

From within the lightless room came a soft glow, a glow brightening slowly to reveal that its source was an old lamp atop a narrow end table. The room was illuminated now, but not well, and gathering my courage, I stepped over the threshold. I saw a low couch, an old-fashioned high-backed chair, a chest of drawers, a bed. There was a window off to the right, but it was covered by closed brown curtains so thick that they let in no moonlight. My nose was assaulted with a sickly scent of decay that made me think instantly of the dogs underneath our vacation home.

A low tapping started up, its origin a closed closet at the far end of the room. The sound was quiet at first, barely perceptible, but it slowly began to increase in volume, and I knew that it would eventually turn into the pounding again.

I wanted to get out of here before that happened—

tap tap

—but I needed to know what was in the closet.

Tap Tap Tap

I moved forward slowly, afraid that any sudden movement would awaken whatever else was in the room. Glancing at the bed to the left of me, I saw that the covers were turned down as though someone had been sleeping there.

TAP TAP TAP TAP TAP

The tapping was louder, not pounding yet but well on its way.

I recognized the closet door in front of me, and it took a moment to place where I'd seen it before, though I should have known it instantly.

Sandy Simmons' house.

It looked like the door to the closet in her "workspace," the one where I'd heard—

Irene's fingernails

—tapping but had been too afraid to investigate.

I was forcing myself to be brave, though I had actually never been so frightened. I stepped closer. In the second before I reached the door, I glanced to the right, where an ornately framed mirror was mounted on the wall. I met the eyes of the figure in the mirror—

But that figure wasn't me.

Instead, looking out from the glass, her face impossibly old and horribly wrinkled, was Irene. She smiled as she saw that I recognized her, and her teeth were so white that they glowed.

I cried out.

I couldn't help myself. I didn't scream like a little girl—it was a fairly manly sound, if I do say so myself—but I cried out nevertheless, and, after stumbling backward, I got myself turned around and sped down the stairs to the first floor.

Where the old lady who ran the B&B was waiting for me, frowning. "What were you doing up there?" she demanded.

I blinked dumbly, my heart still pounding from my upstairs encounter. "Irene...She was..."

"Get out," the old woman said disgustedly, looking at my shirtless chest.

Rationality began to return. "What?"

"We don't want your kind here."

I looked at her, my breathing on its way back to normal. "My kind, huh? And exactly what kind is that?"

She met my gaze with a hard level stare. "Get out."

"I understand now why you're so busy here," I told her. "It's that friendly, welcoming attitude."

"Am I going to have to get my gun?"

"Am I going to have to call the law? I paid for a full night."

She hesitated, and I could see her weighing the options in her mind: getting rid of me and losing out on a hundred dollars versus letting me stay and keeping my money. Greed won out. "I want you gone by morning." She turned, and I watched her walk away, heard her stomp down the stairs to her quarters in the basement.

My kind?

What the hell did that mean?

I didn't know and didn't care. Returning to my room, I locked the door behind me. I actually *did* want to leave. The thought of spending another second here terrified me, but if that old bat could survive here, so could I.

Frank house.

That was the source of everything, the reason behind all of it: the naked kid, the creepy house, the ghostly noises, Irene.

Irene.

I had no explanation for that, and I wanted to believe it was my imagination, but I didn't think it was, and for the first time since I was a child, I pulled the covers over my head for protection and waited for sleep to come.

In the morning, either before the old bitch had awakened or before she'd come up from her basement, I packed up my stuff, left the key on the desk in the living room, and took off.

I drove out of Biscuitville the way I'd come. Past the unbuilt house and the fallen barn, past the drab café and the dusty main street.

Maybe, I thought, Frank's influence had affected the whole town.

The idea gave me no comfort, and I gratefully put Biscuitville in my rearview mirror as I headed west toward New Mexico.

TEN

I SAT AT THE Denny's in Tucumcari, staring out the window.

What had I been thinking?

I'd taken an unspecified leave of absence from my job, and a mere three days later I was already set to pack it in and head home. Las Vegas had been a waste of time, I hadn't learned anything new in Bernalillo, and despite my nightmare experience in Biscuitville, I hadn't gotten any information out of that witch at the B&B. I wanted justice, I wanted closure, but was I going to get it by doing this? Driving pointlessly across the country from house to house? I figured I should just give it up now before throwing away even more time and money.

It was Mike Rivera who set me on the right path. He called me at that moment, as I was drinking coffee and watching a semi pass by on Interstate 40. Mike was not only showing two of the homes I had listed, but he'd spent half of yesterday going through my computer looking for unfinished business. Somehow, I'd forgotten to delete a portion of my recent research, and he had looked up and found a current address for Frank Watkins.

The name he'd used in Randall.

His real name?

I couldn't believe it.

"Yeah, it looked like you were searching for this guy who'd been using a bunch of aliases and had something to do with that Big Bear sale. I figured I could help. He's pretty low-tech, but you can't stay off the grid if you're selling houses and paying utilities. He actually wasn't that hard to track." Mike had a facility with computers that went far beyond mine. At one time, he'd been a low level programmer at a failed start-up, but he'd found he could equal his tech income with real estate, a job it turned out he enjoyed much, much more. I probably should have enlisted his help earlier, but I'd been wary of involving anyone else.

Although, if it had been so easy to find Frank, I wondered why law enforcement hadn't been able to do it.

According to Mike, Frank was back in Nevada. A nowhere town called Feldspar. It was somewhere in the empty center of the state, and I had Mike email me the information so I could access it on my phone.

"I assume this means you'll be back soon," he said.

"Probably," I admitted. "It was stupid for me to take a 'leave.' I should've just banked a few extra vacation days. I don't know what I was thinking."

"That's cool," Mike told me.

I heard the disappointment in his voice and smiled. "You and May can keep those listings I gave you. A promise is a promise. Besides, I owe you for this info."

"Glad you're coming back," he said heartily, and this time he meant it. He lowered his voice. "With only May and Jim here, the atmosphere's a little—"

"Serious?"

"Sterile, I was going to say. I need you around to help loosen the corsets."

We talked a few moments longer. He had questions about one of my listings in Tustin that he was going to be showing later today—the real reason he'd called—and I told him everything I knew. I was anxious to get him off the phone and start off for Nevada, and the second he hung up, I downed the rest of my coffee and called for my check.

My GPS was working again, but the shortest route to Feldspar was through some of the most godforsaken country known to man.

Thank goodness for satellite radio, which allowed me to listen to music while travelling through desert where no regular radio stations could reach.

I spent that night at a real motel, a Holiday Inn Express, and I'd never in my life been so grateful for the bland anonymity of corporate America. After that hellish B&B, the antiseptic atmosphere of a generic Holiday Inn was the most welcome end of the day I could imagine. I ate a dinner of grilled chicken with wild rice pilaf in the adjacent restaurant, took my first shower in two days, and fell asleep in air-conditioned comfort to the sounds of *The Tonight Show.* In the morning, I had a "continental breakfast" that was closer to a real breakfast than anything I'd had since leaving home.

Refreshed, reinvigorated and ready, I set off for Feldspar.

It was mid-morning when I reached the town. Feldspar was only slightly larger than Biscuitville, and I decided then and there that when this was all over, I was going to spend the rest of my life safely within the confines of the endless metropolis that was Southern California.

My GPS was still working, and it directed me to a residential street off the short main drag.

To an empty lot.

I stopped the car.

Not again.

I was filled with a deep sense of disappointment. I wasn't sure what I'd expected to find—Frank holed up alone in a rundown shack or living in a perfectly maintained tract home?—but I honestly thought that I'd see him. I'd even gone over different scenarios in my head, planning out possible conversations and numerous opening lines as I'd driven through the empty arid land. Now, once again, it was all for naught.

Parking in front of the empty lot, I got out to look around. Amidst the dried weeds, empty beer cans, broken glass and windblown detritus, the ground was rough. There were post-sized holes and lengthy trenches that appeared to have been dug for pipes. It was as though the house that had once been here had been ripped up and pulled into the sky, foundation, plumbing and all.

I had a bad feeling about this. On the off chance that one of the neighbors might know what had happened, I walked across the street to where a skinny old man in a dirty tank top was sweeping his porch—a futile exercise in this environment. "Excuse me!" I said.

He looked up, squinting against the sun. "Yeah?"

"Do you know anything about that lot across the street? I'm looking for a man named Frank—"

"Frank?" he said. "Yeah, I know Frank. He used to have a house there."

I could feel my pulse accelerating. "You wouldn't happen to know where he is now, would you?"

"At his new house, I assume."

"New house?"

"Yeah. Built it himself. Been buildin' it for a long time, in fact. I remember when he first started. Took me out to see it once. Back then, it was just one room, hardly bigger'n a storage shed. But he just kept addin' on and addin' on, keepin' nails and pipes and scraps of lumber from other jobs he did and usin' them for to put up his own place. Kind of like that Johnny Cash song about the car. You know, where he steals a little bit at a time from the assembly line and builds himself a one-of-a-kind automobile?"

I didn't know the song, but that didn't matter. I knew Frank's pattern. A thought occurred to me. "Did Frank steal from you?"

The old man laughed raspily. "Hell yeah! Had him put in a new faucet? He bought extra parts, charged them to me and kept the rest. Built a deck for me in the back? Overbought lumber and kept the extra boards. Oh, it was harmless, but he couldn't help himself. That's just who he was. Like this uncle I had. Used to kype somethin' every time he came over: ashtray, lighter, apple, penny, whatever. Nicest guy in the world, give you the shirt off his back, but he just *had* to take stuff when he stopped by..."

"And Frank was like that?" I prodded. "Stole things?"

"Oh yeah. Stole from himself, even. Or *recycled*, I guess. That's why there ain't no house there no more." He pointed his broom toward the lot. "Once he moved out for good, he started tearin' the place apart, takin' wood and siding and plumbing, piece by piece, until there was nothin' left."

"Do you still see Frank?" I asked.

The old man hesitated for a little too long. "Frank don't get out much anymore. I think he mostly just stays inside his house."

"Yeah, he must be pretty old," I reasoned.

There was another weird pause. "I guess so."

"You wouldn't happen to know where this house is, would you?"

"Sure. I even drive by there sometimes, just to see how things're comin' along. I don't stop—Frank likes his privacy—but I do check the place out, and it's...impressive."

"How do I get there?" I asked him.

Another hesitation. "I'm not sure..."

"I need to see him."

The old man looked me over, appraising me. He seemed to like Frank and perhaps thought he was acting as a gatekeeper, so I didn't want to let him know how I really felt. I tried to keep my expression neutral. "Frank knew my family back in Randall, Arizona. I haven't seen him for a long time." I put on my best professional smile, extended my hand. "My name's Daniel. Daniel Martin. I'm in real estate now."

He shook my hand noncommittally. "Petey Bodean." He thought for a moment. "I don't think Frank's interested in selling."

"That's not why I want to see him."

He gave me that appraising look again. "When was it you knew Frank?"

"Mid-eighties," I said.

"Well...Frank hasn't changed. Frank's still Frank."

I wasn't sure if that was a warning or just an acknowledgment that he knew what Frank was like, too. I nodded as though I understood, still smiling, keeping my expression neutral.

Petey must have decided that I was all right. "It's kind of hard to find. His place. I'll lead you out there. Just give me a minute."

He walked around the side of the house to the carport, putting away his broom. I walked across the street to my car. After going into the house to get his keys (but not a shirt), he backed out in his Jeep, and I followed him through the town and down a single-lane road out into the desert.

It was a lot farther away than I thought it would be, and I had plenty of time to go over things in my mind. Since Mike had found the Feldspar property but had not found this new location where Frank had apparently built a house and was living, I wondered if it was in his own name, if he had set up some sort of shell corporation, or if he'd simply used a *new* fake name that had nothing to do with "Frank." I also regretted not asking Petey if Frank was still married. I was pretty sure Irene was dead—

TAP TAP TAP TAP

—but, then again…

Even in the hot light of day, the thought of encountering a *really* old Irene made me shiver.

As fifteen minutes became a half hour, and a half hour became forty-five minutes, I started glancing at my fuel gauge, thinking I should have filled up before we left Feldspar. The road wound through a series of low sandy foothills before finally straightening out and sloping into a flat barren valley containing a single two-story structure that looked like one of those green-shuttered, red-chimneyed homes featured on the cover of elementary school reading books.

Frank's house.

I knew what it was immediately, and when Petey's Jeep sped up, I followed suit. The old man turned around directly in front of the house, honked his horn, pointed at it, waved to me and sped off back the way we had come. I'd expected him to stay, maybe introduce me, at least leave me with some additional information, and the fact that he was in such a hurry to take off left me feeling a little unsettled.

There were no fences enclosing the property, nothing blocking the house from someone on the road who wished to approach. The remoteness of the location and the isolation of the road itself was probably protection enough, but I wouldn't have been surprised to learn that security cameras were trained on me. Hesitating for only a second, I turned onto the short dirt driveway, pulled up directly in front of the structure and got out of the car.

It was a Frank house all right.

What from a distance had appeared to be a stereotypical example of a mid-twentieth century, upper middle class family home was revealed on closer inspection to be a poorly constructed hodgepodge of stucco wall and aluminum siding and wood frame, with a roof that was half shingle, one quarter shake and one quarter plain old tarpaper, all joined together in a manner that was far from seamless. The windows, I saw, were mirrored.

I shouldn't be here alone, I thought. *I should contact the law, let the police handle this.*

I should have, but I didn't. Ignoring my misgivings, I pressed forward, walking up the slanted porch. I looked for some sort of doorbell, saw none, and was about to raise my fist and knock, when the door suddenly swung open, revealing a man standing in the foyer before me.

Frank.

He looked exactly the same as he had all those years ago. He was even wearing those narrow-striped engineer's overalls, and just seeing him sent a shiver down my spine.

Frank hasn't changed.

I knew now what Petey had meant, and what had made the old man so hesitant to answer my questions. I understood, also, why he had taken off so quickly after bringing me here.

He was afraid.

I was afraid, too, and everything I'd planned to say upon meeting Frank once again had fled my head, leaving me tongue-tied and dumb. I could tell from the expression on his face that he knew the effect he had on me and relished it. I could tell also that he recognized me, and that was the most frightening thing. I'd been a child when he last saw me, and I was an adult now who looked nothing like that scrawny young boy, yet he instantly knew who I was. "Daniel," he said. "Come in." And there it was, the stare: awkward and inappropriate and held too long. I was reminded of the times he'd tried to lure me and Billy into his pickup.

I might have been a grown man, but the dynamic between us was the same as it had always been. I felt like a kid with him, a frightened little kid. There'd always been something wrong with Frank; I'd known it even as a child, and the years of experience since had only added a depth of unwanted insight into his words and actions. I walked through the doorway, entering the house, not sure if I was doing so because I wanted to confront him or because I was submissively following his prompt. The sense of purpose that had been driving me up to this point seemed to have dissipated and faded away.

Neither of us had spoken since I'd stepped into the foyer. I glanced around. There was an Oriental rug lying on a floor that was supposed to be hardwood but, in typical Frank style, seemed to be varnished paneling. Like its exterior, the inside of the house was as incompetently put together as everything else the man had worked on. Against the wall, impossibly, I saw our old couch, the one from Randall that we thought Frank had sold at his garage sale. My breath caught in my throat as a wave of unexpected memories washed over me: sitting on the sofa playing Monopoly with Billy during a late summer thunderstorm...unwrapping Christmas presents with my mom...watching *Cheers* with my dad...

Billy, impaled on that triangular board, his open eyes staring up at me from beneath the house through the hole in the floor.

"So how's your brother?" Frank said. Smiling. Staring.

My anger returned, and with it my sense of purpose. I remembered that Billy and I had never gotten into Frank's truck back then; we'd walked away from him.

Frank hasn't changed.

"How's your wife?" I retorted, certain that she was dead and wanting to hurt him.

"I have only the Dark Wife now."

What did *that* mean? The phrase was ominous, and the tone of voice in which Frank said it made my skin crawl.

I needed to get out of here, I realized. I wasn't some movie vigilante; I wasn't going to kill Frank out of revenge or even kick his ass. Now that I knew where he was, I needed to go to the police, tell them where to find him and let them take care of it. There was no statute of limitations on murder, and even if they couldn't pin anything else on him, they had him dead to rights on the boy walled up in his basement.

The door had closed behind me, although whether on purpose in an effort to trap me here, or merely because Frank had not hung the door right or mounted the hinges correctly, I couldn't say.

I was turning to let myself out when he spoke again.

"I hear you've been looking for me."

I swung back to face him. It was out in the open now. I wasn't sure *how* he could have heard that, or *who* he could have heard it from, but he obviously knew that I'd been searching for him, and I didn't bother to deny it. "The police have been looking for you, too," I told him. "You belong in jail for what you've done."

"And what have I done?" he said innocently. "Built a few houses? Worked on some construction projects?"

"Killed a few pets, buried a few bodies, stolen some materials..."

Frank's expression clouded over. "I never stole anything in my life."

It was interesting that that was the only charge he tried to deny. "You stole the paneling that came with our house and you used it to finish your upstairs." I pointed to the sofa. "And you stole our couch."

"Your daddy gave me—"

"My dad didn't give you shit. He went to the cops when he found out what you'd done. And the only reason you're not rotting in jail right now is because they were a bunch of incompetent assholes."

My agitation seemed to make him calmer. "It's been a long time. Maybe it was your mama who—"

"She hated you."

He smiled. "Your mama fed me a dirty breakfast. I saw her eat a filthy sandwich."

I had no idea what he was talking about—it made no sense whatsoever—but the implication was definitely sexual, and when I saw the smutty leer on his face, I wanted to smack it off. "Don't you even mention her," I warned.

He smiled meanly. "Your mama's bones are in my home. I dug them up. In the dead of night. I went to that cemetery in Anaheim, across from the Pancake House, the *Original* Pancake House—"

I felt sick to my stomach.

He knew where she'd been buried.

"—and I paid off a guy, and I dug up her coffin and opened it up and took her bones. I left your daddy there, though. Didn't want the two of them to be together..."

"You bastard!" I yelled, and tried to punch him, but the door opened behind me and somehow Frank was next to me, avoiding my fist and pushing me outside.

"Thanks for stopping by," he said. "Don't come again."

The door slammed shut. I pounded on it, attempted to open it, sought to get back in, even though, only moments before, I had been desperate to leave. My anger overwhelmed my common sense, and though I knew the smartest course of action would be to notify the police, what I wanted to do was kick his ass. Not that I could. He hadn't aged in all these decades, and I was still afraid of him.

I stared up at the facade of the house.

It seemed impossible, but...maybe my mom's bones *were* inside, buried under a floor or interred behind a wall. The thought of it made me crazy. I felt disgusted and depressed and angry all at the same time.

It was best to just get the police out here.

Reaching the car, I got in and turned the key, half-expecting that, as in some bad horror movie, it wouldn't start. It did, though, and I flipped on the satellite radio, starting when I heard a DJ talk about a Dodgers game the night before.

That wasn't possible. They were off last night.

I switched the channel to CNN, where after a rundown of the

hour's top headlines, the anchor announced that it was ten o'clock, Monday, August twenty-first.

Monday? The twenty-first?

I'd been inside Frank's house for six days.

ELEVEN

I DON'T KNOW IF Teri was happier to see me or if I was happier to see her. I'd never believed the adage that absence makes the heart grow fonder, but in this case it had. She was waiting for me when I arrived back in Orange, and before I'd even gotten out of the car in front of her apartment building, she was running toward me, arms outstretched. She ran into me so hard that I would have been knocked down had she not immediately hugged me so tightly. I felt kisses on my cheeks and forehead and then on my lips, and I kissed her back gratefully, happily, passionately.

I'd called Teri immediately after discovering how long I'd been in Frank's house, and found that she was panicked, having left over 30 messages on my phone. She hadn't heard from me, hadn't been able to get ahold of me, and every scenario that ran through her head was either a disaster or a tragedy:

—I'd fallen asleep while driving, crashed into a semi-truck, and had been burned so far beyond recognition that my body could not be identified.

—I'd been forced off the road and over a cliff, where my car had exploded.

—I'd slipped on a wet sidewalk and hit my head and suffered a brain aneurysm.

—I'd choked to death in my sleep in an unknown motel.

She'd contacted the police to report my disappearance, but since she wasn't a relative, I was officially on leave from my job, and the only indication she had that I was missing was the fact that I wasn't answering my phone, the cops told her there was nothing they could do. She would need more proof of my disappearance in order for them to investigate. It had made her frantic, and she'd been calling and emailing every law enforcement and government agency she could think of. While it had been a nightmare for her, I was actually glad that she hadn't succeeded in convincing the police to undertake a big search. Now I wouldn't have to prove that I was really me, not to mention accounting for my whereabouts every minute over the past week.

I told her the truth about what had happened. There was no reason not to, and now I wondered why I hadn't done so before. I left nothing out and made no effort to sugarcoat any part of it. Either I would frighten her off, or she would understand and accept, but either way, everything would be out in the open and there would be no secrets. I was done with secrets.

I was still baffled by what had happened during my five minutes—

six days

—in the house, and was tempted to disbelieve it myself, even though I knew it to be true. The loss of time frightened me more than anything else ever had, more than the trip back to Randall, more than the B&B ghost in Texas. Those, at least, were expected and relatable. This was something entirely different: a complete revocation of the laws of physics.

Even as I described it all to Teri, I was aware of how absurd it sounded, and I would not have blamed her had she gotten mad at me for lying and spinning such an outrageous story, or if she'd run away, thinking me crazy. Thankfully, she did neither. She absorbed what I said and even if she didn't buy all of it, she apparently knew me well enough to understand that *I* thought it was true, and for now that was good enough for her.

"Besides," she teased, "I'll be able to watch part of this on *Ghost Pursuers*, won't I?"

I hugged her tightly, nearly overcome with emotion, not realizing until that moment how important it was to have someone by my side, someone who believed in me.

We talked for hours, going over the details of everything that had happened, examining it all with the thoroughness of grad students analyzing a Faulkner novel. She had questions, of course, but I had questions, too.

Had he really dug up my mom's bones?

That was the big one. That was the question that haunted me, and the only two options, as I saw it, were to believe that Frank had been lying in order to get my goat—or to have my mom's body exhumed to see if it was still there. The first was obviously preferable, but I wasn't sure I'd be able to live with the uncertainty. The thought of having her dug up after all this time, though, made me sick to my stomach.

Teri put her hand on mine. "This Frank's always been a liar, hasn't he? Let her rest."

"But he knew the cemetery!"

"Let her rest."

I nodded tiredly. It was good advice.

I decided to take it.

For now.

Sandy Simmons had died in my absence. I learned what happened when I called to let her know that I had found Frank. I dialed her number, but the connection was automatically switched over to Brad's phone, and when I asked to speak to her, he told me the news. She'd never awakened from her coma, and the official cause of death was organ failure.

But I knew the real reason.

Frank.

I expressed my condolences to Brad but decided to leave it at that. I wasn't going to investigate further, wasn't going to get involved. I was done with all that. It was time to move on. I'd alerted the authorities about Frank, and whatever happened next was up to them. I would testify in court if need be, I would share whatever information

I had, but I was through with any sort of solo quest. I hoped Frank would go to jail, but if not, he could rot out there in his mausoleum in the desert. My part in this was over.

It felt good to concede that. I was starting fresh, beginning anew. I'd dumped all my baggage, and one of my first decisions as a free man involved Teri: I was going to ask her to move in with me.

I did so over dinner in a way that I'd seen in a movie. I made an extra key to my house, put it in a small box and wrapped it up, giving it to her in a nice restaurant right before dessert. There was a slight moment of panic when I realized that she might think this was a proposal and that the box contained a ring, but the idea didn't appear to even cross her mind. She seemed genuinely in the dark about what the box might contain, and she was completely surprised when she saw the key and I explained that I thought we should move in together.

It took some convincing. She'd lived in her apartment for the past ten years and was more than a little attached to it. The location was convenient for work, and she liked the neighborhood. Though she didn't say so, I'm sure she was also afraid that if things didn't work out between us and she gave up the apartment, she would not be able to find a place quite as nice.

So we settled on a compromise: she would move in with me, but keep her apartment for awhile—just in case.

"You're not offended?" she asked.

I laughed. "Not at all. In real estate, we advise people to do things like this all the time. Doubles up on our commissions."

"But you're not selling me anything. Or renting me anything."

"I know. But I understand. It's the unmarried cohabitants' version of a pre-nup. It's smart."

She kissed me. "I'm smart and you're understanding. We make a good team."

"I think we do," I said.

My house was a three-bedroom, two-bath ranch style in a nice neighborhood on the border of Anaheim Hills. I'd been using one room just for storage, but I moved all my crap into the garage, and let Teri have the room for whatever she wanted. Her furniture was nicer than mine, or at least displayed more style, so over the next weekend, using a rented U-Haul truck and the free labor of friends, we switched out my bed for hers, swapped dressers and couches, and the end result was that her now unused apartment looked more like my house while my house—*our* house now—looked more like her apartment. Which was probably for the best.

You get a lot closer to people when you live with them rather than just date, but if either of us were concerned about the implications of that, we needn't have been. Not only were we compatible as roommates, but our relationship was deepened by the increased exposure. We were who we thought we were—only more so. I could imagine us married, in a way that I had not been able to before. I could see us spending the rest of our lives together.

I had nightmares, apparently, but I didn't remember them and only the fact that I awoke to Teri's soothing reassurances and her soft hands on my face clued me in that something was amiss. She told me, after the first time, that she'd been awakened by me thrashing around in the bed and crying out in my sleep, and though I didn't remember anything, I was grateful for her comforting presence. When it happened again, however, and again, I began to feel guilty. I shouldn't have been putting her through this. She didn't seem to mind, though. She was patient. And understanding.

And she was always there.

We started carpooling to work. Her job required her to stay in her office all day, while mine often had me out showing houses, so it made sense that I was the one to drive. She could save on gas money, and wear and tear on her car. Not to mention the fact that we could enjoy each other's company as we commuted. The bank headquarters where she worked was a little out of my way, but not inconveniently so, and we developed a routine, leaving the house around seven, stopping at a Starbuck's near Orange Mall for some coffee, driving past Disneyland, then sitting in the car in the parking lot of her office building, talking until it was time for her to go in.

Life was good.

And except for those nightmares that I didn't remember, I seemed to have put Frank and the past behind me.

A month or so later, we went on a weekend trip to meet her family. I knew Teri had a sister, and I knew that both of her parents were still alive, but they'd never appeared to be close, and I was surprised when she suggested that we visit.

Teri was from a small town in San Diego county called Ramona, a farming community in the mountain foothills some twenty miles past the San Diego Wild Animal Park. Her parents still lived in her childhood home, and both of her sisters' families lived in nearby Escondido. They were all waiting for us when we arrived, the small driveway filled with two pickups and an SUV. I parked on the street, and by the time we got out of the car, we were engulfed in hugs and well wishes. Unbeknownst to me, Teri had sent them my picture from her phone, so I was at a disadvantage; I had never seen anyone before and had to be introduced several times to the same people before I got their names straight.

The house was a late-twentieth century tract home built in a subdivision that appeared to be a buffer zone between the quaint downtown, and the surrounding farms and chicken ranches. Inside, the fireplace mantle and tables were full of framed photos featuring Teri and her sisters, and I examined them closely. I'd never seen what she looked like as a child and was not surprised to see that she'd been the cutest of the three. Both of her sisters were pretty, though, as was her mom, which boded well for Teri's future.

Iced tea and water were distributed to those who wanted them—and then began the serious matter of the inquisition. Julie was the sister with children, and her husband Ron took the kids outside to play, while the rest of us remained in the living room. Under the guise of a casual conversation, my romantic history, financial prospects and intentions toward Teri were extracted, and while I'd definitely had more painful encounters in the past, meeting the family was never fun.

I must have passed the test, though, because they eased off fairly quickly, and as the topic shifted from me to family gossip, I sensed no underlying hostility. Real estate had made me into a facile conversationalist, but there was no need to fall back on my professional skills. Her dad and I genuinely hit it off, and while the rest of the family talked about people I didn't know and incidents I hadn't been a part of, we discussed Humphrey Bogart movies.

Sometime in the middle of the conversation, I heard a baby crying in a back bedroom. Assuming it was one of her sister's, I waited for someone to get up and go to the infant, to comfort it or feed it or change its diaper or do whatever needed to be done, but either no one else heard the cries or they were all ignoring it, so I finally asked, "Isn't someone going to check on the baby?"

Julie frowned. "What baby?"

Sure enough, the sound had stopped. I looked from face to face, confused. "I thought I heard a baby crying."

"No," Teri's mom said.

"Maybe it was next door or something," Julie suggested. "The window's open."

"Probably," I said, nodding.

Everyone went back to their conversations, and eventually we went out to a Mexican restaurant for lunch.

Teri asked me about it that night. "What was that?"

"What was what?"

"That whole thing with the baby."

"Nothing. I just thought I heard a baby crying."

"Don't give me that. It wasn't nothing." I could feel her eyes on me.

"It really was," I told her, but I could tell from the expression on her face when I glanced over that she was suspicious. I couldn't blame her. She'd heard a lot of craziness from me lately, and either she'd bought into it all, or she loved me enough to pretend that she did. Whichever, she was obviously on the alert for any odd behavior that I might exhibit.

"Seriously," I said.

"Okay," she declared after a moment, still not satisfied but apparently willing to let it go.

The rest of the short weekend was spent exploring Ramona and the nearby mountain town of Julien with her family. We had to endure numerous unsubtle hints from her mother about getting married, but though Teri found it annoying (and told her mom so), I thought it was kind of sweet. For the first time in my life, I could actually see myself getting married, and I could tell that Teri, despite her objections, had thoughts along the same lines.

I have only the Dark Wife now.

One thing that spending time with her family made me realize was how much I missed my own family. I wished my parents could have lived to see how I'd turned out, wished they were alive to meet Teri.

And I wished Billy was here, too.

The uptick in housing sales that had started at the end of summer continued into the beginning of fall, and what had begun as a bad year economically was turning out to be pretty good. I sold four houses in a six-week period, one of them a multi-million dollar residence on Skyline Drive in Fullerton, and I listed three properties from past clients that were on very desirable streets in upscale neighborhoods and were bound to go quickly. One of the clients turned me on to some new music I'd never heard before, an ensemble called the Helix Collective, and I found myself downloading their album *All In* and listening to it incessantly, the soundtrack to my fall selling season.

One busy Tuesday, after showing houses to a Korean family who wanted to move into the Sunny Hills High School district, I was washing my hands in the restroom at the office and preparing to eat a late lunch when, beneath the sound of the running water, I thought I heard the wail of a baby. The cry was faint, as though coming from very far away, and the second I turned off the faucet, it was gone. *Had it been there at all?* I wasn't sure, and, just to check, I turned the water on again. There was indeed a high-pitched whine in the pipes. Could that have been it? I didn't think so, but it was possible. It was also the most logical explanation, although logical explanations had been in short supply lately.

I checked with May and Mike, who were both at their desks, but neither of them had heard a thing. Just as with Teri's family, the baby's cries seemed to exist only for my benefit, and I spent the rest of the day in the office, catching up on paperwork, waiting to see if it would happen again. It did not, and when I went to the bathroom a few hours later, even the pipes were silent.

We made love after dinner that night. Teri was on her hands and knees and I was taking her from behind, when beneath her uninhibited screams of pleasure I heard—

a baby cry.

I stopped, pulling out, but the sound did not repeat.

"What are you doing?" she demanded breathlessly. "Put it back in!"

I did, but my concentration was shot, my erection fading, and I hurriedly finished her off without coming myself.

Still breathing hard, she stood, a look of concern on her face. "What's wrong?" she asked, stepping over our pile of discarded clothes.

"Nothing," I told her.

"But you didn't—"

"I thought I heard a baby crying."

Silence greeted my admission.

"I know, I know. I'm probably imagining it—"

"I don't think you're imagining it."

We looked at each other. It felt good to hear her say that. It felt terrible to hear her say that. She put her arms around me, pulled me close. We were both still naked, and the feel of her soft skin aroused me again. Smiling, she pulled me onto the floor and made me finish what we'd started. I heard the baby crying again in the middle of it, but this time I ignored the sound, and by the time we were finished, the noise had stopped.

Was I being haunted? It almost seemed so, as though the ghost of a baby had attached itself to me instead of to the location where it had died. Had I picked up the ghost at the B&B in Biscuitville? Or at Frank's house outside Feldspar?

Maybe it was the ghost of a baby that Teri had lost or aborted before she met me.

I pushed that thought aside, knowing I was being an asshole for even thinking it. This whole thing had me rattled, and I had not been on sure footing since returning to Randall.

The crying baby disappeared—at least for awhile—but a week or two later I inherited a listing from May for a house that was supposed to be haunted. That was not the sort of thing that we would ever acknowledge to the general public, but realtors talk among themselves, and if a residence ever had a cold spot or mysterious shadows or unexplained noises, we all knew about it. I asked for the listing because I wanted to compare the vibe with what I'd felt at the various Frank houses, to see if there was any difference between an ordinary haunting and whatever it was that Frank was involved with. My first impulse was to keep it a secret—I was not used to sharing—but I decided to tell Teri, and over dinner I casually revealed my plan, making it seem like it was no big deal.

It felt like an adventure to her, and she wanted to go with me, so the next day, a Saturday, I stopped by the office for the key to the lockbox before we proceeded to the house. Located in an older section of La Habra, it was a single-story Mediterranean-style home from the 1940s, unusually well maintained for the surrounding neighborhood.

Once inside, I felt nothing. Teri didn't either. We walked from room to room, listening in vain for odd noises, trying to pick up on any uncomfortable sensations, but we encountered nothing out of the ordinary. Disappointed, I turned to Teri. "You sure you don't feel anything?"

She shook her head.

"Me either," I sighed.

"I guess we're not sensitive enough. Maybe you should bring a psychic here. Or at least a Ouija board."

I wasn't sure I believed in psychics, but if there *was* one who was real, I wondered what he or she would make of a Frank house.

I shook my head. Why was I even doing this? Why was I pursuing such a line of thought? I was supposed to be done with it all. I was supposed to have opted out.

From somewhere in the garage, I heard the faint cry of a baby.

The hair prickled on the back of my neck. *That* was why. I might want to be through with all of this paranormal activity, but it clearly wasn't through with me.

The cry came again.

Maybe I should contact the team from *Ghost Pursuers*.

Yes! Why hadn't I thought of it before?

I listened to the crying coming from the garage.

"Do you hear that?" I asked Teri.

She frowned. "No. What is it?" Understanding dawned in her face. "The baby?"

I nodded. "The baby."

She followed me back into the kitchen and through the side door that led into the garage. I reached for the light switch and flipped it on. The garage was empty: an open-beamed room built on an oil-stained slab of concrete. I stood there for a moment, waiting for the baby to cry again, knowing it wouldn't.

"*Wah.*"

It was a single soft wail, coming from the center of the open space before me, and every hair on my body stood on end. I turned to Teri. "Did you hear—?"

She shook her head.

Summoning every ounce of courage I possessed, I stepped into the center of the garage. I heard nothing, but there was a fleeting sensation of cold, as though I'd walked in front of an air-conditioner that suddenly shut off. I looked around the garage, wondering where the baby had gone, wondering if it *was* a baby.

"Anything?" Teri asked.

I shook my head. "Let's go."

As soon as we got home, I emailed the *Ghost Pursuers* team. I'd been given a generic email for the production company, but I addressed my message specifically to Scott Spencer, hoping that the producer would get back to me if he saw my name. I considered giving him a detailed account of my search for Frank, but figured I could go into all that later. Instead, I simply told him that I'd found another haunted house, one built and owned by the same man who'd built the two houses in Randall. I urged him to contact me ASAP. I still hadn't decided whether I would accompany the team to Nevada—

I was supposed to be out of it, wasn't I?

—but I desperately wanted Spencer and his crew to investigate that mirror-windowed home out in the middle of nowhere. The police certainly hadn't come through for me. I wasn't even sure they'd gone to check on Frank's house, because the one time I'd called to find out what they'd learned, the sergeant answering the phone had basically blown me off.

"He's wanted for questioning in a possible *murder*," I told the man, but he informed me in an officious voice that they had nothing new to report at this time, and when they did, *they* would contact *me*.

I had not heard from them since.

"Why a baby?" Teri asked at dinner.

Lost in my own thoughts, I looked up at her. "What?"

"Why a baby? I mean, isn't that kind of a weird thing to hear? And why only you? How does that sort of auditory exclusion work?"

She believed me, I realized. She really thought I'd heard a baby's cry and was trying to reason out the logistics of it. Her support touched me, boosted my confidence, settled me down, and I knew at that moment that I loved her. I was about to tell her exactly that when the phone rang. It was one of her friends from work. She took the call in another room and was on the line so long that the mood was broken. Conditions had to be right for such a life-changing admission. A big reveal like this required the proper frame, and I decided to postpone my announcement and wait for a more opportune moment.

She was still on the phone when I poked my head in the doorway, held up the lockbox key and indicated that I was going to return it to the office. She nodded an acknowledgment, waving goodbye as she continued to talk, and I headed out.

To my surprise, May was at her desk, on her computer, when I arrived. May didn't usually work on weekends—that time was reserved for her family, she said—and I asked her why she was here as I put the key away.

"We're thinking of moving," she told me.

That was unexpected. She and her husband had bought their house in Chino Hills less than a year ago, a no-frills split-level in an upscale neighborhood, and it had seemed a perfect fit.

"Van wants something closer to work; the traffic's really getting to him. Me, too. To be honest, it was just talk at first, we weren't *really* planning to do anything about it, but this new listing in Yorba Linda came up last week—it's not even officially on the market yet—and it's not only this great location, but the monthly payments would be a hundred less than we're paying now."

"Sounds perfect."

"It is. The problem, though, is that if we want to sell quickly *and* maximize our takeaway—which we *do*, which we *need* to do if we're going to scrape up enough for a competitive down payment—we have to have some work done on this storage shed thing that's attached to the garage."

"I remember it."

"We either have to upgrade it or, more likely, tear it down and patch up that garage wall."

"If you tear it down," I told her, "you could plant a little flower garden in that spot. Gardens definitely help."

May laughed. "You're always good on the visuals."

"Part of the job."

"So are you working today?" she asked.

I shook my head. "No. I was just showing Teri that house off Lincoln."

"The haunted house?" She grinned. "See anything?"

"We were hoping to, but no."

"Don't give up."

"Does that mean you—?"

"No. Not exactly." She shivered involuntarily. "But I *really* didn't like the place."

"We felt nothing."

"Not everyone's on the same wavelength. Some people pick up some frequencies, others pick up others. My haunted house might not be yours and yours might not be mine. We all sense different things."

I'd never thought of it that way, but it made a kind of sense.

May picked up her phone again. "I'm going to talk to Van. I think we will tear out that storage shed. And I think we'll steal your garden idea."

"Flowers," I told her. "Bright flowers. Red and yellow. They work every time."

I checked my email as soon as I got home to see if Scott Spencer had replied, but he hadn't, and I leaned back in my chair, closing my eyes. I had a throbbing headache, and there was a burning sensation in the pit of my stomach. Stress. Although I desperately hoped that Frank would be brought to justice, I just as desperately wanted to be left out of it. That did not seem to be possible, however. The crying infant I kept hearing guaranteed that I would be involved in all this whether I liked it or not, and my hope was that my *Ghost Pursuer* buddies could figure out a solution that would let me resume my normal life.

Why had I tracked down Frank anyway?

Billy.

Billy.

I took a deep breath. I wasn't just a part of this—I was right in the center of it.

I went to bed early that night, tired, stressed and longing for rest. Teri stayed up watching some cooking show, but when I awoke shortly after midnight, she was fast asleep next to me. *Why* had I awakened, I wondered? I usually slept through to dawn, especially when I was tired. Something must have—

There was a tap on the window.

Tap

Beneath the blanket, chills ran over the surface of my body. Teri was still sound asleep, an unmoving lump next to me. I wanted to wake her up but knew I shouldn't, so I just lay there for a moment, hoping I hadn't heard what I thought I heard.

Tap Tap Tap

Far more frightened than I wanted to be, I carefully pushed off the covers, slid out of bed and walked across the darkened room to the window. Peeking through a space in the partially parted curtains, I saw a shriveled hand in the night outside, a wizened finger with a long black nail softly rapping against the glass. Behind the ancient hand...

Irene.

She looked just as I'd feared.

Thin white hair blew gently about her wrinkled emaciated face, while somewhere in her sunken sockets were the remnants of eyes, dry darkened orbs too small to fill the empty black space surrounding them. Her mouth could do nothing but grin: the deflated lips were pulled back so far that they were unable to close, and the gums beneath had receded so far that the exposed teeth were huge.

I almost cried out—it was my first involuntary reaction—but recognition that it would wake up Teri caused my conscious mind to override that impulse and kept my cry of terror down. Still, I closed my eyes and, like a child, covered my ears.

Had Frank sent her after me? Or had she followed me of her own accord?

Was *she* the one making noises like a crying baby?

The very idea intensified my fright. I imagined that shriveled skeletal hag hiding somewhere just out of sight in Teri's parents' house or my office, her wreck of a mouth opening and closing to emit the sounds of a distressed infant.

Opening my eyes, I expected her to be gone, but she was still on the other side of the glass, grinning horribly at me, that terrible crooked finger with its sharp blackened nail no longer tapping on the window but beckoning me outside. I took the fingers from my ears, heard nothing.

"What are you looking at?"

I saw Teri's reflection in the exposed section of window at the same time she touched my shoulder, and I jumped, startled.

I exhaled, aware that I'd been holding my breath. "Nothing," I said.

"Don't give me that." She leaned close to the crack in the curtains, squinting at the glass, and it was clear she saw nothing, though Irene's emaciated face was grinning in at her.

How was that possible? And *why* was it happening? I still didn't know, but it didn't really matter because Teri was here and she believed me, and I reached out and pulled the two halves of the curtain shut so I couldn't see out.

I looked into her eyes. "I love you," I told her.

This was the right time.

She smiled back at me, kissed the tip of my nose. "I love you, too."

But she frowned in the split-second that she glanced at the closed curtain before we both went back to bed.

TWELVE

DESPITE MY FEARS, despite my worries, I did not see Irene again. And though periodically I still heard the sound of a baby crying, it was always in the daytime and always far off, and I was almost certain that the wailing infants were real children.

Scott Spencer emailed a response to me several days later, informing me that the *Ghost Pursuers* team was on hiatus. They were finished shooting for the season and wouldn't need to start working on any new episodes for another six months (*if* the show was renewed, he said, which at this point was by no means guaranteed). Hoping to take advantage of what had seemed to me to be a mutual respect, I emailed him back immediately and laid all my cards on the table, letting him know that this was personal, and suggesting that if *Ghost Pursuers* did have another season, I'd be providing his team with an episode that would tie into their two "Most Haunted Town in America" shows and could serve as an easily promotable season opener.

Spencer still wasn't buying what I was selling, even after I went into more detail about the Frank connection. But he was nice enough to provide me with email addresses for Evan and Owen, the show's writers. They were more than happy to discuss ideas with me. Between seasons, they were officially unemployed, and though they were each working on spec scripts of their own, the experience in Randall had made them true believers and put stars in their eyes.

They were both open to collaborating with me on either a *Ghost Pursuers* episode or something totally unconnected to the program. We set up a time and place to meet: next Wednesday for lunch at a Mexican restaurant in Whittier, halfway between their home base in Los Angeles and my Orange County office.

I'd been meaning to look up the whereabouts of Mark Goodwin since my trip to Randall, but events had conspired to put that off. Now, however, I made the effort and, to my surprise, found him easily on Facebook. He was a physical therapist, and he lived now in Tucson. In the displayed photo, he looked older than I expected, older than me, though we were the same age. I searched that lined face in vain for some resemblance to the young boy I knew in Randall. It was the eyes that usually remained the same, despite changes to the flesh surrounding them, but Mark's eyes looked haunted, and I knew that he'd had a hard life since I'd last seen him.

I started off slowly, with a friend request. He responded almost before I was through typing, as though he'd been waiting for this moment. I knew it was a coincidence—he just happened to be online at the same time I made my request—but it seemed like fate, and we IM'd back and forth, quickly catching up on each others' histories. Mark, it turned out, was divorced, with no children ("Thankfully," he wrote). His ex-wife was in jail, doing ten years for drug trafficking. His parents were both dead, though he did not tell me how they'd died, and I did not ask. He had no contact with either his brother or his sister: the last he'd heard, Dean was somewhere in the northwest, doing manual labor; he had no idea where Janine was.

There was nothing self-pitying about his matter-of-fact descriptions, but he seemed to have had a sad life, and I wondered how much of that could be attributed to Frank.

I didn't want to jump right in with that, so I approached the subject obliquely, over a period of days, pretending as though Frank was just one of many childhood remembrances that were returning to me since Mark and I had reconnected.

By now, we were talking to each other over the phone, and to my surprise, he admitted flat out that Frank had ruined his life. "It was that house," he said. "Everything started to go wrong when we moved into that house. I told you it was haunted, right?"

"I saw it for myself," I told him. I thought about mentioning *Ghost Pursuers*, but I wanted to hear what he had to say. I could go into all that later.

"Well, it...affected us. Dean and I both got into drugs, and I'm sure part of it was finding that dead kid in the basement, but that wasn't all of it. Janine turned into a complete slut, started fucking every guy she saw. My parents..." He sighed. "We never really talked in that family, but from what I gathered, what I could piece together from the arguments I heard through the walls and the bits of conversation I happened on, my dad was supposed to have had his tubes tied, but my mom was pregnant again. She swore that it was his, but he never believed it.

"Not that it mattered. She had a miscarriage."

I remembered suddenly that Mark had had a baby sister, though I couldn't remember her name. "What about your little sister?" I asked. "The baby? What happened to her?"

Mark was silent for a moment. "She fell out a window. An upstairs window. Landed on a rock, cracked her head open and died."

"Oh my God."

"That window..." Mark spoke slowly. "Frank made it too low. Kate was only one and barely able to walk, but it was just the right height for her to put her hands on the sill, lean over and fall out. You know Frank had no screens. And the window was open because it was hot and we'd opened it to let the air in. I'm not sure how Kate got upstairs. She was supposed to be in my parents' room in her crib, taking a nap."

"I'm sorry," I told him. I couldn't think of anything else to say.

"Even after we sold that house and moved...it seemed like it stayed with us. The Frank Effect, I called it. Bad luck just seemed to follow us everywhere we went. Did I tell you how my parents died?"

My mouth felt dry. "No."

"It was in the mid-nineties. I was in Phoenix, working, going part time to a JC, and they were living up in Montana, where my dad had gotten a job with some copper mining company. One night, middle of the night, I get this call. It's from the Missoula police department. My parents were in a single-vehicle crash. They smashed into a tree and were both killed on impact."

"Jesus."

"Thing is, they weren't drinking, there wasn't any... No one could find a reason for the accident. But on their answering machine, though, was a call. From Frank."

"Holy shit."

"Yeah. I don't know how he got their number or where he was calling from or even if it was the first time he'd called. But I recognized his voice immediately, even though I hadn't heard it since he sold us the house when I was, what, twelve? He was telling them to drive to Helena and meet him. Didn't explain why or anything. At least not on the message.

"And on the way there is where they were killed."

It was past time for me to come clean, and I told Mark about the disintegration of my own family, and about my recent re-acquaintance with Frank's world, from Brad and his mom all the way up to my trip to Frank's house. I left out nothing, and was glad I didn't.

Because he, too, had seen Irene.

Like me, Mark thought he'd been the only one creeped out by Frank's wife. Frank's negative qualities were so aggressively upfront, and his wife so cowed and submissive, that it seemed wrong to feel anything but pity for her. But though he'd seen her only briefly, Mark had had the same reaction to Irene as me, and he, too, had had recurring nightmares about her as a child.

He'd also seen her recently.

It had been decades since Mark had even thought about Irene, but several weeks ago he'd gone before dawn to the physical therapy center to accommodate a client who'd requested a session before work, and he'd seen an old lady standing beneath a palo verde tree at the edge of the empty parking lot, partially lit by a nearby street lamp. *Irene Watkins* was the name that came immediately to mind, although he had no idea why. Not only had he not seen her in decades, but he could not even remember what she looked like. Still, something in the woman's stance or body type seemed familiar, and the connection his brain made was to Irene.

He *did* remember the nightmares he'd had as a kid, and as a slight warm breeze fluttered the dress she was wearing, Mark hurried inside the building. He might be an adult now, but the thought of Irene still creeped him out, and even if the woman in the parking lot was just some anonymous homeless person, there was something eerie about the way she stood there all alone in the near-darkness, unmoving, her billowy dress flapping gently around her.

Mark made sure to lock the door behind him before walking down the corridor to the exercise room. He turned the lights on as he stepped inside.

Irene was standing outside the floor-to-ceiling window, pressing her face against the glass and grinning in at him.

There was no doubt this time that it was her. He recognized that wrinkled visage, remembered it clearly from childhood, and though he was a grown man now, he was filled with fear. He was glad that he'd made sure to lock the door, and even more glad that he was inside the building while she was outside. Acting far braver than he felt, Mark strode over to the window and rapped on it, his fist directly in front of her face. "You're trespassing!" he yelled, though he was not sure she could hear him through the thick glass. "Get out of here, or I'm calling the police!"

Still grinning, she moved away from the window, backing up without looking until her pale face and fluttering clothes faded into the pre-dawn darkness. There was a blurry smudge on the glass where her face had pressed against it, and Mark stared at the spot, feeling suddenly cold. He had seen similarly blurred imprints on windows at his apartment and on his car over the years, not giving them much thought, assuming they were caused by dew or dust or heat or atmospheric conditions. Unable to take his eyes off the spot, he knew now that they'd been imprinted on the glass by Irene's face.

"She was real, tangible, but I had the same impression you did," Mark said. "That she was dead."

I have only the Dark Wife now.

"I'm pretty sure she is," I told him. "Did you try to go after her or anything?"

"Hell, no! I stayed inside. In fact, I went around checking doors and making sure they were locked just in case she came back. I didn't relax until my client showed up."

"Any signs of her since?"

"No." He was quiet for a very long moment. "So what do we do now? What happens next?"

"I don't know," I admitted.

We left it there, but it made me feel uneasy that he, too, had seen Irene. I didn't know what it meant, but I didn't like it. I didn't like it at all.

For the next week, everything seemed a little bit…off. There was nothing I could point to specifically, nothing I could really put my finger on, but the clothes I chose each morning turned out to be either too warm or too cool for the weather, none of the listings I showed impressed any of my prospective clients, Teri and I weren't in sync sexually, I was twice given the wrong take-out order for lunch, and the Lincoln seemed to be even more sluggish and unreliable than usual. I was grateful for the weekend, and I used my Saturday to rewrite some poorly conceived property descriptions that I'd put on our website a few days earlier. When the phone rang, I let Teri pick it up in the kitchen. A moment later, she walked into my office with a bemused expression, holding the phone in her hand. "For you," she said.

"Who is it?"

"Julie," she said. "My sister."

"She wants to talk to *me*?"

"Apparently so." Teri sounded as surprised as I felt. She handed me the phone.

This was weird. I hadn't spoken to Julie since the trip to Ramona and, truth be told, not much even then. I barely knew the woman. "Hello?" I said.

"Daniel? Hi. Do you have a minute? I have a few questions I thought you might be able to help me with."

"Sure," I said. "What do you need?"

"You're in real estate, right? So you probably know something about home improvement-related issues? I was wondering if you could give me some advice. See, we hired this guy to put in a new toilet. For the past month or so, it would keep running after you flushed it, and you had to jiggle the handle to get it to stop. That's okay, we could live with that. But a few nights ago, the tank started leaking. We found out about it in the morning when we woke up and the whole bathroom was flooded. I mopped it all up, Ron shut off the valve or water pipe or whatever, and we decided to just replace the whole thing. We had this handyman do it, a jack-of-all-trades kind of guy. He charged about half of what the cheapest plumber would've cost us, but he ended up doing a really crummy job. A day later, we had to start jiggling the *new* handle to get it to stop running. Now the guy says he won't come back and fix it unless we pay him again, even though, we think, after one day, there should be some sort of warranty. I thought you might know something about what to do, whether we have any rights here, whether we should file a suit in small claims court or what."

"Is there a way to get in touch with this guy?"

"We have his phone number. He was recommended to us by some friends, who had him work on a deck in their backyard. I guess *they* had no problems. His name's Frank Wharton..."

Frank Wharton.

I didn't hear anything else.

Frank?

It couldn't be.

But it had to be.

I was holding the phone so tightly that my fingers hurt. While it was just barely possible that this was all a coincidence, it was not the least bit probable. This whole thing was *way* too close to home, and my mind was spinning as I traced the connections. Despite what Julie might think, she and her husband had not hired some random handyman. Frank had clearly set his sights on working for Julie—because she was Teri's sister. Hell, he might have even found some way to break that toilet himself just to get the ball rolling. Why? Because he was stalking me, playing with me, going after people in my life, trying to keep me involved after I'd sworn to stay out of all this.

But I couldn't get past the logistics. I'd left Frank in his house in the middle of Nowhere, Nevada, less than two months ago. In that time, he'd not only tracked me down but found out that I was dating Teri, hunted down Teri's sister Julie, then wormed his way into the life of Julie's friends, doing a good enough job building their deck that they had recommended him to her? How was that possible?

There was a pause in the conversation. Julie was obviously waiting for me to respond to something she'd said, and I had to come clean. "I'm sorry. I didn't hear that."

"I said, what should we do?"

Objectively, she and her husband probably *should* take Frank to small claims court—and it would serve him right if they did—but I was afraid of letting him get any more involved in their lives. I knew what Frank was capable of, and without letting on about how much I knew, I told her that lawsuits against itinerant handymen never worked out; even if a judgment went against them, they just pulled up stakes and disappeared without paying restitution. "It's more trouble than it's worth," I assured her. "The best idea is to chalk this up as a learning experience and hire a competent professional to do the job, preferably someone licensed and bonded."

"Oh." I could hear the disappointment in her voice, and I knew she wanted another answer from me, but my goal was to get her as far away from Frank's clutches as I could.

"Here, I'll let you talk to Teri," I said, and handed off the phone.

Teri walked back into the kitchen, the sisters talking for another ten minutes or so while I tried to return to my work. My head was spinning, and though I attempted to write a description for a new listing, the words wouldn't come. I kept thinking about Frank, wondering if he'd stolen anything from Teri's sister. A shadow fell over my desk. "So..." Teri said.

"So?"

"Let it go? That was your advice? She was hoping for something more professional, more specific—"

"It was Frank," I told her. "Frank put in her toilet."

Teri's face grew pale.

I nodded, standing. "I don't know how, don't know why, but it's him, and my thought was to get her as far away from him as fast as possible."

"He's coming after you," Teri said, cutting straight to the chase.

I shrugged. "Maybe."

"Jesus..."

"There's no reason to panic."

"You need to call the police."

I'd been thinking the same thing, and I nodded slowly. She was right. Even if I'd wanted to, I couldn't Hardy Boys my way out of this one. And I didn't want to. I wanted to turn this over to the authorities and have the law toss Frank in jail and throw away the key. I wanted him out of my life, and I wanted him punished.

For Billy.

I looked up the number of the Ramona Police Department and called to tell them about a handyman preying on local homeowners, including, I said, my future sister-in-law. Teri gave me a silent kiss on the cheek for that one.

The sergeant I spoke to didn't seem all that interested in what I had to say, but I couldn't blame him. Even after framing Frank as a scam artist who was wanted for questioning in a thirty-year-old murder investigation, my actual facts were pretty light. And a leaky toilet wasn't that big a deal—even in Ramona. I gave the man Julie's name and number since she was the victim within his jurisdiction, and I told him to call the Randall Sheriff's Office for more information about Frank. I also let him know that he could call me anytime, though that hardly seemed likely.

I wasn't sure how much good it did to complain, but I felt better for having told someone, and I figured, at the very least, it might put some pressure on Frank if he knew the law was sniffing around. Hopefully, he would panic, leave and let Julie alone.

I was able to get back to work and finished rewriting my property descriptions so that they sounded enticing. Casting a wider net, I sent follow-up emails to the handful of Orange County residents who'd filled out our mass-mailed postcards and indicated that they might be interested in selling their homes.

Finally, I took a break. Teri was cooking something in the kitchen, and the smell of it reminded me of my childhood. It was some sort of soup that was simmering on the stove, and though I hadn't thought of it in years, I remembered that my mom often made soups and stews and chilies when I was little, letting them cook all day in a big black pot until the entire house smelled of herbs and vegetables, broth and meat. Billy and I used to love to hang around the kitchen when Mom was cooking, particularly if it was a rainy day and the windows were all fogged up from the heat of the stove and oven, because she used to give us tiny little bowls of whatever she was making so we could taste it ahead of time and let her know how it was.

I felt sad all of a sudden, but I was happy to be sad, grateful to Teri for stirring up memories that I hadn't remembered I possessed.

After dinner, I got in touch with Mark. Like veterans who had been through a war together, we were products of a horrific shared experience, and it somehow made me feel better to confide in him. I didn't call him on the phone because I didn't want to frighten him and make him think it was some sort of emergency, but I did email him, and again Mark IM'd me immediately, as though he'd been waiting for my message. I explained the situation, and he offered to back me up with the Ramona police, if need be. I told him that wouldn't be necessary, and promised to keep him up to date before signing off.

That night, I had a nightmare. Not about Frank, not about Irene, but about my mom. I was sitting in the pancake restaurant across from the cemetery, eating alone next to one of the front windows, and when I looked up from my breakfast, I could see her walking toward me across the street. The clothes in which she'd been buried had rotted away, gaping holes revealing peeling gray flesh underneath. Most of her hair had fallen out, but the sections that hadn't were white and freakishly long. Her blanched face wore an expression of fierce malevolence.

Her pupil-less eyes were trained directly on me.

I quickly got up from the table, the plate of half-finished pancakes falling into my lap. Ignoring the mess, I looked frantically for another way out of the restaurant even as I kept glancing back to the window and seeing my dead mom grow ever closer.

I knew she wanted to kill me.

Pushing my way past a waitress, I ran through a pair of swinging doors into the kitchen. The cooks ignored me as I hurried behind them to the back door, pushing it open and dashing out of the restaurant into the parking lot—

Where my dad's rotting corpse was waiting for me, arms outstretched.

I woke up sweating. I didn't know what the dream meant, but I didn't *want* to know. Teri was sound asleep next to me, snoring. Afraid to go back to sleep, afraid of having another nightmare, I stayed awake the rest of the night, staring up at the ceiling and trying not to think.

ON Wednesday, I was supposed to meet Evan and Owen for lunch. In preparation, I had written out a timeline, the closest thing to a history of Frank that I could piece together. I'd compiled all of his known aliases, all of his known addresses, the names of everyone I could think of who'd had any contact with the man, and I'd listed everything I knew chronologically, hoping the writers could use their *Ghost Pursuers* contacts to dig up additional information and figure out what the hell was going on.

Knowing I'd be gone for the afternoon, I went into the office early, hoping to pick up some new listings. Sales had fallen off in the past few weeks, part of the normal cycle of the business, and I wanted to do everything I could to stave off a longer slowdown. May arrived late, after both Mike and Jim had already come in and then driven out with clients to look at properties. That was unusual for her. She was far more subdued than usual, and when I asked if everything was all right, she seemed vague, distracted and didn't really give me an answer.

"What's wrong?" I pressed.

"Nothing," she said curtly. "I'm fine."

It was clear that she didn't want to talk. We all knew what May was like when she got in one of these moods, and I gave her a wide berth the rest of the morning.

My meeting was for noon, so just to be on the safe side, I left for Whittier shortly after eleven. I was ten minutes early, but Evan and Owen were even earlier. I saw them as I pulled up, sitting on a bench in front of the building, texting on their phones.

"Hey, guys." I said.

"Long time," Evan said, fist-bumping me.

Owen held up his hand in a gesture of greeting.

The restaurant was a windowless hole-in-the-wall with red naugahyde booths, dark paneling and velvet matador paintings. Located on an uncrowded side street between a closed hair salon and a plumbing supply store, it was completely nondescript, and I wondered how the writers had discovered the place. As it turned out, Evan had grown up in Whittier and, as a kid, his family had eaten here often.

The place was surprisingly crowded, and we had to wait several minutes for a table.

"The food here's great," Evan said. "Old school but great."

After we were seated, I slid my printout across the Formica table, thinking I should have brought a copy for each of them. "I wrote down what I know," I said, "to give you a place to start."

Over enchiladas, I came clean about all of it: Frank, Irene, the crying baby. These guys were used to hearing confessions from housewives who thought their laundry rooms were haunted, so there was no reason to hold anything back. Even if they didn't believe something, they could still investigate it.

"This sounds awesome!" Evan said when I was done.

"We could build a whole show just around the search for Frank. Call it ...*The Search for Frank*."

Evan nodded. "Hell, yeah! I'd watch it."

"Movie adaptation would be even better."

They were getting off on their Hollywood tangent. I tried to rein them back in. "Listen, guys, feel free to take anything you want from this for a show or a movie or whatever. But before you do that, I need you to find out as much as you can about what's going on. This is my life here. And it's affecting other people besides me. We're not dealing with some scratching sounds in an attic. People have *died*."

Owen nodded soberly. "Got it."

An attractive young woman in tight jeans passed by our table.

"I'd like to sniff her panties on a hot summer day," Evan whispered.

He and Owen laughed conspiratorially.

Focus! I wanted to tell them. They were acting like giggling high school students, and it made me wonder if they would have the discipline to see this through.

They did ask appropriate questions, though, and Owen actually took notes on a tablet, so I still hoped that something would come of this.

"SO," Teri asked when she got home that night, "how did it go?"

"Okay, I guess."

"You guess?"

"They're…immature. But they definitely have contacts, and they know this ghost hunting stuff." I shook my head. "Jesus Christ. *Ghost hunting*. If you had told me a year ago that I'd be involved with anything like that, I'd've said you were nuts."

"What if I'd told you a year ago that we'd be living together?"

I smiled. "I'd've said you were nuts."

"Things change."

"That they do," I agreed.

It made me wonder what would be happening a year from now. Me and Teri? I could still see us together. Maybe making plans for marriage. Or even a family. But Frank? And all the…*stuff* surrounding him? I had no idea where that would lead.

And that's what scared me.

THIRTEEN

THEY WERE WAITING in the office when I arrived after lunch the following Monday, seated in the two chairs opposite my desk as though they were ordinary homebuyers looking for a property.

George and Betsy.

My heart leaped in my chest the second I walked through the door. I recognized the couple immediately, and the sight of them scared the hell out of me. If May, Jim and Mike hadn't been at their desks, I would've turned around and walked—no, *run*—out of there instantly. Like Frank, George and Betsy had not aged. They had already been old in the 1980s, when I first saw them back in Randall, and they still looked just as they had when I was a kid, even down to the type of clothes they wore: old-fashioned, old people's clothes that even today's elderly didn't wear anymore.

I stood rooted in place, wondering what to do. Should I try to hold them here and call the police? The law in Randall had been looking for them, but that was decades ago, and the officers involved were probably not even on the force anymore. Would whoever was there now want to speak with them?

I wasn't sure how that worked, but judging by my recent experiences with law enforcement, I figured George and Betsy had probably fallen through the cracks so successfully that they were no longer wanted or known by anyone.

I decided to play this by ear. Affecting a nonchalance that couldn't have been further from the way I actually felt, I strode across the office to my desk. May was on the phone, both Jim and Mike were on their computers, and as far as any of them were concerned, there was nothing out of the ordinary here. Walking around my desk and sitting down in my chair, I faced George and Betsy, opting at the last second to pretend I didn't recognize them. "What can I do for you?" I asked.

Betsy smiled in a way that let me know she saw through my attempted ruse. "We're here about Frank," she said.

Hearing her speak his name sent a shiver down my spine.

"You're George and...Betty?" I said, still pretending I wasn't sure who they were.

"Betsy," she corrected me, wearing that same knowing smile.

I dropped all pretense. "How is Frank?" I asked.

There was no response.

"I've been investigating him, you know. That man has done a lot of damage to a lot of people." I looked at them, struck once again by how neither of them had changed over the years. There was something unsettling about that, something wrong. "You lied to us back then," I said. "I've learned that much. You said you'd both grown up with Frank in Randall, but he was working on homes in Texas and Nevada and New Mexico when he was supposed to be there with you in Arizona."

It was George who spoke this time. "You're right. Frank wasn't from Randall. Neither were we. But we did grow up together."

I looked at Betsy. "Were you really Irene's sister?"

"No."

"*Where* did you grow up together?"

"That's not important—" George began.

"It is to me," I said.

We looked at each other across the desk.

George sighed. "Plutarch, Texas."

"And everything else you told us?"

"I don't remember what all we said."

"For one thing, you said that Vietnam made Frank into what he is."

They looked at each other. "Frank *did* change after Vietnam," George said. "We didn't lie about that." There was a pause. "But the truth is that there was always something wrong with Frank. He was always...off. Even as a little boy. I remember once, we were about eight or nine—"

"And what year was that?"

He ignored me. "—Frank had what he called his 'killing box.' A lot of us had killing jars back then. For insects. We'd put some alcohol or something onto some cotton and seal it up in a mason jar, then catch bugs in it. The bugs would die and we'd pin them on a board for our collections. But Frank's box was for animals: mice, squirrels, sometimes even cats. And he didn't have alcohol in there to put them to sleep. He'd capture them, put them in the box...then beat them to death with a hammer. He'd toss the bodies afterward. It was almost as though he killed them just to decorate his box. Because the box was what really mattered to him. It was heavy and made of wood, and inside it was brown with dried blood and red with wet blood, and he would open it up and show it off, and expect everyone else to admire it as much as he did."

"He was a bad kid," Betsy said, and something in her voice told me that she knew stories about Frank far worse than the one about his "killing box."

"So what happened in Vietnam?" I asked.

"We weren't there," Betsy said quickly, before George could respond.

"But how was he different?" I pressed. "I remember you saying he was more secretive when he came back."

"You remember a lot for a little kid," George said.

I didn't respond.

He sighed. "Yeah, he was more secretive. And it seemed like he had more to be secretive about, like he *learned* things over there."

Things man wasn't meant to know.

My mind filled in the cliché, and it seemed completely appropriate. I tried for the next several minutes to get one of them to expand on what they thought Frank might have learned in Vietnam, addressing most of my questions to George since he seemed more likely to answer, but neither would open up to me.

I changed tack. "What happened to Irene?" I asked.

They looked at each other.

I frowned, picking up on an unstated subtext. "What?"

"She died," Betsy said simply.

"I figured. But how? And when?"

"She died." Betsy fixed me with a flat stare, and I understood that nothing more would be forthcoming. A shiver tickled my spine.

"I thought I saw her..." I began.

"Why are you investigating Frank?" Betsy interrupted.

I ignored her. "I saw Irene. In Texas. Recently."

"No, you didn't."

"I did. In a house that Frank built."

That look passed between them again.

"I went into Frank's *actual* house," I said. "In Nevada."

"Oh, that's not his house," George assured me.

"What do you mean, 'That's not his house?' I saw him. I talked to him."

"Well, he did build it, so I suppose it is his house, but it's not his *real* house; it's not where he lives."

"So you know where his real house is? You know where he lives?"

They looked at each other again.

I came out and said it: "Okay, why are you here? What do you want?"

Neither of them answered.

"I haven't seen you since I was a kid. Now you track me down where I work and show up and tell me you're here about Frank? So tell me what you came to tell me, or ask me what you came to ask me, because I have work to do."

"Stop," George said.

"Stop?"

"Stop '*investigating*' Frank."

"Why should I?"

"Frank wants you to."

"Why?" I asked. A thought occurred to me. "Is he afraid?"

"Yes," George said without hesitation. Betsy shot him a look that made it clear she thought he'd given away more than he should.

"So he sent you two all the way out here—"

It was Betsy who went off script this time. "We didn't want to come here. We don't want to do...a lot of things. But there are tradeoffs. And Frank has a way of..." She trailed off, and beneath that hard exterior, I saw for the first time a trace of vulnerability—and fear.

George nodded.

Betsy stood, clasping her purse, and George quickly followed her lead. "We've said what we've come to say," she said. "The rest is up to you."

They'd come to threaten me, and despite my show of defiance, I was rattled. Frank had kept George and Betsy—not to mention himself—from aging. And he'd forced them to come and deliver his message.

His threat carried weight. He'd made inroads into my life already, doing work for Teri's sister.

I decided to drop my tough guy act. "I'm out," I said. "I'd stopped even before you came here. I told the police everything I know, but that's it. I'm done."

Betsy leaned forward. "No, you're not," she said. There was both fear and sadness in her tone. "And you never will be."

I knew she was speaking as much about herself as she was of me.

The two of them turned and, without another word, strode through the office, past the other desks, and out the door. I thought of following them, but a client walked in at that moment, one of *my* clients, and I was forced to greet her as George and Betsy walked down the sidewalk and disappeared beyond my line of sight.

Why should I want to follow them anyway? I *was* out of it.

Wasn't I?

Billy.

Billy.

While I might not want to be directly involved, might want to protect the people close to me, I still wanted to see Frank caught and punished, wanted him to pay for what he'd done.

Betsy was right. I never would be free of Frank, and after my client left, I called Evan. I had both of the writers' phone numbers, but Evan was the more talkative of the two and seemed to be the leader of the team. I told him what had happened, letting him know that I had some additional information about Frank. "He was supposedly born and raised in Plutarch, Texas. Maybe that'll help you find something out about him."

"We'll keep looking," he promised. "And if there is a show in this, would you be willing to be on camera if—"

"No," I told him.

"Just checking."

I walked over to the coffeepot and poured myself a cup. I noticed May watching me. There was a strange expression on her face, and she glanced quickly away when our eyes met. I stirred some sugar into my coffee and walked over to her desk, where she was pretending to be engrossed in a flyer from a rival realtor.

"So what's with you?" I asked her.

She shook her head.

"May..."

"It's nothing."

"It's not nothing. What?"

She took a deep breath. "I heard you talking. When those old people were here. They mentioned Vietnam."

I didn't know what to say. I never knew how to react when that subject came up. I knew May's family had fled the country after the fall of Saigon and had come to the U.S. as refugees with nothing but the clothes on their backs. I knew also that her mother was dead, although I didn't know any details. Mike had speculated once that her mom had committed suicide, since she had died here in the United States and to May any mention of her mom seemed to be taboo.

"Yeah," I said, not wanting to go into detail. "A friend of theirs, someone I met when I was a kid, was over there."

She nodded. "Oh," she said, as if that explained it all.

I sat down in the empty chair on the side of her desk. "You've been acting weird for the past week," I told her. "What is it? What's wrong? And don't give me that 'nothing' B.S."

"We hired someone to tear down that storage shed and fix the garage wall, so we could put in a flower garden." May was silent for a moment. "The contractor was in the war. And he keeps trying to *talk* to me about it. I wasn't even born then, you know? It's just...uncomfortable. And weird."

"Did you tell him that?"

"Of course. But he's a chatty guy. I try not to even talk to him, but sometimes Van isn't home, and there's only me, and I need to deal with him..."

"Can't you just change the subject?"

"I do. But I guess I've been acting weird because he reminded me of things. Things I'd forgotten I even knew. Things I haven't thought about since my mother..." She broke off, wiped away a tear.

"It's okay," I told her.

Mike had come back into the office halfway through the conversation. "You should report him to his supervisor."

"He's an independent contractor." She looked sheepish. "He's not even licensed."

Alarm bells went off in my head.

I took a deep breath. I didn't want to know the answer, but I had to ask the question: "What's his name?"

"Walters. Frank Walters. Why?"

No.

My mind did some quick calculations. It couldn't be. Frank had been over in Ramona with Teri's sister when work started on May's project. Then again, Ramona was only two or three hours from Chino Hills. Conceivably, he could have traveled between them during the course of a normal workday.

Frank Walters.

As much as I might want to believe it was coincidence, I knew it wasn't. He was targeting the people around me, warning me that he could easily do more.

Maybe I should have followed George and Betsy.

"Do you know him?" May asked.

I shook my head.

"You shouldn't use someone who's unlicensed," Mike said. "You oughta know that."

"We were trying to save money. It's just a teardown job anyway." Her defensiveness with Mike was automatic, but it disappeared almost instantly. "You're right, though. If we'd used a real contractor, I wouldn't've had to listen to..." She swallowed audibly, wiped her moistening eyes.

"Is he still there?" I asked. "At your house?"

"No, he's done." May smiled slightly. "It does look better. We'll definitely fetch a higher price."

"Do you have a business card or something? A phone number where he can be reached?"

"A phone number. Somewhere. But it's no big deal. I'm probably just oversensitive."

"Can you get me the number?"

"He's gone, it's done, I don't want you stirring things up."

"I need some work done," I told her.

She sensed the lie, and held my gaze for a moment before giving in and nodding tiredly. "I'll find it."

May did find the number when she went home that evening, and she texted it to me, but when I called, the number was out of service. He'd probably used a disposable phone, I reasoned. A burner.

I told Teri what had happened with May, as well as describing my visit from George and Betsy, and her reaction was reliably sensible: call the police. I did just that, informing the Randall PD in Arizona that the two of them had been spotted in Orange, California; calling the Orange PD and explaining that the couple was wanted in the questioning of a possible cold case murder in Arizona. In what was beginning to seem like standard operating procedure, neither department seemed particularly interested in what I had to say, but out of duty or politeness, they listened, assuring me that they were taking everything down.

I wanted all of this to end. The events of my childhood—

Billy

—had affected everything in my life, but it had all remained in the background until recently, until I'd sold the Big Bear cabin to Brad and Connie and gotten drawn into this nightmare. I wanted it to be that way again. I was sorry I'd ever started looking into the history of Frank, and right now I wanted to just forget it all and move on.

No, that wasn't true. I wanted revenge for what Frank had done. I wanted vengeance.

I wasn't sure what I wanted.

I dreamed that night that Teri had hired Frank to renovate our bedroom, and I returned from the office to find that the floor and ceiling were plywood, the walls were cardboard and everything was painted black. Frank had already gone, and Teri told me to get undressed because we were having a housewarming party. We both stripped down to our underwear and went out to let in our first guests, who, I suddenly realized, had been ringing the doorbell for quite some time. Teri pulled her thong tighter, opened the door, and George and Betsy were standing there. "Grandma!" Teri cried. "Grandpa! Welcome to our home!"

The next day, I received a call from Detective Johnson of the Ramona Police Department. I was meeting Teri for lunch, having just shown a condo in Anaheim, when the call came in, and the news could not have been more surprising. "I just wanted to let you know that we have Frank Wharton in custody," the detective told me after a brief introduction. He said that they'd sent in the suspect's prints to both the FBI and the Randall Sheriff's Office to check whether "Frank Wharton" and "Frank Watkins" were the same man. "You've seen this Watkins," Johnson said. "I was wondering if you could come down and make a preliminary ID, help us get a head start on this."

"I'll be there in an hour or two," I said.

Teri's phone had rung while I was talking. It was Julie. She, too, had been informed of Frank's capture and had been asked to come down to the station to identify him, to see if he was the handyman who had cheated her and her husband. It didn't seem right that she would have to do that for what was essentially a small claims case, Julie said, but Teri assured her that the police were just trying to dot all the i's and cross all the t's. He'd conned other people as well, she told her sister.

Teri made no mention of the fact that he might be connected to a 30-year-old murder.

I'd hung up by this time. Listening in, it was clear that Julie was hesitant about going to the police station to identify the man, so I told Teri to let her sister know that we were speeding down to Ramona and would go in with her and her husband.

My mind was spinning as we raced down the Santa Ana Freeway. Frank was caught? It seemed unreal. It seemed anti-climactic. I was glad he was locked up and hoped he would spend the rest of his life in jail, but at the same time, this outcome seemed too easy. Contradictory feelings wound together in a Gordian knot inside me.

Julie and Ron met us in the parking lot of the police station. Teri had called her sister and brother-in-law to let them know when we were almost to Ramona, and they were standing in front of their van waiting for us as we pulled in.

"I don't know if I can do this," Julie said. Her voice was shaky. "What if I identify him and he doesn't get convicted? He could come back and—"

"And what?" Ron asked roughly. "Install another toilet incorrectly? He's a con artist not a murderer. Don't worry about it. We're not ID-ing a mob boss here."

Teri shot me a glance, warning me to keep my mouth shut, and though my feelings were closer to Julie's than her husband's, I remained silent as the four of us walked into the station.

Detective Johnson stood up from a gray metal desk as we were escorted through the squad room by a uniformed officer. Introductions were made. Johnson explained that the man had been picked up breaking into the house of a couple whose garage he had been painting. Both the husband and wife had been at work, and the attempted break-in had been called in, as was so often the case, by a nosy neighbor. Although the suspect had no form of identification on him, when asked by the arresting officer, he admitted that his name was "Frank Wharton."

Teri had gone to great lengths to make sure I didn't share any details about Frank with her sister, but Johnson was under no such restrictions. The detective explained to us all that in addition to cheating local residents, Frank was also wanted for questioning in Arizona regarding a 30-year-old murder. Glancing at Julie out of the corner of my eye, I saw her face turn pale.

"I...I'm not sure I can do this," she said nervously.

Johnson smiled reassuringly. "Of course you can. And you and your husband can make the ID together if that'll be easier for you."

I frowned. "Shouldn't they do that separately?"

"We have five more couples coming in to identify him," Johnson said. "We won't have any problem." He turned back toward Julie. "So, Mrs. Coburn, are you ready to go in and see if we got the right man?"

She nodded hesitantly.

"Wait here," he told me. "I'll be back in five minutes."

It was quicker than that, and when he returned with Julie and Ron in tow, Julie was sobbing. "That's the man!" she said with a hiccupping snuffle. Her face was drained of color, and I could see the fear in her wet eyes. "Oh my God, we had a murderer in our house! He might've... He could've..." She broke off, crying. Ron held her so tightly he seemed to be holding her up.

Sheepishly, Johnson rubbed the back of his neck. "Kinda screwed up here," he admitted. "I should have kept you all separated until after you made your independent IDs. Sorry about that. This isn't going to influence you is it?" he asked me. "Contaminate the results?"

I wasn't so sure the detective *had* made a mistake. I had the feeling he knew exactly what he was doing and was attempting to reinforce my positive identification. "Don't worry," I assured him. "I can't be influenced. Either I recognize him or I don't."

Moron, I thought. *Now even a halfway decent lawyer will be able to get these IDs thrown out in court.*

"Good," he said, clapping me on the back. "Step right this way."

I followed him out of the squad room through a back door. I was expecting one of those situations like I'd seen on TV, where there'd be a lineup against a wall, and I'd be looking through one-way glass. But I was brought into a short hallway and told to look through a small mesh-reinforced window in the center of a green steel door.

Where a bearded man who was definitely not Frank sat on a cot against the wall of the small room.

The anxious anticipation I'd been feeling disappeared instantly, my hopes crashing to earth.

"It's not him," I said.

"Look carefully. Take your time."

"It's not him."

Johnson shrugged. "Well, we have one positive ID so far. He might not be *your* Frank Wharton, but it seems pretty clear he's the guy who's been rooking our local populace."

We walked back into the squad room. Seeing Teri's expectant look, I shook my head. Nodding, she turned to Julie, holding her sister's shoulders and speaking directly into her face, no doubt telling her that the handyman who'd cheated them was not a murderer, just a con artist. I could see the relief flood Julie's face.

So her Frank wasn't my Frank.

Maybe none of the Franks were connected, I thought. Maybe all this time I'd been seeing links where there were none, chasing chimeras across the Southwest in a quixotic search that had more to do with me than Frank.

But, no. I'd seen the man. I'd been to his house.

A house where time didn't work? Where I'd lost six days in ten minutes? After encountering his wife's ghost at a bed-and-breakfast in Texas?

Maybe *none* of it had happened. Maybe it was all in my head. Maybe I'd imagined everything.

I glanced over at Teri, wanting to talk about this with her, needing to know what she thought, but she was nodding at something her sister was saying, not looking at me, the expression on her face unreadable.

We drove back to Orange County in silence.

PART TWO
INCIDENTS

ONE

SAN DIEGO, CALIFORNIA 1979

HE SAW HER in the line outside the theater.

Cheryl Hinson.

Steve Fisk shifted position to hide behind Roland. He, Roland and their other friend Brian had been looking forward to seeing *Alien* for months, since they'd first read in *Starlog* that the monster was designed by the same artist who'd done the cover for ELP's *Brain Salad Surgery*. But why in the world was Cheryl here? She didn't even like these kinds of movies. Was she doing this just to torture him?

No. She was here with someone. Another boy. On a date. Steve looked over Roland's shoulder and saw a guy he didn't recognize. A surfer-looking dude. Tall, tan, with an OP shirt and Shaun Cassidy hair, he had his arm around Cheryl's shoulder, and both of them were laughing easily at something one of them had said.

Steve felt as though he'd been kicked in the stomach. He had spent most of the past two weeks in his room, lying on his bed, listening to depressing music and running through an endless series of what-if scenarios in his head, wondering what he could have done to keep her. Ever since Cheryl had broken up with him, he'd been lost; even his school work had been affected.

She, apparently, was fine.

She was wearing a blouse he recognized: the white one with little purple flower things all over it, the one she'd worn the first time she let him touch her breasts. He remembered fumbling with the little plastic buttons in the cramped back seat of his mom's Datsun and pulling open that thin material to reveal the smooth velvety bra beneath. It was a moment of his life he would never forget.

Tonight, someone new was going to be unbuttoning that blouse.

Steve no longer wanted to see the movie. He wanted to go home. He wanted to be back in his bedroom, in the comfort of his bed, far away from Cheryl and her studly new boyfriend who, in the car after the movie, was probably going to take off that bra, gently massage her pert little breasts, and then, as he was kissing her, sneak his hand down her pants and slide a finger inside her.

Maybe she'd let him do more than that.

He felt sick to his stomach. Right at that moment, Cheryl happened to glance in his direction, and for a second their eyes locked. She looked away, but not before he saw the expression of satisfaction on her face. She made a big show of kissing the new guy, and Steve turned his head.

Brian must have seen it, too. "Hey, isn't that—?" he began, pointing.

Steve knocked his hand down. "Yeah," he said. "Ignore her."

Brian and Roland exchanged glances, but neither of them said anything. Once inside, in their seats, in the center of the theater far away from the back row where Cheryl and the guy with the hair had stationed themselves, Roland leaned over and whispered, "Fuck her, man. She's a bitch. You're better off without her."

It was still too soon. He wanted to agree with his friend, but his first impulse was still to defend her, and he forced himself to pretend as though he didn't care one way or the other and simply nodded.

The movie was good (*Great!* both Roland and Brian excitedly pronounced on the way out), but Steve had a hard time focusing on it. All he could think about was Cheryl, and it took every ounce of willpower in his body not to turn around during the show and try to see what she was doing. Afterward, they went to Pup 'n' Taco to get some drinks and fries, and talk about the flick. Pup 'n' Taco was *the* Friday night hangout for kids from their school, but neither Cheryl nor her date showed up at the fast food joint, and Steve couldn't help wondering where they were.

They left Pup 'n' Taco, and after an hour of aimless cruising, the three of them decided to call it a night. Brian, who had borrowed his parents' station wagon, was the driver, and he dropped Steve off first. "Sorry about Cheryl, man," he said as Steve got out.

"Me, too," Roland told him.

Steve waved them away, pretending it was nothing, though they all knew it wasn't. He slammed the door shut, then cringed as his friends peeled out loudly, knowing that in the morning he'd get an earful about that from old Mr. Hopkins next door.

The house was dark, the driveway empty. His parents were gone, at a party with friends, so he walked around to the back of the house to get the extra key his dad kept hidden under a rock. As soon as he opened the side gate, however, he sensed movement, a man-sized shadow that disassociated itself from the house and started across the backyard.

Steve's heart leaped in his chest, and a vision of the alien popped into his head. He was about to turn and run, when the man drew closer, waving at him.

Mr. Walton.

The handyman.

Steve stood nervously in place while the man approached. What was he doing here when no one was home? Especially at this hour. Was he planning to rob the house? His parents had hired Mr. Walton to put in a new sprinkler system, and though Steve hadn't said anything, it seemed to be taking a long time to finish the project, and he thought his parents were getting rooked.

Now the man was lurking around the backyard in the middle of the night? Something was definitely not right about this, and Steve was fully prepared to run like hell, screaming his head off, if anything weird happened.

Mr. Walton stepped closer. He was wearing his usual attire, what looked like an engineer's uniform: black-and-white pin-striped overalls with matching cap. It was odd in the daytime but downright creepy at night. "Your friends dropped you off, huh?"

"Yeah," Steve said. It was the first time Mr. Walton had talked to him, which made this conversation all the stranger.

The only thing he wanted was for the man to leave so he could get the key out from under the rock and go inside.

There was a long awkward pause. "I can give you a ride if you ever need one," the handyman said. "Plenty of room in my pickup."

Alarms were going off in Steve's head. This wasn't just a *little* creepy. It was full out Polanski, and he was about ready to haul ass when Mr. Walton brought things back from the brink. "I finished those back sprinklers today. Put them on a night timer to help your parents save water. I just wanted to check and make sure they were working."

Steve nodded. It was plausible. And it did explain why the man was here at this hour.

But Steve still didn't believe him.

Mr. Walton smiled, and in the darkness his teeth looked too white. "I'll get out of your hair now. Let your parents know that everything seems to be working. I'll be back in the morning to finish off the front."

Steve stood there, unmoving, watching him go. He was surprised when the man reached the sidewalk and started walking down the street. Where was that pickup? Maybe he had parked down the block.

Or maybe he was homeless and spent his nights wandering the city, looking over the odd jobs he'd done.

The thought didn't seem as ludicrous as it should have.

Steve waited a few more minutes to make sure the handyman wasn't going to return before heading into the backyard to get the extra key from under the rock. He quickly let himself in and locked the door behind him, turning on every light in the house. Placing the key on the kitchen counter so his dad could put it back under the rock later, Steve frowned. Where was Harpo? He looked around.

The cat always came out to meet him when he walked inside, but tonight the house was silent, and there was no sign of the tabby.

"Harpo!" Steve called.

Silence.

That was weird.

He opened the cupboard and took out the Friskies box, shaking it. That always made Harpo come running, but this time there was no response.

"Harpo!" He walked from room to room, looking under furniture, opening closets.

Nothing.

The front door opened as his parents returned, and the sound made him jump.

"Steve," his mom said, surprised, "what are you doing up?"

"Harpo's gone," he said accusingly. "You let him out."

His dad had the pleasant, half-amused tone that indicated he was drunk. "He was sleeping on the couch when we left. We didn't let him out."

"He was," Mom confirmed.

"Well, he's not here now. He must have gotten out somehow—"

The handyman.

Steve cut himself off in mid-sentence. Why hadn't he thought of that before? Mr. Walton may not have had a key to the house, but that didn't mean he couldn't have found some way to let the cat out. He wanted to tell his parents that he had encountered the man in the backyard tonight, but something kept him from it.

"Harpo's around," his dad said. "We'll find him in the morning." Giving a distracted wave, he started down the hall.

Disgusted, and more than a little worried, Steve went into his own bedroom, slamming the door behind him.

By the next morning, there was still no sign of Harpo, and the family spent until noon searching the house, yard and nearby neighborhood with no luck. Mr. Walton *did* return to finish the front sprinklers, and this time he came in that pickup truck he'd mentioned. Where had the truck been last night? Steve wondered.

After lunch, they went to the pound to see if anyone had found Harpo and turned him in, but no one had, and though Steve helped his mom make flyers and put them up on trees and telephone poles around the neighborhood, he'd already begun to resign himself to the fact that their cat was probably gone for good.

It was a quiet, depressing dinner they had that evening, and after halfheartedly watching TV for awhile, Steve decided to turn in early and go to bed.

THE sprinklers came on in the middle of the night.

With his windows open to let in the cool air, Steve heard the sprinklers the instant they started, the *tss-tss-tss* sound loud enough to awaken him from a fairly deep sleep. But that wasn't what caused him to sit up. There was a splashing/dripping noise as well, and even before he knew what it was, he knew it was not supposed to be there. Opening his eyes and looking over at the source, he saw, backlit by the street lamp in front of the house, water shooting through his window screen, hitting his drapes and dripping onto his desk below.

With a cry, he bounded out of bed, pulled the cord to open the curtains and slammed shut his window.

But not before he could see, outside, on the grass, behind the sprinklers, the silhouette of Mr. Walton.

Steve quickly shut the drapes. He told himself that the man had only come to make sure everything was working properly, although he knew that was a lame rationalization. The handyman could have and should have tested the timers before leaving earlier today. He also should have tested the arc of the sprinklers to make sure water wouldn't hit the house.

But he hadn't.

Or maybe he had.

Steve had the feeling that the sprinklers had been specifically set to *hit* his bedroom window, and that the man had come over tonight to watch it happen.

Was he still out there?

Steve was afraid to look. In even, ten-second intervals, spray hit the glass, the splashing sound even louder than before. In the spaces in between, the *drip-drop* of water from the soaked curtain continued to dribble onto his desk.

Why was the handyman doing this? Steve had no idea, but seeing Mr. Walton out there tonight, after that bizarre encounter the previous evening, left him feeling like a frightened little kid. He thought of calling for his parents, but he knew he was too old for that, and the prospect of embarrassment was more of a deterrent than his fear was an incentive. Hopping back into bed, he pulled the covers over his head, plugging his ears with his fingers so he couldn't hear the sound of the water hitting the window. It seemed as though an hour had passed, and his fingers were tired, by the time he finally fell asleep again.

IN the morning, he lay in bed after he awoke, not knowing how to tell his parents that the sprinkler had come through his window in the middle of the night and soaked his drapes and desk. They would blame him, even though it was not his fault, lecturing him that he should have kept his window closed, that he should not have put his desk by the window in the first place, that he had done *something* wrong.

Steve could hear them in the kitchen, chatting in alternating currents beneath the monotonic drone of the news radio they listened to while eating breakfast. It would be easier to tell his dad, Steve decided. His old man wouldn't care as much about the drapes and might understand that the real problem was that Mr. Walton had screwed up the alignment of the sprinklers, a distinction that would probably make no difference to his mom. He'd just wait until she went to the bathroom or something, and catch his dad alone.

Steve sat up in bed and looked toward his desk. He'd been hoping the damage wouldn't be as bad as he feared, but he could see in the morning light that it was actually worse. Water had ruined the books and papers on top of his desk, and sitting puddles had already discolored sections of the wood. He should've gotten a paper towel and wiped all that up last night. Now it was too late.

His parents stopped talking, and moments later he heard the click of the front door being unlocked. His dad was going outside to get the newspaper, and Steve leaped out of bed, pulling on his pants. His old man had to walk all the way across the lawn to the sidewalk where the paperboy threw the paper, then walk all the way back to the house. If he intercepted him in time, he could point out the errant sprinkler and explain what had happened without his mom getting involved at all. If his dad was the one to tell his mom about it, he might even get off scot free.

He hurried down the hall, through the living room and pushed open the screen door—

Just in time to see his dad trip over a raised metal sprinkler, fall forward and hit his head on another sprinkler.

He lay still, bleeding into the grass, onto the lawn.

"Dad!" Steve rushed forward, calling for his mother even as he did so. "Mom! Mom!"

The whole neighborhood probably heard him, but he didn't care. He just hoped that somebody had the presence of mind to call an ambulance. He couldn't do it because he had to see if his dad was okay—

still alive

—and he dropped to his knees, grateful to hear a wet gurgling sound coming from his father's throat. The sound was horrifying, but at least it meant that his dad wasn't dead. He tried to roll his dad over, away from the sprinkler, so he could see the damage, but it was harder than he thought it would be, and when he did finally manage to roll his dad onto his back, blood gushed from his split forehead. Steve put his hand over the wound to try and stop the bleeding, but the feeling of warm sticky wetness made him gag.

He was still screaming for his mom. She had come out by now and was running over, as was Mr. Hopkins from next door and Mr.

Gonzalez from across the street. His mom took over the first aid, pushing Steve aside and wadding up the hem of her bathrobe, pressing it against the wound to staunch the blood flow.

Had someone called for an ambulance?

Now that his mom was here, he no longer had to yell for her, so he started shouting, "Someone call an ambulance! Someone call an ambulance!"

His hands were wet and sticky with blood. He wiped them on the grass, not wanting to get his clothes dirty, and his gaze focused on the metal sprinkler next to his dad's head. Something was wrong here. He glanced around the lawn. Shouldn't the sprinkler heads have been spaced farther apart? And more evenly? Looking at them now, they seemed almost haphazardly installed...

No.

Not haphazardly.

One sprinkler was aimed at his window. Another was apparently aimed at their car in the driveway. They were all too high, easy to trip over; it was no wonder his dad had stumbled. Several sprinklers, in fact, seemed purposefully placed so that they would facilitate just such an accident.

Steve looked toward the street, suddenly overcome by the certainty that he would see Mr. Walton in the growing crowd of people congregating on the sidewalk. Although it was the last thing he wanted to do, he scanned the gathered faces, looking for the handyman, grateful not to find him there.

Suddenly, the sprinklers came on again, and, as if by intent, a stream hit Steve full in the face. Another hit his mom and dad. Still more were aimed directly at the neighbors. People were shouting, backing up, moving away.

From somewhere not so nearby came the sound of a siren—someone *had* called for an ambulance.

"Turn it off!" his mom cried. He could hear the panic, fear and frustration in her voice. "Turn it off!"

The manual sprinkler controls were next to the hose and faucet in the backyard, and Steve stood up and ran to turn off the water.

The spray had washed some of the blood from his hands, but not all of it, and thin pink drips followed him as he dashed across the grass, up the driveway and along the side of the house. He found the controls, but had no idea how to shut off the water, so he did the only thing he could think of to do: he unplugged the timer.

He heard the hiss of the sprinklers stop and the tumult of voices from the front subside. The approaching siren grew ever louder, but instead of immediately rushing back to check on his dad, Steve stood where he was for several seconds, shocked and staring. Because in the dirt next to the series of metal and plastic switches connected to each other and the timer by crisscrossing wires, jutted a little gray cat leg.

Harpo's.

The ambulance had arrived, and Steve tore himself away from the sight of his dead pet's limb, speeding back out to the front of the house. Standing neighbors were wiping water from their faces and pulling cold wet clothes away from their skin, but his mom was where he'd left her, kneeling by his dad and holding the section of blood-soaked bathrobe to the wound. Two paramedics rushed from the ambulance onto the lawn, one wearing a stethoscope, the other carrying a white case with a red cross on it. They not-so-gently pushed his mom aside and crouched down to check his dad's condition, the one with the stethoscope listening to his dad's heartbeat, the other opening his case and quickly applying some sort of bandage.

A third paramedic had unfolded a gurney from the open rear of the ambulance and was wheeling it across the grass, moving quickly. In his mind's eye, Steve saw the three paramedics rapidly and efficiently transporting his father to the nearest hospital, where calm professional doctors immediately diagnosed the head wound as nothing serious. He understood almost instantly, though, that that was not going to happen. The man with the stethoscope was shaking his head slowly, removing the twin-pronged instrument from his ears, and at that signal the man pushing the gurney almost imperceptibly slowed down.

Steve dropped to his knees next to his father and noticed that he didn't hear that wet breathing sound anymore.

"No!" he screamed.

And started crying.

THE next several days were a blur, a hazy half-understood amalgam of disjointed images from various places around the city: his home, a mortuary, his home, a church, his grandma's house, a cemetery, his home, his home, his home...

The pain of seeing Cheryl with another boy faded into insignificance against the loss of his dad, and even looking back at how he'd felt at the theater that night, he realized how shallow and naïve his feelings had been.

The funeral was set for Friday, and all of the important decisions had been made, so it was a surprise when the funeral director called Wednesday night and said an emergency had come up. Steve was the one to answer the phone, because his mom had fallen asleep on the couch shortly after dinner, but the man would not tell him what the problem was and would only speak to his mom.

"Hold on," Steve said, and hurried back into the family room to wake her up.

She seemed groggy and out of it—as she had been since his father's death—but she took the call. What she heard on the other end of the line made her wake up immediately. "What?!" she shouted into the phone. "How is that possible?!"

Steve couldn't hear what the funeral director was saying, but he heard his mom's responses. "Then who could have?...I don't believe this!...Well, you better, or you're going to be facing a lawsuit so fast your head will spin!"

She slammed the phone down.

Steve had a knot in the pit of his stomach. "What happened?" he asked.

His mom burst into tears, grabbing him and hugging him tightly.

"Mom?" he said, worried.

"It's your father! They can't find him!"

The funeral home had lost his dad's body? How could that even happen? Different scenarios ran through his head. Had he accidentally been cremated? Had they accidentally taken him to the wrong funeral and buried him under some other name?

"Don't worry," he reassured his mom. "They'll find him." He had no facts to back that up with, no reason to even think it was true, but the words seemed to help, and her grip on him lessened, her sobs quieting down.

It had to be an accident, Steve reasoned. Some snafu involving the wrong paperwork or something. No one could have stolen the body.

Stolen the body?

That was ridiculous. How could he even allow his mind to go there? No one would *steal* his dad's dead body. It was a mix-up at the mortuary, that was all. It probably happened more often than people knew. Everything was sure to be put right before Friday.

The funeral would be fine.

So why, Steve wondered, did he keep thinking about Mr. Walton?

And why could he so easily imagine the handyman carrying his dad's body off into the night?

TWO

EUGENE, OREGON 2010

ZORAIDA KNEW THE apartment was haunted the first time she stepped through the doorway.

Kelsey, on the other hand, was completely clueless, and it was only because their relationship was so young and in such a fragile transitional stage that Zoraida hadn't put her foot down and insist they find someplace else to live. She'd given up her own rented duplex when Kelsey, on a whim, had suggested the two of them move in together, but Kelsey's apartment had proved too small, and after a week, they both decided that, since they each had a lot of stuff, they needed a place with more rooms. It was Kelsey's ex, Shari, who said she knew of a two-bedroom apartment that was near downtown with reasonable rent.

Zoraida wondered now if Shari's suggestion had been part of an intentional effort to get back at Kelsey.

"This'll definitely work," Kelsey had said happily, walking with the landlord through the open rooms.

And against her better instincts, Zoraida had agreed.

She wished she had spoken up at the time. They'd been here a month already, and there was not a single night that she'd been able to sleep more than four hours. Kelsey was oblivious. Invigorated by a new bedroom, she initiated lovemaking almost every night, although Zoraida had grown increasingly inhibited. She couldn't shake the feeling that they were being watched, and while Kelsey wanted to stretch out in bed and try new things, she just wanted to hurry up and get it over with. Afterward, Kelsey would fall instantly asleep, snoring within minutes, and would remain dead to the world until morning, while Zoraida found it almost impossible to fall asleep. Only after hours of tossing and turning would her exhausted body finally give in and allow her to drift into a light, easily interrupted doze.

Haunted.

She wished she had a reason for her feelings, but she didn't. She hadn't seen anything, hadn't heard anything, had only felt a sort of vague unease. She was certain that the apartment was haunted, but didn't know how, didn't know why, and on Thursdays when their schedules diverged, when Kelsey was at work and she was home alone, she would walk from room to room, trying to figure out what was wrong and where it was centered. Sometimes she'd start in their bedroom at the rear of the apartment, but more often than not, she'd start at the front door, trying to recreate her initial impression of the place. She'd walk slowly through the front room, past the couch, past the TV, into the small kitchen with its even smaller breakfast nook, then back out into the front room and into the microscopic hallway, peeking into the bathroom, opening the shower curtain to make sure nothing was behind it, checking out the room that was their shared office. She'd end up in the bedroom, on the bed, looking around, wondering how anything so normal could feel so wrong.

The only time that anything close to concrete occurred was one Saturday, at lunch. They were both home, crammed into their tiny breakfast nook, eating macaroni and cheese.

"Do you think time's speeding up?" Kelsey asked.

Zoraida was getting used to her girlfriend's idiosyncrasies. What would have once seemed a bizarre left-field query that had nothing to do with anything she now took in stride as a normal topic of conversation. "Not really. Why?"

"I always heard that things seem to go by more quickly when you got older, that a kid's summer seemed to last longer than an adult's. But my whole life's gone by quickly. I never had a slow period. There were no endless summers for me; they all sped by. I'm wondering if the same thing's true for you, for everyone our age, if we didn't have those slow years like other generations because time's speeding up."

The phone rang at that moment, and since Zoraida was closer, she reached over and grabbed the handset from the wall. "Hello?"

The voice at the other end of the line sounded as though it was coming from an old Victrola. There was the same foreground crackle and hiss, the same faint tinny timbre to the spoken words. "*I'm lost.*" It was a woman speaking, sounding plaintive even from so far away. "*I'm lost.*"

Zoraida hung up quickly.

"Who was it?" Kelsey asked.

Zoraida shivered. "I don't know."

Her girlfriend frowned. "What did they say?"

"It was a woman. And she just kept repeating, 'I'm lost,' in this creepy, otherworldly kind of voice."

"Prank call," Kelsey determined. "Don't worry about it."

Zoraida did not think it was a prank...but she wasn't sure what it was. Kelsey had already forgotten about the call, and she tried to forget about it, too, but she couldn't. Remembrance of that tinny voice recurred throughout the day, and going to bed that night, she was glad she wasn't alone, glad Kelsey was here with her.

On the two-month anniversary of their moving in together, they attended a "Diversity Rally" downtown, a protest against news coverage of public policy by both the local and national media which left Asians and Latinos out of nearly every discussion of race. As a Filipino-American, Zoraida was tired of not being part of the cultural conversation, and she thought it was long past time that when matters of race were addressed, when poverty or education reform or crime statistics were discussed, the media did not just poll whites and African-Americans about their opinions. As impossible as it would have been to believe ten years ago, these days her sexuality gave her a better seat at the table than her ethnicity, and one of the purposes of this rally was to draw attention to the entire spectrum of the rainbow that lived in the United States.

After signing petitions and listening to a host of activist speakers on the college campus where the rally was to start, the entire group of 500-plus began marching downtown, taking a strategic route that passed by the local ABC, NBC, CBS and FOX affiliates.

"Diversity's not just black and white!" they chanted. "Diversity's not just black and white!"

They added to their numbers as they moved through the city, and got a lot of honking support from passing motorists, but there really was no planned ending, and after chanting in front of city hall for the benefit of reporters and cameramen covering the event for the six o'clock newscasts, people just started gradually drifting away.

Zoraida and Kelsey had run into some mutual friends, and after walking back to the campus and their cars, the six of them went out for drinks and dinner.

They didn't get back until late, and the second they walked through the doorway into the apartment, Zoraida knew something had changed. They hadn't expected to be gone so long and hadn't left any lights on. The apartment was dark when they entered, and even after Kelsey had reached around to find the wall switch next to the door. The front room had no ceiling light, so the switch was connected to an outlet and turned on a standing lamp next to the television. They'd recently replaced the lamp's burned out bulb with one that was more eco-friendly, and though Zoraida had not noticed the difference until now, she saw that the glow given off was weaker and yellower than the bright white of before.

There were far too many shadows in the room.

She glanced over at Kelsey to see if she was noticing anything unusual, and was chilled to see a look of apprehension on her girlfriend's face.

This was real.

There was another lamp on the end table next to the couch, and Kelsey instinctively hurried over to turn it on. Zoraida went into the kitchen to turn on the lights in there. But that was where they stopped. Neither of them, it seemed, wanted to go into that short hallway or the bathroom or the office or the bedroom.

They looked at each other. Kelsey laughed a little to cut the tension, but it wasn't a real laugh, and it didn't work. The feeling—whatever it was—was still here, and Zoraida picked up the remote to turn on the television, needing to hear a little noise in the apartment.

She heard more noise than she wanted.

They both heard it.

Above the irritating *Access Hollywood* music on the television came a high-pitched whine so loud that it hurt their ears. It was not electronic but did not sound natural either. Zoraida could think of nothing that could possibly make that squeal, and her impulse was to turn around and leave, get out of the apartment as quickly as possible.

Then the sound disappeared, the lights went out, the television switched off, the apartment was thrown into darkness, and suddenly the source of the uneasiness they'd felt when they'd walked through the door, the cause of the haunting that had disturbed Zoraida's sleep ever since they'd moved in, was right there before them. It wasn't invisible, wasn't even some vague amorphous shape. It was an old Asian man, a short dark figure wearing what looked like green pajamas. Glowing, lit from within, he was rocking back and forth on his bare heels, laughing through a mouth crowded with crooked overlapping teeth. His laughter was silent, no sound emerged from that open maw, and his eyes burned with a malevolent ferocity that was the furthest thing possible from mirth.

The juxtaposition of the hatred in those eyes and that wide laughing mouth was not merely unsettling but terrifying.

Screaming, practically knocking each other over in their efforts to escape, like two characters in a primitive slapstick comedy, they ran from the apartment, instinctively trying to get as far away from that—

ghost

—figure as quickly as possible, although Kelsey did take the time to close and lock the door behind them before fleeing to the car.

Rent was paid up through the end of the month, but they moved out the next day. They'd spent the night—in separate bedrooms—in Kelsey's parents' house, and in the morning they gathered together what friends and family they could, and with a rented U-Haul returned to the apartment complex. Zoraida's brother Alex was the first one inside, and they let him scope out the place to make sure it was empty before either of them entered. Assured that the rooms were clear, the rest of them swarmed in and, as quickly as they could, carried away the furniture, boxed up the possessions and cleaned everything out.

Two days later, they were installed in a new apartment—an apartment that actually *was* new—close to the college.

And that should have been the end of it.

But it wasn't.

While they did not see the Asian man again, they both experienced...incidents. This place was smaller (smaller than Zoraida's old duplex, which made her wish she had never moved out). There was only one bedroom, and the apartment was sparsely furnished since half of their belongings were now crowding Kelsey's parents' garage. But whatever had been behind the events in their old place seemed to have followed them here. The television now turned off and on at will, as did the light in the kitchen, though both of them pretended not to notice and neither of them mentioned anything about it.

Kelsey did mention the fact that she sometimes heard voices, coming from the closet, what sounded like a man and a woman talking low in order to keep from being overheard. It happened both when she was by herself and when Zoraida was with her, though Zoraida heard nothing and whenever Kelsey pulled open the closet door the voices stopped and there was never anything there.

But it was Zoraida who had it the worst. Waking up in the middle of the night to go to the bathroom the week after they'd moved in, she flipped on the light and saw what she thought was a face in the toilet, the reflection of a leering old man looking up at her from the water.

The man grinned at her and winked.

After that, she was afraid to go to the bathroom in the apartment by herself. Kelsey had to check first and then stay in there with her. If Kelsey was gone, she would hold it until she went to work, or, if necessary, use the bathroom at the McDonald's down the street.

All of this put a strain on the relationship.

Their formerly vigorous lovemaking trailed off to nothing, and even casual displays of affection like kisses goodbye and hugs somehow fell by the wayside without either of them noticing.

Then, one day, Kelsey was gone.

Zoraida awoke in the morning to find that her girlfriend was not there. She thought little of it at first, assuming that Kelsey had merely left early for work and had rudely not informed her. But when she came back to the apartment that night to find Kelsey still gone, when a call to Kelsey's cell not only rang and rang, but did not go into voicemail, Zoraida knew something was wrong. Her hope was that Kelsey had just needed a little space and was taking a few days off, or even that Kelsey was breaking up with her and leaving.

She was afraid that something bad had happened.

Kelsey's parents did not know where she was when Zoraida called, were not even aware she was missing, and for Zoraida that was the last straw. She immediately called the police, and two detectives came to the apartment to get her statement. They took a photo of Kelsey, looked around to make sure there were no signs of foul play, then left her with a case number and told her they would be in touch.

They were in touch the next day, when the same two policemen arrived not to follow up on her report, but to drag her down to the station for questioning.

"I don't understand how you can bring me in," she said in the car. "I haven't done anything."

That was when one of the detectives let slip that she was being questioned at the behest of Kelsey's mom and dad, who apparently blamed her for their daughter's disappearance. The police had been filled with homophobic falsehoods from the family, and Zoraida realized that the tolerance she'd experienced from Kelsey's parents up to this point was only the thinnest of veneers. She'd seen enough movies and TV shows to know that she shouldn't answer any questions without the presence of a lawyer, but she didn't have a lawyer, didn't even know how to go about finding one, and all the way to the station she obsessed over whether she would have to sit in a cell and wait until a lawyer showed up.

What she learned at the station, once she was in an interrogation room and cameras were trained on her, was that Kelsey was dead. Her body had been found this morning next to a forest control road by a mountain biker. The cyclist had been speeding down the dirt trail when he'd noticed what looked like a naked woman lying in the adjacent runoff ditch. He'd braked to a halt, circled back, and found the bruised and battered body of what was almost immediately determined by law enforcement, once the bicyclist had called them, to be Kelsey Edwards.

"Hope for the best, expect the worst" was a motto Zoraida had always claimed to live by, but this *was* the worst, and she found that she hadn't expected it and definitely wasn't prepared for it. She sat there, stunned, acutely aware that the detectives were watching her reaction. Instead of being allowed to honestly respond to the news, she was under scrutiny, forced to wonder if she was acting in a sufficiently innocent manner, and she burst into tears, not only at the thought that Kelsey was dead, but also from the stress of being under suspicion of murder.

Murder!

It didn't even seem possible.

She thought of Kelsey, her brain forcing her to imagine what her girlfriend's body, her beautiful body, had looked like crumpled up by the side of the road, beaten, bloody and black-and-blue.

Zoraida's sobs intensified. Who could have hurt her? And why? She'd been stripped. Had she been assaulted as well? Entered against her will by some gross pig?

One of the detectives, the older one, a stern no-nonsense looking guy, told her wearily that this was just pro forma, that she wasn't really a suspect, that they had to do this, and the sooner she answered their questions, the sooner they could all get out of here. She knew she was innocent, knew none of her responses would implicate her, and she decided to answer honestly. If it looked like they were trying to trick her into saying something incriminating, she'd shut up, but if she could clear up any suspicions they had about her, they would be free to pursue the *real* murderer.

The questions were generic: where was she at this time, at that time; had she and Kelsey had a fight; did she know of any enemies Kelsey might have had.

What disturbed her most about the interview, what really brought it home to her, was the way the detectives kept referring to Kelsey in the past tense. Kelsey didn't exist anymore, she was dead, and though the rest of the world seemed to have caught on to that fact, Zoraida's brain was still a step behind, and the words remained jarring.

She was released fairly quickly, and she returned to the apartment feeling numb. The first thing she noticed when she walked inside was how many of their furnishings and possessions were Kelsey's. The sight of a book her girlfriend had been reading, lying on top of the end table, made her burst into tears again, and she plopped down on the couch, feeling overwhelmed. Were Kelsey's parents planning a funeral? If so, would she be invited? To her knowledge, Kelsey had no will (why *would* she? She was only twenty-six). So what would happen to her belongings? Would they go back to her parents? Kelsey's name was on the rental agreement. How was that going to work? There were too many things to consider, and Zoraida felt completely unprepared to deal with any of them.

It was the middle of the day, but she felt tired and just wanted to go to bed. Part of her thought that maybe if she went to sleep and woke up, she would find that this had all been a dream, that everything was back to normal. She knew that was wishful thinking, but she also thought that it couldn't hurt to try, and she dragged herself into the bedroom, fell onto the bed and pulled the covers over her head.

The pillow still smelled like Kelsey.

She dozed off, crying, and when she awoke several hours later, it was dark and Kelsey was still dead. It hadn't been a dream. She tried to fall back asleep again but couldn't, and after a half-hour of tossing and turning, she sat up, feeling hungry, intending to go into the kitchen and get something to eat.

Then she saw it.

There in the dark corner, looking at her.

A small huddled figure with the face of a wrinkled old woman.

Screaming, Zoraida ran from the bedroom, outside, into the courtyard of the complex. Lights were turning on, other people coming out of their apartments to see what was going on, perhaps thinking there was a fire. Luckily, Zoraida had fallen asleep with her clothes on, but she didn't even care about that at the moment. All she cared about was getting away from that...*thing*, and she ignored her emerging neighbors, running all the way out to the street before stopping.

She bent over, breathing deeply. What the hell was she going to do now?

She wasn't going back, that's for sure. And she certainly couldn't expect to stay with Kelsey's family. Maybe she'd be able to crash at a friend's house for a night or two, just until she could sort things out.

Her purse, car keys and pocketbook were back in the apartment.

Zoraida's heart dropped as the realization came to her. She hurried back into the courtyard. Maybe some of her neighbors were still out, still curious about what was happening. She didn't really know any of them, but one or two of the braver men might be willing to accompany her back inside while she picked up her purse. It was on the floor next to the magazine rack, if she wasn't mistaken. That's where she usually dropped it before plopping herself down on the couch. She'd be able to get in and out quickly.

She looked at the open door of the apartment. The idea of seeing that *thing* again terrified her. She didn't know what it was or why it was there, but it frightened her even more than the ghost of the Asian man had, and she wasn't sure she had the strength to face it.

Most of her neighbors had gone back indoors; the fireworks were over, there was nothing to see, no reason to stay outside. But an older man in the apartment above theirs—

hers

—was leaning against the railing, smoking. He looked down as she entered the courtyard. She didn't know his name, was not even sure she'd seen him before, but she stopped, addressing him. "Hi. I'm Zoraida. I live in the apartment below you."

"Heard you screaming. Saw you running out," he said. He took a long slow drag on his cigarette. "What was that about?"

"I think someone's in my apartment. I was wondering if you could just...walk in there with me. I need to get my purse, and just in case..."

He looked at her disinterestedly. "Call the police." He pinched the end of his cigarette, then flicked it down at her and turned to go back into his apartment.

"Asshole!" she called out.

His apartment door closed.

She considered knocking on another door, asking someone else to help her, but the brief confrontation had boosted her courage, and she thought she'd be able to do this herself. She'd just rush in, take the two steps to her purse, grab it and run. Besides, that *thing* was in the bedroom. She wouldn't even have to see it.

Fear gripped her as she approached the open doorway. It was dark inside. She'd fallen asleep when it was day and hadn't turned on any lights. Gathering what was left of her rapidly dwindling courage, she reached the doorway and stretched her arm around the side of the jamb, reaching for the light switch.

Maybe it's gone, she told herself. *Maybe I imagined it.*

She flipped on the light, intending to grab her purse and go.

But there it was.

It had moved to the sitting room. Still in a corner, it was shaking, vibrating, and there was a toothless smile on the wrinkled old woman face.

Something pushed her from behind, knocking her forward. The door slammed shut. Zoraida's hands landed on her purse, breaking her fall. She heard something crunch inside (*sunglasses*? *Tic Tacs*?), then she was pushing herself to her feet, grabbing the purse.

The small huddled figure was next to her, its wrinkled face looking up into her own.

She was alive until it touched her.

KIMBER Edwards looked at her husband, mouth set in a straight hard line. "Didn't I tell you? When Kelsey first got involved with all those...*lesbians*, didn't I say things would turn out this way? I knew it. I knew it! But, *n-o-o-o*, you knew *better.* 'Leave her alone,' you said. 'Let her find her own way.' Well, are you happy now? Huh? Are you happy? If you hadn't allowed her to—"

"SHUT UP!"

Kimber blinked, stunned into silence. She could not recall the last time Tom had raised his voice to her, and his outburst cut her off in mid-diatribe. She narrowed her eyes. "*What* did you say?"

"SHUT UP!"

There was danger in his expression, and the thought crossed her mind that if she continued, he might hit her.

But that was crazy. *Tom*? *Hit her*? He couldn't hit anyone.

"You're the one—" she began.

"I TOLD YOU TO SHUT UP!"

He pushed her back on the couch. Hard. She bumped her head on the wall behind the sofa, causing a framed photo of Kelsey to fall, but before she could even cry out, he was pulling down his pants, and she saw that he was harder than he'd been in years. She was both shocked and disgusted. How could he be aroused at a moment like this? Their daughter was dead, for God's sake! It was not only nauseating, it was incomprehensible. "You sick—" she began.

He grabbed her midsection in mid-sentence, roughly flipping her over and pushing up her dress, ripping her underwear.

Furious, she tried to get up. Then his weight was on her and she couldn't move. "What are you—"

In one brutal movement, he forced his hardness inside her, intentionally shoving it up the wrong hole. "No!" she screamed at the top of her lungs, but he rammed it in deeper and began pounding away. She cried out in pain—it felt as though she was being ripped apart—but his hand went over her mouth to muffle the sound, and he continued thrusting so violently that she thought she would pass out. There was a disgusting grunt of release in her ear, his body stiffened as he finished, and then he was finally off her, pulling his pants back up. She could feel that she was bleeding back there and wasn't even sure she'd be able to stand, but she managed to roll over and stagger to her feet. The pain was unbearable, and she hobbled, sobbing, into the bathroom, where she locked the door and sat on the toilet, mingled sperm and blood dripping into the water below.

She didn't know how long she sat there, but morning became afternoon, and afternoon became evening. Throughout the day, she could hear Tom moving around the house, but he never spoke to her, and she didn't call out to him. She heard the microwave bell and smelled re-heated chili when he made his lunch, heard the microwave ding again later and smelled the hot dogs he made for dinner. He made no effort to use the bathroom, though they had just the one, and she wondered if he was holding it, going outside in the backyard or pissing in the kitchen sink. The thought made Kimber's stomach churn.

The bleeding had stopped for the most part, but she knew she still might need medical treatment. She would have herself checked out later, but for now she'd gooped a bunch of Neosporin on her finger and gently slathered it in and around the hole. What was going to happen when she had to poop? Would that open the wounds again? Would everything get infected?

She didn't even want to think about it.

Tom had not interrupted his after-dinner routine for her. She could hear, from the front of the house, the muffled sound of the television, and several hours later (probably after he'd fallen asleep in his chair and woken up several times) the TV finally shut off. She heard him coming down the hall. The bathroom door was locked, and she braced herself against it, just in case he tried to force his way in, but he passed by and went into the bedroom, where she heard the rattle of his belt buckle, the thump of his shoes hitting the floor. He was getting ready for bed, and moments later there was no sound at all as he lay down and tried to fall asleep.

Kimber had turned on the lights in the bathroom when it started to get dark outside, but the lights were dimmer now than they had been. In fact, they seemed to be fading by the minute, as though they were connected to a dying generator whose power was gradually diminishing. She didn't see how that was possible, but it was happening, and she tried to look through the frosted glass window to find out whether any of her neighbors' homes were being similarly affected.

Movement glimpsed out of the corner of her eye caused her to turn, and in the mirror over the sink she saw the reflection of a figure that wasn't in the room.

Startled, she sucked in her breath. She thought her heart would burst through her chest, and for a moment she even forgot the pain and what had happened to her. She almost called out for Tom but stopped herself at the last second. *He* was real; *this* was not. He could actually hurt her, while this was merely a reflection.

Of what, though? She wanted to believe it was a figment of her imagination, but it was still there, even though she'd looked away and looked back. She hoped that it was a misperception on her part, the confluence of objects in the bathroom that *looked* like a figure when viewed from a certain angle. But she'd changed angles, moved closer and it was still there.

In fact, the figure had the face of an old lady...and it reminded her of someone. She couldn't think of who at the moment, though it came to her later: the wife of Mr. Wilbert, the handyman who'd built their back patio. At that instant, however, she was too scared to think about whose appearance the phantom resembled. Her priority was getting out of the bathroom and away from that thing without waking up Tom in the bedroom.

And then it spoke.

Just as she thought of Tom, it spoke.

"Kill him," the old lady mouth whispered.

There were scissors on the counter next to the sink, the scissors she occasionally used to trim her bangs. She didn't remember putting them there, hadn't trimmed her bangs for awhile, but she picked them up and looked at them in the dim half-light.

Kimber glanced up at the thing in the mirror.

It was grinning.

As if on autopilot, she unlocked the door and walked out of the bathroom. The hallway was dark, but there was a blue light coming from the bedroom. The TV. Tom couldn't fall asleep without that flickering light, though he always turned the sound off because he also needed silence. She walked into the room. He was on his stomach, in his underwear, the covers pushed down, dead to the world.

Dead.

She held the scissors above his bare back for several minutes... but in the end she couldn't do it. She hated him, yes, but she realized as she stood there that she didn't want to live without him. She didn't want to sleep in an empty bed. She didn't want to go to jail, either, but that wasn't even part of the consideration. She was at that moment in a world with no legal consequences, where she was free to act as she pleased, and though her rectum was still bleeding, though she was still in terrible pain, she decided to let him live.

Taking a deep breath, Kimber returned to the bathroom to put away the scissors. The lights were again at full power, and the only person reflected in the mirror now was herself. Back in the bedroom, she took off her clothes, put on her nightgown and crawled into bed. She faced Tom, still not comfortable with turning her back to him, but it was nice to feel his warm body next to hers.

When she awoke in the morning, he was gone.

Was he consulting with the police to see if they'd found Kelsey's killer? Had he headed off to work? Was he down at Dunkin' Donuts getting coffee? None of those felt right. He was *gone*, and she knew he was *gone*, but she decided to wait a few days to see if he came back before reporting him as missing.

Getting out of bed, Kimber walked over to the bathroom. There was nothing in the mirror, though the scissors were again on top of the counter. Had she put them back in the drawer? She thought so, but couldn't remember. For some reason, apropos of nothing, she found herself wondering what had happened to the vial of Billy Bob Thornton's blood that Angelina Jolie used to carry around with her. Had it been thrown away—or was it sitting around somewhere, growing moldy, turning *into* something?

She'd probably never know.

There were a lot of things she'd never know.

Staring into the mirror, Kimber looked for the figure, but it was not there, not standing in the foreground as it had been before, or hiding in the background. It was not in the shower, not in the window. It was nowhere to be seen, and she stood in that same spot and stared that way many times over the following days, weeks and months, patiently waiting for the figure to come back.

But it never did.

THREE

SEATTLE, WASHINGTON 1995

IT WAS RAINING again—it *always* rained here—and Laurie Skeffington stared out the wet window at the blurry world stretched out beneath the gray sunless sky. She should have put her foot down, she thought now. When Patrick's company had transferred him, she hadn't wanted to move, but it was a key promotion and he was really excited, so she went along with it and said nothing. A year later, she still hadn't found a full-time job, hadn't made friends with any of her standoffish neighbors, and with Patrick gone most of the day, it was difficult finding something to do with all the hours at her disposal.

No wonder this region had such a severe drug problem.

To top it off, the roof was leaking.

It had started yesterday, a drip in the center of the upstairs bathroom that at first she'd put down to ordinary condensation. Water was *everywhere* in Seattle, and sometimes the mirror, fogged up from the shower, did not clear up all day no matter how many paper towels she used to wipe it. But when she'd returned to the bathroom later and nearly slipped on the growing puddle on the tile floor, Laurie knew something was wrong. She mopped up, put down a plastic wastepaper basket to catch the drips, and called Patrick at work. He could not get off until lunch, and by that time, she'd emptied the wastepaper basket three times into the tub. It was a serious leak, and they needed to get it fixed before it spread and caused some real damage.

Patrick called every roofer in the phone book, but the storm had created a lot of business, and the only company that could come over within the next week charged twice as much as its most expensive competitor. Asking around at work in the afternoon, while Laurie continued to empty the wastepaper basket and keep an eye out for new leaks, Patrick managed to find an unlicensed, independent, off-the-books roofer whom one of his colleagues had used last year. The quote was reasonable, and the man, who worked alone, said he'd be able to come over this morning. They'd thought their problem was solved.

But...

Laurie didn't like being home alone with the roofer. It was an intuition thing, but the man rubbed her the wrong way, and when he arrived she asked Patrick if he couldn't take a day off and stay home. He couldn't, he said. They were right in the middle of an important project and he was the project coordinator. He had to be there.

He had at least gone in late, staying long enough to explain what needed to be done. But then he'd left her alone with the man, and she'd spent the morning staying out of his way. He'd been on the roof for an hour or so before ringing the doorbell and asking to come inside. "Shakes at the top're patched," he explained, "But there's probably water damage inside. I need to access your attic and come at it from underneath."

Laurie had nodded her assent, and he'd been nothing but professional as he courteously took off his raincoat and boots in the foyer, but she still felt uncomfortable having him in the house, and after showing him the attic entrance and pulling down the ladder, she'd retreated to the kitchen at the far end of the house. The polite thing to do would have been to offer him some coffee, but she didn't want to do that, and she sat here looking out the window as he worked upstairs.

She wasn't quite sure when she realized that there'd been no sound up there for a while. She glanced up at the ceiling. *What could he be doing?* They'd stored a lot of things in the attic, and it suddenly occurred to her that he might be looking through boxes, peeking at their private belongings. Even if that wasn't what was happening, however, the roofer shouldn't be slacking off. It was still raining outside, and that leak needed to be fixed.

The hammering started again a moment later, but Laurie still found herself curious as to what was going on up there, and, despite her trepidation, she walked upstairs, stopping at the foot of the ladder that led into the attic. It sounded as though he was hard at work, and it occurred to her to announce her presence, but something kept her from it, and she said nothing as she climbed the rungs and poked her head through the trapdoor opening.

There was a bare bulb light hanging from the ceiling, and its yellow illumination was so weak that she didn't see the roofer until her eye caught sight of movement in the darkness.

She squinted to focus her vision.

He was nailing the body of a dead squirrel to the underside of the shake roof. Two other squirrels had already been nailed into the wood, and there was a small sack of more dead animals on the floor next to him. He must have seen her in his peripheral vision, because he stopped hammering in mid-swing and looked over at her, caught.

The second their eyes met, she was screaming, and she jumped down off the ladder, running through the house and outside, leaving the front door open as she took off down the street.

TAG McKellips had worked at Ammon's Lumber for the better part of two decades, and he was not surprised at all when he read in the paper about the psycho roofer. He'd had his eye on that weasel from day one. A lot of people came through the lumberyard gates, and Lord knows the construction business did have a high level of transient workers, but there'd been something about that guy in the engineer overalls that had set off Tag's internal alarm. It was nothing specific, not his appearance or anything he said. But just watching the man walk up and down the aisles, picking out roofing supplies, made Tag feel uncomfortable.

And his instincts had been correct.

After reading the article this morning, he had called the police to let them know the roofer had bought his supplies from Ammon's. Tag wasn't sure how the man had paid, but if it was with a credit card, the cops might be able to track him. There might also be other employees who saw and remembered what type of car, truck or van he drove.

The cops had come later in the afternoon and interviewed everyone, but they didn't seem to have found out much that would help. After all the publicity, Tag figured that the man had probably skipped town. Which was just as well. There was definitely something wrong with the guy, and it was probably only a matter of time before he did something far worse than butcher small animals and nail their body parts to a roof.

It was Tag's night to close, and after John, Ray and Stuart tallied up their registers, cleared the aisles and made sure no customers were in either the store or the yard outside, he unlocked the front door, let them out, and then locked the door behind them before heading back to the office to turn on the security camera and alarm. The sound of his shoes on the cement floor echoed far out of proportion to its actual volume.

But that was not the only noise in the building.

Somewhere in the semi-darkness, an electronic *whirring* started. Then stopped. Then started. Then stopped.

As though someone was testing out a drill.

Had someone been hiding when the store was cleared? Tag felt a flash of anger. "Hey!" he called out in warning.

The *whirring* stopped. But from the last aisle, where the lights had already been turned off, came a loud crash. Something heavy had fallen from one of the shelves.

Fallen...or been pulled.

Seconds later, there was another crash, from further up the aisle.

And another.

Whoever—

whatever

—was pulling items off the shelves was coming closer and would soon be in the same rear section of the store that he was.

Tag felt unaccountably chilled. It was probably some punk-ass teenagers. Or maybe it was the psycho roofer, who'd seen the cops here earlier and was pissed at Ammon's because someone here had ratted on him.

Those were best-case scenarios.

Worst-case scenario?

It wasn't even human.

Was he in third grade? How could he even come up with an idea so idiotic and patently ridiculous? Because the hair standing up on his arms and the back of his neck said the idea *wasn't* so ridiculous. There was a gigantic floor-shaking crash from the front of the aisle.

Tag knew instantly what it was—a bathtub.

But the bathtubs were on a shelf six feet up and so heavy that they could only be moved by a forklift.

He ran quickly into the office, closing and locking the door behind him, turning on the alarm.

All of the power in the building shut off.

Thrown instantly into darkness, Tag looked toward the alarm control panel, assuming that the alarm had a backup battery and that he would still see a lit red light. No such luck. There were no lights on in the building at all, no illumination...except for a soft bluish glow somewhere near the head of the store's first aisle.

Where something heavy crashed in the stillness.

Through the window of the office, he could see the blue glow pulsing gently, as if in time to a heartbeat. It shone above the top of the first aisle, partially lightening the exposed beams of the open ceiling high above. Reaching the end of the aisle, it moved out into the open.

It was a ghost.

Tag knew it instantly, though he had never seen a ghost before and had not even believed in their existence until this moment. But the sight triggered a latent recognition in his brain, and his instinctive reaction was to duck below the level of the window so he would not be seen. It seemed suddenly hard to breathe. Though possessing a vaguely human shape, the glowing figure that emerged from the aisle was so fundamentally wrong, so horrifyingly unnatural, that he was afraid in a way he had never been before. Panicked, he scrambled through the darkness, crouching low, hands in front of him to keep from running into any furniture. He knew there was a door to the lumberyard on the opposite side of the room, and his goal was to reach it, run outside and escape. A rational part of his brain knew that he should find the phone and call the police, but there was nothing rational about the terror coursing through his veins. As quickly as he could, he scuttled across the floor, maneuvering around an unseen desk, knocking over a wastepaper basket and passing to the right of a filing cabinet before reaching the door.

Standing, Tag opened the door, closed it behind him and dashed outside.

Boards of various size were stacked on metal frames against the wall of the building within a chain-link fenced yard that opened onto the parking lot. No lights were on out here either, but the sky was clear, the moon was full, and the soft illumination from the sky mingled with the diffused light of the surrounding city, allowing him to see where he was going.

Running as fast as he could, he passed the railroad ties and posts, the four-by-fours, the two-by-fours—

And stopped short when a dark figure lurched out in front of him.

Blacker than the surrounding darkness, it emerged from between two stacks of lumber, comprised of shapes that were not supposed to go together, emitting a low noise that sounded like a cross between a moan, a mumble and the hum of a powerful diesel engine. He could feel the sound in his bones, as though the vibrations were passing through him, but he didn't stop to analyze the situation. He backtracked, ran into another row and, heart pounding crazily, zigzagged between piles of wood toward the front gate and the parking lot beyond. Behind him, he could hear boards falling, that low noise rising in volume as though the entity producing it grew in anger.

He reached the gate.

It was locked.

Tag's heart sank. He only had keys to the *building's* door. The *gate* key was back in the office. He felt overcome with exhaustion, knowing that his only option was to go back the way he'd come. Breathing deeply, he turned around.

And the lumberyard was empty.

He saw boards that had been knocked over or strewn about, but there was no sign of the dark figure he'd seen only moment before or of the glowing ghost from inside the building.

The lights suddenly came on, the alarm blaring.

He breathed an honest-to-God sigh of relief, letting out all of the air his lungs had been holding in one grateful exhalation. It was over. Whatever it was, it was finished, and once again the world was back to the way it was supposed to be.

Before something else could happen, he ran back down the length of the yard to the office, closing and locking the door, shutting off the alarm and using the phone to call the police. He explained who he was and where he was, telling the dispatcher at the other end of the line that someone had broken into Ammon's and asking her to send some officers down here. There was no way in hell he was going to describe what he saw, but he hoped that if the cops got here in time, they might see something for themselves.

Hanging up, he hurried back through the building to the entrance, unlocking and opening it before stepping gratefully outside.

Two officers arrived fairly quickly in a patrol car with lights and sirens on. In Tag's telling of the story, he had just set the alarm when it went off. He heard a series of loud noises from down the first aisle and quickly called the police. Running out to the front door, he locked it to keep the intruder or intruders inside.

Tag accompanied the officers as they canvassed the inside of the building as well as the adjacent lumberyard. They discovered plenty of vandalism, saw objects big and small thrown from shelves onto floor, but there were no signs of the perpetrators.

Of course not. They were ghosts.

Henry Ammon himself was called. The owner sped down to the store in less than ten minutes, but it was still nearly two hours later before all questions were asked, all reports taken, and Tag was allowed to go home. Although he was tired, at least the fear had faded, and he drove through the wet streets to his neighborhood, anxious to get into bed and grab some shut-eye.

That wasn't going to happen, though. He was halfway down the block when he noticed that the lights in his house were flashing on and off. It looked almost like the house at the end of *Poltergeist*, and he slowed the pickup, his heart pounding so hard he could hear the blood pulsing in his head. He had no intention of pulling into his driveway—he was going to head straight for the police station—but he looked at the house as he drove past and saw a pickup truck almost identical to his own parked in front of the garage. On the roof, clearly visible in the light from the streetlamp, was a man tearing off shingles and throwing them onto the lawn below.

The psycho roofer.

It had to be. He'd found out somehow that Tag had called the cops to help identify him, and he had come for revenge.

Bringing ghosts with him?

None of this made any sense, but Tag didn't care. He was going straight to the police. Let them handle it. Let them figure out—

His steering wheel was yanked to the left by an unseen force, putting the truck on a collision course with the massive oak tree in front of Nora Domberg's house. Something pushed his foot down on the accelerator.

He neither saw, heard nor felt the crash. His foot was being pushed down against his will...and then he was opening his eyes to find himself standing in his own hall closet.

Except that he wasn't really standing. He was being held up. By long thick nails that had been driven through his hands into the closet's back wall. He felt no pain, though, only numbness. His vision was blurry, but he could see that the closet door had been taken off, and a man crouching down in front of him was meticulously screwing in a wooden panel that covered the bottom third of the open doorway.

Tag knew he should scream, should try to free himself and fight, but his brain was foggy and he didn't have the will to do anything other than stare.

The man finished affixing the bottom panel and picked up another that he fitted above the one he'd already installed. This one came up to Tag's neck.

He was being walled in.

The man saw that Tag was awake, and he smiled pleasantly. He was wearing what looked like a train engineer's outfit: striped overalls with a matching billed cap.

"Nice to meet you," the man said. "My name's Frank."

And he started screwing in the second panel.

FOUR

DENVER, COLORADO 1988

RANDY ARMSTRONG WAS grateful for Frank. Ever since he'd gotten out of prison, it had been damn near impossible to find a job—even though obtaining gainful employment was one of the requirements of his parole. As Christian as everyone always claimed to be, none of them *really* believed in rehabilitation or giving a guy a second chance. The minute they found out he'd done time, he saw that familiar look pass over their faces, the one that said there was no way in hell they were going to hire him, and he knew that even though he'd paid his debt to society, they were going to lie and say the job was filled, or not pick *anyone*, rather than put him on the payroll.

So thank God for Frank.

An independent contractor, Frank didn't have to answer to anyone but himself, and he wasn't afraid to take a chance on someone who maybe didn't have the most upstanding background. He knew that Randy was good with his hands and familiar with construction, and that's all that mattered. Randy had come clean right away, had even ended up spilling details, but Frank hadn't cared. In fact, he'd *understood*. Smiling sympathetically, Frank said he knew how sometimes little girls would flirt with you. Didn't matter how old they were: sometimes they *wanted* it. And when they started screaming afterward, playing the victim once they'd gotten their jollies, well, they might *need* to be beaten, shut up for their own good so that other people wouldn't get the wrong impression.

Frank knew the score. Which was why it was such a pleasure to work for him. Although...

Although sometimes he did things that were a little bit strange.

One time, for example, a neighborhood dog found its way onto the site where they were working, and, grinning, Frank hit it with a hammer. The dog ran off, limping and bleating, and Frank laughed. "Next time," he said, "that mutt's going into the cement."

Another time, Frank showed up in the morning with a bag full of pelts. That's what he called them, *pelts*, as though he was some sort of trapper back in the 1800s. Again they were laying concrete, and Frank spread the *pelts* over the rebar lattice before pouring the cement. "What does that do?" Randy asked. Frank only smiled mysteriously and put a finger to the side of his nose, wiggling his eyebrows up and down like Groucho Marx. It was an odd and unnerving response, and Randy, feeling creeped out, had had to look away.

Frank also liked to tell stories. They were good stories, mostly, and he insisted they were true, but Randy had his doubts. One time, Frank said, he'd been working in California and had been called in to oversee the construction of an addition to Johnny Carson's house. Johnny was pissed off one day because the night before he caught his wife blowing George Hamilton in the bathroom at a party. He'd gone in to take a leak and had found the tan man sitting on the toilet, pants around his ankles, while his wife knelt on the floor before him, her head bobbing up and down. "I can't let that stand," Johnny said, and Frank was with him. So, under the talk show host's supervision, he put together a Mousetrap-like device that appeared to be part of the construction, but when a smiling George Hamilton toured the site so Johnny could show him how things were coming along, he stepped on a spot that, through a series of what appeared to be coincidences, caused a board with a long nail poking out of it to slap him in the crotch. "You should have heard the bastard scream," Frank said, laughing. "Sounded like a woman getting her ass reamed." Randy said that he thought the wife should have been punished, too, and Frank said that she had been—Johnny had divorced her and cut her off with no money.

Another story involved a drunk Ronald Reagan who'd hired Frank to install an alarm system in his house. "This was well before he was president," Frank said. "But after he was governor of California. He was in kind of an in-between stage, and I don't think he knew what to do with himself. So he drank a lot. Anyway, he tells me that he wants to go joyriding in this crappy old pickup the gardener drove. It was parked in the driveway, and the gardener was in the back. The moron left his keys in the ignition because he thought it would be safe there at Reagan's estate, and we just hopped in and took off. Reagan was driving, and he was drunk off his ass, almost hit the gate on the way out. We went careening down the road and ended up crashing into a fountain in front of Anthony Quinn's house. Luckily Anthony Quinn wasn't home, because Reagan pulled his pants down and took a shit in the fountain. We left the truck there and walked back, where the gardener was panicking and running around, wondering where his pickup was." Frank laughed. "Then Reagan told me to get back to work and wandered off, said he needed to take a piss."

These were all tall tales as far as Randy was concerned, but most were funny as hell, and he always enjoyed hearing Frank tell them.

Overall, he thought, he had a good thing going here.

Overall.

He'd been working with Frank for a little over three months the first time it happened.

It was late at night, and he was half-asleep in his lounge chair when there was a loud knock on the door of his trailer. Randy jumped, startled. He wasn't expecting anyone—and who showed up at this hour anyway? He was more than a little drunk, but even through the fog of alcohol he had enough wits about him to know that it was most likely his parole officer with a spot check. Use of alcohol was prohibited as part of his parole, and he quickly ran into the bathroom, poured some Scope in his mouth, gargled, then swallowed. Looking in the mirror to make sure his eyes weren't too red (although he could always claim to be tired), Randy hurried to answer the door.

It was Frank.

He let out a huge sigh of relief, a sigh that turned into a belch. "Hey," he said.

"I need your help," Frank told him.

"Okay," Randy said warily. The fog was coming back in as adrenalin receded. He thought that it seemed awfully late to show up asking for a favor. "Help with what?"

"With a girl."

"A—"

"*Girl,*" Frank said. "A *little* girl."

Randy's brain was buzzing. Whatever this involved, it was definitely prohibited. He was not supposed to have any contact with minors. Any violation and he could be sent back inside, no questions asked. But he was well-oiled, and right now a little girl sounded really good, so he asked Frank exactly what he needed.

"Help," Frank repeated.

"Yeah, but, I mean, what do you want me to do?"

"Help me."

They were going around in circles, and Randy was starting to feel confused. "The girl..."

"She's in the back of the truck, under a tarp."

"The back of the truck?"

"I accidentally killed her."

That sobered him up. Randy started backing away, tried to close the door. "Nuh-uh, dude. I can't—"

"Can't what?" Frank's eyes bored into his. "I'll dump her out right here, call the cops and tell them you fucked her before you killed her. Is that what you want?"

Randy shook his head, frightened.

"Good. Then help me. We need to take her to the site and put her in the cement where no one'll find her. We'll pour a layer tonight, then add on tomorrow, and once the building's up, no one will ever be the wiser."

He accompanied Frank out to the pickup, where he lifted a section of tarp to take a peak. Underneath, the girl's body was broken, as though it had been folded in on itself. He had never seen anything like it and didn't even know how such a thing could have been done. What blood he saw was dried, although there seemed to be very little considering the damage. "Cover that up," Frank said harshly. "We have to get going. There's a lot to do before morning."

They reached the site ten minutes later, a half-house they were building that would connect to an existing shotgun shack and hopefully make the place saleable. Randy hadn't realized it until now, but Frank had left a section of the cement foundation unpoured, and within the open square of dirt was a deeper hole lined with pelts.

Pelts.

He'd obviously planned this ahead of time. Working by moonlight, they carried the girl's twisted body from the trunk to the hole (if Frank had gotten her *into* the truck by himself, Randy wondered, why was *he* needed to help get her *out*?). The concrete was already mixed and ready (when had Frank done *that*?), and they poured it over the girl, filling up the hole, then the entire frame, before smoothing it out.

Randy was completely sober by this time. Sober and scared. Despite what Frank had said, there was no way the concrete would be set by morning. It would be two days, at the least, before the cement would be dry enough to add another layer. What if some neighborhood kid came by in the meantime and poked a stick in there or something? What if the body was discovered?

Frank seemed to know what he was thinking. "It'll be fine," he said. "Let's go."

"I just—"

"It'll be fine."

And it was fine.

The cement dried. They put in posts and added another layer. They started on the walls and the wiring, and, as Frank had promised, no one was the wiser.

It happened again about a month later.

Another late night knock. Another child in the back of the truck. This one a boy. They were drywalling the half-house by this time, so the boy's body could not be buried in the floor.

Frank had plans, though.

He'd already rented a tar kettle, though they wouldn't be roofing for at least another week, and he'd heated up the tar. "We just throw him in," Frank said. "Let him simmer for a week or two. There'll be nothing left of him by then, and anything that *is* left will be gluing down shingles."

Randy had not asked any questions the first time, and he didn't this time either. They carried the kid—about four or five, staring blankly at nothing, dried rivulets of blood descending from both ears—out of the truck, tucked him into the tar kettle, closed the lid and let the body burn.

Who were these kids? Randy wondered. Why had Frank killed them? Randy didn't know, and he didn't want to know, but working for Frank was getting to be too heavy, and he needed to find a way out. If it were up to him, he'd just leave and relocate, go to another part of the state or another part of the country, even. But the terms of his parole decreed that he could not leave the area. And he doubted that his truck could get him more than sixty miles away without breaking down. And...

And he was afraid of Frank.

That was the main reason. It wasn't logical—would Frank really skip out on a paying job to hunt down an easily replaceable day laborer?—but it was how he felt. The man was *wrong*. Sure, Randy liked little girls. He even liked to be rough with little girls. But Frank was on a whole other level.

Frank was scary.

The third time Frank showed up at his trailer at night, the child with him was still alive. It was a girl and she was naked, and Randy liked that. But he knew what Frank was going to do to her, and the thought made him feel sick inside. He was in way over his head, and for the first time he considered trying to kill Frank. He could save the girl, be a big hero, tell the cops about the other two kids, and...

"What are you thinking?" Frank said softly. He looked as though he knew *exactly* what Randy was thinking.

Taking a deep breath, Randy tried to smile. "I'm thinking about how cute she is."

"*Was*," Frank said, and twisted her neck. There was an audible *crack!* and then the gagged child in his hands went limp. "You can do what you want with her, then we'll plaster her up in my basement."

"I can't do *anything* with her," Randy responded. "She's dead."

Frank shrugged. "We'll put her away, then."

He didn't want to. He didn't want to have anything to do with this. But he had no choice.

They were partners.

Frank had made sure of that.

Over the next several months, they "put away" three more little kids, incorporating one into the wall of a house they were remodeling, coating the other two with plaster and putting them in Frank's basement, where they stood with two others like statues against the wall. Part of him wanted to get caught and put an end to it all. But another, scarier part, was actually beginning to enjoy the process. The missing children were all over the newspapers and the television. The last one had even made the national news, an example of a large and frightening pattern in contemporary America. He was astonished that it seemed so easy to get away with such heinous acts when he had been caught so quickly for his own earlier transgressions, but obviously Frank knew something he didn't. Maybe it was the relatively straightforward simplicity of it all, the hide-in-plain-sight aspect of Frank's deeds that kept them from being caught.

Did he still *want* to be caught?

Randy wasn't sure.

But he continued to feel uneasy around Frank, and if the contractor happened to die in a construction accident or a car crash, Randy certainly wouldn't shed any tears.

He was deep asleep, dreaming his usual dream, a nightmare of his mother beating him with his own baseball bat, when he was awakened by a crazed pounding on the outer wall of his trailer. The noise traveled, as though someone was running around the trailer and pounding on it as he did so. "Asshole," Randy muttered. He got out of bed and, still in his underwear, hurried out to the living room, grabbing the ax he kept for just such occasions. He swung open the door, ready to run off whoever was out there.

A sharp and terrible pain hit his stomach at the same time he heard the familiar piston-like click of a nail gun. He looked down to see a long framing nail protruding from his midsection, blood welling around it, soaking his t-shirt and dripping over his boxers. Another click, another horrible stab of pain, and a nail was sticking out of his right thigh.

Those first two had been intentionally staggered, their shooting deliberately paced, but the nails came at him fast and furiously now, hitting his legs, his arms, his chest. *ClickClickClickClickClick*. He screamed in agony, dropped the ax, tried to go back inside, but as he turned, nails embedded themselves in his side, in his back, in his buttocks.

ClickClickClickClickClick...

He stumbled, falling forward, against the wall next to the door.

"Sorry," he heard a man say beneath his screams, and the man's voice was Frank's.

Then Frank was in front of him, holding the nail gun. "I'm almost done here in Denver, and I'm afraid I can't trust you to—"

"You can trust me!" Randy yelled through the pain. "You can trust me!"

Frank leaned forward, smiling. "But I need you for attic insulation."

And he pressed the flat metal of the gun against Randy's forehead and shot a nail into his brain.

FIVE

AMARILLO, TEXAS 1999

COOPER MICHAELSON HAD never seen anything like this.

He'd been a fire inspector in Amarillo for the past half-decade, in Galveston for eighteen years before that. But nothing had prepared him for the house on Calvin Street.

It was a code enforcement officer, signing off on a newly built patio across the street, who had noticed the state of the house and had called it in. Cooper had already been scheduled to inspect carbon monoxide and smoke detectors at a nearby nursing home, so he was drafted for this assignment as well.

Even pulling up out front, he knew why the code enforcement officer had called, and he was surprised that none of the neighbors had lodged a complaint. For the low slung brown house had a wood shake roof that was completely covered with a layer of dry sycamore leaves, and a front yard consisting of dead grass grown waist-high.

The outside was a mess, but it was the interior of the home that was so shocking. Inside was a pack rat's dream—or nightmare. Scraps of wood, lengths of pipe and other construction site castoffs were nailed, screwed, soldered, welded or otherwise affixed to windowsills, doorways, and the beams that were exposed through holes torn in the walls and ceiling. Tables, chairs and couches were piled high with newspapers and magazines. The floors were littered with garbage, and there were bones amongst the debris—including several that appeared to be human. In the kitchen, in cloudy water within a glass pickle jar, floated a small severed penis.

He had been let in by an old man who looked more like an old woman, a bent-over figure with long hair, long fingernails, and delicate facial features beneath deep intersecting wrinkles. As Cooper stepped in, the old man stepped out and from that point disappeared. Where did he go? There was no car in the driveway. Did he just walk away, or did he scurry to some hiding place? Was he afraid he would be arrested? Cooper didn't know, but the old man had not given him a name, and he wondered now if the guy was a squatter rather than the owner.

Immediately after entering the house and seeing that appalling interior, he first phoned his supervisor to lay out the situation, then called the police. The rubbish and wreckage were too overwhelming for him to be able to conduct anything close to an orderly inspection, but he went through the rooms while waiting for the police to arrive. The smell within the house was powerful but not nearly as unpleasant as it should have been, competing odors of rot and decomposition combining into a single immersive stench that, like some landfills, was vaguely redolent of mint. This was when he found the bones, and the penis in the jar, though it would take another full week before everything in the house could be sorted out and those looking through the debris would discover the desiccated remains of a long dead woman shoved into the back of a closet stuffed with bags of rags and paper napkins.

Police easily found the creepy old man who'd been living in the house, but Cooper's instincts had been right: he was a squatter. It turned out that the owner of record, a Chilton Teager, had been dead for over a decade.

His wife was the desiccated corpse at the rear of the closet.

Eventually, crews were called in to clean out the house and haul everything away. Over the next several months, the house itself was auctioned off, and the new owner had it repainted, remodeled and the yard landscaped before putting it up for sale.

Cooper continued along as he always had, inspecting buildings throughout the city.

But the pack rat house haunted him.

He found himself driving past it whenever he was in that part of town. Sometimes he would even go out of his way to go down Calvin Street, just to see it. The place might be all cleaned up now, but he still remembered the way it looked when he'd been called in. He even had dreams of wandering endlessly through those narrow maze-like passageways winding between the piled boxes and bags. In some of those dreams, he ended up in rooms piled high with body parts. In others, he wound up in a black empty space with no walls, no ceiling, no floor, only the sense that he was not alone, that *something* sat in the darkness with him.

It felt wrong taking such an interest in the house on Calvin Street, though he couldn't put his finger on exactly why. He did notice that he'd started to accumulate extraneous items in his own home. Not to the extent that there was a fire hazard—his house would still pass any objective inspection—but though it could never have been said about him before, such an eventuality was now definitely within the realm of possibility. He had a stack of magazines piled on top of his coffee table that he'd picked up for a quarter at the tail end of a library book sale, and a broken VCR on the kitchen counter that he'd taken from the station before it was thrown out. It was comforting to have things in his house that only he appreciated, and though Cooper knew he should be worried by that attitude, he was not. If Amy were still with him, things might have been different, but they'd divorced over six years ago, and now he was all alone.

And haunted by the pack rat house.

Haunted.

It was his friend Lewis, one of the city's building inspectors, who first told him about the ghosts.

"There have been sightings of the dead," Lewis told him.

Sightings of the dead.

It was, as much as anything else, the stilted formality of his friend's statement that made Cooper take it seriously. That and his own unexplainable obsession with the house on Calvin Street.

Something was happening in Amarillo, something that couldn't be explained in ordinary terms. He'd always been a rational man, a practical man. He was neither superstitious nor religious, but he was not closed-minded, either. And when he encountered things he did not understand, he was willing to admit it. He knew he'd been acting strangely since entering that house, and he sensed that his behavior was being influenced by something outside of his control.

Either that or he was going crazy.

But if he was going crazy, everyone else was, too. For Lewis was not the only one talking about ghosts. Cooper heard it from another firefighter as well. All over the city, it seemed, people were seeing spirits—

sightings of the dead

—and they weren't all flakes and weirdoes. An accountant, a cop, a married couple, a mechanic, an entire family had all admitted to supernatural encounters. These weren't people looking for publicity, and ordinarily, most of them wouldn't have confessed to anything as potentially embarrassing as glimpsing a ghost, but what they'd encountered had frightened them so thoroughly that they were willing to risk public humiliation in an effort to find out what they'd really witnessed.

Cooper slightly knew the cop, a patrolman named Terry Hutchings, and he made a special effort to talk to the man when he saw him one day at city hall. He waited until they'd both finished their business inside, then caught up with him on the lawn on the way to the parking lot.

"Terry!" he called.

The policeman turned around. "Cooper. Hey."

He wasn't sure how to ask what he wanted to ask, so he just blurted it out. "I have a question about the ghost."

Terry's face hardened, and he turned away, walking purposefully toward his patrol car.

"Wait! I'm not making fun of you. I saw something, too," he lied.

Terry stopped, turned toward him. "What? What did you see?"

It was a challenge, not a question, but Cooper had an answer ready, and he described in detail the pack rat house. Even if he hadn't actually seen anything supernatural, the feeling was the same, and what he'd encountered in that house had affected him the way the ghost had affected the policeman. He knew that close wasn't good enough, though, not with Terry, so he threw in a wavy black shape that he claimed to have seen moving around the edges of the room with the penis jar.

The policeman relaxed considerably. "We're not the only ones, you know," he confided. "A lot of other people have seen things."

"What did *you* see?" Cooper asked.

They continued their walk toward the parking lot, albeit more slowly. "Shadows," Terry said, and his tone of voice made the hairs prickle on the back of Cooper's neck. "I saw shadows."

Cooper said nothing, giving him space.

The policeman inhaled deeply before he spoke. "It was in that old Yellow Front building past the corp yard. The one they're tearing down now for The Store. It's been empty for a long time, but some lady reported seeing teenagers breaking in. So I went over to check it out." There was a brief pause. "The shadows were in there."

He didn't seem inclined to say more, so Cooper pushed him. "What happened?"

Another deep breath. "Oh, kids had been in there. Probably over a period of years. There were broken bottles, junk food wrappers, used condoms, graffiti on the walls. The usual. I was shining my light around and there, out of the corner of my eye, I saw something move. I thought it was an animal at first, a cat or a dog, but my light couldn't find it. Then I saw the shadow of a man...or a woman. Something with wild hair. It was dancing in the circle of my light, but there was no...there was nothing there that could *make* a shadow. I was shining my light against the wall, and there was *nothing* between me and the wall—but the shadow was there, dancing." Terry licked his lips. "Then there were more shadows. A small person with a big head. That cat thing I thought I'd seen. A skinny stick figure." He shivered. "I ran away. I'm not proud of it, but there it is. Those shadows scared the *shit* out of me, and I haven't stopped thinking of them since." He nodded toward Cooper, acknowledging the kinship of their experiences. "You know what I mean."

Cooper thought of the narrow aisles winding through the debris in the house on Calvin Street. The bones. The penis. "Yeah," he said honestly. "I do."

They'd reached the parking lot. There seemed little more to say, so Cooper bade the policeman goodbye, and the two of them walked separately to their cars.

The rest of the workday was normal, and he managed to drive home without swinging down Calvin Street, which he counted as a victory. Once inside his own house, he flipped on the TV, switching it to CNN, then grabbed a beer and a bag of Doritos from the kitchen. Settling on his couch, he checked his phone for messages.

There was a voicemail from Amy.

Cooper hadn't talked to his ex-wife since the divorce, and it was weird hearing her voice now. He recognized it, but just barely, and he wondered if her voice had changed or if he'd just forgotten what she sounded like.

"*Coo?*" she said (she was the only one who'd ever called him "Coo"). "*Can you hear me? Can you hear me, Coo? Coo?*"

And that was the extent of the message.

How had she gotten his phone number? he wondered. It was unlisted, and not only did he live in another city now, but he'd moved several times since they'd last had contact. He didn't know her number, either, but it apparently wasn't blocked and so was displayed on his list of incoming calls. He listened to the message again, unsure of why she'd called him, unsure if she wanted him to call her back.

Did he *want* to call her back?

Not really.

He put the phone down, finished his bottle of beer. Their breakup had been hard, and it had been final. He'd never been one of those modern liberal people who stayed on good terms with his exes and remained friends. As far as Cooper was concerned, once it was over it was over, and he could not remember the last time he'd even thought about Amy.

Besides, it was his fault the marriage had ended.

Because he hadn't been able to get over the rape.

It had happened in the parking structure of the office building where she'd worked, and the assault had been hard on both of them. He'd understood her feelings after the attack because they were the same emotions he was experiencing: rage, hate, hurt. And he'd been there for her, supported her. He hadn't insisted on intimacy, was willing to let that aspect of their relationship come back whenever it did, whenever she felt comfortable. He'd held her hand and hugged her when she needed reassurance, backed away when he knew she needed space.

Then he'd found out that she'd had an orgasm.

He wasn't sure why he'd asked about that and didn't know why she'd answered, but she'd admitted that she'd come when the man had been inside her. It was a purely physical response, she insisted. She hadn't *wanted* it to happen; it was something that had been horrifically forced upon her and had occurred completely against her will. But, still, the fact remained that sometimes when Cooper was in bed with her, she *wasn't* able to have an orgasm, even though she *did* want to, even though she was *trying* to, and the idea that the rapist had made her climax was something he had not been able to get past. It had led to arguments, led to tears, led to accusations and recriminations, led to the end.

He thought after all these years that he'd put all of that behind him, but hearing her voice again, it all came back.

But *was* it her voice?

There still seemed something different about it, though he did not know what exactly had changed. It was probably just a fault of memory due to the years that had gone by, but he replayed the message again and the discrepancy between how her voice sounded and what he *thought* it should sound like nagged at him.

That seed of doubt was why Cooper called back the displayed number. He couldn't believe he was so nervous, but his palms grew sweaty as he listened to the phone ring, and he thought he might hang up once she answered. But she didn't answer. The ringing was interrupted by three discordant tones, and the recorded voice of a robotic woman informed him that the number he'd dialed was no longer in service.

He tried again, just in case he'd pressed a wrong digit, but the result was the same. *Just as well,* he thought. He wasn't sure what he would have said to her anyway. Putting the phone down, he reached for a Dorito. The phone rang again, and he picked it up. "Hello?"

"*Coo?*"

It was the same voice. *Her* voice, he knew, though it still sounded different.

"*Can you hear me?*"

It was the same message as before, and from the same number.

"Amy?" he said.

"*Why am I back?*" she asked. "*How did I come back?*"

A chill raced down his spine. No. It couldn't be.

"*Can you hear me, Coo?*"

She was dead.

She was calling him from beyond the grave.

He switched off the phone, throwing it away from him on the couch as though it was contaminated with a plague virus. He didn't want to believe it, but he knew it was true, and he was more scared than he'd ever been in his life.

What if she didn't just try to call him but tried to visit him?

There have been sightings of the dead.

He checked to make sure the door was locked and the windows were closed, but beyond that, he didn't know what to do. Should he call Lewis? His friend had been the one to tell him about the rash of ghosts that had been seen around the city and might have some ideas about what he should do, but Cooper was afraid to use the phone in case he heard *her* voice when he tried to call.

He finished off the Doritos and dropped the bag on the floor where it joined a growing pile of cans, bottles and wrappers that had been accumulating over the past several days. He turned up the television to mask the sound of anything that might be trying to get into the house, even though he was pretty sure that ghosts could not be kept out by physical barriers like walls, windows or doors.

Ghosts.

It was amazing how quickly his worldview had adjusted to include a supernatural world that until recently he'd been certain did not exist.

Keeping the channel on CNN, comforted by factual accounts of the events of the day—a murder, an earthquake, weather, a presidential veto—he turned on all of the lights in the house and made himself a quick sandwich before plopping himself back on the couch for the rest of the evening.

He went to sleep early.

And dreamed of a maze of piled boxes in a dark dirty house. At the end of the maze was a filthy bed. Next to the bed, the wild-haired squatter from the Calvin Street house was pulling up his pants. On the bed, naked and spread-eagled was Amy. "I *came*," she moaned. "I *came*."

The next morning, after checking in at the station, he headed out to a junior high school for a scheduled annual inspection. It was summer, so the school was empty. A janitor unlocked the gate and let him into the rooms, and he dutifully checked the pressure of the fire extinguishers and determined whether the smoke detectors were functional. Everything went smoothly, as expected.

Until it didn't.

He was in one of the locker rooms, opening the "In Case of Emergency Break Glass" cabinet to check the status of the folded hose. The janitor had left to attend to his own duties in another part of the school, having unlocked both the boys' and girls' locker rooms, the PE offices, and the gym so that Cooper could continue with his inspection. There was no one in the locker room but him.

So who was laughing?

He stopped what he was doing, stood still and listened. The long room was dark, the aisles between the rows of lockers lit only by the muted illumination seeping down from a series of clouded skylights, the showers at the rear of the space shrouded in a gloom that might as well have been night.

And from somewhere undetermined came the disturbing sound of cracked laughter.

Gooseflesh covered his body. Moving slowly and quietly, as though afraid of being discovered, he closed and locked the door of the glass cabinet without even bothering to look at the hose. All he wanted to do was get out of there.

The noise seemed to be coming from one of the shower stalls, but sound echoed in this empty space so it was impossible to determine its actual origin. Just to be on the safe side, he decided to exit through the gym, in the opposite direction of the showers. Accompanying the laughter, beneath and between it, he could now hear another noise, fainter, higher. It was almost a creak, and something in its timbre grated on him.

Cooper grabbed his materials and, as softly as he could, padded out of the locker room into the gym.

Where he saw a shriveled figure in a wheelchair facing him from center court.

He stopped where he was. The laughter hadn't been coming from one of the shower stalls. As impossible as it seemed, this was the origin of the sound, and in the openness of the gym, the laughter was loud and frantic, tinged with madness. Even in the dim light, he could see that the withered figure in the chair was an elderly woman, and with a squeak of long-unused wheels, she began pushing herself in his direction. Her arms moved faster, and faster, and faster until she looked like a bird flapping its wings, the wheelchair gaining speed, until the crone was *racing* toward him, cackling insanely. One eye was bigger than the other, he saw now, and her off-center mouth had many missing teeth.

He tried taking an officious attitude. "Excuse me," he said. "What are you doing here? This is—"

And then she was gone.

He didn't know how—had he blinked and missed it?—but something had happened, and she was suddenly nowhere to be seen. The gym was dark, silent and empty, and he hurried out, through with the school. Quickly tracking down the janitor, Cooper told him he was done with the inspection, then retreated to his car in the parking lot, where, for the first time in his life, he falsified the results of an inspection.

But that was not his only odd encounter.

In the restroom of a crowded bar where he'd been sent to assess the maximum number of occupants, he was frightened by the silent presence of someone—

something?

—in one of the stalls. He'd only gone in to wash his hands, but he'd instantly known that the second stall was occupied. The metal door was closed, although that was not the reason for his certainty. It was a sense of *presence* that emanated from behind the door. There was no noise at all in the restroom. It was as if he'd entered some type of soundproof cubicle. Chilled, he decided that his hands didn't need to be washed that badly—he had Purell in the car—but before he turned to go, he ducked down and took a quick peek under the stall door. In the space between the dirty floor and the bottom of the metal, he saw black dress shoes, gray pant legs—and caught a split-second glimpse of a wrinkled ankle that appeared to be made of dried wood.

He hurried out of the restroom, out of the bar and drove away from the area as quickly as possible.

Later in the week, he ran into Terry outside city hall. The policeman looked pale and gaunt—

haunted

—and he wasn't in the mood to talk. He barely acknowledged Cooper's greeting and quickly hurried away to avoid any interaction.

The shadow stretching out behind him was not his own.

For some reason Cooper could not put his finger on, he was convinced that all of these incidents were connected to the pack rat house on Calvin Street. He became increasingly sure in his mind that if the house had been left as is, none of this would be going on. There was absolutely no reason to think such a thing: he had no proof to back it up, not even anything that amounted to a coherent theory. But Cooper began to believe that all of the mess, all of the clutter—the newspapers and bones, the pipes and boards, even the jar with the penis—had acted as a type of counterbalance to ward off the intrusion of the dead.

It was why he had started to work on his own house.

In truth, he had already started, if completely unintentionally. But it was now a conscious decision to pack his house with as many diverse items as he could, to build up a fortress of protection between himself and the spirit world. While he was not a timid man, the supernatural occurrences he'd heard about from others and encountered himself terrified him like nothing else ever had. He was constantly on edge now, waiting for the moment when something utterly horrifying and completely unknown would casually reveal itself to him.

On his days off, on his lunch hours, he scoured junkyards, garage sales, thrift shops, even the dump, looking for items that caught his eye and that would help him fill up the house. By the end of the month, the living room was almost impossible to navigate, with narrow pathways leading from the door to the couch to the kitchen, and his bedroom was piled high with clothes, towels and bedding, both his own and those he'd been buying in bulk from Goodwill and the Salvation Army.

He never answered the phone, just let it go into voicemail, because Amy kept calling.

Dead Amy.

"*Can you hear me, Coo?*"

He did keep going to work, however, hanging out at the station, maintaining his normal life. He was determined to keep adding to his defenses without succumbing to obsession like the people on Calvin Street had. He just wanted to reverse what he feared he had set in motion by his inspection of the pack rat house.

Another week went by, and it actually seemed as though his plan might be working. He encountered nothing out of the ordinary during his daily routine, nothing *supernatural*, and he thought perhaps that he'd been successful in rebuilding the wall that he had helped tear down. He was reflecting on that as he lay in bed, wondering when he could quit collecting and storing. This couldn't be an endless proposition. He had only so much room in his home, and at some point, he had to stop.

A soft sigh sounded from the corner of the room.

The hair on his arms bristled. The bedroom was dim, a large pile of linens partially blocking the floor lamp that provided his only source of light. The sigh came again, and though he could see nothing, he sensed movement, as though something was moving from the corner into the center of the room, toward the bed.

Cooper had no idea whether any of this was real, but he quickly decided that the best course of action would be to get out of the bedroom. Better safe than sorry. He threw off the covers and took a single step down the narrow pathway toward the door—

Before it was blocked.

He stopped in his tracks, staring at the thing before him. It was made of dirty laundry, a shuffling shambling figure three feet high, moving blindly through the room. There was a noise coming from deep within the pile of filthy clothing, that soft sigh again, and something about the sound chilled him far more than any piercing shriek could have.

It was then that he saw the shadows.

They were shapes that were almost, but not quite, recognizable, and they danced on the walls against a wavering light as though they were the silhouettes of creatures cavorting around a fire. Only there was no flickering fire, just the standing lamp. And there were no creatures. In fact there was nothing in the room that corresponded even remotely to the shapes on the walls, and Cooper thought of what Terry had told him.

The small linen figure had turned in his direction, as though sensing his presence, and was shambling toward him, changing as it did so, sloughing off a dirty handkerchief that floated to the floor, adding a sock that attached itself to the pile as though it were made of Velcro.

There was power in this room. He could feel it, and he knew that there were other entities here he could not see. He'd been wrong, he realized. The house on Calvin Street had not served to ward off the dead.

It had contained them.

Now they were being contained in *his* house.

He needed to get out of here. His mind raced. He'd spend tonight in a motel, and tomorrow he'd throw out all of the crap he'd been collecting, clean house. He had a sneaking suspicion that it was the dismantling of the accumulated debris at the Calvin Street home that had unlocked and unleashed these spirits onto the community, and perhaps that would happen again when he threw out all of the collected garbage from his own house, but that was someone else's concern. He needed to purge his own residence before—

There was a sharp stabbing pain in his leg.

Crying out, Cooper looked down to see what appeared to be a snake wrapped in a rose-colored sheet. It was attached to his ankle. Those were teeth he was feeling, and he kicked at the sheet only to see it crumple and collapse. There *was* no snake, nothing within the sheet but air, though his calf was bleeding profusely from a deep bite.

All around him, there was movement, shadows dancing on the walls and ceiling, mounds of cloth and bedding creeping over the floor. Wincing in pain, the blood streaming down his leg, Cooper hobbled toward the door.

But the door closed before he reached it, and at the same time the light went out. No illumination shone from outside because the windows were blocked by piles of blankets. He was enveloped in softness as supple pillowcases and silky sheets and downy bedspreads wound themselves around him in the dark, sliding up his legs, dripping on him from above. He was held gently in place, and for the first few seconds the sensation was comforting.

Then a towel wrapped itself around his head and what felt like cloth fingers pushed themselves against his nose and into his mouth. He was unable to breathe, but he was also unable to fight back, and as the pain in his constricted throat and lungs grew greater than the pain in his leg, he thought he heard Amy's voice, filtered through fabric.

"*Can you hear me?*"

"*Can you hear me, Coo?*"

"*Coo?*"

SIX

AUSTIN, TEXAS 2003

THE WORLD HAD changed. And Alex wasn't sure when it had happened. He'd been in the army for four years (stationed in Germany, thank God), and he'd kept abreast of everything going on, knew the music and the movies, certainly knew the politics, but when he got out and decided to resume the life he'd lived before enlisting, he found that that life was gone. A new generation had come up, with new interests and new definitions of hip, and his former peers had disappeared from the landscape, seamlessly blending into mainstream society, vanishing into families and careers.

Wanting to get back into practice, he thought he'd check out a few poetry slams, jump in and throw it down—

(A dirty dong
Dingle dangling
Feed it to your sister! Feed it to your mom!)

—only there were no poetry slams anymore. People didn't seem to do that these days, and he wondered when that change had occurred. People weren't even buying CDs much, he discovered, not the way they still did in Germany. Instead, they were downloading their music off the Internet. He felt lost in this new world, out of place, out of time. Everything he knew and loved seemed to have faded away. He found that he missed Germany, and if there hadn't been a good chance that he'd be sent to Iraq or Afghanistan, he would have up and re-enlisted yesterday.

As it was, he needed to find a job, and while soldiers were always being portrayed as heroes, their virtues constantly extolled in the media and by politicians, here on the ground it was damn near impossible for a vet to find work. He finally ended up at a temp agency—a Kelley girl!—working a week here, a day there, mostly for minimum wage.

It was at one of those jobs, a two-day stint as a carpet cleaner, that he first found evidence of The Conspiracy.

He was on his break, smoking outside in the patio of the office building where he'd been assigned. Two other men were on their breaks as well, drinking coffee at a table, and one of them was talking about the body of a strange white-skinned creature that had been discovered behind the wall of an old house that was being renovated on the south side of town. "They're keeping it quiet. Someone posted a picture, but it was taken down almost immediately, and all photos have since been destroyed or deleted."

"Enough with the *X-Files* crap. Every time you—"

"I told you before; this has nothing to do with aliens."

"But there's still a big government cover-up of mysterious events..."

"There's a cover-up all right, but I'm not sure it has anything to do with the government. I don't think the government even knows about it. In fact, I think these things are being covered up to keep them *from* the government. The government *and* the public. So there's no accountability."

"Who is it, then? An evil corporation?"

"Possibly. I don't know. All I know is, these things are happening. And that white creature was here in Austin, but it was hushed up, so you're never going to hear a word about it except from me. Keep your eyes and ears open, bud. Keep your eyes and ears open."

Alex remembered the conversation because it was so strange, but he didn't believe a word of it. There were a lot of wacky people out there now. He'd known some of them in the army: Art Bell listeners, conspiracy theorists, people who believed the government was behind the September 11 attacks, people who thought the president was some sort of Muslim Manchurian candidate. Such craziness was par for the course these days.

But...

As he traveled from temp job to temp job, he heard more. Whispers of things that shouldn't be, that couldn't be. Unrelated, all of them, but when taken together, they formed a sort of tapestry that seemed a little harder to discount.

Although he *still* wouldn't have believed any of it had he not come across an example of it himself.

He was working that week as a file clerk in the corporate office of a six-store chain of Texas supermarkets. It was an old school filing system—they actually had *files*. In *folders*.—and he was sorting through a batch of complaints while everyone else was at lunch. As a temp, he was allotted only a half-hour to eat as opposed to a full hour for actual employees, and since the office was empty, he took a moment to open the folder in his hand and glance at the complaint.

The referenced store was the original Austin branch, just down the street from where he lived, the place where he usually bought his groceries. Curious, Alex sorted through the papers in the folder. A sales clerk and a customer both claimed to have been attacked in the men's restroom by a skinny gorilla with the head of a dog. *A gorilla with the head of a dog?* How could such a thing get into the bathroom? How did it get out? Because there was no mention of it being seen by anyone other than the two victims, and no indication that law enforcement or animal control were notified. There must have been wounds sustained by the clerk and the customer, however, because there was a recommendation attached to the complaint that generous money should be offered for a settlement before either issue was pursued through legal channels.

From the front of the building, Alex heard the voices of workers returning early from lunch, and he quickly closed the folder and continued with his filing.

He was curious, and he stopped by the store on his way home, ostensibly to buy milk and orange juice, although the real reason was to see where this bizarre attack had occurred. Pretending he had to use the restroom, he asked a cashier how he could find the men's room. A strange look came over the girl's face, and she said nervously, "It's, uh, closed right now. I mean out of service. For repairs."

"Thanks anyway," he told her.

He wandered up the nearest aisle as though he were shopping for groceries. Supermarket restrooms were usually located near delivery entrances, adjacent to storage rooms or loading docks rather than in the central part of the store, so he made his way to the rear of the building. Spotting an unlit corridor next to the butcher's counter that headed back into an area not open to the public, Alex walked in a few steps and saw a door in the left wall with a mounted plaque that read *Women*, as well as a door next to it marked *Men*. Beneath the word *Men*, someone had used masking tape to affix a handwritten sign stating, "Closed for Repairs."

Alex tried the restroom door. It was not locked, surprisingly, and before anyone told him he could not go inside, he pushed open the door and entered.

Like most such facilities, the restroom was small: a sink, a urinal and a single enclosed stall. He didn't see how a gorilla-like animal could fit in here, let alone hide and jump out at a person, and he started to think that the two attacks were part of a scam—

Until he heard a low growl coming from the stall.

Before he could back up and exit, the creature had slammed open the stall door. It was an impossible animal—if it even *was* an animal. Yes, there were elements of German shepherd in the snout-like protrusion of its mouth, and the hairiness of its anthropoid form did resemble that of an ape. But even a quick glance revealed human components in its makeup, particularly its hands and eyes, and from the top of its head protruded a series of reptilian spikes.

Alex stumbled backward, pulling open the door and falling onto the floor of the corridor outside. He expected the beast to burst out and tear him apart, but the men's room door remained closed, and the only noises he heard were the sounds of rattling shopping carts and fragmented conversations from the aisles of the store. There were no growls coming from the bathroom, no sound at all.

He wanted to peek in there again, wanted to check, but he was afraid to do so and quickly hurried back out into the store.

Why wasn't there anything about this on the TV news or in the papers?

Because the company was paying out hush money.

The Conspiracy.

He sped out of the supermarket and back to his car, not realizing how frightened and rattled he truly was until he tried to put his key in the ignition. His hand was shaking so much it took him over a minute to get it in and get the car started.

He kept his ears and eyes open after that, even more than he had before, and in the margins of the workaday world he encountered a supply room in an insurance office that everyone in the company was afraid to enter; a photofinishing department in a chain drugstore that was closed because all of the photos it developed were of the same smiling old lady; a radio that played even when it was unplugged and its batteries removed; an air conditioning system that remained off because every time it was turned on the voices of dead people could be heard in whispered discussion through the vents.

He actually discussed the haunted air conditioning with another temp from the agency, an older retired man named Bud who was working part-time in order to supplement his Social Security income. Bud, too, had seen things he wasn't supposed to see, and, like the man at the office where he'd worked as a carpet cleaner, Bud firmly believed that there was a well-organized conspiracy to keep such things from the public. Alex found that he believed it, too, and the more places he worked, the more he encountered, the more he saw evidence of The Conspiracy.

He started asking questions casually, obliquely, surreptitiously, and word must have gotten back to someone because, at a wholesale nursery where he spent the day loading citrus trees onto landscapers' trucks, he was approached by a gardener who told him that a man named Frank Wheatley wanted to meet him to talk about some things he might have seen.

Alex had built up The Conspiracy in his mind until he was convinced it was made up of a cabal of the nation's most powerful men. So it came as something of a surprise when the gardener's directions led him not to some rich businessman but to a nondescript construction worker in striped overalls installing window boxes at a remodeled cottage. Unsure of how to approach the man, Alex stood on the lawn in front of the cottage, cleared his throat and said, "Excuse me, are you Frank Wheatley?"

The construction worker did not turn around. "I am."

"I'm Alex Kroeger?" (Why was saying that as though it were a question? He *was* Alex Kroeger.) "I was told you wanted to see me?"

The man finished tightening a screw before silently turning toward Alex and walking onto the lawn. The screwdriver he'd been using was held out in front of him almost like a weapon, and when he finally spoke there was an undercurrent of menace in his voice. "So what is it you think you know?"

"I'm not sure what you're talking about," Alex said, but he did.

"You've been *asking* about things, I hear."

"Like what?" Although his impulse was to run, he was determined to stand his ground.

The man—Frank—crooked his finger and bade Alex follow him into the cottage. With only a slight hesitation, he did so, walking through the front door into an empty living room.

Where the corpse of a Corgi was splayed, its furry limbs screwed into the wall.

Smiling, Frank used the screwdriver to gesture toward the dead animal's body.

A shadow passed over the room. Or sped around the room. There was a brief diminution of light, and Alex might have ascribed it to a cloud passing over the sun, but it happened too quickly and was accompanied by a localized sense of movement. Chills surfed down his arms. He had never been so frightened. Not because of a physical threat but because this—whatever it was—went so far beyond the merely physical. Maybe there was a Conspiracy and maybe there wasn't, but whatever was going on, this Frank was at the center of it.

"Leave," the man said, as though reading his thoughts. "And make sure you stay away from my business. I don't want to have to see you again."

Alex left as quickly as his legs would carry him. His knees felt weak, and his mouth was drier than it had ever been. He realized he'd been given a second chance, and he practically ran out to his car, locking the doors the second he got inside and speeding away down the street.

He was done with this, he decided. He was going back in the army.

Even if it was to Iraq or Afghanistan.

Because things there were a lot less dangerous.

SEVEN

From *The Arizona Republic:*

Body Parts Found in Abandoned House

Workmen made a gruesome discovery Wednesday at a condemned house in South Phoenix. The severed limbs of at least three individuals were found within the walls, floor and ceiling of the structure by a demolition team that had been hired by the city to tear down the house.

The body parts had been incorporated into the construction of the building, police reported, with legs and arms hammered into the frame of the house in place of boards, and peeled skin stretched over a hole in a shower stall...

From *The Fresno Bee:*

Rash of Pet Kidnappings in East Fresno

The sixth pet kidnapping in as many days has east Fresno residents up in arms. As reported previously, a rash of dog and cat abductions has targeted the residential neighborhood, with animals being stolen from fenced yards in broad daylight.

Although there have been no witnesses to any of the abductions, home security footage of the most recent dognapping—a pit bull named "Pit bull"—appears to show a bald man wearing overalls carrying the animal in his arms as he walks toward the street, according to Fresno police. The dog's owner, Oscar Hijo, 39, expressed surprise that someone was able to pick up his pet. "Pit bull's a fighter, and he don't like anyone but me," Hijo stated. "Someone must have drugged him."

Police are searching for a white male, medium height, medium build...

From *The Salt Lake City Gazette:*

Unlicensed Contractor Sought in Fraud Investigation

An unlicensed contractor accused of bilking senior citizens out of thousands of dollars is being sought for questioning by Salt Lake City police. According to a police department spokesman, Frank Wilkins has been named by eighteen elderly homeowners as the man who conned them into paying for home remodeling work that he never performed.

Wilkins, who is suspected of using an alias, allegedly provided free estimates for home improvements, convincing those residents planning to have work done to pay him half of the amount ahead of time with the balance due upon completion. Wilkins never showed up to perform the work.

"He gave me a receipt," said Ida Castle, 79. "I thought it was real."

The address Wilkins provided homeowners turned out to be that of an abandoned gas station, and police are currently looking for...

From *The Albuquerque Journal:*

Son Accused in Parents' Homicide Blames 'Ghost' for Murders

Francesco Covarrubias, 22, of Albuquerque, claimed in court Monday that the gruesome dismemberment of his parents last April was performed by a "ghost" that killed his mother and father while he was forced to watch.

In an attempt, prosecutors claim, to lay the groundwork for an insanity plea, the accused asserted that he was held in place by "invisible hands" while an unseen assailant used tools from the family's garage to torture, mutilate and murder his parents "before my eyes."

Covarrubias broke down crying in court and his lawyer asked for a recess while the accused murderer composed himself...

EIGHT

DOUC SONG PROVINCE, VIETNAM 1966

PFC TEX HENDERSON stood within the perimeter, looking out at the jungle, wondering if he was going to die today. He wondered the same thing *every* day, and it was not an idle worry. Fully half of the men who'd flown out with him six months ago were either dead, injured or MIA, and he was acutely aware of the fact that he could join them at any time. The training they'd received back in the States had in no way prepared them for this, and it was only through sheer dumb luck that he was still in one piece.

He remembered what the CO at the camp had said to him on his first day in country, after they'd drawn fire and a kid who'd flown over with him on the transport had fallen at his feet, a bullet in his head, his blood pumping into the mud. Tex had knelt to pray for the boy after the shooting stopped, but the CO had pulled him to his feet, saying: "Don't waste your time. There ain't no soul there to pray for. There's only alive and dead, and anyone who's ever killed a man'll tell you the same."

That was blasphemy as far as Tex was concerned. He'd been brought up Baptist, had always said his prayers and trusted completely in his Lord and Savior. His daddy had died when he was ten, and he and his momma had known ever since that the old man was up there in heaven, smiling down on them. He'd never questioned that or any other aspect of his faith until he'd come to Nam, and he'd been shocked when he'd been told not to pray for the boy.

But all these months later, he'd come to learn that the CO was right. He'd seen a lot of men die, and when they did, they just shut off. Their spirits didn't leave and go to a better place; they just stopped living, and that was the end of them, like machines that suddenly quit working.

There was only alive and dead.

From far off came the sound of gunfire, from farther off explosions.

He turned away from the jungle, looking back at the tents of camp.

Where's Frank? he wondered.

It was a question he'd had to ask a lot lately. The other private was seldom where he was supposed to be at the time he was supposed to be there, and if this had been stateside or anyplace other than Nam, Frank would probably have been court martialed by now. But they were so shorthanded that every man was needed, even the fuck-ups, and things were tolerated that ordinarily would not have been.

Tex looked at his watch. Frank was supposed to have relieved him from sentry duty forty-five minutes ago.

There was movement in the jungle before him, and he swung his weapon into position, heart in his throat, adrenaline coursing through his system.

This is where I die, he thought.

And then Frank emerged from the wall of green, running out from behind a leaf the shape and size of an elephant's ear.

Tex lowered his gun, exhaling. "What the fuck were you doing?" he demanded.

"I went out. It's no big deal."

"You can't go out! You have to stay within the perimeter! And what do you mean it's no big deal? It's a *huge* deal! Did you get permission? Were you on some sort of—"

Frank looked at him. "I went out on my own. Nobody knows but you."

That flat affectless stare made Tex shiver and took some of the intensity out of his tirade. "You could've been killed out there. *I* could've killed you."

Frank shrugged.

"You were also supposed to be on duty almost an hour ago."

"Thanks for covering for me."

"This is the last time!" Tex vowed before storming off.

But it probably wouldn't be the last time. And he suspected Frank knew it, too. Almost anyone else would have cut him loose long ago, but Frank was really his only link to home. Not only had they both gone through Basic together, but they were both from Texas, he from Amarillo, Frank from Plutarch. They had a lot in common.

Or they used to.

Tex trudged over to the mess for breakfast.

Mess.

It was an appropriate word since the slop they were given to eat could not be described, even on its best day, as food. He picked up a cup of coffee and a bowl of some sort of rice porridge, then sat down at a crowded lopsided table next to Jerome Powell, one of the five men who shared a bunk in his tent. "Where you been?" Powell asked. "Damn near done eating."

"Waiting for Frank." He took a sip of the bitter coffee.

Powell laughed. "Shit. No wonder."

Tex leaned in to keep the conversation private. "Thing is, he was out. I almost shot him when he came back in. Thought he was VC."

"What was he doing?"

"Hell if I know, but it almost got him killed."

"You ask me," Powell said, "the fucker's going native."

Tex had not considered that, but it was conceivable. It had happened once before, with Jed Balcomb, who'd deserted nearly a month ago, building a lean-to where he lived and a bamboo shrine where he worshipped, until he died in a firefight with the men who'd come to arrest him.

Tex could see Frank doing something like that.

He forced himself to take another bite of the disgusting porridge.

He needed to keep closer tabs on Frank, keep him tethered so he didn't go floating away on his own and do something stupid.

Powell leaned forward, lowered his voice. "Better get some sleep. I heard we're going out tonight. Recon."

Tex's heart was in his throat, and he felt as though he was going to throw up what little porridge he'd swallowed. "Us?"

"The team. So tell that asshole Frank he'd better straighten up and fly right."

Tex nodded, trying to ignore the butterflies in his stomach.

"I'm not going down because he fucks up. If it's a situation where it's him or me, it's gonna be him."

"Any idea where we're going?"

"Back to that last village, I heard. Guess it's not as innocent as we thought."

"That was a two-day march!"

"This is all thirdhand, nothing official. Maybe it's not true. We'll find out what's what at the meeting."

Downing the rest of his coffee, Powell left. Tex finished his own coffee, leaving the rest of the porridge. His hands were shaking. He hated recon. Something always went wrong, and he had a gut feeling that Powell's concerns were legit: with Frank along, the odds of ending up in a shitstorm were probably going to be far higher than they would be otherwise.

Knowing he'd need to catch some Zs if they were going out, he bussed his cup and bowl, then headed back to the tent. Hanging from a wire above his cot was his countdown calendar, and he looked at it before lying down. Three years, five months, two weeks and six days.

If he lasted that long.

The gunfire, which had calmed down sometime while he'd been at breakfast, had started up again, closer. His muscles tensed. He was officially off-duty, but that didn't mean shit out here. If the gunfire continued, he *would* be called.

Hoping to at least get a few minutes of sleep, he closed his eyes.

THE village looked different this time.

It was all perception, Tex knew, but the beleaguered buildings, ramshackle huts and fallen fences seemed ominous now rather than just sad, a false front meant to fool them into thinking it was merely a harmless backwater community rather than a VC refuge. Spying with binoculars from various vantage points, they maintained silence, communicating with each other using only their bastardized version of semaphore. He didn't know what exactly they were looking for—he doubted any of them did—but the sergeant told them that they'd know it when they saw it.

Powell saw it.

Tompkins noticed Powell's frantic gesturing first, and he stole around the edge of the village, gathering the rest of them until they were all assembled at Powell's position. "What'd you find?" the sergeant whispered.

Powell raised his binoculars. "First building on the left. That barn thing next to the corral or whatever the fuck it is. Old woman brought food over, and when the door opened the guy had VC pajamas. Not only that, but there're weapons in there. Couldn't see what, but the light was reflecting off a lot of black metal."

"What do we do?" Carrera asked. "Take 'em?"

The sergeant shook his head. "We don't know how many are in there or how many are nearby." He glanced over his shoulder at the jungle. "Could be an even bigger cache within a click in any direction."

"Call it in?" Tex asked.

The sergeant nodded. "But we pull back first. Get to a safe vantage point. A *defensible* vantage point."

Stealthily, they retreated. The land here was flat, so Tex wasn't sure what sort of vantage point they were supposed to find, but the sergeant obviously knew the region better than he did, because they were soon on a hill overlooking the section of jungle they'd just passed through and the small village beyond. Frank had the radio, and he called in the strike coordinates.

They waited.

And waited.

The bombers weren't close, but they weren't far, and Tex was beginning to worry that the message hadn't gotten through. There'd been no confirmation, as per regulation, so it was impossible to tell whether or not—

There they were.

The team heard the planes before they saw them—and the villagers did, too. There was a sudden scrambling as men and women, many of them holding onto children, dashed in different directions, trying to lose themselves in the jungle and get as far away from their homes as possible. The VC came running not just out of the first building but nearly every building, carrying weapons. Two of them attempted to set up an anti-aircraft gun. Carrera, their designated sniper, took both men out. Thrown into panic, the VC began firing indiscriminately into the air, into the trees, and Carrera calmly took aim and managed to hit two others, killing one and sending the other crawling off into the underbrush using the single arm he had left.

After all that, the bombers missed.

Instead of hitting the buildings, bombs were dropped on the cemetery and an uninhabited area just south of the village. From their vantage point, they could see everything, the rush of villagers and VC in the opposite direction, the utter destruction of the cemetery and a wide swath of jungle. Before smoke and dust obscured the scene, Tex saw through his binoculars how bodies—or pieces of bodies—flew out from graves once they were hit. They were everywhere: hands, arms, feet, heads. A lot of the corpses were new, because of the war, and blood the consistency of poached egg yolk rained down from the sky.

Frank was trying to contact a pilot to let him know that the village was still standing, but the radio was unable to get through, and suddenly, with a tip of the wing, the lead bomber was gone, the other two following.

"Disaster!" the sergeant was fuming. "Fucking disaster!" He twirled his arm, motioning for them to gather everything up. "We're going down there," he ordered. "Clean 'em out. Move!"

The villagers and VC had fled to the north, so the team moved quickly in single file around the side of the hill, intending to approach the village from the south. This was exactly the sort of thing Tex had been afraid was going to happen, and he was filled with panic. He felt as though he had to take a shit but held it in as they followed the sergeant through the jungle, wishing he had written to his mom before leaving camp, wondering if his previous letter to her would be his last. How would she find out about his death? he wondered. Would she get a letter, a telegram or a phone call? Or would they dispatch someone to inform her in person? What about his body? Would someone come back for it or would they just leave him out here? If they did try to retrieve his body, how would anyone from camp be able to find him?

And then they were there.

Weapons drawn, they stood within the green perimeter, hiding behind oversized leaves, trees and bushes near the bombed-out cemetery. The VC fighters were the first ones back in. No one had kept track of their numbers, so the team waited in position for nearly two hours, until sure that most or all of the fighters had returned, before cutting them down in the road.

The women of the village were wailing, running out to the bloody bodies heedless of potential gunfire. The team waited in place for what seemed like forever just in case more fighters emerged, and when none of them did, the sergeant sent Powell and Carrera out to canvas the village. They knew they were targets, there to draw fire, but they went in regulation style, covering each other, both covered by the men who remained in the brush, and when neither of them were fired upon, they knew it was over.

The rest of them broke cover.

Frank kicked aside a glop of bloody flesh at his feet, a fragment of the recent dead blown out of the cemetery ground. "Where do they go now?" he asked. There was curiosity in his voice and also a sense of wonder.

Tex frowned. "Who?"

"The dead. Where do they go now?"

"To hell," Tompkins said with a laugh.

"They're dead," Tex said. "They're not going anywhere." He motioned toward an isolated hand on the ground in front of them. "Especially not now."

"This was their home," Frank said, looking toward what had been the graveyard. "Now they have no home."

"They're dead," Tex repeated. "Jesus, Frank, get ahold of yourself."

But he seemed distracted by the blasted graves, and while the rest of them moved through the village, Frank wandered about on his own.

They took as many weapons as they could carry from the barn-like VC hideout, torching the building when they were through, scattering villagers in front of them and escaping into the jungle as the explosions rocketed behind them.

"Good mission," the sergeant kept repeating. "Good mission. Good mission."

It was on the way back to camp that they were ambushed.

They were completely unprepared. Although they were walking with their weapons drawn, as always, they weren't on alert. They'd come through here on the way over, and there'd been no sign of anyone in the area, VC or otherwise. It must have been escapees from the village, because less than two clicks out, they were fired upon. Powell was hit and instantly down, but the rest of them were miraculously spared in that first burst and immediately crouched into firing position, back-to-back, facing outward and firing round after round in every direction. Within seconds, all return fire had stopped, and by the time they stopped shooting more than a minute later, the only sound was a man screaming in agony from the jungle off to the left. Without saying a word, without even looking at each other, they turned as one and fired in the direction of the screams, tearing apart leaves and bark and everything in their way. When they stopped again, the jungle was silent.

A bullet had grazed the sergeant's chin, and Tompkins had been hit in the right shoulder, but they'd gotten off impossibly light. Powell was the only casualty, and when Tex looked down, he saw that his friend's body had been shot to pieces. Chunks of this morning's breakfast rations floated on top of a puddle of blood in his midsection where the contents of his stomach had been blown out.

Lurching to the edge of the path, Tex threw up.

"Alright, ladies!" the sergeant announced. "Let's pick him up and keep moving!"

"But it's—" Carrera began.

"Pick. Him. Up. And keep moving."

They nodded. They had no body bag with them, but Tompkins took the tarp out of Powell's pack, and they wrapped him in it, tying it up. Tompkins and Carrera used ropes to carry Powell's bound body between them. It was awkward and heavy, the terrain was tough, and they had to keep switching off with the rest of the team until, sixteen hours later, completely exhausted, they staggered back into camp.

A week later, Tex was on sentry duty, waiting to be relieved by Armando Serra, the one man in camp he truly hated, when he heard Frank call his name. He turned to look behind him, but there was no sign of the man. Swiveling back around, he saw Frank emerging from the jungle.

"What the fuck?" Tex demanded. "I told you—"

"I need you to come with me," Frank said, walking up to him.

"No way. Nuh-uh. I'm not getting busted for something that stupid."

"Powell wants to see you."

Tex just stared at him.

"Come on. Come with me."

Armando was suddenly there on his left, and, startled, Tex jumped at the sight of him. Armando laughed disdainfully. "Pussy." He nodded. "Hey, Frank."

Officially relieved of sentry duty, Tex hoisted his gun over his shoulder and, without a word, started back toward his tent. Frank followed close behind, speaking lowly. "Powell wants—"

"Powell's dead!" Tex shouted, too loudly. "Jesus, Frank!"

"I have his body."

Tex stopped walking, staring at him. "What do you mean you have his body?"

"I kept it. What was left of it." There was a pause. "His head."

"Holy shit! You could be court-martialed for this!"

"I can talk to him, Tex. And he talks back."

Everything stopped. Whatever he had been about to say fled his brain and never made it anywhere near his lips. He was suddenly aware of the heat of the day, the humidity of the jungle, the low drone of the soldiers in camp doing what they did.

Frank's gone crazy.

That one thought superseded all else, and his brain raced, trying to calculate when eccentricity had escalated into madness, and wondering what he should do about it, who he should inform. He liked Frank, and he owed the man something, but this...*body snatching* was beyond the pale, and if Frank really believed that he could talk to Powell's ghost, he was a danger to himself and others and needed to be stopped.

"Powell said he was right, he went first, and you owe him a hundred dollars."

Tex blinked. "What?"

"Powell says you owe him a hundred dollars."

There was no way Frank could know that. It was a joke between the two of them, a bet as to who would die first, and it had been said as they were gathering their gear together for the trip to the village. They'd been completely alone in the tent, and Frank and the rest of the team had been eating in the mess. There was no way Frank could have heard them. No way *anyone* could have heard them.

So how...?

"Powell wants to see you," Frank said again.

Tex looked at the other private more carefully. He noticed, for the first time, that Frank seemed to be quite a bit older than the other soldiers, even most of the enlisted men. Since Basic, he'd thought of Frank as a peer, but he looked more like a parent, and he wondered how he could have not picked up on that before.

"Powell's dead," Tex rebutted him again, but there was no shouting this time, and he was not even sure he believed it.

No, he did believe it.

He knew Powell was dead.

But he no longer entirely disbelieved Frank when he said that he'd talked to the man.

"It's close by," Frank said. "It'll only take ten minutes."

The camp was technically in a combat zone, but not a hot zone, so it was possible to get permission to go outside the perimeter. Tex chose to go through proper channels rather than follow Frank's example and just wander about indiscriminately. It took him half the morning, but he petitioned his way up the ladder until a sergeant major able to make an executive decision granted him permission to leave the camp for an hour. Frank followed no such protocol but simply waited on his bunk for Tex to return.

It took longer to get there than the ten minutes Frank promised, longer than the hour for which Tex had gotten approval, and it was farther away than he'd been led to believe. But he did not back out, did not turn around. He followed Frank through the jungle, into gullies and up hills, down narrow intersecting footpaths that were barely there. Somewhere along the way, they gained a companion, an old Vietnamese man Frank referred to as his "teacher."

Powell had been right, Tex thought. Frank *had* gone native.

The little man was the size of a child but wizened beyond belief. Slitted black eyes stared out from between wrinkled folds, and the few teeth visible in his open mouth were black and rotted. He spoke a sort of rudimentary English, Frank spoke the Vietnamese equivalent, and apparently that was enough for them to communicate.

"Where are we going?" Tex asked more than once, and, like a child, "Are we almost there?"

"There" was a place whose location had apparently been forgotten even by the locals, whose name was not even known by the old man, a clearing amongst boulder-sized rocks that was ringed with human rib bones. In the center of the clearing was a small stone structure, housing a single closet-sized room. There were no windows in the structure, but the doorway was open and inside the light of a candle flickered, though Tex couldn't see how that was possible since there was no one here to tend it and a rather stiff breeze was blowing through the clearing.

If it had been night, he would have turned around then and there. He was not a superstitious person—was no longer even a *religious* person—but something about this place chilled him to the bone. He didn't like the circle of human ribs demarcating the circle in the center of the clearing, didn't like the flickering candle lighting the dark interior of the stone hut. He didn't even like Frank or that wizened little man.

They were walking slowly now, across the grassy ground, toward the small structure. The Vietnamese man was mumbling something in what sounded like the cadence of a prayer.

"Powell wants to talk to you because he *knows* things," Frank said. "He's *seen* things."

"Where is Powell?" Tex asked, though he was sure he already knew the answer.

"He lives *there* now," Frank said, nodding toward the open doorway and smiling blissfully.

This close, Powell's blackening, shriveling head could be seen in a stone alcove in the back wall of the hut, dimly lit by wavering candlelight.

From within the little room came an audible whisper.

"Tex."

He backed away. He didn't want to know about this, he decided. He didn't want any part of it.

"*Tex.*"

He turned and ran.

"Where are you going?" Frank called after him. "Powell can help us! He can tell us things!"

But Tex was speeding out of the clearing as fast as he could.

IT was two days before a search party found him.

PART THREE
DANIEL

ONE

I DIDN'T HEAR FROM Evan and Owen for nearly a month, and when I did, they didn't do their usual call-and-set-up-a-meeting routine. They showed up at the real estate office. First thing in the morning. In fact, they were waiting in a car outside when I arrived and hurried over before I could even pull out my key to unlock the door. "News," Evan announced.

I looked from one to the other. "Good news or bad news?"

"News," Evan repeated.

We walked inside. My heart was pounding. For the past several weeks, I'd been semi-successful in pushing everything Frank to the side and concentrating on the ordinary business of living, but it all came back in a rush, and I felt the full force of the stress and anxiety that had been with me since Big Bear. I motioned for Evan and Owen to sit down in client chairs as I walked around to the other side of my desk. Evan opened a laptop and put it on the desk in front of me.

"So what have you got?" I asked.

The case laid out by the writers was astonishingly thorough. Those two knew how to do research, and they'd dug up an impressive amount of information involving addresses associated with Frank. There were incidents dating back decades, and Evan pressed a key on his laptop, shifting from screen to screen as he showed me what they'd found.

"There's bankruptcies, accidents, robberies, miscarriages, suicides, murders. Almost any bad shit you can think of that involves a house has happened to people who've hired or bought from Frank."

"But that's only the beginning," Owen added. "It's the supernatural events that are really impressive."

I shook my head. "How did you guys find all this?"

"It's what we do, dude. It's our job."

"The thing is..." Owen began.

They looked at each other.

"We have a theory," Evan offered. "It sounds crazy, I know. And it probably is."

"And we don't have the resources to check it out."

"But there's been a tremendous increase in psychic activity over the past several decades."

"Ever since Frank got back from Vietnam."

Evan shot his partner a look. "I'll get to that. Let me tell it, will you?" He turned back to me. "There's been a *huge* increase. Hence all of the ghost hunting shows. Like ours. But it's an increase in activity that only seems to be taking place in America. It's not happening in other countries. So we got to thinking, what if it's related to Frank? Imagine a map of the United States, with little red dots marking each of the locations where hauntings or psychic experiences occurred. Like I said, we don't have the resources to prove this, but it's possible—"

Owen nodded. "More than possible."

"Okay, we actually did get out a map. And we did some rough correlations with what we knew about Frank's whereabouts in certain years, and, the thing is, there's been an exponential increase in, if not psychic activity, at least reported sightings that seem to correspond to buildings worked on by our buddy Frank. I've never seen anything like it. Never *heard* of anything like it."

"An exponential increase," Owen repeated.

I was doubtful. "All because of Frank?"

Evan nodded. "I know it sounds crazy..."

"It does," I admitted. "I mean, one guy...?"

"Maybe he's doing something or is tapping into something that triggers all this. I don't know. What I do know is that Vietnam seems to be the key. You told us that George and Betsy said Frank was changed when he came back. Yeah, there was something wrong with him even before he went over, but it was after the war that all *this* started happening around him."

I nodded.

"Well, we have a lead on that—"

Owen grinned excitedly. "This is pretty impressive."

"We emailed a guy whose father served with Frank in Vietnam. Back then, he was Frank Watkins—and we think that's his *real* name."

"I think so, too," I said.

"Anyway, this guy's dad told him stories about Frank, who was apparently into some sort of local Vietnamese religion." Evan paused dramatically. "A religion that involved communicating with the spirits of the dead."

"Unfortunately," Owen said, "his dad's dead."

"But the thread's not. Right now, we're trying to track down someone else from that unit, or anyone who can shed some light on his time in Vietnam, which we think was from late 1967 to early 1969."

"The dates are murky, though," Owen said. "There seems to be some discrepancies in Frank's official record."

"Communicating with the dead?" I said.

"Oh yeah. And the freaky thing is, the dad said it worked. Frank could do it."

"There are witnesses."

"Which is why we're looking for guys from his unit."

"What about that town in Texas? Did you find out if he's there or not?"

They looked at each other.

"What?" I said.

"Frank's there. The town's not."

Before I could ask what that meant, Evan was going to Google Earth and zooming in on an overhead view of what was supposed to be the town of Plutarch. Only there was no town. There was only a single structure.

A house.

I was reminded of the Winchester Mystery House, which I'd seen as a child on a trip with my parents. From above, there was the same sort of random conglomeration—peaked roofs connected to flat roofs, shakes and shingles, tarpaper and skylights—and I realized that Frank had constructed his house from the town, connecting the buildings until they made one enormous edifice.

"Jesus," I breathed.

"I'd guess he's somewhere in there," Owen said drily.

"But that's the last episode of the show," Evan said. He saw the expression on my face and immediately backtracked. "What I mean is, we don't know enough to go after him at this point. It'd be like the last time you saw him. We need more information before we confront him."

"We can call the cops," I said.

They both looked disappointed. "Sure," Evan said. "You can do that."

I did so. Immediately. In front of them. I took a business card out of my wallet and dialed the number of Detective Yamamoto, the cop I'd spoken to after returning from Frank's house—

six days

—telling him that Frank's address had been found. I called the Randall sheriff's office to tell them the same thing.

Hanging up, I felt vaguely dissatisfied. I realized that I didn't think the law would be able to capture Frank or stop him. Because even if police officers or sheriff's deputies were able to take him in, there was no way they were going to address the *real* problem. They didn't know about it and wouldn't believe it if they did. As much as I wished I could step away from this and pass the responsibility on to someone else, Evan and Owen were right. I had to confront Frank myself.

For Billy.

"All right," I said after putting down the phone. "Tell me what else you found."

There wasn't much else, as it turned out, but they were still following up leads, and with the amount of information they'd uncovered already, I was sure there was more to come. I copied what they'd brought on a flash drive so I could look at it more carefully later, and they promised to let me know if they unearthed anything new.

That night, Teri put extra effort into making sure all of the doors and windows were locked before going to bed.

That was odd.

"Did something happen?" I asked.

"Better to be safe than sorry." She cuddled next to me under the blanket, slipping her hand beneath the elastic waistband of my underwear to hold me.

"Are you sure—" I began.

"Julie called today."

The erection that had started growing under her fingers reversed itself, shrinking again. I wasn't sure I wanted to hear what came next. In fact, I was pretty sure I didn't.

"*Their* Frank didn't show up in court this morning. Now there's a warrant out for his arrest."

I pulled back to look her in the face. "Why didn't you tell me this before?"

"Well, you had so much going on with all that stuff those writers gave you—"

"It's all connected!"

"*Is* it?" she asked, meeting my gaze.

"Yeah. I mean...maybe." I shook my head. "Who knows? The point is, if there's anything about *any* Frank, you need to let me know."

I glanced over at the windows she'd just closed and locked. She saw where I was looking. "Okay," she admitted. "I think it's connected, too."

I held her close. It made no rational sense, and I had no idea how it was possible, but I knew it was true. We both did.

I slept only fitfully that night.

And there were dreams.

I followed up with the police the next day since they hadn't bothered to call me back. According to Yamamoto, Orange County had coordinated with local law enforcement in Texas in an effort to pick Frank up for questioning—only he hadn't been at the address I'd given. *Nothing* had. There *was* no gigantic house where the town of Plutarch used to be, only open desert. Yamamoto sounded pissed. "I don't know what kind of game you're playing here, but it's a crime to—"

"I'm not playing any game!" I insisted. "That's Frank's address."

"There *is* no such address."

"It used to be a town, an entire town, the town where Frank grew up, only now he's made it into one big house, connecting all the buildings—"

"Do you think this is funny?"

"I'm not joking!" I told him.

"Then there's something wrong with you."

"It's on Google!" I said. "I saw it!"

"There's nothing there. The police went out—"

"There's a satellite photo!"

"If there is, it's a mistake, a glitch."

I hung up on him, angry and frustrated. I stared at the blank black screen of my phone. There was no way I was going to convince Yamamoto or anyone else in officialdom about the crazy truth that was Frank. I should have known that from the beginning. Hell, the only people helping me out on this were two writers for a basic cable TV series about ghost hunting who were hoping to turn Frank's story into a show of their own.

That ought to have told me something.

I was so upset I was shaking. It felt as though I was trapped in one of those maddening dreams where it was impossible to move forward and everything I did set me back.

Not knowing what to do, I contacted Mark, figuring he'd want to hear what we'd discovered. I called him rather than emailing him, knowing he'd want to talk about it, but he was at work, so

I got his voicemail. I left a message, however, and he called back within ten minutes.

"That was quick," I said. "I hope you're on break and not blowing off some poor guy who's had knee surgery and needs to learn to walk again."

"It's fine," he assured me. "What's up? You have news about Frank?"

"That I do." I gave him a quick rundown of what Evan and Owen had dug up. "I can send it to you if you want."

"Definitely." Mark was silent for a moment. "So what now? I assume you told the cops where he is. Are they going to arrest him?"

"It's not as simple as that." I sighed. "The cops here contacted the police or sheriff or whoever out in Texas, and they went out to where Frank's house is—but they said there's nothing there. Only there is. You can even download a satellite image of it. Like I said, he took over a whole town. Turned it into one gigantic house. Except somehow the law can't find it."

"So you're going to go see him yourself." It was a statement, not a question.

"I guess so. Yeah." I hadn't admitted it even to myself, but it was true.

"I'm coming with you."

That was a bolt from the blue. Although I probably shouldn't have been surprised. It would have been more surprising had Mark *not* wanted to come. His family had been damaged by Frank almost as badly as mine had, and I knew he was looking for closure.

"When are we going?"

"I don't know," I admitted. "I have to work some things out. I need to...prepare."

"What are we going to do when we see him?" Mark asked, and I could hear in his tone of voice what he *wanted* to do.

"I don't know," I said again, and we both let the words hang there.

"Call me when you're ready," he said finally. "And keep me up on anything new."

"I will," I promised.

On the way home from work, I drove to the cemetery in Anaheim where my parents and my brother were buried.

I could not remember the last time I'd gone there. I'd never been the type of person to bring flowers or talk to a burial plot. Billy and my parents were never far from my thoughts, but seeing their graves depressed me, and, as far as I was concerned, the only things in the ground were their lifeless bodies. I was only going now to see if my mom's gravesite had been disturbed. Frank's taunting had been in the back of my mind ever since I'd left Nevada—

Your mama's bones are in my home. I dug them up. In the dead of night.

—and I wanted to make sure he hadn't been telling the truth.

To my relief, there was no indication that her body had been exhumed. The grass atop all three graves was not only intact but thick and had obviously been growing for a long time. There was no difference in the level of earth over the three graves, or between them and the adjoining plots.

I knelt down, touching the engraved letters on my father's stone, looking at the dates that measured the length of his life. I was almost as old as he had been when he'd died in the car crash, I realized.

I touched Billy's stone. If he were still alive, he'd be as old as my parents had been when he died.

I could barely bring myself to look at my mom's grave. I had known her the longest, known her the best, and her loss seemed fresher to me.

There were tears in my eyes, and I turned away, heading back to my car, feeling heavy and hurt and alone.

EVAN and Owen called again the next day. I was prepping a house for sale—adding a couple of new throw rugs to the bathrooms, putting some flowers in a vase on the kitchen counter, placing some upscale magazines on top of the living room coffee table for display—but I stopped what I was doing and sat down on the sofa to talk when I found out Evan was on the line.

"We're both here," Owen announced. "Conference call."

They must have found something.

"Did some more research," Evan confirmed.

"And?"

"We have access to a program that's kind of a spreadsheet deal—"

"An algorithm," Owen offered.

"We don't know what the hell it is," Evan admitted, "but it sorts and analyzes data about hauntings and sightings and supernatural events. We use it all the time for *Ghost Pursuers*. I don't know who came up with it—some university's parapsychology department, probably—but it's kind of an industry standard. Which means that not just us but researchers from all over are putting in information about their findings for others to see."

"And?" I repeated.

"And our theory about Frank seems to be more right than we thought. Like we told you, there's been an increase in psychic activity wherever he's hung out his shingle. But it's bigger than that. Because it's not *just* in those places. His movements have been pretty much confined to the western half of the United States, but in that exact same time period, there's been an increase in activity all over the country."

"The correlation's there," Owen said.

"Think of an open faucet, spilling out all over, water spreading far away from the original source."

I was skeptical. "And you attribute it to Frank?"

"Oh yeah."

"Without a doubt."

"And it's *still* spreading. That's why we have our show, why there are *all* those haunting shows out there. There's a lot going on. We ran everything by Kayley Samhoe, one of the psychics we use on the program, to see if she had some ideas. She had an interesting theory. She also agreed with us that it'd make a great show, just following this thread, and I guarantee you that if Scott doesn't want to do it for *Ghost Pursuers*, we can probably get something going with Travel or NatGeo. I mean, this is solid stuff—"

"But..." Owen prompted.

"Oh, yeah. Well, Kayley came up with the idea that all this activity might be leading up to something." He couldn't help himself. "Which would also make a great show. I mean, the arc's already built in..."

"Kayley's theory," Owen interrupted, "is that these events aren't just becoming more frequent, they're getting bigger. And, eventually, there's going to be...an explosion."

"Something major."

"*Major.*"

I shook my head, though they couldn't see it. "That'd make a good movie, but I can't see some apocalyptic event triggered by Frank's house repairs. The whole idea's ridiculous."

"But what if it's true?"

"That's just stupid."

"But what if it's true?"

"It can't be."

"But what if it *is*?"

What if it was?

I didn't want to believe it. I told myself I *couldn't* believe it.

But I could. I thought of that house the size of a town, thought about all of the people whose lives had been destroyed, remembered my six minutes that had been six days.

"Did you discover anything else?" I asked.

I could hear the grin in Evan's voice. "Oh, indeed we did."

In a truly heroic bit of sleuthing, they'd managed to track down Dang Nguyen, a former South Vietnamese soldier who had known Frank during the war. Old and frail, he now lived in a rest home in the Little Saigon area of Westminster, right here in Orange County.

"A rest home?" I said dubiously.

"His grandson said he has health problems, but his mind's sharp. He remembers Frank and he's willing to talk to us."

"When?"

"Tomorrow, if you can make it."

"Give me a time. I'll be there."

"Want to meet at your office and carpool, so we can discuss things on the way?"

"Let's do it," I said.

They texted me later with the name and address of the rest home in which the ex-soldier was living, and the time we were to meet, which was ten-thirty.

Evan and Owen had said that the old man's English was sketchy, and I figured he could express himself better and go into greater detail if he spoke in his native tongue, so I decided to invite May along as a translator. She had been moody lately, ever since her chatty unlicensed contractor—

Frank Walters

—had brought up bad memories about Vietnam. I'd left her alone, hadn't pressed, but I thought perhaps, in addition to translating, she might open up a little if we were all in a car discussing Frank. She knew only that the guy who'd torn down her storage shed was an insensitive jerk. It was going to be a real eye opener to find out Frank's history, and even if she didn't believe it all—or believe it *at* all—she still might tell me something I could use.

Teri, when I told her about it later, thought it was a mistake to get May involved. She was already involved, I reminded her. She'd been targeted by Frank.

I wanted to find out why.

We were supposed to meet at the real estate office at nine, but Evan and Owen were late. They called from the middle of a traffic jam on the Santa Ana Freeway in Norwalk, telling me that as soon as they got past construction in the right lane some two miles ahead, it would be clear sailing. Mike, Jim and May were already at their desks and working, and though I wanted to pull May aside and give her some background on Frank, I didn't want to do it in front of my other agents. I wasn't even sure how to bring up what had happened without making myself sound like a total lunatic. So I let her work, and figured she could get up to speed in the car on the way over.

It was nearly ten by the time Evan and Owen pulled up in front of the office. I told Mike and Jim to hold down the fort for a few hours as May and I went outside to meet them. The only thing May knew was that I needed her to help translate for an ex-South Vietnamese soldier, but I explained to her on the sidewalk that we were questioning the man about a person named Frank, who I believed was responsible for my brother's death.

She looked curiously and suspiciously at me when I mentioned Frank's name.

"I'll explain in the car," I said.

Evan and Owen had arrived in a new black SUV. It was better than either of my crappy vehicles or May's Volvo, and she and I got into the backseat. I introduced everyone, and when I told May that Evan and Owen worked on *Ghost Pursuers*, she said, "Van and I watch that show!"

The two writers were as voluble as usual—well, Evan was—and after basking in May's praise, they began laying out what they'd learned about Dang Nguyen. Apparently, he was the one who had introduced Frank to the primitive local beliefs that had led him to seek out banned practitioners of this indigenous faith. "Like we said before, one of the main tenets? Talking to the dead."

As I'd hoped, May spoke up and asked what this had to do with my brother's death, and that gave me the opening I needed. I decided to start from the beginning. "You're not going to believe this," I prefaced my explanation.

"But it's true," Evan butted in.

"All of it," Owen seconded. "We were at those Arizona houses. We experienced it."

As we drove, I told her an abbreviated version of events, sticking to the highlights. She didn't ask questions, merely listened, and when I was done, she said, "And you think this is my contractor." It wasn't a question.

I nodded, glad she'd made the connection on her own.

May was silent for a moment, and I wasn't sure whether she was going to tell us we were all crazy and demand to be driven back to the office, or admit that she, too, had had some sort of supernatural experience involving Frank. Her reaction was somewhere in the middle, but she didn't reject the premise entirely, and for a civilian that was good enough.

Traveling south on Brookhurst, we passed through an area of Middle Eastern shops and restaurants, then block after block of lower middle class homes. Houses gave way to businesses again, and as we passed from Anaheim into Garden Grove and then into Westminster, the ethnicity of the communities gradually changed. We passed an old Taco Bell that had been converted into a banh mi shop, a Burger King that had become a restaurant called Saigon Noodle House, strip mall after strip mall whose signs were in Vietnamese. I remembered, a decade or so back, when California had gone through one of its periodic bouts of immigrant bashing, that there'd been a push to have all business signs in the state be in English. I'd been approached by a right wing group outside the post office to sign a petition that would put such a measure on the ballot. "It's a free country," I told the signature gatherers. "The government shouldn't be telling private businesses what they can put on their own signs."

"This is America," one of them responded. "You're supposed to speak English."

"This *is* America. And the government can't dictate what language I can or cannot speak. I can talk in any damn language I want. It's a free country," I repeated.

I didn't sign the petition.

We turned onto Bolsa, into the heart of Little Saigon.

"We should've brought cameras with us," Owen said. "Gotten all this on film."

"You're right," Evan agreed. "Damn!"

"We could go back—"

"We're not going back," I told them.

"Is your phone charged up? We can use it to record the interview."

"Close enough for rock and roll," Owen said.

The rest home was even more depressing than those places usually were. Two stories of ugly gray, it was a stucco cracker box, its entrance flush with the uneven sidewalk, with no sign of a lawn. The few windows facing the street had wrought iron bars over them, although whether that was to keep criminals out or keep residents in was impossible to tell. We parked in a narrow lot on the side of the building next to a white cargo van with the name of the rest home written on the side in faded brown letters.

Dang Nguyen was a small wrinkled man living in a narrow room barely big enough to accommodate his bed, a dresser and a television. There was no way the four of us could fit inside or even stand in the doorway, so an attendant helped him walk down the short hall to a dark empty dining room barely bigger than the living room in my house. There were three round tables, each ringed with six chairs, and we sat down at the closest one, the attendant turning the light on for us before leaving.

Evan and I looked at each other to determine who would ask the first question, while Owen turned on his phone to record the encounter. Evan nodded at me, throwing the ball in my court, and I addressed the old man, speaking loudly and slowly. "Mr. Nguyen? My name's Daniel. I understand that you knew Frank Watkins? Back in Vietnam?"

He nodded. "We meet in Duoc Song. He in army. I guide."

"I heard that he was interested in..." I looked at May. "The occult," I said.

She translated the word for me.

Nguyen nodded again. "That why I tell him about wandering dead."

"Wandering dead?"

He said something to May in Vietnamese, and she nodded. "I'm going to interpret for him," she explained. "It's easier."

He began speaking a sentence at a time, giving her time to translate. "The dead wander if they are taken from their home. If a person is not buried or cremated in his own village, his spirit will not remain with his body. The spirit will wander, searching for home, and will be forever lost because the body has no home. There are many wandering ghosts during wartime."

"And Frank wanted to contact these wandering ghosts?"

Nguyen was silent for a moment, considering how much he wanted to say.

"We need to know," I told him. "Frank is a bad man."

"Frank bad," he agreed.

"*Very* bad."

He sighed, resuming again in Vietnamese.

"We believe that the dead have power," May translated. The old man gestured toward the corner of his room, where framed black and white photos of an Asian man and woman stood between two sticks of incense in front of a red backdrop decorated with gold lettering. "We rely on the dead. We ask our ancestors to watch over us, and they remain in our lives, helping when they are able and doing whatever they can to make our days happy."

I saw May wipe a tear from her eye.

"Frank," Nguyen said, and it was jarring to hear the name because it was the only word not spoken in Vietnamese. "He did not honor *his* ancestors," May translated. "He talked to the wandering ghosts of *our* people. He wanted to *use* them. For what, no one knew, but he thought he could control them and make them do what he wanted them to do."

The old man looked remorseful. "It was my fault," May translated. "I introduced him to Thanh Ngo, a..." She frowned. "Hold on. I don't know that word."

She and Nguyen spoke briefly in Vietnamese.

"I guess he was like an excommunicated priest or some sort of disgraced religious leader, only for a local religion that was native to that part of Vietnam."

Nguyen nodded, then continued, May translating: "I took him to see Thanh Ngo, although I do not remember why. He probably paid me. I needed money in those days.

"It was said that Thanh Ngo spoke to the dead—*and the dead spoke back*. He had abilities that good men did not possess and that he used for wrong purposes. Even the VC were afraid of him and left him alone. He was supposed to be over a hundred years old, and he lived in the ruins of an ancient temple, in the land where the old gods still walked." May met my eyes and shrugged as if to distance herself from his words, to indicate she had no connection to this Vietnam. "The war was not happening there, even though it was not that far from the Americans' camp. I brought Frank to Thanh Ngo, and he became his pupil. Frank visited Thanh Ngo whenever he could, and finally he abandoned his army. He left the Americans and lived in the temple. The last time I saw Frank, before I left Duoc Song, he was..." Nguyen shivered at the memory.

"What?" I asked.

"He was *younger.* I heard later, when I asked, that there was no more Thanh Ngo, only Frank."

"Do you mean he killed him?" I asked.

Nguyen nodded, answering me in English. "I think so, yes."

We had more questions, a lot of them, but the old man didn't seem to know much more than he told us, although he did provide more detail. He also grew tired fairly quickly, and, soon after, one of the rest home attendants who popped in to check on us decided that Mr. Nguyen had had enough excitement for one day, and told us we would have to leave.

On the drive back to the office, May grew increasingly quiet, as the writers and I discussed what we'd learned. "That was great stuff," Evan said excitedly. "'The land where the old gods still walked?' You can't make that shit up."

"There's a *series* there," Owen said. "And not just reality. *Scripted.*"

"That's where the money is," Evan explained.

It seemed to be Frank's involvement with this dead religion, and what he had learned from its banished leader that had made him what he was today.

"Mr. Nguyen didn't seem to know many specifics," Evan said, "but from what we've learned already, it must involve sacrifices. All the bodies and bones. Pets. Children."

Billy.

"I think he knew more than he let on," Owen posited. "I mean, if he was aware of this Thanh guy and knew where to find him..." He looked over at May. "What say you?"

"Maybe," she said quietly.

"This is a gold mine," Evan said. "Exciting stuff."

May didn't speak again until we were back at the office. "It's true, isn't it?" she asked, once Evan and Owen had dropped us off.

I met her eyes. "Yes," I said. "It is."

The rest of the day was busy. There were walk-in clients as well as previously scheduled meetings, and I did not even have time for lunch, let alone time to discuss what had happened with May. I tried talking to her at the end of the day, but she held up a hand before I'd even gotten half a sentence out. "Tomorrow," she told me. "I need time to...*absorb*."

"Understandable," I said.

I picked up Teri on my way home from work and told her about our trip to Little Saigon. She said nothing until I was finished. "What have you stumbled onto?" she wondered.

It was a good question, and not for the first time I wished that my dad had never read *Blue Highways*, that we'd taken the interstate back from the trip to see my cousins in Colorado, bypassing Randall, and that we'd never met Frank and Irene. My life would be completely different today—better—and I would know nothing about any of this but would be living a blissfully ignorant existence devoid of any hint of the supernatural.

But that was magical thinking, like praying for God to turn back time and undo events that had already happened. This was my world, and I could only deal with it as it was.

I didn't feel like going out to a restaurant and Teri didn't feel like cooking, so we stopped off to pick up a pizza on the way home. There was too much to talk about, but neither of us were up to it, so we vegged out in front of the television, eating our pizza and catching up on shows we'd recorded earlier in the week.

If I'd never encountered Frank, would I still be with Teri? I wondered. Or would I be with someone else? Would I be married by now? Would I have children?

The rabbit hole was deep, I thought.

For the first time in a long while, we did dishes together. Afterward, we took a shower and made love.

Lying in bed, arms around each other, we discussed Frank.

"So he was mentored by some kind of Vietnamese witch doctor who taught him how to communicate with the dead," Teri said.

"Pretty much," I allowed.

"And you believe that?"

"Don't *you*?"

Teri exhaled deeply. "Yeah. I do."

"The question is, what's next? Where do we go from here?"

"Nowhere," she said firmly. "We stay out of it."

"You know that old saying that the only thing evil needs to triumph is for good men to do nothing? We can't just stay out of it and hope someone else does something. *I* can't, at least. I'm involved, I'm in the middle of it all, and waiting for it to go away just isn't going to work."

"Then what *is* going to work?"

"I don't know," I admitted.

"Look, you've got those *Ghost Hunter* guys—"

"*Ghost Pursuers*."

"Okay, *Ghost Pursuer* guys involved. They *know* this stuff. It's their job. And you've told several police departments about it. What more do you think you can do? I mean, no offense, but you're a real estate agent. This is a little out of your comfort zone."

What she said made sense, logical sense, but emotionally it felt wrong. I was probably just fooling myself—in the same way that I felt safer driving a car than I did flying in an airplane, even though statistics said I was much more likely to be killed in a car crash—and I honestly had no idea what to do about Frank, but I wanted to be the one to stop him, I *needed* to be the one to stop him.

For Billy.

I let the subject lie, held Teri tighter. Reaching over, she grabbed the remote from the nightstand and turned on the TV. It was later than I thought. The eleven o'clock news was already on, and a red, white and blue graphic came swooping out from the screen.

"Breaking news in Chino Hills," the anchor intoned. "News chopper Four is over the scene of a brutal home invasion. Chris, what do you have?"

There was a night shot from above: an upper middle class neighborhood, police cars with flashing red and blue lights parked in the street in front of a well-kept house, officers keeping back local onlookers. Above the oscillating drone of the helicopter blades, a male voice encased in static said: "*No details yet, but neighbors who called police reported hearing screams coming from the home of Van and May Tran...*"

I sat up in bed.

"*...At least one victim has been airlifted to UCI Medical Center...*"

"Oh my God," Teri breathed.

We watched the rest of the report in silence, though there was no additional information.

Teri's frightened eyes met mine. "Do you think it's—"

"Yes," I said.

"You're going to tell the police, right?"

I was silent.

"Oh, no," Teri said, understanding. She shook her head. "No, you can't."

"I have to," I told her.

"You don't have to do anything."

"May? Your sister? He's doing all this to get to me."

"And what do you think you can do about it?"

"I don't know. Yet. But—"

"But nothing," she said, furious. "You're not going."

"My mom might be there." It was the first time I'd said it out loud, and I realized that even though I'd seen her intact grave, I was still not sure that Frank hadn't been telling the truth.

Your mama's bones are in my home. I dug them up. In the dead of night.

The words, and the image, had been in the back of my mind all this time, and it felt strangely freeing to admit my fears aloud. I thought of what Dang Nguyen had said about wandering ghosts. Not being religious, I had never believed there were such things as spirits or souls, but that had changed, and now I couldn't help worrying that my mom was not at rest, that Frank had interfered with what was supposed to have happened to her and that she was lost somewhere.

I looked into Teri's face. "I have to go there."

"You're not going alone," she warned me.

"*You're* not coming."

"Dumbledore's Army."

I frowned, confused. "What are you talking about?"

"In the movie *Harry Potter and the Order of the Phoenix*?"

"Never saw it," I admitted.

"It's on every other week."

I shrugged. "Never saw it."

"Okay, well, in the movie, Harry spends half the school year training students to fight Voldemort and forming Dumbledore's Army. But when it comes time to confront Voldemort, Harry wants to just take off by himself. Hermione convinces him to take a couple of his friends along with him. They hold off the Death Eaters, but people still die. If he'd brought the entire army, all the kids he'd trained, as originally planned, they might have been able to save everyone."

"I get it. There's safety in numbers."

"Yes. Which is why I'm coming with you. And you should try to bring your ghost hunters. Ghost *pursuers*. And maybe your friend Mark or some of Frank's other victims who have a score to settle. But not my sister," she added quickly.

"Which is the same reason I don't want you—"

"I'm coming," she said simply.

We were at a stalemate.

"Call the police," Teri suggested gently.

"They've done such a great job so far."

"What can *you* do, though? You still haven't answered me that."

"Something," I said, and though I didn't know what that might be, I believed it. "Something."

TWO

TERI AND I were eating breakfast in the kitchen, searching the internet through our respective phones, looking for news about May and Van, when we were interrupted by a knock at the front door. I went out to see who it was.

Mark Goodwin.

I was stunned to see him. I'd been planning to call Mark this morning and let him know that Teri and I were going out to Frank's house, certain that he'd want to come along. But I didn't understand why he was here now.

"Mark," I said, surprised.

He grinned. "Long time no see."

"Come in, come in." I reached out to shake his hand at the same time he tried to hug me, and we ended up in an awkward shoulder-patting half-embrace.

"It's been awhile," he said, smiling, and for a brief second, underneath the years, I saw the old Mark. I suddenly remembered a time when I'd been staying overnight at his house and we snuck downstairs to watch *Saturday Night Live*. It was something his parents had expressly forbidden—their family had a strict no-television-after-ten o'clock rule—but we made it into the living room without anyone hearing us, and we turned on the TV, keeping the volume so low that we had to almost press our faces against the screen. Mark had had that same smile on his face back then.

I still would not have recognized him had I met him on the street, but, happily, he looked better than he did in his Facebook photo. He definitely seemed older than me, but his eyes were not as haunted as they were in the picture, maybe because he no longer had to carry his burden alone but had me to share it with.

"I found that satellite photo of Frank's place, just like you said. Then I got your email about the Vietnam stuff. I figured you were getting ready to go over there, and I wanted to be in on it. So I drove all night and...here I am."

He'd known what I was planning to do before I did.

Teri emerged from the kitchen. "Teri," I said, "this is Mark Goodwin."

She smiled. "Nice to meet you. Daniel's told me so much about you."

"And your house," I added.

"You are going to see Frank, aren't you?" Mark asked.

Teri and I both nodded.

"Good," he said. "Good."

We'd been eating cereal, but when Teri asked Mark if he'd eaten anything this morning, and he admitted that he hadn't had anything except coffee, she offered to make him an omelet, and he gratefully accepted. "You want one, too?" she asked me.

"Sure," I told her.

"Three omelets, coming up."

I realized how lucky I was to have her. We'd shared the cooking duties when we'd first moved in together, but once it became obvious that her culinary skills far surpassed my own, she pretty much took over those responsibilities, while other aspects of household maintenance became my job. We were settling in, smoothing off rough edges until we fit together like pieces in a jigsaw puzzle, and while it just so happened that our abilities tended to fall along traditional gender lines, neither of us felt put upon or in any way constrained by our roles.

Maybe Teri was right, I thought. Maybe I should just be happy with what I had and let someone else deal with Frank.

But he was taunting me.

And I couldn't live with myself if someone else's life was ruined due to my inaction.

Could I live with myself if something happened to Teri?

I pushed that thought aside.

We talked as we ate breakfast, Mark filling Teri in on more details of his family's house in Randall and the repercussions of their time living there. It was a depressing story, and she gave my thigh a reassuring squeeze under the table as Mark described how his dad had died in a freak accident, slipping on a spot of oil at a gas station, falling and cracking his head open on the concrete next to his car. His mother had committed suicide less than a year later, swallowing oven cleaner, and Mark had been the one to discover her bloody lifeless body on the floor of her kitchen.

"Oh my God," I said.

He had gone through the same sort of mental anguish that I had after the death of my parents, coming to the conclusion that if they had not moved into Frank's house, circumstances would not have led to his father being at *that* gas station on *that* day. He would not have slipped and fallen and died, and his mother would not have committed suicide. Of course, there were a million other variables that could have also changed the outcome, but Frank was the only one that mattered to Mark. Or to me.

Because it was intentional.

I filled in more detail for Mark about what we'd learned regarding Frank.

"So what's the plan?" he asked. "We go out there and burn the place down?"

Arson? It was illegal, and it hadn't occurred to me, but it was the first course of action that anyone had come up with. I glanced over at Teri, who shook her head, frowning.

"It's an option," I said. "Definitely not our first choice, but maybe it's an idea we should keep on the back burner."

Mark smiled. "So to speak."

"No," Teri said firmly.

"So what then?" Mark asked.

"I don't know exactly. But Teri's right," I told him. "We need to go out there in force, with as many people as we can. I'm going to ask Evan and Owen, the two writers and researchers from *Ghost Pursuers*, and see if they can bring along the psychic they work with and anyone else they know who might be interested."

I'd thought about what Teri had said regarding inviting some of Frank's other victims. I'd even considered calling Brad Simmons, who'd started all this back in Big Bear, but, safety in numbers notwithstanding, I could not justify bringing in anyone else when there was a strong likelihood that this might prove dangerous. Or deadly.

"I don't know how long it might take to get everyone together," I told Mark, "but it could be a few days. Maybe you should go back home and back to work and let me call you."

He shook his head. "I have vacation time saved up, and this is it. When you're ready, I'm ready."

"Where are you staying?" Teri asked politely.

"Here," I answered for him. "No reason to waste money on a motel. We have room."

"No," he said. "I'll find someplace nearby."

"But—"

"I have night terrors. Not all the time, but it does happen. I don't want to be waking you guys up with my screams. Besides, I feel more comfortable on my own, not sharing space."

Mark had an adult's voice now, but the cadences and rhythms were the same as they had been when he was a kid, and, just like back then, I could tell when he was being honest.

He was being honest now.

I didn't try to argue him out of it. "If you've been driving all night, you should probably get some sleep. There's a decent motel about a mile away. Cheap, fairly clean. I can show you where."

"I *am* tired," he admitted.

Mark drove a Kia, and he led me out to where he'd parked on the street, opening his trunk. "I brought baseball bats for both of us," he said, showing me. "Just in case."

"Holy shit!" I picked up a red aluminum one. "Is this Mr. Sluggo?"

"The one and only."

Mr. Sluggo had been Mark's bat when he was a kid. Neither of us had been particularly athletic, and though Mark's dad had bought the bat so that Mark could practice hitting balls, Mr. Sluggo was actually used by us to ward off his brother Dean and to practice for imaginary run-ins with local redneck teenagers.

Mark picked up the other bat, hefted it. "And if I see Frank..." He left the thought unfinished.

I drove to the motel in my van, Mark following in his Kia. After checking in, we went up to his room. I told him to get some sleep and call me when he awoke. "I'll try to get things going," I said. "Hopefully, there'll be plans in place the next time we talk."

"We're really going to see Frank again." There was a combined sense of dread and wonder in his voice, as though for the first time the idea was actually sinking in.

"We really are," I told him.

Back home, I called Evan.

"Dude," he said. "I was just about to call you."

My heart started racing. "Why? Did you find out something else?"

"Not really, no. Well, sort of. But that's not the reason I was going to call. We did look up information about those wandering ghosts, and apparently it is a thing. I mean, it's not totally unknown in Vietnam; it's kind of an accepted belief. I'll email you what we found. But the reason I was going to call is because I think we should head out to Frank's place." He paused dramatically. "We have a development deal."

"You have a...development deal?"

"Damn right. We sold our concept. Told you it was a winner. We didn't want to jinx it, so we kept quiet, but after our little excursion yesterday, Owen and I had a meeting scheduled with the head of programming for the network and a bunch of big honchos. We laid out the Frank story, explained a couple of ways it could go, and they bit. Best part of all? Owen and I are the show runners. Scott's not even involved—it's all us! Hey, you want to be a creative consultant? *Executive* creative consultant? After all, you're the one who started this ball rolling."

"I just want to find Frank."

"Well, we can do that. We can definitely do that. We have a budget. We can *fly* to Texas. Hell, there's no reason we can't shoot the season backwards. Start off with the big Frank confrontation, then fill in the backstory later. They're giving us time to shoot the entire series—thirteen episodes—before the first show even airs. That's a luxury we've never had with *Ghost Pursuers*."

I was starting to get excited, but not for the same reasons Evan was. I didn't give a damn about a TV show. But with money and people behind us, it seemed to me that we had a legitimate shot at bringing Frank's misdeeds to light and maybe getting some semblance of justice.

"I want to bring a couple of people along," I said.

"The more the merrier."

"My girlfriend's one."

"Cool."

"The other is a guy who used to live in that house in Randall—"

"Kick ass!" Evan said excitedly. "Do you think he'd be willing to talk? Think we can get him on camera?"

"I don't know," I admitted. "You'd have to ask him."

"Excellent, dude, excellent. Of course he's invited."

"Do you think you could ask that psychic—"

Evan laughed. "Already done. She's part of the package. She'll be in every episode." He started talking about his vision for the show, how the fact that it was not an episodic supernatural reality show but had a continuous through-line was going to give it more weight than something like *Ghost Pursuers*, and I listened politely, but for me this was merely a means to an end. For him, it *was* the end. We were almost exact opposites of each other, Evan and I, but it was a complementary relationship, and we were both getting what we needed. Before I hung up, I reminded him of how scary Frank's house in Randall had been, and warned him that this trip was going to be dangerous.

"Excellent!" he said. "Excellent!"

I was pretty sure he'd missed my point.

Later, he called back to let me know that a plane had been booked for the next day. "Time flies when you have money at your disposal," he said. "Be there or be square."

Both Teri and I had a hard time sleeping that night. I was more angry than scared, but she was more scared than angry, and she tried to talk me out of going. It was something I needed to do, I told her. I let her know that she didn't have to come along, that I would *prefer* it if she stayed, but she adamantly insisted that wherever I was going, she was going—although *she* would prefer it if we both stayed home.

The next day, Mark met us at the house for an early breakfast, and the three of us drove in Mark's car to the Burbank airport, where Evan, Owen and their team had arranged for a flight to San Antonio. They had arrived first, and we were filmed walking into the airport.

"Cut!" Evan said as we approached. He walked up, grinning, slapping his arm on the back of the ponytailed cameraman. "Here's our shooter. You remember Twigs? From *Ghost Pursuers*?"

Twigs nodded disinterestedly at me. "Hey."

"The same deal applies," I told Evan and Owen. "I don't want to be on camera."

"I know, I know," Evan said. "But just in case..."

"There is no case."

"Got it." He turned toward Teri. "How about you? Do you mind if we—"

"Yes," she said. "I mind."

Mark was the person they really wanted on the show, so they stopped there, not wanting to be rejected off the bat, thinking they could approach Mark at a more propitious time. Introductions were made all around. I finally got to meet Kayley, the psychic, and she gave me an enigmatic smile as she daintily shook my hand. "So you're the one," she said.

I had no idea what that meant, so I just shrugged. "I guess I am."

There were seven of us on the small plane, fully half of the passengers on the flight. As we checked our bags, Owen suggested that we rent a van in San Antonio that could hold us all, in order to save money, but Evan and I argued for two vehicles. "We'll be hundreds of miles out in the boonies," Evan said. "What if we break down? We need a backup vehicle. Who knows how well-maintained rental vans are in Texas?"

"And if we did break down," I pointed out, "who's to say there'll be cell service? We might not be able to call for help."

But that wasn't the real reason I wanted two vehicles.

I was thinking we needed an escape car.

In case something happened at Frank's house.

No one talked much on the plane, other than Evan and Owen, who chatted happily with each other about their TV show. One of the civilian passengers overheard their conversation, made the mistake of asking about it, and, over Arizona, Evan conducted an hour-long infomercial for what they were tentatively calling "The Hunt for a Monster." Toward the end of the flight, the two writers cornered Mark, who, despite my warnings, agreed to tell his story and be filmed.

"We need to get this out," he told me.

"Exactly," Evan agreed.

We'd called ahead to the rental car agency, and there was a van and a full-sized car waiting for us when we landed. Evan, Owen, Kayley and Twigs grabbed the van, while Teri, Mark and I took the car. It was already noon, California time, and according to my GPS app, Plutarch was a two-hour drive away. I didn't like the timing. We'd be getting there in the late afternoon and wouldn't have time to do much before dark.

"Perfect," Evan said, Owen nodding. "Night shots are exactly what we want."

"We're staying the night here," I said firmly. "We'll go out in the morning."

Teri, Mark and the psychic agreed. Twigs didn't seem to care one way or the other.

I faced the writers. "I don't think you understand the danger..." I began.

"Fine, fine," Evan said, annoyed. "Cheap lodgings, though. This is costing us an extra day."

"You're sounding more like Scott by the minute," Owen told him, grinning.

Evan punched his partner's shoulder. "Asshole."

We checked into a single-story courtyard motel called The Pioneer Inn. All of the rooms had HBO, and there was a pool in the center of the complex, although no one had thought to pack a bathing suit. Still, the weather was nice, and Teri, Mark and I sat out by the pool, sharing a six pack, while the others went off somewhere to shoot background footage. Teri eventually got bored and went in to see if there was something on the Food Network or Travel Channel for her to watch, but Mark and I stayed outside.

"Doesn't seem like they have much of a budget for their show," Mark noted. "This motel isn't exactly The Reata. And only one cameraman? No other crew?"

I shrugged. "Travel fast and light, I guess."

"Seems like it should be more professional."

"I don't really care, to be honest. I'm just after Frank. Whether they get a TV show out of it is up to them."

Mark nodded. "I hear you."

We continued talking, catching up on old times, and the conversation gradually turned more personal as the sun went down.

"Is this where you thought we'd end up when you were a kid?" Mark asked, finishing off his last beer.

"At a motel in Texas?" I laughed. "No."

"No. I mean...our lives. Is this what you thought you'd be doing when you grew up? Is this how you thought things would turn out?"

There was a wistfulness in his voice, and I knew exactly what he meant. It was the same conversation I'd had with myself many times. I shook my head.

"I sure wouldn't have expected you to become a real estate agent," Mark admitted. "You were the smartest kid I ever met. You knew all that stuff about old movies, and you were into rocks and shells and science. You had that insect collection."

I'd forgotten that.

"You were just into a lot of things. You had a lot of interests. I thought…I don't know. You didn't seem like someone who'd go into real estate."

"What about you?" I asked.

Mark smiled sadly. "Did you know my dad wanted me to be a lawyer? His dad was a lawyer, and he was hoping I'd go into corporate law, be one of those guys paving the way for companies to do business overseas, have offices in New York, Paris, Brussels, Hong Kong. Then…Frank came along. Now I teach people how to exercise their leg muscles in Tucson."

"Physical therapists do a lot more good in the world than corporate lawyers," I said.

He stood. "Yeah. Let's keep telling ourselves that." He dropped his beer can into a recycling container next to the fence. "I'm getting hungry. It's about dinnertime, isn't it?"

WE were on the road early the next morning. Owen had stopped by each of our rooms the night before, telling us to set our alarms for five. Apparently not trusting us to follow through, he pounded on our doors before dawn to wake us up. He and Evan had coffee and donuts to pass out by the time we were packed and ready to go, and our two-vehicle caravan was heading out of the city before San Antonio's rush hour even started.

The landscape was flat, barren and unbearably monotonous. West Texas has some of the most god-awful scenery known to man, and along the side of the road dozens of small white crosses adorned with plastic flowers indicated where bored drivers had been lulled into sleep and crashed their vehicles.

An hour out, we turned off on a narrow barely paved road that was unmarked and probably would have been missed had we not known what we were looking for.

"Shouldn't there be a sign for that town?" Teri asked.

"Plutarch? Probably," I said. "But there is no town anymore, and I don't think Frank wants to make it easy for people to find him."

"It's not *that* hard," Mark pointed out.

He was right. It wasn't that hard. The road did not disappear, and there were no washed out sections of asphalt, no locked gates to finesse, no impediments of any kind.

After an hour and a half of travelling through a land of wind-swept desolation, seeing no other cars, no sign of human existence other than the thin strip of bleached macadam, we passed over a small rise to see a wide basin dominated by a single massive structure that towered over the rocks and desert vegetation surrounding it.

Frank's house.

I stared at the structure in awe.

It seemed so much bigger in real life than it did in the satellite photo. Five stories tall at its peak, with turrets and gables located at odd and inappropriate junctures that gave the entire building a weirdly off-center appearance, it stretched to the left and right for over a mile. I had no idea how far back it went, though I was certain that it stretched behind a considerable distance.

It had, after all, once been the town of Plutarch.

It was not merely the size of the house that was impressive, however, but the complexity of its construction. The building contained multitudes. In it, I saw the stores and homes that it had overtaken as well as echoes of every structure that Frank had ever worked on, all of it incorporated into one monstrous edifice.

How was this possible? He had to have had help constructing it; there was no way a single person could do all this, especially one with Frank's sub-par skills. But who'd assisted him? And where had he gotten the money for all the materials? Sure, he'd stolen a few items here and there, but he could not have stolen this much lumber and concrete in a dozen lifetimes.

There was nothing about this situation that made any kind of rational sense, and that made me wary.

Had this always been Frank's end-game? I wondered. Was this the point of it all? To build a big house? It seemed senseless to me. A lifetime of cheating and stealing—

and killing

—had all led here, to this bizarre white elephant in the middle of the Texas desert?

The road curved to the right in front of the house, continuing on until it disappeared around the side of the structure. We'd been following the van since leaving San Antonio, and when Evan pulled to a stop in front of what seemed to be the entrance, I parked next to him.

Teri instinctively hated the house. Mark did, too. I could see the looks of revulsion on their faces, as though they were looking upon something disgusting. I understood how they felt, though I did not experience that reaction myself.

We got out of the car. Evan, Owen and their cameraman were having a field day. They were already dashing about, shouting at each other about things to film and angles to shoot. The psychic remained in the van.

The air here felt...heavy. I don't know how to describe it other than that. The temperature was hot, and there was no wind, but that didn't account for the *thickness* of the air. If normal air was water, this was syrup, and indeed there was a sense in which it seemed more liquid than gas.

Wrong, I thought. *It feels wrong.*

Did anyone else feel the same way? I looked around to gauge the others' reactions but was distracted by something I had not noticed before: three law enforcement vehicles abandoned on the drive that ran along the side of the house, a line of empty cars and trucks stretching beyond that.

"Where are their owners?" Teri's voice was soft, but I didn't expect to hear it so close to my ear, and it startled me, making me jump.

I glanced up at the house. "Lost," I replied, and imagined the drivers wandering endlessly within that structure, thinking they'd been in there for only an hour or two when they'd really been inside for months.

"*Now* call the police," Teri suggested. She nodded toward the abandoned cars. "I'm pretty sure this classifies as probable cause.

Tell them we're here. Send them a picture. Let them know that if they don't get off their asses and do their job..."

"I knew there was a reason I kept you around," I said.

She punched my shoulder, and this playful display of normalcy lightened the mood enough that it gave me strength. The air was still thick, the edifice in front of us still gigantic, but I felt stronger, less nervous, and hearing Evan and Owen ordering Twigs around gave me even more confidence. I could do this. I could handle it.

Taking out my phone, I punched 911.

There was no signal. Whether that was because we were so far out here or because there was something in the house that blocked it, I did not know. But I can't say that I was totally surprised. I tried the same thing with Teri's phone, with the same result.

"So much for that," I said.

"We'll bring someone back."

"After," I told her.

She blanched. "You're not actually thinking of—"

Mark walked up. "So are we going to go in?" he asked.

"I guess so," I said.

"No," Teri insisted.

It was as if Mark hadn't heard her. "Do we just...knock?"

"We could try it."

Teri was hurrying off to tell Evan and Owen, hoping to find an ally, though I knew the writers would be the first ones to advocate entering the house. That was the whole reason they'd brought us here.

"We need a little backup first," Mark told me. He'd been allowed to bring his baseball bats on the plane as long as they were stashed in the luggage compartment where they could not be accessed, and right now they were in the rear seat of our rental car.

I walked over with him to retrieve the weapons.

"You can use Mr. Sluggo," he said, handing it to me. "I wouldn't be here if it wasn't for you. You deserve it." He closed the car door and swung the other bat in an arc. "But I get first crack at him. I deserve *that*."

"He's all yours," I promised.

We faced the house's entrance, a large intricately carved wooden door that looked like it belonged on a cathedral, that Frank had probably *stolen* from a cathedral. The Texas desert was hot, and although in the deep shade cast by the mammoth house, the temperature was much cooler, the goosebumps on my arms were not generated by the chilliness of the air.

Was there a back door to this place? I wondered. Or a side entrance? Even if there was, it didn't matter. There was no way to sneak up on the building. With only the one road, anyone approaching would be instantly seen.

Maybe Frank wasn't even home.

He was, though. I knew it. I felt it.

And he was watching us.

Teri was standing next to the open side door of the van with Evan, Owen and Twigs, talking to Kayley. Mark and I walked over.

The psychic looked shaken. "I'm not going in," she said. "I can't."

Evan motioned for the cameraman to start filming. "Why can't you go in?" he asked, lowering his voice to what he undoubtedly considered interview mode. "What do you sense?"

Kayley turned toward him angrily. "Goddamn it! I'm not doing this, Evan!"

"We need a more professional host," Owen noted. He addressed Twigs. "Just film her, don't get him. We'll have someone overdub your voice," he told Evan.

"What's wrong with my voice?"

"This is *real*!" Kayley shouted. "Don't you assholes get it? There's no way in hell I'm stepping foot in that place, and you shouldn't, either!"

"*I* get it," Teri said softly. She shot me a disapproving look.

"I get it, too," I told her. I gestured toward Mark. "*We* get it."

Kayley looked at me, peered into my eyes and nodded slowly. "I can see that you do," she said. She turned her attention back to Evan. "We need to leave. This place is not safe."

"Why?" Evan pressed, motioning with his right hand for Twigs to use his camera to zoom in.

"The dead—"

There was a noise unlike anything I had ever heard, a deep pervasive rumbling that seemed to come from the earth itself, though we all knew its origin was the house. It was a sound so immersive I could feel it in my stomach, and my instinctive reaction was to turn tail and run. This wasn't just conjured up by a crazy contractor, this was the growl of something so massive and elemental that there was no humanly way to go up against it.

That was undoubtedly the point. That's what Frank *wanted* us to think, and I was filled with a resolve to come at him with everything at my disposal.

"Look," Teri said. Her voice was hushed.

I followed her pointing finger.

The front door of the house was open.

A chill passed through me, and my grip tightened on the baseball bat, which I'd been holding like a cane. Through the open door, I could see a foyer identical to the one in Frank's other house in Nevada. Our old couch was there again, and I wondered if Frank had had it moved, if one couch was real and one a fake, or if both were illusions.

"Do not go in there," Kayley said from within the van, her voice commanding yet at the same time deeply frightened. "Do. *Not.* Go. In. There."

But Evan and Owen were already hurrying toward the doorway, Twigs between them, each instructing the cameraman about what to film.

"Why shouldn't we go in?" Teri asked the psychic.

"There's too *much.*" I moved closer to the van to better hear Kayley's answer. Her voice was quiet now. "It hurts just being this close. I need to get away."

"Too much what?" Teri wanted to know.

"Everything." She sucked in her breath. "The dead are not at rest in that building."

Evan, Owen and Twigs were already walking inside. I shifted my position so I could see better, searching for Frank within the foyer, but I saw no sign of him.

"I need to get out of here," Kayley said. "You need to get out of here."

"This is amazing!" Evan called from within the house. I could no longer see any of them, but the door remained open.

I took out my car keys, offered them to Teri. "Go with her," I said. "Get help."

Teri shook her head. "I know your plan. You're not getting rid of me that easily."

I stepped forward, offering the keys to Kayley. "Here," I said.

The psychic grabbed them instantly. "I'm not coming back. But I'll get the police over here." She looked into my eyes. "Not that it will help."

I turned. "You want to go with her, Mark? Make sure she's okay?"

He swung his bat. "Not happening. I'm here to see Frank."

"I don't need any help." The psychic stepped out of the van, pushed past me and headed toward the rental car. "Don't go in there!" she called over her shoulder. "You won't come out!"

Teri ran after her, opened the passenger side door and took her purse off the front seat. The two of them spoke briefly for several seconds, something I could not hear, then Teri closed the door and Kayley started the car, spun backward on the drive and took off the way we'd come. I watched the car speed away, feeling strangely abandoned.

I turned back toward the house.

The door was still open.

I walked forward, keeping my eye on the room beyond the doorway. "Evan?" I called. "Owen?"

No answer.

"Twigs?"

Silence.

"Are we going in?" Mark asked.

I hefted Mr. Sluggo. "We're going in."

Teri took my hand. "Lead the way."

The two of us stepped over the threshold.

Behind us, Mark screamed at the top of his lungs.

And the door slammed shut, locking us in.

THREE

WE TRIED DESPERATELY to open the door, but there was no knob or handle on the inside and of course it did not budge. It also appeared to be soundproof. Mark's scream had been cut off in mid-cry, and even putting our ears to the door we could hear nothing. I pounded on the wood, calling Mark's name, but there was no response. What had happened to him? Was he injured? Was he dead? There was no way to tell, and I kicked the door as hard as I could with my right foot, trying to break it down the way I'd seen cops do in television shows, but all I got for my efforts was a hurt heel and a sore shin. I might as well have been kicking a concrete wall. Moving into a batting stance, I used Mr. Sluggo to whale away on the door, swinging as hard as I could, but though a few slivers of dried paint disengaged themselves from the spot I was hitting, the wood itself was not even scratched.

We were trapped in here, and Mark was...was...I had absolutely no idea.

Teri looked at her watch, obviously thinking about the last time I'd been inside one of Frank's houses. "Look," she said, holding out her hand and wrist.

I glanced down at the watch, which had stopped dead.

Dead.

I pushed that word out of my mind.

"Evan!" I called. "Owen!" The two writers and Twigs were somewhere in this house, and finding them was our first priority. Teri was right: there was safety in numbers. And we were *not* safe. An active air of menace hung over not only this room but the entire structure, permeating the atmosphere. There was very real danger here. I understood why Kayley had felt the need to flee, why she had not been willing to enter the house, and even though my perceptions were much less acute, I felt overwhelmed by all that confronted us.

Teri was trying to use her phone, but there'd been no access outside the building and there was none inside either.

"Evan!" I called again. "Owen! Twigs!"

The house was silent.

Either they were so far away that they could not hear me, or...

I refused to even consider it.

"What do we do?" Teri asked.

I had no idea. I glanced toward the open archway at the other end of the foyer and saw only darkness beyond. As though responding to my thoughts, a series of lights and lamps switched on in the next room.

Up close, the interior of the house did not appear to be as professionally constructed as the outside. Even in the well-appointed foyer, I saw the outline of a bulging board behind the wallpaper, a section of uneven floor, gaps where segments of molding did not meet. The couch, I noted, *was* a replication of ours, and, from this vantage point, not a very good one. Fabric similar to that covering our couch had been inexpertly tacked onto an entirely different sofa in order to make it appear as though the furniture was ours, only the fabric had not been measured properly, and near the bottom, the original material showed through.

Typical Frank job.

"Evan!" I called again. I paused. "Frank!"

"Maybe we should try to find a window," Teri suggested. "I know I saw windows from outside."

Moving slowly and carefully, with me in the lead and Mr. Sluggo ready for action, we stepped out of the foyer into an old-fashioned, western-looking drawing room. There was a writing desk and a piano, a bookcase, some sort of fainting couch, and, in the center of the space, tables and high-backed chairs placed in a formal seating arrangement. On the walls were paintings of cattle drives and cowboys, interspersed with the mounted heads of buffalo and javelina. Nothing about this room seemed even remotely familiar, and certainly nothing in it put me in mind of Frank.

There was no one in the room, but there was a doorway at the far end that opened onto darkness. Another room? A closet? Something else? I had no idea, but the darkness made me nervous. "Evan?" I called out. "Owen? Twigs?" No one answered, but from somewhere came the sound of faint music, a song that was familiar but that I could not immediately place.

"I don't like this," Teri whispered.

"I don't either," I told her, holding tight to the bat.

"Is this some sort of—" *Joke*, I thought she was going to say, but she went with "trap?"

Both seemed appropriate.

"I don't know," I said.

I didn't want to go through that dark doorway, but there were no other options. It was either that, or remain in the drawing room or the foyer while waiting for a rescue that, judging by the abandoned cars outside, was never going to come.

I peered into the blackness, trying to make out the outline of... something. "I wish we had a flashlight."

"The phones," Teri said, taking hers out.

"You're right!" Our phones might not have cellular access, but they had lights, and I immediately turned mine on, adjusting the settings until the screen emitted a white luminescence. Together, we faced forward, moving slowly, aiming our beams into the dimness, but most of the light was swallowed by the gloom, allowing us to see only the vague outlines of what looked like furniture. I'd given up calling out names, but let out a generic "Hello!" to see if there was a response from anyone—

anything

—in the room ahead.

"Do you think Frank's in here?" Teri whispered.

"Somewhere."

Phones extended, we walked through the doorway—

—and were home, sitting on the couch, watching TV. We were in the middle of a *Breaking Bad* marathon, and Teri had just made popcorn. I turned to her and said, "After this one's over, let's go to bed. I'm getting tired."

I *was* tired, and I had the sense that I'd just drifted off for a few seconds and dreamed that I was trapped in some funhouse version of a home that Frank had built.

No.

That was wrong.

It was close—but wrong.

"I'm tired, too," Teri said. "Let's finish watching in the bedroom."

She used the remote to shut off the TV, I switched off the living room lights, and we walked down the hall to the bedroom, where we each took off our clothes before climbing under the covers. We were both too tired to make love, but that wasn't to say that it wouldn't happen sometime tonight if one of us awoke aroused, and we snuggled together as we finished watching the episode.

I dozed off during a commercial, my mind sinking into a strange half-dream in which I saw Mark Goodwin for the first time since childhood and the two of us took a trip somewhere. I awoke seconds later with the feeling of Teri's soft fingers between my legs. Apparently, we *weren't* too tired, and once she'd gotten me hard, she climbed on top of me, using her hand to guide me in. She was moaning breathlessly, but when I looked into her eyes, I saw a disassociated confusion, the same sort of confusion I was feeling myself. I wondered what that meant, but my brain was foggy, and then we were both climaxing, and I forgot all about it.

At work the next day, May was at her desk before I arrived, talking to Miles and John. I was surprised to see her because in the back of my mind, I'd thought she was either in the hospital or dead. I was glad to be wrong, though, and I sat down at my own desk to check my daily calendar.

Miles and John?

I frowned. Weren't my other agents Mike and Jim? I glanced across the office, but there seemed nothing out of the ordinary, and the two men were exactly who they were supposed to be.

Miles and John.

That still didn't seem right.

I spent the morning driving an entitled older woman all around Orange County to view properties that were "not quite right" for her, and the afternoon hosting an open house in Tustin. I returned home shortly after five to find that Teri had not left the house all day. Not only had she not gone in to work, but she had not bothered to call in sick. Strangely, no one from the bank had called to see what might be wrong.

"Are we supposed to be here?" Teri asked me. She seemed genuinely confused, and I understood her feelings perfectly because they were identical to my own.

It was obviously something she'd been thinking about, and I was honest with her when I said, "I don't know." My gaze fell upon a framed Ansel Adams photograph of the Grand Canyon above the couch. I didn't remember that picture. In fact, I didn't remember half of the pictures on the wall. Suddenly even the couch seemed unfamiliar to me.

A cat came walking out from the hallway, and this casual illustration of normalcy made me feel more at home, though I was vaguely aware of the fact that we didn't have a cat. I called out to it, "Here, kitty, kitty," and it did not run away but turned to look at me, sitting down on its haunches. I reached out my hand as I approached, intending to pet it—

—and the cat smiled.

Animals weren't supposed to smile, and the effect was unnerving. The eyes that appraised me were knowing and sly, and I backed away as the diminutive monstrosity giggled in the voice of a little girl.

"Teri?" I said, backing away.

She grabbed my hand, and I saw the look of terror on her face.

"What's going on?" I felt as though I knew the answer, but that it was locked somewhere in my brain. I was hoping she could jog my memory, make me see what was right in front of my face but eluding me. Teri was even more bewildered than I was, however, and we both backed away from the hideously cackling cat as I looked around the room, searching for clues to...something.

We moved into the kitchen.

And there was a door I did not recognize next to the refrigerator.

I was about to ask Teri about it, but just as I opened my mouth, she said with a frown, "What's that, a closet?"

She didn't recognize it, either.

We'd stumbled onto something, and I stepped forward, reached for the knob and tried to turn it. The door would not open, and I was reminded of another door that would not open, though I could not recall where or when that was. Shoving my shoulder against the edge, I tried to make it budge, but there was no give.

"Maybe I can find a key," Teri offered, and she started looking around the kitchen for a hook or nail that might have keys on it.

From back in the living room, the girlish giggling had stopped, but I heard a loud plaintive meow.

What I need's a weapon, I thought. *Something to use on the cat and to batter down the door.*

Mr. Sluggo.

I glanced down at my hands. It seemed to me that I'd had a baseball bat at some point, Mark's bat from childhood, but it was gone, something had happened to it. I couldn't remember what, however, and couldn't remember when.

"I think I found something!" Teri announced. She was holding up what looked like an old-fashioned skeleton key. The door seemed too modern to require such a contrivance, but when I looked more closely, I saw a large antiquated keyhole beneath the knob, and when we put the key in, it fit.

Because of the door's location in the kitchen, both of us expected to see a pantry or closet. But behind the door was some sort of workshop, a primitive plywood-lined room with an uneven floor, a too-low ceiling and walls with visible gaps where the wood did not meet. It looked like something Frank would build.

Frank.

Frank.

It all came back, everything, and I turned to Teri and saw the recognition on her face. We were in Frank's house, that terrible gargantuan structure he had built over the bones of Plutarch, Texas. We had somehow been lulled or hypnotized into thinking that we were back in our regular lives, but we'd been here all along.

How long had that been?

I was afraid to even think about it, and, holding Teri's hand, I walked into the workroom. There were not just tools on the sagging shelf that ran along the opposite wall and the beat-up, paint-stained table that took up the center of the space before us, but bones and the dried carcasses of small animals. A drill and handsaw lay next to a beagle's head and what looked like a pile of feline leg bones. Hammers and nails, screws and screwdrivers were scattered about, sharing the tabletop with desiccated squirrels and the skulls of mice. A stack of lumber in one of the corners butted up against what appeared to me to be a bovine ribcage.

"My God," Teri breathed.

I picked up a hammer to use as a weapon should I need it. The grip felt sticky. *Blood* was the first thought that crossed my mind, but I didn't want to look down and check. Searching around, I found a small hatchet, and I wiped off the handle on my pants before passing it to Teri. "Just in case," I said.

She turned back toward the kitchen, into our house. "You went to work," she said. "You drove a car there, through the city."

"I don't know what I did," I admitted. "But I never left Frank's house. I couldn't have."

We were both silent after that, overwhelmed by the sheer power of what we were up against. Teri recovered first, and her voice when she spoke was strong, as though she had simply decided not to give in but to continue on as always. "How do we get out of here?" she said.

I did not want to go out the way we had come in; that would only lead us to where we'd been, and I had a suspicion that were we to re-enter our house, our perceptions might once again be manipulated. This room was not that big, though, and I did not see any other doors. I shook my head.

"How does Frank get in and out?" she wondered.

It was a good question, and I looked toward the stack of lumber in the corner, thinking there might be some sort of trapdoor behind it.

There was a rumbling beneath our feet, what felt to me, as a Southern Californian, like an earthquake. I saw movement out of the corner of my eye, and when I swiveled my head in that direction to find out what it was, I saw the entire kitchen descending on the other side of the doorway. There was a moment's darkness, what looked like bare drywall, and then another room came into view beyond the doorframe, a dim antechamber lit by flickering gas wall lamps.

The workroom was some sort of elevator, which was perhaps how Frank navigated this immense edifice he had created. But neither Teri nor I had pushed any buttons or worked any controls. Did that mean that we had been summoned to this new room by someone else?

By Frank?

I held the hammer in front of me, moving slowly toward the open doorway, alert for any sign of movement. Following my lead, Teri held her hatchet at the ready, but we saw no one as we stepped carefully over the threshold.

If the chamber before had been a workroom, this was what the work had gone into. Bones and body parts were incorporated into the walls of the room we entered. It seemed almost alive, an unholy hybrid of biology and architecture, and though nothing moved, I had the sense that it *might*, and our short silent trip to the door on the other side of the antechamber was a jittery and unsteady walk. To our right, segments of skin had been stretched and stitched together, forming a sort of wallpaper. Skeletal hands protruded from dark stained wood that was merged with the metal of the gas lamps, and the dancing flames revealed faces and feet used to close gaps in the wainscoting.

We emerged into a long corridor resembling that of a mid-range hotel, lit by recessed fluorescent bars in the ceiling. I didn't know where we were in the house. Neither of us did. Without a view of the outside world to set our bearings by, we were lost. We could have been anywhere inside the structure. Teri suggested that we try every door until we found a way out, but I was hesitant to use that approach. What if the same sort of thing happened again, and we ended up trapped in some fictional scenario we didn't even recognize?

"Only one of us looks into the rooms," she said. "The other stays grounded in the hallway here."

"And we never let go of each other," I said, "keep in contact at all times."

She nodded. "I'll open doors, peek in, and you look away and hold onto me. Pull me back if you need to."

"It's as good a plan as any."

The first few doors were locked, but the next several weren't, and we could clearly see how the house was a conglomeration of different parts of the original town, the linoleum floor of a grocery store fusing with the concrete of a neighborhood sidewalk, the metal siding of a service station melding with the wooden planks of a barn, which were nailed on the other end into the rock-and-mortar wall of a root cellar. It was as if bits and pieces of Plutarch had been disassembled and thrown haphazardly together, with staircases that led nowhere, doors that opened onto walls, storefront windows that overlooked closet space. Church altars existed side by side with bar counters, fireplaces with urinals.

Each room we encountered was empty of people and most were without furniture. There was no indication of occupancy, and the only noises were the ones we made: our footsteps and voices, the clicking of door handles and squeak of hinges.

Despite the superficial trappings of vacancy and abandonment, I knew Evan, Owen and Twigs were here somewhere.

And Frank.

Beyond that, or below that, I could *feel* the presence of others, could tell that we were not alone, despite the silence, despite the absence of any sign of habitation. It made my skin crawl because I wasn't sure if those presences I felt were living beings...or the wandering dead.

Several yards later, around a downward sloping curve, the corridor ended at a red barn door.

Teri and I looked at each other. It would have been funny if it had been anywhere else at any other time, but nothing was funny here. "Should we…?" I began.

She nodded, though I could feel her trembling. It was going to need both hands to pull aside the bolt, so I let go of her and slid the hammer into my belt, moving forward. She stayed with me, holding the hatchet out in front of her with two hands. "Ready?" I asked.

"Yeah."

Taking a deep breath, I pulled the bolt aside as quickly as possible. Behind the barn door was…

The B&B from Biscuitville.

It was like walking onto a movie set. Identical down to the pattern on the worn carpet, the combination living room/lobby looked as tired and depressing as I remembered. I glanced up the stairs, remembering my stay, and as if to taunt me, I heard a pounding from one of the floors above that sounded like a baseball bat being hit against a wall.

An impossibly skinny form crawled quickly on all fours across the landing.

I jumped, startled.

Another followed, just as skinny, scuttling just as quickly, and I thought of the naked boy who'd thrown rocks at me. I looked to the left, across the living room, through the sheer curtains that covered the closest window, but on the other side of the glass was not the plains outside of Biscuitville, but other rooms within Frank's house, as if the bed and breakfast had been picked up and dropped intact in the middle of the enormous building.

Teri gasped. "I saw—" She was staring up at the landing.

"I know," I said. "I saw it, too."

"It looked like a child."

"Maybe it was."

"Like that kid who threw the rocks?"

I nodded.

"Let's get out of here," she said.

"Wait." I watched the top of the stairs but saw no additional movement. How many were there? I wondered. I had seen two, Teri another. So there were at least three, maybe more. At least they weren't coming down. I was gripping the hammer so tightly my fingers were numb. As long as they stayed upstairs, we should be okay.

But what to do next? We could go back the way we'd come, see what was at the opposite end of the corridor. Or we could continue through the B&B and find out what was beyond the back door.

We definitely weren't going upstairs.

I thought for a moment. My impulse was to ascribe a purposeful pattern, a premeditated design, to the layout of the house, though the rooms, despite the professional construction of sections like this, betrayed the random haphazardness of the Frank I knew. Had he just thrown all this together, building willy nilly as the mood struck him? Or was there a method behind the madness? Had he designed the layers of this mazelike structure in a specific way so as to ensnare those who dared enter?

Had he designed it for me?

As narcissistic as it might be, the idea did not seem out of the realm of possibility, and I could not help thinking that if I unlocked the pattern of design, if I decoded the puzzle he had made, I would know what Frank was up to and would be able to find him. The different types of rooms, the *things* within them, had meaning to Frank, I believed. It all meant something to him, and if I could figure out the *why* of it, I could go after him on a more equal footing.

Upstairs, the pounding noise had stopped, replaced by whispers that were louder than any whisper had a right to be.

Another childlike figure scuttled spiderlike across the landing, its arms and legs spindly and far too thin.

Four.

There were at least four of them.

"Come on." I led Teri forward, down the hall, past the bathroom and supply closet, past the door to the basement. I peeked into the shabby kitchen on the way, and saw the same gas stove and ancient

Frigidaire that had been in Biscuitville.

The door at the end of the hall that should have led to a backyard opened instead onto a formal dining room. Oversized and opulent, it had a long table in the center, with at least a dozen chairs lined equally on each side. On the table, instead of place settings, was a body, half-eaten. Naked and obviously a woman, it had been decapitated and the head was nowhere to be seen. Chunks of flesh had been ripped from the thighs, chest and abdomen, and while the body looked fresh, there was no blood.

I could still hear the whispers behind us, and in my mind I saw those spindly children seated at the table, tearing off pieces of the corpse for their meal.

I was glad I wasn't alone here, but I wished Teri had not come. There was no guarantee that either of us would be able to get out, and I would have felt better knowing she was safely back in California.

"This is sick," she said. Her voice was stronger than I expected, disgusted rather than frightened, and I wondered if Teri thought the corpse was some sort of prop or mannequin. I wasn't about to check, but I was certain it was real, despite the lack of blood, and before she came to the same conclusion, I hurried her through the room where, on the opposite end, we walked through an open vestibule that led into a storage area. There were cobweb-embraced boxes and dust-covered trunks, ladders and saw horses, irregularly shaped items covered with tarps and sheets. I pulled up a corner of the sheet nearest to me and saw beneath it the disassembled frame and headboard of an old bed.

Teri lifted a section of tarp to reveal an antique printing press. "What do you think happened to Mark?" she asked, apropos of nothing.

Neither of us had mentioned that awful scream we'd heard in the seconds before we'd been locked in here, though I suspect it had been on both of our minds.

"I think he might be dead," I said.

"Eaten?" she asked.

She'd known the body on the table was real; she was simply tougher than I thought.

"Maybe," I admitted.

"What about the others? Owen and Evan and Twigs? Do you think they're still in here?"

"They pretty much have to be; I don't think they escaped. I doubt they followed the same path we have, but I'm sure they're in here somewhere."

"Alive?"

"I hope so."

But at this point I didn't think that likely, and neither did she.

Teri looked down at the hatchet in her hand, then up at me. "So what are we doing?" she asked. "Are we looking for a way out? Or are we looking for Frank?"

"Whichever comes first?" I smiled feebly.

"We're in over our heads. This is definitely more than I expected, and I have a feeling it's more than you bargained for, too. We can't go up against—" She gestured around us. "—all *this*. At this point, we're just...wandering around. Reacting. We need to be more proactive. We need to find a way out of here, bring in an *army* if we have to, and tear this thing down to the ground."

She was right, and that sounded good from where we were standing, but out in the real world, the same obstacle was there as before: no one was going to believe us. All the cell phone photos in the world would not be enough to convince law enforcement officials that, out here, in the middle of the desert, over the town of Plutarch, a handyman had constructed an architectural monstrosity encompassing multitudes that was home to horrors out of a scary movie.

She squeezed my hand. "He got the rest of your family," she said softly. "Don't let him get you."

He had already, and she knew it. That was why we were here. That was why my life was my life.

Still, I nodded, agreeing. With everything we'd encountered, there had to be some way to convince the authorities that something terrible was going on, even if they didn't buy the specifics. Hell, a shot of the abandoned cop cars alone should bring the law swarming down on this place.

"Let's go," I said.

Past the storage room was a passageway. Unlike the hallways and corridors we'd previously encountered, the passage was narrow and claustrophobic, lit by dim bulbs hanging occasionally from a wire that ran down the center of the cement ceiling. A concrete floor and unadorned walls stretched forward several yards before turning right, then continued several more yards before turning left, then turned left again, then right, then left...

Even if we *had* known where we were in the building, even if our sense of direction had been correctly oriented upon leaving the storage room, we would have been hopelessly lost within moments of entering the passageway. It seemed deliberately designed to confuse. There were no side corridors we could have taken, no doors in the walls, and the only thing we could do was continue on or turn back. I felt more uncomfortable the farther along we went, not just mentally but physically. It may have been my imagination or merely the fact that I was out of shape, but I was sweating profusely. The air felt warm and damp, as though we were approaching a furnace room, and after several moments, I stopped walking, glancing over to see if Teri was having the same experience.

She was visibly hot, her face red and drenched with sweat, but before I could say a word to her about it, I heard a noise from within the passageway behind us. A low, quiet noise barely audible above the sound of our breathing.

The soft pad of bare feet on concrete.

The sound chilled me to the bone. Teri heard it, too, because I saw her eyes widen, and I put my finger to my lips, warning her to remain silent.

Pat-pat.

Pat-pat.

Pat-pat.

It was growing closer. Or at least louder. Now I was not certain that it *was* coming from behind us. Maybe the footsteps were coming from in front of us. It was impossible to tell in this directionless labyrinth, and as much as the soft insistence of the sound, it was the fact that its source was so indeterminate that frightened me.

Teri and I huddled closer together, weapons extended, afraid to proceed, afraid to retreat.

Pat-pat.

Pat-pat.

The bare feet continued to approach.

"What is it?" Teri whispered.

I shook my head. And then I saw the source of the noise. An Asian girl, not more than five or six, appeared from around the corner in front of us. Dressed in a dirty shift, eyes vacant and staring, she marched desultorily forward, arms stiff at her sides, lanky hair parted in the middle and hanging down, framing her bruised face. I should have felt concern for her, should have felt sympathy for the fact that she was in this place and had clearly been abused. But I felt none of that, and it was the fact that she *was* here that caused my heart to race and the hairs to stand up on the back of my neck.

Teri, I noticed, was not rushing to give her aid either. She must have felt the same way I did, and without even asking the girl if anything was wrong or if we could help, we hurried back the way we'd come, trying to get away from her.

Another figure emerged from around the corner.

This one was a man, a thin, heavily mustached, white trash-looking man who was shuffling toward us like a zombie. There was something off about his appearance, about the *texture* of his form, and it took me a second to figure out what it was.

I could see through him.

Not completely. There was still some *there* there, but his substance was not as solid as it should have been, and behind the vaguely flesh-colored face I could see the grayness of concrete wall.

Turning in the opposite direction, I saw the girl coming toward us.

She was not merely abused, I realized, she was dead. Her form, too, was translucent. How could I have not noticed that immediately?

"Ghosts," Teri said, stating aloud what I was thinking. "They're ghosts."

Knowing we couldn't make it past the man, we opted to try and go around the girl. We hugged the wall as we neared her, flattening ourselves against the cement. She paid no attention to either of us but continued walking forward, and as she passed, the hem of her shift brushed against me. I felt coldness, as though I'd been touched by ice.

We hurried away in the direction she had come, hoping we wouldn't run into anything else.

Were these the people Frank had killed? I wondered. It occurred to me that maybe the wandering ghosts of Frank's victims didn't actually wander. Maybe he had found a way to capture and keep them. Maybe this house was like a prison or a—

"Venus flytrap," Teri said.

It was as if she had read my thoughts, and I looked at her, a little spooked by the coincidence. She must have mistaken the expression on my face for one of confusion, because she said, "This house. It's like a Venus flytrap. It attracts people here, then traps them inside and...kills them, I assume. Although that better not happen to us." She didn't sound as worried as I thought she should have been.

"If he builds it, they will come," she continued, knowing I would get the reference. "And if they die here, out in the middle of nowhere, and they're not buried or cremated or interred where they're supposed to be...then they wander. Or they're Frank's."

"I was thinking the same thing," I said. "Exactly."

There was a pause.

"Which means he's going to try and kill us," Teri said.

I nodded.

"And we don't have any secret spells or mystical chants that can stop him."

I hefted the hammer. "Just his own tools."

"As fitting as that might be, I don't think it's going to work."

I didn't either.

"We need to get out."

We were walking away from those two—

Had they passed through each other? Were they even aware the other was there?

—but not exactly hurrying, knowing that we might encounter more figures, other ghosts, at any time. If the house was a trap, I was thinking, maybe it didn't just lure in people, killing and entombing them away from their intended burial sites, people like those policemen whose cars were outside...

and us.

Maybe it sucked in ghosts who were already wandering. Maybe it stored them here, using their energy. Maybe the entire house was one big battery that Frank could use for...what?

Anything seemed possible, and the range of alternatives was dizzying.

We still had not encountered anything else, and we turned the next corner—

—and were in Sandy Simmons' house.

The passageway ended where her front door should have been. We were facing the living room, and what really unnerved me was the fact that the furnishings were identical to those in Sandy's actual home. Had Frank been there? He had to have seen it. How else would he know where she placed her television and her couch and the rest of her furniture? Even more unexplainable was how he had replicated those items, brought them out here to Texas and installed them deep within this impossible building.

The Simmons house meant nothing to Teri—she'd never seen it—and she pulled me forward as though we were passing through another generic room. We passed into the kitchen, and I sucked in my breath. On the floor was a white woman's handbag I recognized.

My mom's.

Your mama's bones are in my home.

It was not only hers, it was the one with which she'd been buried, but I didn't want to go there, and I didn't say anything to Teri as we stepped over and moved past it. My mind was spinning. The B&B? The Simmons home? I knew what this meant. Somewhere within this gigantic warren of rooms was our Randall house, the place where, for me, it had all started. Where Billy had died. Where perhaps the bones of my mom had been taken.

But where was Frank?

I imagined him sitting in some sort of control room, staring at video monitors, watching all of our movements through hidden cameras, though I knew that was highly unlikely. I'd never seen such a no-tech environment as this house, and while Frank might be watching us, I doubted it was through cameras. Behind everything here was not the machinery of science fiction but the supernatural powers of horror.

Past the kitchen, where the door to the back patio should have been, was an archway that led into another kitchen. It might have been a mirror image of Sandy's, but it was not. It did face in the opposite direction, but in place of modern appliances there was a wood-burning stove, an old-fashioned ice box and a gigantic sink with a hand-pump for water. In the center of the room was an unadorned wooden dining table.

We exited through the kitchen's only other door into a plain primitive shack completely devoid of furniture. There were only two things within the shack: a man and a woman, naked, arms and legs spread wide, nailed to the wall on our left.

George and Betsy.

They had not succeeded in scaring me away, and they had clearly been punished for their failure. They were still alive, but barely, sections of skin flayed from their bodies, visible bites taken out of their arms and legs. Unlike the last time I'd seen them, they both looked their current age, faces thin and sunken, more heavily wrinkled than anyone I had ever seen. The sounds they made were pleading, heart-rending, and I had the sense that what was left of them was waiting for the arrival of a god, a savior, something to redeem their suffering.

This location had to have some meaning. Was this the house where one of them had lived as a child? Had they played here with Frank when he was nothing more than a bad little boy, torturing bugs and animals? Was this where their lives had first become entwined with his?

"Jesus," Teri breathed. She turned toward me. "We have to help them. We have to get them down."

The thought hadn't occurred to me, and I wasn't sure if that was due to the unreality of this place and everything in it, the fact that I feared and resented George and Betsy because I considered them Frank's co-conspirators, or simply a lack of common humanity on my part. But I understood what Teri was saying, and I moved across the uneven plank floor to where they were nailed onto the wall. This close, I could see the spikes that had been driven not only into their hands and feet, but into their necks and stomachs. I stopped before George, wondering how it could be possible that he and Betsy were still alive and thinking that, if by some miracle they really *were*, moving them could very well be a death sentence.

"I can't do it," I said.

"You have to!"

"They'll die if I try. Those spikes are through their *necks*. And *organs*."

In my ears, their individual whimperings combined into a single line that had the cadence of a prayer. Only a god *could* save them now, and I could tell from the tears rolling down Teri's face that she understood this, too. Then I saw her face harden beneath the tears, and as she subconsciously raised her hatchet, I knew she was thinking of Frank, and that any man who could torture people like this did not deserve to live.

I wasn't convinced they were not already dead, but even if they were, if Frank was somehow tormenting them beyond the grave, it was still an act so evil that it could never be forgiven.

"Let's get out of here," Teri begged.

We turned to leave through what was positioned as the front door of the shack. The door was actually closed, and I pulled it open to reveal a round room beyond, a strange room with multiple doors, and walls, floor and ceiling that were all painted a strange sickly yellow. Throughout the cylindrical chamber, there were shadows where shadows should not have been, and in their inky blackness I sensed life. Perhaps not life as I'd always understood it, but, still, a consciousness, a claim to sentience that was completely at odds with such unformed shapes.

It was not the shadows that captured my attention, however, but the female figure suspended upside down from the center of the ceiling.

Irene.

"I can't take much more of this," Teri said, and I could tell from the sob that caught in her throat that she was telling the truth.

Slowly, I approached the hanging body. Frank's wife was definitely dead and had been for some time. Her remains were skeletal, almost mummified, though the aspects of her face that had frightened me as a child were still there and scared me even now. The shadows in the round room grew visibly active as I drew nearer to Irene, one of them along the edge of the wall swirling in such a way that it almost coalesced into a shape I recognized. I stopped walking and the shadows stopped moving.

Something did not want me getting too close to Irene.

Glancing around the circular chamber, there seemed to be a purposefulness to its setup, a reason for its existence. The doors were evenly spaced in the curved walls, and Irene hung in the center like a pendulum. I was reminded of a clock, and though I knew the room was not a clock, I could not help thinking that it served a definite function in Frank's world.

I took a step back, away from Irene, and the shadows simmered down.

"Which door?" I asked.

Teri shook her head, beyond caring, but before I could choose a route to take, one of the doors opened, and an old man wandered into the room. Bearded and disheveled, dressed in raggedy clothes, he looked furtively around upon entering, saw us, then made his way around the edge of the wall, carefully avoiding all shadows.

Teri squinted at the old man as he approached, and I felt her grip on my hand tighten. "Oh, God," she said. "Oh, God."

"What?"

"It's Evan."

She was right. I saw it now, and gazing into his wrinkled bearded face made me wonder how long we had been in here.

Years? Decades?

The thought filled me with dread and panic. Maybe everyone I knew was already dead. Maybe I'd been a missing person for so long that my house and belongings had been sold at an estate sale. A feeling of hopelessness and despair washed over me.

Evan reached us, still glancing around as if afraid he might be overheard. His voice was little more than a hoarse whisper. "Daniel?"

"Evan?"

He nodded. "You look the same," he rasped. "Both of you." He looked from me to Teri and back again. "How's that possible?"

"How long do you think you've been in here?" Teri wondered.

"I have no idea, but—" He pulled on his long beard, ran a hand through his wild hair. "—a long time."

"Where's Owen?" I asked. "Where's Twigs?"

"I haven't seen them in years."

Years.

As in Frank's other house, the laws of physics, the realities of time, apparently did not apply here.

"Two days," I calculated, taking at face value the disorienting time we'd spent in our own house in those sham lives. "We've been here for two days."

Evan started crying.

I didn't know what to do or how to respond. I turned to Teri for help, and she handed me her hatchet and gave him a hug. "It's all right," she said. "It's all right."

"No," he sobbed. "It's not."

I glanced around. The shadows weren't moving, but they were still in places they should not have been, and they still gave off an aura of consciousness. A slight breeze was blowing in through the doorway Evan had entered, and Irene's upside down body was swaying a little, spinning on the rope from which she was suspended. The sight disturbed me, and I had to look away.

Evan was drying his eyes. "Sorry," he croaked. "Sorry."

"No reason to be sorry," I told him.

Teri patted his back. "You're with us now. We're going to get out of here."

Even amidst all this craziness, I felt compelled to understand the practical aspects of Evan's existence. "What have you been eating?" I asked. "Where do you get your food? Or sleep? Or go to the bathroom?"

He sighed wearily. "There are plenty of kitchens, plenty of bedrooms, plenty of bathrooms."

"What about Frank? Have you seen Frank?"

"No. I haven't seen him. I've been avoiding him. But I know where he is." There was a pause. "I can take you there."

Teri and I shared a glance. Was this part of the trap? No. One look at Evan's devastated face told me that the suffering he'd experienced was real. There was no way he had been co-opted. He wanted out of here as much as we did. Probably more.

I reached out and put a hand on his shoulder, and he flinched at my touch. I could feel the bones beneath his skin. "Let's go," I said. "Let's find Frank and put a stop to this once and for all."

FOUR

EVAN KNEW HIS way around. He did not roam aimlessly, as we had been doing. He lived in this house and was familiar with its rooms and hallways; he knew which doors led where.

Following his steps, avoiding the shadows, we exited the round room through the same door he had used. He stopped us before we walked through. "We have to stay away from the Little Man," he said. "Whatever you do, don't let him see you."

The Little Man.

Something about the appellation sent a shiver down my spine. "Who is the Little Man?" I asked.

"I don't *know* who he is. I don't know *what* he is." Evan shuddered. "I just know what he does. Stay away from him. Don't let him see you."

He led us through a maze of passageways. The air grew warm again and fetid, as it had in the other passage, and I was suddenly struck by the absurd notion that these concrete corridors were not hallways for people to pass through but heating ducts supplying warm air to different parts of the house. If that were true, the inhabitants of this dwelling would have to be giants, and though I knew the rooms were built for people of normal size, it was an image I could not shake.

Several times, I thought I heard footsteps behind us, though when I looked back, I saw no one there.

I was struck once more by not only the elaborate construction of the building, the way it incorporated disparate elements of the forgotten town of Plutarch into its composition, but by the professionalism of its assembly. Yes, there were parts that were clearly the result of Frank's substandard skills, but others were astoundingly well-made. How could the incompetent handyman who'd lived across the street from us in Randall have created such a perfectly fused amalgam of styles? It was inconceivable to me, and it reinforced the idea that he had access to a power we could not even comprehend. I imagined a scenario in which Frank kept adding onto the house, never stopping, until the structure spanned the surrounding desert, reached San Antonio, and continued on, engulfing other cities until the entire country was incorporated within its walls. It sounded crazy—and it was—but when I thought about all we'd encountered, recalled what Owen had said about Kayley's theory of increased supernatural activity building up to something, the impossible didn't seem quite so impossible.

Where *was* Kayley? I wondered. Had she managed to contact the law and bring someone back? If she had, it hadn't mattered. We'd been here for God knew how long, and no one had come to rescue us.

Maybe the rescuers had become trapped as well.

There seemed no end to this nightmare, and I was convinced that the only way to stop it was to dispatch Frank and burn this house to the ground.

Dispatch Frank.

Did I really think I would be able to kill the man if it came down to it? I was a suburban real estate agent who had never even fired a gun. Was I really going to use the hammer tucked in my belt to smash in Frank's head? If given the opportunity, could I actually perform such a brutal act?

I thought of Billy.

Yes, I could.

Evan had led us to a large dark gallery that reminded me of the Hall of Mammals in the Natural History Museum. At the museum, dark wood walls were broken up every few yards by lighted dioramas populated with taxidermied animals placed in scenes that resembled their native habitats. Here, the layout was the same, only instead of nature scenes, the lighted squares revealed offices and bedrooms, kitchens and art studios, family rooms and libraries. There were people living in the displays. Ensconced in rooms that were essentially their own little living quarters, they ignored us as we passed. We saw a well-heeled woman primping in front of a dresser mirror, a middle-aged couple sitting on a sofa and staring blankly into space, an older man at a workbench whittling something out of wood, a younger man in a rocking chair reading a book. Were they alive or dead? People or ghosts? Did they know where they were, or were they trapped as Teri and I had been, living in their own alternate reality?

"Who are they?" I asked.

Evan shrugged.

"Did you ever talk to them?"

"I tried. Years ago. They didn't want to talk to me. I'm not even sure they talk to each other. Or know where they are."

It was odd conversing with this sober Evan. There was no sign of the showbiz obsessed, easily excitable television writer I knew, and I wondered when that spirit had been leeched out of him.

Teri approached a room on the right, where a young woman using a treadle sewing machine was making a flower-print dress. Dozens of other dresses hung on racks behind her. "Excuse me," Teri said. "Can I ask you a question?"

The woman looked at her, confused. She did not answer, and there was a haunted look in her eyes that belied the work her busy hands were doing.

I turned to a man in the room opposite, a guy about my age in a bare monastic cell furnished only by a cot. The man was on his knees, praying. "Hello," I said. He looked up. For a brief second, I saw a flicker of hope in his eyes, then it was washed away by what seemed like bafflement and an overwhelming despair. Immediately, he returned to his prayers.

Evan was right. They did not seem to know where they were. I got the same sense from them as I had from those ghosts we'd encountered in the passageway, that they were lost and searching for something: meaning, purpose, a redeemer, a god. Ultimately, it didn't matter that they were here. No matter where they were, they would have felt trapped and lost in a pointless existence, and Teri turned to me and said, "They're not going to give us any help."

We kept walking. Between two of the rooms was a stairwell, and Evan took us up the steps one flight, two flights, three flights, four, until we were in a large empty space that looked like the floor of an abandoned factory. Suspicious ambient light illuminated the vast room, and within the accordion ceiling I saw glowing skylights. Were we at the top of the house? Was there a way to break through those windows onto the roof and find a way out and down?

Evan didn't stop but continued on, certain of where he was going, and Teri and I followed. We could always come back here, I reasoned. Far off, from some other room, came the faint but unmistakable sound of infants screaming in agony.

"Those are babies!" Teri cried, distraught.

Evan did not respond.

"They're torturing babies!"

"They're just crying," I said placatingly, but I knew she was right. We both did. As faint as they were, the screams were unlike anything I'd ever heard.

Evan's voice was sober. "It's the Little Man. That's what he does."

We strode quickly across the empty floor, and while there was no fluctuation in temperature, no variation in the feel of the air, nothing physical that was in any way changed, something had altered, although I had no idea what it was, or where or when it had happened.

I grew gradually more aware of my arms as I walked. They felt awkward to me, and I wasn't sure if I was walking the way I usually did. Was I swinging them out too far? Not far enough? I couldn't tell. Everything I tried felt wrong, and I started wondering about my steps. Was my stride too long? Too short? Something about the way I was walking felt off, and I glanced over at Teri, unnerved to see a disconcerted expression on her face that perfectly mirrored the way I felt. Evan was walking so fast he was practically running, and it occurred to me that he was moving quickly through the room on purpose, so as not to let whatever we were experiencing affect us or sink in.

"Hurry up," he croaked. "We're almost there."

We were rapidly approaching the opposite end of the room, and in the center of a bleak industrial wall was a perfectly round opening that looked as though it belonged in a submarine.

"Through here," Evan said.

We ducked through the doorway.

And...

Teri and Evan were gone.

I was in the living room of our A-frame as it had looked in the 1980s. My dad and my brother were sitting on the couch, playing with the primitive electronic game Simon. Wedges of primary colors lit up randomly on the circular toy to the accompaniment of synthesized musical tones, and the two of them took turns pressing down on the colors, trying to replicate the pattern.

A painful pang wrenched my heart. Billy looked just as he had when we'd first gotten the vacation home, but it surprised me how much I had forgotten about his appearance. His hair was lighter than I recalled, his smile more innocent. Time and memory had made him seem more mature in retrospect, perhaps because I'd been close to that age myself. But I saw now that he'd been a true child, a little boy. He'd had his whole life ahead of him, a life he'd been denied, a life that had been taken away from him.

By Frank.

I'd never been entirely sure whether Billy's death had been intentional or the result of Frank's incompetence, but at this point it didn't matter. After all I'd learned about Frank, I knew he was guilty of far more than I ever could have suspected.

My dad looked up at me, and he smiled in the way that he had before Billy's death but that I had never seen after. "Daniel? You want to play?"

I wanted to more than anything else in the world. I wanted to sit on the couch next to my dad and my brother and be with them again.

But even though they were pretending I was still ten years old, I was an adult, and it was this heartbreaking discrepancy that kept me grounded in reality, that made me realize they were not really there and this was a false echo of a reunion that could never be.

"I'll beat you this time!" Billy told me, grinning as he held up the Simon, and my eyes teared up.

There was a noise from the rear of the A-frame, what sounded like someone bumping against a wall.

"Are you okay?" my dad called out, glancing in that direction.

"Mommy?" Billy said, Simon lighting up red-yellow-blue and making beep-bop-boop noises in his hand.

It emerged from my parents' bedroom into the short hall beyond the kitchen and turned in my direction.

The clothes it wore were my mother's, but the being inhabiting those clothes was unformed, pale arms ending not in hands and fingers but in vaguely rounded stumps, the pallid face so ill-defined that I was not even sure it had features.

I froze at the sight of it, and realized that any fear I had felt before this moment was nothing compared to the all-encompassing terror that unformed figure instilled in me. It began creeping toward the living room, moving slowly, and I was reminded of the way a snail propelled itself forward through undulations of its slimy body.

Descending footsteps sounded on the stairway that led to the loft where Billy and I had had our beds, and seconds later Frank stepped into the living room. He was dressed as always in engineer's overalls, and his eyes peered out at me from behind his thick black-framed glasses. "Daniel," he said. "Glad you could make it."

He did not seem as arrogant as he had at the other house. There was a subdued quality to his voice, a subservience in his manner, and when he stepped forward so he could peek around the corner and see into the hall, I realized what that thing masquerading as my mom had to be.

The Dark Wife.

It continued to creep slowly forward, and Frank awaited its arrival in the room with a mixture of anticipation and submissiveness. He didn't go to meet it, though. He *waited*, and that told me a lot. On the couch, Billy and my dad remained unmoving, like two robots whose power had been suddenly shut off. The Simon in Billy's hands was the only sign of life, its flashing lights and electronic sounds continuing unabated.

And still the Dark Wife advanced with its snail crawl, faceless and utterly silent. Frozen in place, frightened beyond words, I could do nothing but watch in horror as the thing approached. I could feel its power, rolling over me in unseen waves. I did not know what it was. I *could* not know what it was. The explanation for its existence was utterly beyond my comprehension. I believed it was the god for which those lost souls we'd encountered were searching, a god that Frank had been serving since he discovered it in Vietnam.

At the last minute, self-preservation trumped fear, and I found myself backing up, toward the front door of the A-frame through which I'd entered. Behind me, my fingers found the knob, but it wouldn't turn. I was trapped, with no way to escape, and I instinctively reached for the hammer in my waistband.

The Dark Wife had reached the edge of the kitchen counter, and in a strangely formal, oddly courtly move, Frank reached for its hand. There was a sickening fusion of flesh where his rough fingers met the white rounded stump.

I had to get out of here. Filled with an almost animalistic desperation, I turned to the side, keeping one eye on the horrifying couple, and used the hammer to shatter the window to the right of the doorway.

The reaction was instantaneous. The Dark Wife visibly blanched, and Frank's face contorted with rage. "What are you doing?" he yelled, apoplectic.

There was nothing beyond the glass other than an inky blackness so thick that it seemed to have mass. I could not get out through there, but I was still desperate to escape, and, remembering how cheap the walls of our pre-fab home had been, I shifted my efforts to the space between the window and the door, swinging the hammer as hard as I could and using it to punch a hole in the painted drywall.

"I built that!" Frank screamed.

I hit the wall again.

And again.

The house around me flickered, and behind our vacation home I saw the bones of the surrounding structure, a primitive hodgepodge of beams and supports, rafters and planks. Teri and Evan were there as well, nearby, and they saw me at the same instant I saw them, just before the A-frame reasserted itself around me.

I hit the wall again, then swung the hammer hard at the door itself.

"Stop!" Frank ordered, and there was not just anger but fear in his voice. I'm sure he wanted to attack me and most certainly would have if he'd been able to do so, but his hand was attached to the Dark Wife, and the Dark Wife was not doing well. Each swing of the hammer was like a blow to its body, and it was rooted in place, even its slow progress halted.

The Dark Wife was connected to the building, I realized. Not just our little vacation home but the enormous outer structure in which it was enclosed.

A broader realization came to me. It was the house that was holding *all* of this together, Frank's construction that had trapped us and everyone else in this place. It had *always* been Frank's handiwork—his interred bodies and stolen materials—that had been at the root of everything, that had summoned whatever power granted him the ability to do what he had done.

My hammer punched another hole in the drywall, and then Teri and Evan were by my side, using the opportunity of that flicker to pass through the temporarily dissolved walls. For the first time since we'd found him again, Evan seemed confident and enthusiastic, sensing possibility in the weakness we'd found.

Frank had not stopped screaming a profane string of threats, but he was sidelined and impotent, and I told Teri to use her hatchet to start whaling on anything she could find. I quickly led Evan over to the boxy 1980s entertainment center against the wall opposite the couch. My dad had kept tools in a junk drawer below the shelf holding the television, and I opened it, gratified to find that the replication of our house was accurate down to the level of cabinet contents. I found a claw hammer, handed it to Evan, and we began attacking the nearest wall in earnest, working in tandem to create and widen an opening in the cheap building material.

Drawing back my arm, I swung again and practically fell forward when I encountered only air. The wall was gone, the A-frame was gone, and Evan, Teri and I were in that other room I had briefly seen through the flickering walls. Billy and my dad were gone, too, and their absence wrenched at my heart. I knew they weren't real, but the fact that I had not been able to say goodbye to...whatever they were...filled me with a deep sense of sadness. I had lost them again, though I had not really had them back, and that loss filled me with regret.

It also renewed my hatred for Frank and made me determined to stop to him once and for all.

This room was far more crudely constructed, like a clubhouse a not-particularly-handy dad would make with his son. Ill-fitting sheets of plywood were hammered with too many nails onto randomly joined two-by-fours that acted as an off-center frame. On the unpainted walls were random letters and strange symbols drawn in red. This was a room I could tell Frank had actually built, and without pausing, the three of us assaulted its walls. We needed to tear down as much as we could as quickly as we could. It was the only way to fight back.

Frank and the Dark Wife had disappeared, although whether that was for their own safety or in order to prepare for an attack I had no way of knowing. I also couldn't afford to wait and find out. Assuming that those letters and symbols had some sort of mystical purpose, I called Teri over to where Evan and I were bashing our hammers against the wall and told her to use her hatchet to obliterate as much of the red writing as she could.

The results were remarkable. From behind the plywood came the sounds of lumber falling and concrete cracking, and when I looked through one of the interstitial breaks in the badly built wall, I saw the collapsing of other rooms beyond. Teri kept chopping, smashing into splinters a circle connected to the letter X. There was a whoosh of air, a sensation of falling, as though the rudimentary room we were in was dropping down an elevator shaft, but there was no resultant crash that followed. The feeling of movement simply stopped, and when Evan and I managed to knock a hole in the plywood and then pull off a section of wall, we saw what looked like a crypt or vault, a chamber with a dirt floor and stone sides, dim flickering light issuing from a kerosene lantern hanging from a hook.

With a creak of nails, we pulled off another piece of ply board, tossing it aside. I pounded off the two-by-four behind it, and the way was clear to exit the room we were in and enter the larger darker chamber. Was it a basement? It looked and felt like it, but there was no way to know. The room had a permanence, however, that had been lacking in the other rooms we'd encountered. Even the concrete corridors had seemed less substantial than this dark rock vault, and I realized that we were in what had to be the heart of the house.

There was a huge hole in the center of the dirt floor in front of us, and, sticking close together, the three of us approached. Glancing into its inky depths gave me a disorienting sense of vertigo, and I stepped back, afraid of falling.

"What...What is it?" Teri wondered.

We both looked toward Evan, but he shook his head. As familiar as he was with the house, even he was stumped.

"What do you think's down there?" Teri asked.

"I don't know," I admitted.

Evan had moved over to the wall on our left, and he began chipping away at the stone with the claw end of his hammer. It was a good idea. If vandalizing the A-frame and taking apart that plywood room had started things unraveling, destroying what we could of this vault should speed up the process even more. That mysterious hole had convinced me that this room was the key to whatever Frank was doing, and the fact that the room had been built like a fortress around the pit, as though to protect it, made me confident that this was indeed the key to the house.

I raised my own hammer, about to strike at the stone, but a hint of movement off to the right revealed the presence of another man, watching us. He'd been standing so still that I had not noticed him before, but as I glanced in his direction, I saw others as well, immobile against the wall, their skin bleached of all color, as if they had been bred in the darkness of the pit. They were wearing the uniforms of police officers, and I knew they belonged to those abandoned patrol cars outside. I didn't know what was wrong with them or what they were, and while I did not believe they were dead, I did not think they were alive either.

Teri was hitting the wall now, too, using the dull edge of her hatchet to attack the stone, and though I kept my eye on the cops, they made no effort to stop us. I was chipping away at the wall myself, gratified to see small chunks of rock break off and fall to the dirt, but I was making no real progress and neither was anyone else. The room was too well-constructed.

Which led me to believe that Frank had not made it himself.

Where *was* Frank? Hiding? No, that was not his style. He was watching, waiting, planning something. Tearing down what he'd built had enraged him, but it also seemed to have weakened him. His strength was connected to the durability of his creation, and judging by what we'd seen of the disappearing rooms around us, Teri's obliteration of the writing and symbols on the wooden walls had probably debilitated him further. Was there something in here that we could employ to similar effect? I looked over at Teri and Evan, all of us with our puny little tools masquerading as weapons, and thought that we'd better find something. And quick. Because when Frank did return, he would be armed for bear.

We weren't gaining much traction attacking the stone wall, and I was about to say that we should go back into the previous room and wipe out what was left of the red—

blood?

—markings on the plywood, when I glanced in that direction and saw movement behind the open beams, a small dark figure that seemed to emerge from the wood itself, from a complicated scribble that took up a large lower section of a ply board sheet. Evan saw it, too, and cried out in fear at the sight, clearly recognizing it for what it was. The figure moved slowly around the other room, disappearing for a moment, and was out of sight until emerging into the opening through which we'd come, illuminated by the dim light of the kerosene lamp.

I knew instantly who it was and understood why Evan had screamed.

The Little Man.

He was ancient and Asian, and he had to be the excommunicated cleric who had mentored Frank in Vietnam. He was wearing Vietnamese peasant clothes, what Americans had always derisively referred to as "pajamas," and he clutched what looked like some type of ceremonial knife in his tiny hands. Had he shrunk, I wondered, or had he always been this small? He poked his head into the vault and looked carefully in all directions to make sure there was no attacker lying in wait. He seemed to be neither dwarf nor midget, although his proportions were those of a child. He was an evil man, I knew that, and the expression on his face was one of undisguised malevolence.

I glanced from Evan to Teri. Could we take him? There were three of us and we were bigger. Two of us had hammers and one a hatchet.

But he had emerged from a wall, clutching some sort of ceremonial knife in his hands, and was God knew how many years old, with who knew what powers. No doubt he could kill us easily, and our wandering spirits would be absorbed into the house, with no one ever the wiser.

There was nowhere to run, no way to escape, but as the Little Man approached the edge of the pit, glanced dismissively at us, then stared into the blackness, I understood that he was not going to kill us. He didn't care about us at all.

He was here to kill Frank.

He hated Frank.

The realization shocked me. My assumption had been that everything within the walls of this structure was working together as one cohesive unit toward a single common goal. But I remembered how in the rest home Dang Nguyen had told us that the outcast cleric who had been Frank's mentor had been killed by his disciple. So, if indeed this was him, he had a definite reason to hate Frank. Not only that, but, if he was here, that meant he had been taken from his country and installed in this Texas monstrosity. Talk about the wandering dead. He could not have gotten any farther from where he was supposed to be than where he was.

The Little Man began chanting. The words were in Vietnamese, and even though I did not know the language, I could tell there was something off about them. This was not the musical dialect Dang and May had exchanged; it was harsher, darker, with accents and cadences that seemed dissonant and discordant.

The chanting was answered by a voice from the pit, a smooth, almost *liquid* voice that responded in a manner that I had never heard before, that *no one* had ever heard before. These were new words, words that had been spoken before only in Hell, and the sound of them rocked me to the core, grating against everything I knew or thought I knew, conjuring images I would not have believed myself capable of imagining.

I staggered back against the stone, feeling as though my brain was about to explode. From the agonized expression on Teri's face, I could tell that the words had the same effect on her, and she dropped her hatchet, using both hands to cradle her head. On the other side of me, Evan was whimpering, and when I turned toward him, I saw that he had fallen to his knees.

From the center of the pit rose the Dark Wife. Or what *had* been the Dark Wife. It was not wearing clothes anymore but was nude, and despite the fact that Frank had dressed it as my mother, its unadorned body possessed no feminine features. It was neither mother nor wife but some sort of embryonic...creature. What I felt in my bones to be an emergent god. For there was something distinctly larval about its appearance, and I realized that it was not yet fully formed, not completely finished. What would happen when it was, I did not even want to guess.

I only knew that Frank needed to die in order to stop its evolution.

The would-be god was still speaking in that abhorrent tongue, its hateful language drilling painfully into my brain. The Little Man continued his chanting as well. The two were not engaged in a dialogue but were talking at each other, around each other, past each other. He was summoning it from the pit, and it arose from the darkness as though stationed atop a rising platform. There was no platform, however, and seconds later the slimy white stumps of its unformed feet floated above the hole's edge and alighted on the dirt floor.

The cacophony was becoming unbearable, and I was forced to drop my hammer in order to plug my ears. It helped only a little. Even muffled, the hellish duet bored, unwanted, into my skull.

The Little Man stepped forward, ceremonial knife extended. With no preamble, no muss, no fuss, he thrust it into the creature, its point entering the slimy white flesh just above the thigh. He moved the knife to the left, to the right, up, down, carving a symbol into the being as its liquid voice devolved into a series of disgusting grunts. The nascent god's substance was like butter, the blade slicing through it with seemingly no resistance, and the Asian mystic stepped back as sections of flesh slid away from that carved symbol in gelatinous segments, slipping to the dirt where they reformed into four smaller facsimiles of the original figure. Those repulsive grunts, like the sound of gargling glass, were issuing from four mouths now, in a higher pitch than before but in perfect synchronization.

Suddenly Frank was standing next to the split forms of the god. Had he been there all along, had he come through some concealed door in the room, or had he just appeared out of thin air? I didn't know, and it didn't matter. He was here now, and while he looked frighteningly old—the age he *should* have been—he was by no means enfeebled. He started purposefully toward the Little Man, an expression of undisguised wrath on his sallow wrinkled face.

Ignoring the pain in my head, I reached down, grabbing my hammer for protection.

The Little Man definitely wanted to kill Frank. Until now, he'd been unable to do so—otherwise he would have finished off the man long before now—but he appeared to have faith in the weapon he wielded. His face filled with rage and hate, he held the knife with supreme confidence. Having stopped chanting, he shouted at Frank in Vietnamese, and Frank responded calmly in the same language. Frank had killed his mentor the first time, so the Little Man was already dead, but I was still hoping for an epic fight. It was not to be. The Asian man thrust quickly with the knife, but Frank easily stepped aside and avoided the blade. Bellowing with fury, he picked up the Little Man from behind and threw him into the pit.

And that was it.

There was no prolonged battle between two powerful necromancers or whatever-they-were. There was only a brief one-sided attack: a lunge, an apprehension, and then the Little Man was tossed into the black hole, disappearing instantly, the whole thing literally over and done with in seconds.

But the knife fell onto the dirt in front of the pit.

Had he dropped it accidentally or had it been intentional? I had no idea. I only hoped Frank had not seen it. Because that thing did seem to have power. It had cut the embryonic god into pieces, and the Little Man had obviously thought it had the capacity to take out Frank as well.

The kerosene lamp dimmed for a moment. If it had been an electric bulb, I would have assumed a power surge, but this was something else, and when the illumination brightened again seconds later, the miniature gods looked more fully formed and actually female. There were chest protuberances that hinted of breasts, budding clefts where the thighs met, separations in the formerly solid appendages that were supposed to be hands and feet.

My eyes were on that knife.

Teri, Evan and I were huddled together. We had all retrieved our weapons, and either the sounds assaulting our ears were not as horrible as they had been or we were getting used to them, because we were able to speak. I nodded toward the knife, making sure Frank was not looking in my direction, and, speaking low, said, "Spread out. Evan, go to the left. Teri, go to the right. Kick the dirt, scratch the walls, make noise, do whatever damage you can. I'm going after that knife."

Teri shook her head furiously. "You can't. It's too close—"

"Go!" I whispered, and pulled away from them.

They had no choice but to follow my orders. I hung back as they drew Frank's attention with their cries, and was gratified to see him flinch as Evan clawed stone with his hammer, as Teri used her heels to dig indentations in the dirt floor and randomly struck sections of the wall, both of them circling around the edges of the room. All four incarnations of the god did that flickering thing from the A-frame, and their cries slipped out of sync.

"No!" Frank yelled. "Stop it!"

The hole in the floor was between him and Teri, but Evan was easy to reach across an open space, and Frank lurched toward him. "You bastard!" he screamed. "I'll make sure you *never* fucking escape!"

This was my opportunity, and the instant he stepped away from the pit, I dove forward.

The knife was near—*too* near—one of the miniature gods, and the back of my hand brushed the creature as I grabbed the handle of the blade. I felt searing heat and excruciating cold, a repugnant texture against my skin that made me think of congealed mucus.

Without thinking, without stopping to ponder options or consider strategies, I raised the knife and drove it into the midsection of the small figure. Acting on instinct, I drew the blade through the soft flesh, cutting the body in two. Maybe there were words I was supposed to say, symbols I was supposed to carve, but I knew nothing about any of that, and I trusted in the power of the blade itself to extinguish the creature's life.

No such luck.

I successfully cut the form in half, but the god did not die. Its white flesh quivered and flowed, rearranging itself, and then there were two of them instead of one.

I needed to kill Frank.

Looking up from the still-developing bodies, I saw that this might be easier than I thought. Frank had indeed grabbed Evan, but Evan was defending himself with his hammer, landing blows to Frank's midsection that seemed to be doing actual damage, and Teri had come around from the other side of the pit and was attacking with her hatchet from the rear. I saw no wounds, no blood, but Frank was being battered, and his wrinkled face was grimacing, pain evident as he winced with each strike.

Teri landed a blow with her hatchet, slicing into his shoulder, causing him to scream with fury.

Could they kill Frank? Possibly. But this was my fight. I had started us on this journey, I had brought us all here, and it was my responsibility to finish it. In my mind, I could still hear the voices of Billy and my dad as they'd sat on the couch playing with Simon, voices I had not heard for decades, that I'd almost forgotten, and it was the silencing of those voices, the loss again of my family, that spurred me forward.

If anybody was going to kill Frank, it was going to be me.

Did I have any moral qualms? No. I had never killed anyone, could not even remember ever getting into a fight or hurting another person, so this went against everything I'd ever stood for, everything I was and wanted to be.

But I didn't care.

I rushed toward him, knife at the ready.

"You can't—" Frank began.

And I stabbed him in the throat.

There was a *shift* in the air around us. His voice dissolved into a drowning gurgle as blood spurted and he collapsed, the life draining from his body. The figures on the dirt twisted and withered, white flesh darkening to gray and then to black, the no longer humanoid forms emitting high-pitched sounds like the screaming of dying squirrels, their substance leeching into the dirt and creating a muddy mess.

Frank stopped moving, blood trickling now instead of spurting from the wound in his neck. Above our heads, the ceiling disappeared, and, past it, I could see the house, Frank's house, the rooms shifting, changing position, walls and floors gradually fading. It was not an instantaneous process. We stood there unmoving while the activity continued, and at the end of it, the only thing left was the open stone room we were in and the adjoining plywood construction that we had managed to partially demolish. In back of that, we could see the world outside, the rental car in which we'd arrived, and the dirt road through the desert beyond.

Holding Teri's hand, I hurried out, in case the opportunity to leave was once again taken away. Evan followed quickly. From this vantage point, I could see bits and pieces of the house that were still extant. There was no gigantic pile of rubble as might have been expected from a building that size, only individual sections of wall, occasional freestanding doors and a few stairway segments. Here and there, men and women were staggering about, freed from whatever trap, cage or dream in which Frank had had them ensnared.

Mark's body lay just outside the door we had used to enter the building, which was still standing strong within its frame. He was dead, mutilated by some sort of wild animal—

or monster

—but he had not been dead for long. There was a lot of blood, and the blood was still fresh, not dried. I walked over to where he lay, grief-stricken with the knowledge that he had been another victim, that he had not lived to see our victory over Frank. The one goal of his life had been denied him, and my eyes filled with tears as I recalled the little boy who'd lived across the street, my friend. If I'd had a jacket, I would have placed it over his face, but I didn't, and I turned away disconsolately, leaving his open, permanently terrified eyes to stare vacantly up at the sky.

"Hey!" One of the wandering men was waving at us, trying to get our attention, and as he approached, I saw that it was Twigs. He held up his camera, grinning hugely. "I got some amazing shit, here, man! *Amazing* shit! This is going to be one hell of a show!"

I wiped the tears from my eyes, scanning the remaining individuals stumbling about, but saw no one I recognized. There was no sign of Owen, and I assumed the worst. Teri was on the same wavelength. "I don't see Owen," she said.

I shook my head. "I don't, either."

"Holy shit," Twigs said, recognizing Evan beneath the years. "What happened to you?"

I didn't hear the writer's response. I was looking down at the bloody knife in my hand. In the bright sunlight, I could see a lined pattern tempered into the blade, intricate carvings in the handle, which appeared to be made of ivory or bone.

Amidst the chaos, practical considerations reasserted themselves, and I realized it was entirely possible that I could be charged with murder. Beyond the remnants of the rickety plywood room, the roofless stone chamber still stood, an island of permanence among the ruins of insubstantiality. There seemed no threat to it now, and I let go of Teri's hand and retraced my steps, intending to toss the weapon into the pit. The hole was still there, but Frank's body wasn't, and almost as soon as my mind registered that fact, he lunged for me.

Like the stoic bleached policemen still standing against the stone, Frank had blended into the wall, as motionless as a corpse, waiting for me. He was dead, as the gaping hole in his throat and the blood that covered his clothes attested, but somehow he had become reanimated, and he attacked me with a ferocity I had never seen before. The expression on his face was frozen—and the unsettling half-smiling countenance reminded me of nothing so much as the way he had looked peeking out of his pickup window the first time he had offered me and Billy a ride—but his arms and legs were flailing like a madman's. It was luck more than intent that allowed the knife to strike home when I lashed out to defend myself. I stabbed outward, and the blade passed between Frank's grasping hands and into his chest. I twisted it, pulled out and was ready to strike again, but his body collapsed in front of me and lay still, crumpled on the ground. No blood spilled from the new wound, but through his torn shirt, I could see that the skin around the gash had turned a deep black.

I backed up, afraid he was going to come to life yet again, but his body remained unmoving. On impulse, I did throw the knife into the hole, then grabbed Frank's right arm, the one on top, and dragged him out of the stone room, thinking *it* might have had something to do with reviving him.

Police cars were arriving. I could hear their sirens approaching, see the dust from their tires. The psychic *had* made her way back to San Antonio and contacted the law.

I pulled Frank over the ply board floor of the adjoining room and left him on the desert ground beyond, his head hitting a rock where I dropped him.

Teri had taken my hand, pulling me away, and I suddenly realized that I was crying again. Police cars, sheriff's SUVs, county jeeps, pickup trucks, a whole convoy of vehicles had arrived and were braking to a halt next to our own rental car. Uniformed officers emerged, moving slowly, obviously confused.

Eventually, I knew, they would find Frank's body and take it back to San Antonio, where it would be cremated or receive a proper burial. Either way, it would be hundreds of miles away from this place, the onetime location of Plutarch, the location where he was supposed to be interred.

He would wander, then, yet another homeless spirit, and that made me feel good. The bastard did not deserve to be at rest, and I hoped that whatever afterlife he had was wretched, unbearable and endless.

Teri held me close. I was still crying, but there was a sense of gratification mixed in with the tears.

A man in a sheriff's uniform approached, a bewildered expression on his face.

Whatever had been here was gone, and the only things left were aftereffects and questions.

I glanced over at Frank's lifeless body. He was dead, and I was glad. He would never repair another roof, fix another floor, remodel another room, build another house.

For Billy, I thought proudly, the tears rolling down my cheeks.

For Billy.